Churchill

3rd August 1956.

MAIGRET
AND THE YOUNG GIRL
and
DANGER AHEAD

"A blessed companion is a book"—JERROLD

MAIGRET
AND THE YOUNG GIRL
and
DANGER AHEAD

*

SIMENON

THE COMPANION BOOK CLUB
LONDON

*Made and printed in Great Britain
for The Companion Book Club (Odhams Press **Ltd.**)
by Odhams (Watford) Limited
Watford, Herts*
S.856.ZT.

CONTENTS

*

MAIGRET AND THE YOUNG GIRL   *page* 9

DANGER AHEAD, *comprising:*
    Red Lights   123
    The Watchmaker of Everton   239

MAIGRET

AND THE YOUNG GIRL

(*Maigret et la Jeune Morte*)

Translated from the French by
DAPHNE WOODWARD

CHAPTER ONE

MAIGRET yawned and pushed the papers across the desk.

"Sign those, boys, and then you can go to bed."

The "boys" were probably the three biggest toughs that had passed through the hands of Police Headquarters in the year. One of them, the one called Dédé, was built like a gorilla; and the frailest of the three, who had a black eye, could have earned his living as an all-in wrestler.

Janvier handed them the papers and a pen; and having at last spilt the beans, they made no further attempt to argue, did not even read their interrogation-statements, and signed with sullen resignation.

It was a few minutes past three by the marble clock in the office, and most of the offices at the Quai des Orfèvres were in deep darkness. For a long time the streets outside had been silent, save for the hooting of a distant horn or the screech of a taxi's brakes as it skidded on the wet cobbles. When they came in the day before, the offices had been deserted too, because it was not yet nine in the morning and the staff had not arrived. It was raining then, with a thin, melancholy drizzle that was still coming down.

For over eighteen hours they had been within the same walls, sometimes together, sometimes apart, while Maigret and five of his subordinates took turns to bombard them with questions.

"Fools!" the Chief-Inspector had said the moment he set eyes on them. "It's going to be a long job."

Fools, being pig-headed, are always the slowest to make a clean breast of things. They imagine they can save themselves by refusing to answer questions—or by answering at random and even contradicting themselves every five minutes. Believing themselves to be exceptionally astute, they invariably begin by boasting:

"You needn't think you'll get anything out of me!"

For several months these three had been working in the neighbourhood of the Rue La Fayette, and the newspapers had nicknamed them "the wall-borers". Thanks to an anonymous telephone call, they had at last been caught.

There were still some dregs of coffee in the cups, and a small enamel coffee-pot stood on an electric ring. Everybody was grey-faced and drawn. Maigret had smoked so much that his throat felt sore, and he planned that once the three men had been taken away he would ask Janvier to come and eat onion soup with him somewhere. His longing for sleep was past. He had felt suddenly tired at about eleven o'clock, so he had gone away to his own office and dozed for a few minutes. But now he felt wide awake.

"Ask Vacher to take them along," he said.

Just as they were leaving the Duty Room, the telephone rang. Maigret picked up the receiver and a voice asked:

"Hullo, who are you?"

He frowned and did not answer at once. The voice at the other end queried: "Jussieu?"

That was the Sergeant who should have been on duty, whom Maigret had sent home at ten o'clock.

"No. Maigret," he growled.

"I beg your pardon, Chief. This is Raymond, at the Exchange."

The call came from an enormous room in the other building, where all emergency calls for the police were received. The moment the glass was smashed in one of the red-painted alarm-signals which are scattered throughout Paris, a tiny lamp would light up on a map covering a whole section of the wall, and a man would put a plug into one of the holes of the telephone switchboard.

"Exchange here."

The call might be to report a street-fight or a recalcitrant drunkard, or, again, to ask for help for a policeman on the beat.

Then the Exchange man would put his plug into another hole.

"Is that the Station in the Rue de Grenelle? That you, Justin? Send a car to the Quai, outside No. 210. . . ."

Two or three men were on duty all night in this Exchange room, and they, too, probably made coffee for themselves. Now and again, when there was something really serious, they would warn Police Headquarters. And at other times they might simply ring through to have a word with a friend. Maigret knew Raymond.

"Jussieu's gone home," he explained. "Did you want to speak to him specially?"

"Only to tell him that a girl's body has just been found in the Place Vintimille."

"Any details?"

"The men from the Second District are there by now, I expect. The call came through to me three minutes ago."

"Thank you."

The three thugs had left the office by this time. Janvier came back; his eyelids were rather red, as they always were when he stayed up all night, and he had a stubble of beard which gave him a sickly look.

Maigret put on his overcoat, looked round for his hat.

"Coming?"

They went downstairs, one behind the other. Ordinarily they would have gone off to the Central Market for their onion soup. But when he saw the small black police cars lined up in the courtyard, Maigret hesitated.

"They've just found a girl's body in the Place Vintimille," he said.

Then, like someone who wants an excuse for not going to bed, he added:

"Shall we go and have a look?"

Janvier took the wheel of one of the cars. Both men, after the hours they had just spent interrogating, were too tired to talk.

Maigret had completely forgotten that the Second District was Lognon's sector—Lognon, whom his colleagues called Old Grouch. Even if he had remembered, it would have made no difference, for Lognon was not necessarily on night-duty at the station in the Rue de la Rochefoucauld.

The streets were drenched and deserted, with the drizzle making a soft halo round each gas-lamp, and occasional figures keeping close to the walls. At the corner of the Rue Montmartre and the Grands Boulevards a café was still open, and farther on they noticed the lighted signs of two or three night-clubs, and taxis drawn up along the kerb.

The Place Vintimille, though only just off the Place Blanche, seemed a little island of calm. A police car was standing there. Near the iron railing that surrounded the tiny garden, four or five men were standing round a light-coloured form which lay stretched on the ground.

Maigret at once recognized the short, spare figure of Lognon. Old Grouch had left the group to investigate the new arrivals, and now, in his turn, recognized Maigret and Janvier.

"That's torn it!" muttered the Chief-Inspector.

For of course Lognon would again accuse him of having done it on purpose. This was his district, his own territory. A crime had occurred while he was on duty, bringing him, perhaps, the chance to distinguish himself for which he had been waiting for so many years. And a series of coincidences had brought Maigret to the spot almost at the same moment as himself!

"Did they ring you up at home?" he asked suspiciously, already convinced that a plot had been hatched against him.

"I was at headquarters. Raymond put a call through. I came up to have a look."

Maigret was not anyhow going to leave without knowing what had happened, just to placate Lognon.

"She's dead?" he enquired, pointing to the woman who lay on the pavement.

Lognon nodded. Three uniformed policemen were standing there, together with a man and woman, passers-by who, as Maigret learnt later, had seen the body and given the alarm. If all this had happened only a hundred yards farther on, a large crowd would have gathered already, but not many people go through the Place Vintimille at night.

"Who is she?"

"We don't know. She has no identity papers."

"No handbag?"

"No."

Maigret took three steps forward and bent down. The girl was lying on her right side, her cheek against the wet pavement. One of her feet had lost its shoe.

"You haven't found her other shoe?"

Lognon shook his head. It was peculiar to see the girl's toes showing through the thin stocking. She was wearing a pale blue satin evening dress which, perhaps because of the way she was lying, looked too big for her.

The face was young. Maigret thought she could not be more than twenty or so.

"What about the doctor?" he asked.

"I'm expecting him. He ought to be here by now."

Maigret turned to Janvier.

"You'd better ring up the Identity people. Tell them to send the photographers along," he said.

There was no sign of blood on the dress. Borrowing an electric torch from one of the policemen, Maigret turned it on the girl's face, and it seemed to him that the one visible eye was slightly bruised and the upper lip swollen.

"No coat?" he asked.

It was March. The weather was mild, but not warm enough to

go about at night, especially in the rain, with nothing but a thin dress, which left the shoulders bare except for the narrow straps that held it up.

"She probably wasn't killed here," muttered Lognon in a glum tone which conveyed that he was in duty bound to help the Chief-Inspector, but had lost all personal interest in the affair.

He had purposely drawn a little apart from the others. Janvier had gone off to telephone from one of the bars in the Place Blanche. Before long a taxi pulled up, bringing a local doctor.

"You can have a look, Doctor," said Maigret, "but don't move her at all until the photographers get here. There's no doubt whatever that she's dead."

The doctor bent down, felt for the girl's pulse, her heart, straightened up again, indifferent, without saying a word, and waited like the others.

"Are you coming?" asked the woman, who was holding her husband's arm and was beginning to feel cold.

"Wait a bit longer."

"Wait for what?"

"I don't know. I expect they'll do something soon."

Maigret turned towards them.

"Have you given your name and address?"

"Yes—to that gentleman."

They were indicating Lognon.

"What time was it when you found the body?"

They looked at each other.

"It was three o'clock when we left the night-club."

"Five past three," corrected his wife. "I looked at my watch while you were waiting for your coat."

"Well, anyhow, it can't have taken us more than three or four minutes to get here. We were going to walk round the Place, when I noticed a light-coloured shape on the pavement. . . ."

"She was already dead?"

"I suppose so. She didn't move."

"You didn't touch her?"

The man shook his head.

"I sent my wife to 'phone the police. There's a police-alarm at the corner of the Boulevard de Clichy. I know, because we live in the Boulevard des Batignolles, only a step from there."

Janvier was soon back.

"They'll be along in a few minutes," he announced.

"Moers wasn't there, by any chance?"

Though he could not have said why, Maigret had a feeling that this was the beginning of a pretty complicated affair. He stood waiting, pipe in mouth, hands in pockets, glancing from time to time at the body on the ground. The blue dress was far from new and not even very clean, and the material was tawdry. It was the sort of dress that might be worn by any of the host of bar-girls who work in Montmartre night-clubs. And the shoe, a silver shoe with a very high heel and a worn sole, might have belonged to one of them too.

The first idea that sprang to mind was that one of these women, on her way home, had been attacked by somebody who had gone off with her handbag. But in that case one of the shoes would not have disappeared, and they probably wouldn't have troubled to strip her of her coat.

"She must have been killed somewhere else," he said to Janvier in an undertone.

Lognon heard, for he was keeping his ears pricked; and his lips curled slightly, since he had been the first to put forward this theory.

If she had been killed somewhere else, why should her body have been brought here? The murderer could hardly have carried the young woman over his shoulder. He must have used a car. In that case, he could easily have hidden her in some patch of waste ground or thrown her into the Seine.

Maigret would not admit to himself that what intrigued him most of all was the girl's face. So far he had only seen one side of it. Perhaps the bruises gave her that sulky expression? She looked like a bad-tempered child. Her soft brown hair, which was pushed back from her face, was naturally wavy. Her make-up was slightly smudged by the rain, but instead of having an ageing or ugly effect, this made her look younger, more appealing.

"Come here a minute, Lognon."

Maigret took him aside.

"Yes, Chief?"

"Have you any ideas?"

"You know I never have an idea. I'm only a District man."

"You've never seen the girl before?"

Lognon was the great authority on the Place Blanche and Place Pigalle neighbourhood.

"Never."

"A bar-girl?"

"If so, she isn't one of the regulars. I know pretty well all of them."

"I shall be needing you."

"You don't have to say that to please me. Now Police Headquarters has taken up the case, it's out of my hands. Mind you, I'm not complaining. It's quite natural. I'm used to it. Just give me your instructions and I'll do the best I can."

"It mightn't be a bad thing to begin right away by questioning the doormen at the night-clubs?"

Lognon glanced at the outstretched body and sighed:

"I'll be off, then."

To him this meant that he was being got rid of on purpose. They watched him cross the road, with his usual weary gait, and he took care not to look back.

The Technical Branch car arrived. One of the policemen was trying to get rid of a drunken man who had joined the group and was indignant because they were not helping "the little lady".

"You're all alike, you cops are. Just because someone's had a drop too much. . . ."

Once the photographs had been taken, the doctor could bend down to the body and turn it on its back, revealing the whole face which, seen thus, looked even younger.

"What did she die of?" enquired Maigret.

"Fracture of the skull."

The doctor's fingers were feeling about in the girl's hair.

"She was hit on the head with some very heavy object, a hammer or a wrench, or a piece of lead piping or something that kind. Before that, she'd received several blows in the probably from a fist."

"Can you say approximately the time she was kill

"In my opinion, between two and three o'clock Doctor Paul will tell you more exactly after h

The van from the Medico-Legal Institut The men were waiting for permission t stretcher and take it away towards the

"Go ahead!" sighed Maigret.

He looked round for Janvier.

"Shall we go and get somet'

Neither of them felt hung they went to a restaurant an decided an hour earlier, ordere instructions for a photograph of the dead girl to be sent to the newspapers, in the hope that there might still be time to get it into the morning editions.

"Are you going down there?" asked Janvier.

Maigret knew he was referring to the morgue, now known as the Medico-Legal Institute.

"I think I'll just drop by."

"Doctor Paul will be there. I 'phoned him."

"A *calvados*?"

"If you like."

At the next table sat two women eating sauerkraut and frankfurters, both of them bar-girls, both in evening dress, and Maigret watched them closely, as though trying to discern the most subtle differences between them and the murdered girl.

"Going home?"

"I'll come with you," Janvier decided.

It was half-past four when they entered the Medico-Legal Institute, where Dr. Paul, who had just arrived, was putting on his white overall, a cigarette hanging from his lower lip, as always when he was about to start a post-mortem.

"Have you examined her, Doctor?"

"I've just taken a look."

The body was lying naked on a marble slab and Maigret glanced away.

"What do you think?"

"She was between nineteen and twenty-two years old. She was in good health, but I rather suspect she was undernourished."

"A bar-girl?"

Dr. Paul glanced at him with his small shrewd eyes:

"You mean a girl who goes to bed with the clients?"

"More or less."

"Then the answer is no."

"How can you be so positive?"

"Because this girl has never been to bed with anyone."

Janvier, who was gazing absent-mindedly at the body, lit up strong electric-lamp, turned away, blushing.

e you sure?"

tain."

ulled on his rubber gloves, began to lay out his ts on an enamel-topped table.

u staying?"

it in the next room. Will you be long?"

18

"Less than an hour. It depends on what I find. Do you want an analysis of the contents of the stomach?"

"Better have it. One never knows."

Maigret and Janvier went into a neighbouring office and sat down, looking as ill at ease as in a waiting-room. In his mind's eye, each of them was still seeing that young, white body.

"I wonder who she is," murmured Janvier after a long silence. "A woman doesn't put on evening dress unless she's going to a theatre, to some of the night-clubs, or to a social function."

They had evidently both reached the same conclusion. Something didn't make sense. Social events that call for evening dress are not very frequent, and it would be unusual to see there a frock so cheap and worn as the one on the unknown girl.

On the other hand, after what Dr. Paul had just stated, it seemed hard to imagine that she could have worked in a Montmartre night-club.

"A wedding?" suggested Maigret without conviction.

It was another occasion for that kind of dress.

"Do you think so?"

"No."

Lighting a pipe, Maigret added with a sigh:

"We'll wait and see."

For the next ten minutes neither man said a word. Then Maigret asked:

"Would you mind fetching her clothes?"

"You really want me to?"

The Chief-Inspector nodded.

"Unless you funk it."

Janvier opened the door, vanished for scarcely a couple of minutes, and came back looking so pale that Maigret was afraid he was going to be sick. He was carrying the blue dress and some white lingerie.

"Has Paul nearly finished?"

"I don't know. I preferred not to look."

"Give me the dress."

It had often been washed, and when the hem was pulled undone, they could see that the colour had faded. There was a tab with the words: "Mademoiselle Irène, 35b, Rue de Douai."

"That's close to the Place Vintimille," observed Maigret.

He looked at the stockings—the foot of one of them was soaking wet—the panties, the brassière, the narrow suspender-belt.

"Is this all she had on?"

19

"Yes. The shoe comes from a shop in the Rue Notre-Dame de Lorette."

All in the same district. If it weren't for what Dr. Paul had said, everything would point to a bar-girl or to a young woman on the make in Montmartre.

"Perhaps Lognon will discover something?" suggested Janvier.

"I doubt it."

They were both feeling uncomfortable, since they could not shake off the thought of what was going on beyond the door. Three-quarters of an hour went by before it opened. When they looked in the next room, the body had disappeared and an employee was shutting one of the metal drawers in which corpses are kept.

Dr. Paul took off his overall and lit a cigarette.

"I haven't found out anything much," he said. "Death was due to a fracture of the skull. She was hit not once but several times, at least three violent blows. I can't say for certain what weapon was used. It may have been a tool, a brass fire-dog, a candlestick—anything heavy and hard. She fell on her knees first and tried to cling to someone, for I found shreds of dark-coloured wool under her finger-nails. I'll send them straight off to the laboratory. The fact that it's a woollen material suggests that it was a man's clothes she had clutched."

"So there was a struggle."

Dr. Paul opened a cupboard in which, together with his overall, rubber gloves and various other things, he kept a bottle of brandy.

"Would you like a glass?"

Maigret made no bones about accepting. Seeing this, Janvier nodded in his turn.

"What I'm going to say now is just my personal theory. Before being hit with the weapon, whatever it was, she received several blows in the face—from a fist, or maybe with the flat of a hand. I wouldn't be surprised if she had her face well slapped. I don't know if that was when she fell on her knees, but I think it's probable, and that would be when it was decided to finish her off."

"In other words, she can't have been attacked from behind?"

"Certainly not."

"And so it won't have been a scoundrel jumping on her as she turned a corner?"

20

"I don't think so. Besides, there's nothing to prove that it happened out of doors."

"The contents of the stomach didn't give you any information?"

"Yes. So did the blood analysis."

"What?"

Dr. Paul smiled slightly, as though to say: "Look out, this will come as a shock."

He paused, as was his way when telling one of the anecdotes in which he excelled:

"She was at least three-quarters drunk."

"Are you sure?"

"You'll find in my report to-morrow the percentage of alcohol in her blood. And I'll send you the result of the full analysis I'm going to make of the contents of the stomach. She must have had her last meal about six to eight hours before she was killed."

"What time did she die?"

"At about two o'clock in the morning. Earlier rather than later."

"That puts her last meal at six or seven in the evening."

"But not her last drink."

It was unlikely that the body had lain long in the Place Vintimille before it was discovered. Ten minutes? A quarter of an hour? Certainly not more.

So at least three-quarters of an hour must have elapsed between the time of her death and the time when she was dumped on the pavement.

"Any jewellery?"

Paul went back to the other room to fetch it. A pair of gold ear-rings with a flower design outlined in tiny rubies, and a gold ring with a slightly bigger ruby. It was not cheap, but it was of no great value. To judge by the style, the three pieces were about thirty years old, or perhaps more.

"Is that all? Did you look at her hands?"

One of Dr. Paul's specialities was to deduce what work people did from the rough indications of the shape of their hands, and this had often led to the identification of a body.

"She must have done a little housework, but not much. She wasn't a typist or a dressmaker. Three or four years ago she was operated on for appendicitis by a second-rate surgeon. That's all I can tell you so far. Are you going to bed now?"

"Yes, I think so," said Maigret vaguely.

"Well, good-night. I'm staying here. You'll get my report in the morning, about nine. Another drop of brandy?"

As Maigret and Janvier left the building, there were already slight signs of activity on board the barges tied up along the quay.

"Shall I run you home, sir?"

Maigret assented. They went past the Gare de Lyon, where a train had just come in. The sky was growing paler. The air was colder than during the night. A few windows were lit up, and every now and then they passed a man on his way to work.

"I don't want to see you at the office before the afternoon."

"What about you?"

"I shall probably get some sleep too."

"Good-night, Chief."

Maigret went noiselessly upstairs. As he was trying to fit his key into the lock, the door opened and Madame Maigret, in her nightdress, switched on the light and blinked at him with dazzled eyes.

"You are late! Whatever time is it?"

However sound asleep she might be, he could never get upstairs without her hearing him.

"I don't know. Past five."

"Are you hungry?"

"No."

"Hurry up and come to bed. A cup of coffee?"

"No, thank you."

He undressed and slipped into the warm bed. But instead of falling asleep he went on thinking about the dead girl in the Place Vintimille. Outside, he could hear Paris gradually awakening—isolated noises, more or less at a distance and separated at first, but mingling, as time went by, into a kind of familiar symphony. The concierges began to drag the dustbins to the edge of the pavements. He heard the little servant-girl from the dairy clattering upstairs to leave the bottles of milk outside each door.

Finally Madame Maigret got up, taking immense care to make no noise, and he had to make an effort not to give the show away by laughing. He heard her in the bathroom and then in the kitchen, where she lit the gas; and soon a smell of coffee pervaded the flat.

He was not lying awake on purpose. He simply could not get to sleep, probably because he was overtired.

His wife jumped when, clad in dressing-gown and slippers,

he came into the kitchen where she was having her breakfast. The electric-lamp was still burning, though it was already daylight outside.

"You're not asleep?"

"As you see!"

"Do you want your breakfast?"

"If possible."

She did not ask why he had been out for most of the night. She had noticed that his overcoat was damp.

"You didn't catch cold?"

After drinking his coffee, he went to the telephone and rang up the Second District police-station.

"Is Detective-Sergeant Lognon there?"

The night-clubs had all closed long ago, and Lognon could easily have gone to bed. But he was in the office.

"Lognon? Maigret here. Any news?"

"None. I've been the whole round of the night-clubs and questioned the drivers of all the cabs in the ranks."

Maigret was expecting this, after those few words of Dr. Paul's.

"I think you might as well go to bed now."

"What about you?"

Coming from Lognon, this meant:

"You're sending me to bed so that you can handle the case in your own way. So that people will say later on, 'That fool Lognon didn't manage to discover a thing!' "

Maigret thought of Madame Lognon, a thin, whining woman whose ill-health confined her to their flat in the Place Constantin-Pecqueur. When Lognon went home he would be greeted with groans and recrimination, set to do the housework and the shopping.

"Did you remember to sweep under the sideboard?"

He felt sorry for Old Grouch.

"I've got one small clue. I'm not sure if it's any help."

There was silence at the other end of the line.

"If you really don't want to get some sleep, I'll call for you in an hour or two."

"I shall be at the office."

Maigret telephoned to Police Headquarters for a car and for it to go first of all to pick up the girl's clothes at the Medico-Legal Institute.

In his bath he did almost fall asleep, and for a moment was tempted to ring up Lognon and ask him to go round by

23

himself to see Mademoiselle Irène in the Rue de Douai.

It had stopped raining. The sky was white, with a yellowish glow which gave some hope of sunshine later in the day.

"Will you be home for lunch?"

"Probably. I don't know."

"I thought you were expecting to finish your case last night?"

"That one's finished. This is another."

He didn't go out until he saw the little police car pull up in front of the house. The driver hooted three times. Maigret waved from the window to tell him he was coming down.

"Good-bye."

Ten minutes later, as the car was on its way up the Faubourg Montmartre, he had already forgotten that he had not slept all night.

"Stop somewhere so we can have a white wine!" he said.

CHAPTER TWO

DETECTIVE-SERGEANT LOGNON was waiting on the edge of the pavement in the Rue de la Rochefoucauld, and even from a distance he looked as though his shoulders were bowed beneath the burden of his fate. He invariably wore mousey grey suits, which were never pressed, and his overcoat was also grey, his hat an ugly shade of brown. His sallow face and air of having a cold in the head were not due to the fact that he had been up all night. He always looked like that, and even when he was just out of bed his appearance was no doubt quite as depressing.

Maigret had said on the telephone that he would call for him, but had never suggested that he should wait outside. But Lognon had purposely planted himself on the kerb, as though he had been there for hours. Not only had he been robbed of his case, but his time was being wasted and after a sleepless night he was kept hanging about in the street.

Opening the car door for him, Maigret cast a glance at the police-station, outside which the faded flag drooped in the motionless air. This was the building where he had begun his career, not as a detective but as secretary to the District Superintendent.

Lognon took his seat without a word, refrained from asking where he was being driven. The driver, who already had his orders, turned left, towards the Rue de Douai.

Conversation with Lognon was always awkward, because whatever one might say he always found some reason for taking offence at it.

"Have you seen the papers?"

"I haven't had time."

Maigret had just bought one, which he now took out of his pocket. The front page carried a photograph of the unknown girl—just the head, with the bruised eye and lip. All the same, she should have been recognizable.

"I hope by this time headquarters will be beginning to get some 'phone calls," the Chief-Inspector went on.

And Lognon was thinking:

"In other words, I've spent my night out for nothing, tramping from one night-club to another and one taxi-driver to the next. All that's really necessary is to print a photo in the papers and wait for the telephone to start ringing!"

He never sneered. It was difficult to describe. His face took on a dour, resigned expression as though he had decided to serve as a living reproach to his unkind and inefficient fellow-men.

He asked no questions. He was only a humble cog in the police machine, and nobody gives explanations to a cog.

The Rue de Douai was deserted except for one concierge standing in her doorway. The car pulled up in front of a mauve-painted shop-front above which was written, in large script: "Mademoiselle Irène". Below, in smaller letters: "Model Gowns".

In the dusty window were only two dresses—one white, with spangles, and one black silk day dress. Maigret got out, signing to Old Grouch to follow, told the driver to wait, and picked up the brown-paper parcel which had come from the Medico-Legal Institute.

When he went to open the door, he found it was locked, and the handle was off. It was after half-past nine. Peering through the glass, the Chief-Inspector saw a light in the room behind the shop, and began to knock.

Several minutes went by, as though there were nobody inside to hear the racket he was making—while Lognon waited at his side, motionless and silent. He did not smoke, had given that up years ago, when his wife first fell ill and began to say that it made her cough.

At last a figure appeared in the inner doorway. A youngish girl, in a red dressing-gown which she held wrapped round her,

25

stood looking at the two men. She vanished, no doubt to speak to someone, came back, threaded her way through the shop, which was cluttered with dresses and coats, and at last consented to open the door.

"What is it?" she asked, looking suspiciously from Maigret to Lognon and then at the parcel.

"Mademoiselle Irène?"

"I'm not her."

"Is she here?"

"The shop isn't open yet."

"I want to speak to Mademoiselle Irène, please."

"Who are you?"

"Inspector Maigret of Police Headquarters."

She showed no surprise or alarm. On close inspection it was clear that she could not be more than eighteen years old. Either she was still half-asleep or else she was listless by nature.

"I'll go and see," she said, and went back to the inner room.

They heard her speaking to someone in a low voice. Then there were sounds of this person getting out of bed. Mademoiselle Irène took two or three minutes to run a comb through her hair and put on her dressing-gown.

She was a middle-aged woman with big blue eyes in a moonish face, and sparse fair hair that faded into grey at the roots. She began by poking her head out to take a look at them, and when she finally emerged she was carrying a cup of coffee.

It was not Maigret she spoke to, but Lognon:

"What are you after this time?" she inquired.

"I don't know. It's the Inspector who wants to talk to you."

"Mademoiselle Irène?" asked Maigret.

"Is it my real name you want to know? If so, it's Coumar, Elisabeth Coumar. In my line of business, Irène sounds better."

Maigret, who had gone across to the counter, now opened his parcel and took out the blue dress.

"Do you know this dress?"

She didn't even step forward to look at it more closely, answered unhesitatingly:

"Certainly."

"When did you sell it?"

"I didn't sell it."

"But it comes from your shop?"

She did not ask them to sit down, seemed neither impressed nor uneasy.

"So what?"

26

"When did you last see it?"

"Is it important to you to know that?"

"It may be very important."

"Yesterday evening."

"At what time?"

"Soon after nine o'clock."

"Your shop is open at nine o'clock in the evening?"

"I never close before ten. Almost every day customers come in to buy something at the last moment."

Lognon must have known all this, but he assumed an air of detachment, as though it was none of his business.

"I suppose most of your customers are bar-girls or cabaret performers?"

"That and other things. Some of them don't get up till eight o'clock in the evening, and they're always short of something when they want to get dressed—stockings, a suspender-belt, a bra—or they find their dress got torn the night before. . . ."

"You said just now that you didn't sell this dress!"

She turned to the girl who was standing in the doorway of the inner room.

"Viviane! Get me another cup of coffee."

The girl came to fetch her cup with the swift obedience of a slave.

"Is she your maid?" asked Maigret, watching her go.

"No. My protégée. She turned up, just like that, one evening, too, and she stayed on."

She did not bother to explain. Lognon, at whom she glanced now and again, probably knew what she meant.

"To get back to yesterday evening——" said Maigret.

"She came——"

"Just a minute. Did you know her?"

"I'd seen her once."

"When?"

"About a month ago."

"She bought a dress from you then?"

"No. She hired one."

"You hire clothes?"

"Sometimes."

"Did she give you her name and address?"

"I think so. I must have written them on some scrap of paper. If you want me to look——"

"Presently. Was it an evening dress the first time?"

"Yes. The same one."

27

"Did she come as late that time?"

"No. Directly after dinner, about eight o'clock. She wanted an evening dress, and she admitted to me that she couldn't afford to buy one. She asked whether it was true that I hired them out."

"She didn't strike you as different from your other customers?"

"They always start out by being different. After a few months, they're all alike."

"You found a dress to fit her?"

"The blue one you have there. It's size twelve. It's been worn for a night by goodness knows how many girls in this district."

"She took it away?"

"Yes—the first time."

"And brought it back next morning?"

"Next day at noon. I was surprised to see her so early. They generally sleep all day."

"She paid the fee?"

"Yes."

"And you didn't see her again till yesterday evening?"

"I told you that already. It was soon after nine o'clock when she came in and asked if I still had the dress. I told her yes. Then she explained that this time she couldn't leave a deposit, but that if I was willing she would leave me the clothes she had on."

"So she changed here?"

"Yes. She needed shoes and a coat as well. I found her a velvet cape, which did all right."

"How did she seem?"

"Like a girl in desperate need of an evening dress and a coat."

"In other words, it seemed to be important to her?"

"It always seems important to them."

"Did you get the impression she had an appointment?"

She shrugged her shoulders and took a sip of the coffee Viviane had just brought her.

"Did your protégée see her?"

"She helped her to dress."

"Did she say anything in particular to you, Mademoiselle?"

It was the elder woman who replied:

"Viviane doesn't listen to chatter. She isn't interested."

It was true that the girl seemed to be right in the clouds. Her eyes were blank. She moved without a sound, and beside the fat shopkeeper she really reminded one of a slave—or rather of a dog.

"I found shoes for her and stockings, and a silver brocade handbag. What's happened to her?"

"You haven't seen the papers?"

"I was still in bed when you knocked. Viviane was getting my coffee."

Maigret held the paper out to her and she looked at the photograph without showing any surprise.

"Is that her?"

"Yes."

"Aren't you surprised?"

"It's a long time since anything's surprised me. Is the dress spoilt?"

"It's got wet in the rain, but it isn't torn."

"That's something. I suppose you want to take away her own clothes? Viviane!"

The girl had understood and was already opening one of the cupboards where dresses hung. She put a black wool dress on the counter, and Maigret at once looked for a maker's label.

"It's a dress she made herself," said Mademoiselle Irène. "Bring her coat, Viviane."

The woollen coat was of rather shoddy material, beige with brown checks, and came from a department store in the Rue Lafayette.

"Cheap, as you see. Her shoes are no better. Nor her slip."

These items were lined up on the counter. Then the slave produced a black leather handbag with a white metal clasp. Except for a pencil and a pair of shabby gloves, it was empty.

"You say you lent her a handbag?"

"Yes. She wanted to use her own. I pointed out that it didn't go with the dress, and I found her a little silver evening bag. She put in her lipstick, powder and handkerchief."

"No note-case?"

"Perhaps. I didn't notice."

Lognon still had the air of listening to a conversation from which he was excluded.

"What time was it when she left here?"

"It took her about a quarter of an hour to change."

"Was she in a hurry?"

"She seemed to be. She looked at the time once or twice."

"By her watch?"

"I didn't see any watch. There's a clock on the wall."

"It was raining when she left. Did she take a taxi?"

"There wasn't one in the street. She went off towards the Rue Blanche."

"Did she give you her name and address again?"

"I didn't ask her to."

"Will you try to find the piece of paper which you wrote them down on the first time?"

She heaved a sigh as she went to the other side of the counter, where she opened a drawer crammed full of note-books, bills, pencils, samples of material and innumerable buttons of all sorts.

Groping half-heartedly among this jumble, she explained:

"You see, there's really no point in keeping their addresses, because most of them live in lodgings and they change them more often than their undies. When they've no money left to pay the rent, they just clear out and. . . . No, that's not it! I seem to remember it was somewhere quite near here. A well-known street. I can't find it. If you insist, I'll keep on hunting and ring you up. . . ."

"Please do."

"He works with you, does he?" she asked, pointing to Lognon. "He'll have plenty to tell you about me! But he can tell you I've been going straight for years now. Haven't I?"

Maigret began to wrap up the clothes in the brown paper.

"Aren't you going to leave me the blue dress?"

"Not now. You'll get it back later."

"All right."

As he was going out, Maigret thought of another question.

"When she arrived yesterday evening, did she just ask for a dress, or for the dress she'd worn once before?"

"The one she'd worn before."

"Do you think she'd have taken another if you hadn't still got that one?"

"I don't know. She asked me whether I still had it."

"Thank you."

"You're welcome."

They got back into the car, and the slave closed the door behind them. Lognon still remained silent, waiting to be questioned.

"Has she been to prison?"

"Three or four times."

"Receiving?"

"Yes."

"When was her last sentence?"

"Three or four years ago. First, she was a dancer, then a madame of a brothel, until they were closed down."

"Has she always had a slave?"

The driver was waiting to be told where to go.

"Are you going home now, Lognon?"

"If you've no urgent orders for me."

"Place Constantin-Pecqueur," said the Chief-Inspector.

"I can walk there."

Of course! He must look humble, resigned!

"Do you know Viviane?"

"Not her. They change from time to time."

"She throws them out?"

"No. The girls clear out. She takes them in when they're flat broke and don't know where to go for a bed."

"Why?"

"Perhaps so as not to leave them in the street."

Lognon seemed to be saying:

"I know you don't believe it, that you suspect all sorts of sinister motives. But it's perfectly possible that a woman like that may be kind-hearted and do something out of sheer charity. That's just the way people misjudge me too. . . ."

Maigret sighed.

"You'd better get some sleep, Lognon. I shall probably need you to-night. What do you think about the case?"

The Detective-Sergeant did not reply, merely shrugged his shoulders. Why pretend to believe that he was capable of thinking, when, he felt sure, everybody regarded him as an idiot?

It really was a pity. Not only was he intelligent, but he was one of the most conscientious men in the entire Force.

The car stopped in the little square, outside a block of flats.

"Will you 'phone me at the station?"

"No, at home. I'd rather you'd wait there."

Half an hour later Maigret was back at the Quai des Orfèvres, and appeared in the Duty Room with his parcel under his arm.

"Anything for me, Lucas?"

"Nothing, Chief."

He frowned, surprised and disappointed. It was hours now since the photograph had appeared in the papers.

"No 'phone calls?"

"Only about the theft of some cheeses from the Central Market."

"I mean about the girl who was killed last night."

"Absolutely nothing."

Dr. Paul's report was waiting on Maigret's desk, but he only gave it a glance, noticing that it added nothing to what the police doctor had told him during the night.

"Send Lapointe in, will you?"

While he waited, he looked at the various garments which he had spread out on an arm-chair, and at the girl's photograph.

"Good morning, Chief. Anything for me?"

Maigret showed the young man the photo, the dress, the underwear.

"First, you'll take all that up to Moers and ask him to make the usual tests."

This meant that Moers would put the clothes into a paper bag; shake them to loosen the dust, which he would then examine under the microscope and analyse. Sometimes this gave useful results.

"Tell him to look at the handbag, the shoes and the evening dress as well. You understand?"

"Yes. We still don't know who she is?"

"We don't know a thing, except that she borrowed this blue dress yesterday, for one night, from a shop in Montmartre. When Moers has finished, you'll go to the Medico-Legal Institute and take a good look at the body."

Young Lapointe, who had only been two years in the police, pulled a face.

"It's important. Then you'll go to a model agency; it doesn't matter which. There's one in the Rue Saint-Florentin. Get hold of some young woman who's about the same height and figure as the dead girl. Size twelve."

For a moment Lapointe wondered whether his chief spoke seriously or was teasing him.

"And then?" he asked.

"Get her to try on the dresses. If they fit, take her upstairs and ask them to photograph her."

Lapointe was beginning to understand.

"That's not all. I want a photo of the dead girl, too, with make-up and so on, a photo that looks as though she were alive."

The Technical Branch had a photographer who specialized in this kind of work.

"They'll only need to fit two photos together, to have the dead girl's face on the model's body. And hurry. I'd like this in time to catch the last edition of the evening papers."

Alone in his office, Maigret signed a few documents to be sent off, filled a pipe, and then called Lucas and told him to find the file dealing with Elisabeth Coumar, alias Irène, just in case. He felt sure it would yield nothing new, that she had been telling the truth, but she was the only person up to now who had recognized the murdered girl from the Place Vintimille.

As time passed he grew more and more surprised at receiving no telephone calls.

If the unknown girl lived in Paris, there were several possibilities. First of all, she might have lived with her parents, in which case they would have rushed to the nearest police-station, or to the Quai des Orfèvres, the moment they saw the photograph in the morning paper.

If she lived alone, she must have had neighbours, a concierge, and probably she did her shopping locally.

Perhaps she shared with a girl friend, as many of them did? That meant one more person to worry about her disappearance and recognize her photograph.

She might have lived in a students' or working girls' hostel, of which there were several, and that increased the number of people who would know her.

The final possibility was that she had had a room in one of the thousands of small hotels in Paris.

Maigret rang through to the Duty Room.

"Is Torrence there? He isn't busy? Ask him to come in here."

If she lived at home, it was just a question of waiting. The same thing if she had a room in a private house, whether alone or with another girl. But in the other cases it was possible to hurry things up.

"Sit down, Torrence. You see this photo? Well! We shall have a better one towards the end of the afternoon. Imagine that girl wearing a black dress and a beige checked coat. That's how people are used to seeing her."

Just at that moment a ray of sunshine came slanting through the window and made a bright streak across the desk. Maigret broke off for a second to look at it with pleased surprise, as one watches a bird that has perched on the window-sill.

"First go down to the Hotels Section and ask them to go the round of the cheap hotels with the photo. They'd better begin with the ninth and eighteenth *arrondissements*. See what I mean?"

"Yes. Do you know her name?"

"We don't know anything. Meanwhile, you make out a list of hostels for girls and go round to them yourself. There'll probably be no result, but I don't want to neglect any possibility."

"I understand."

"That's all. Take a car to save time."

It had suddenly turned warm, and he went across to open the window, turned over a few more of the papers on his desk, looked at the time, and decided to go to bed.

"Wake me about four o'clock," he said to his wife when he got home.

"If it's necessary."

It was not necessary. There was nothing to do but wait. He fell asleep almost at once, a heavy sleep, and when his wife came to the bedside, carrying a cup of coffee, he stared at her, surprised to find himself there with the sun pouring into the room.

"It's four o'clock. You said . . ."

"Yes. . . Has anyone rung up?"

"Only the plumber, to tell me that——"

The first edition of the evening papers had appeared about one o'clock. They all carried the same photograph as the morning papers.

The girl was a bit bruised, yet Mademoiselle Irène had recognized her at the first glance, though she had only seen her twice.

There was just the chance that she didn't live in Paris or stop at an hotel, but that both times she came to the Rue de Douai she had arrived only a few hours earlier.

But this seemed unlikely, for all her clothes came from shops in the Rue Lafayette, except the dress she had made herself.

"Will you be home for dinner?"

"Perhaps."

"Well, take your big overcoat in case you're kept out late; it'll turn chilly after dark."

When he got back to his office, there was no message on his pad. He was annoyed at this, and called Lucas.

"Still no news? No 'phone calls?"

"Not a thing, Chief. I've brought you the Elisabeth Coumar file."

Still standing, he turned the pages without finding anything more than Lognon had told him.

"Lapointe has sent the photos to the newspapers."

"Is he here?"

"He's waiting for you."

"Send him in."

The photographs were masterpieces of their kind, so good that they gave Maigret a start. Here, before his eyes, was the girl's picture—not as he had seen her in the rain in the Place

Vintimille, by the light of electric torches, not as he had glimpsed her later, on the marble slab in the Medico-Legal Institute, but as she must have looked the evening before when she came into Mademoiselle Irène's shop.

Lapointe, too, seemed to be struck by it.

"What do you think of it, Chief?" he asked hesitantly.

And after a pause he added:

"She's pretty, isn't she?"

That was not the word he wanted, nor did it really describe her. True, the girl was pretty, but there was something more about her which was hard to define. The photographer had even managed to give a life-like expression to her eyes, which seemed to be asking an unanswerable question.

In two of the proofs she wore only her black dress; in one she had her brown checked coat, and in the last she was in evening dress. One could imagine her on the Paris streets, where so many like her slipped through the crowds, pausing for a moment in front of a shop-window, then going on again towards some unknown destination.

She had had a father, a mother, and later on, at school, friends among the other children. People—men, women—had known her as she grew up. She had talked to them. They had called her by her name.

Yet now she was dead, no one seemed to remember her, no one was concerned, as if she had never lived at all.

"It wasn't too difficult?"

"What?"

"To find a model."

"Only embarrassing. At least a dozen of them came crowding round me, and when I showed them the dresses they all wanted to try them on."

"In front of you?"

"They're used to it."

Lapointe could still blush, after two years in Police Headquarters!

"Have the photos sent to the rural divisions."

"I thought of that and took the liberty of sending them without waiting for instructions."

"Splendid. Did you circulate them to the Paris stations as well?"

"They went off half an hour ago."

"Get Lognon on the 'phone for me."

"At Second District?"

"No. At his home."

A few seconds later, a voice at the other end of the line said: "Detective-Sergeant Lognon here."

"This is Maigret."

"I know."

"I've had some photos sent to your office, the same ones that will be appearing in the papers in a couple of hours."

"You want me to go the round again?"

Maigret could hardly have explained why he thought it useless. The girl's visit to Mademoiselle Irène, the way she obtained the evening dress, the hour at which the crime had been committed, the place, everything seemed to indicate some connection with the night-club district.

Why should the unknown girl have suddenly wanted an evening dress, at nine o'clock at night, unless she had to go to some place where they dress?

It was too late for the theatre; besides, evening dress is not compulsory there, except at the opera or for a first night.

"Try it on the off-chance. Concentrate on taxis that work the night-shift."

Maigret hung up. Lapointe was still there, waiting for instructions, and Maigret didn't know what instructions to give him.

Again on the off-chance, he rang up the shop in the Rue de Douai.

"Mademoiselle Irène?"

"Speaking."

"Have you found that address?"

"Oh, it's you. . . . No! I've hunted everywhere. I must have thrown away the piece of paper, or used it to write down a customer's measurements. But I've remembered her Christian name. I'm almost sure. She was called Louise. And her surname began with an L too. 'La . . .' something. Something like 'La Montagne' or 'La Bruyère'. . . . Not that, but something of that kind."

"When she took the things out of her own bag and put them into the silver one, you didn't notice whether there was an identity-card among them?"

"No."

"Any keys?"

"Wait a minute! I seem to see keys. No, not *keys*. Just one small brass key."

He heard her calling:

"Viviane! Come here a minute."

He could not hear what she said to her slave (or protégée).

"Viviane thinks she saw a key, too," she assured him.

"A flat one?"

"Yes—you know; like most of the keys they make nowadays."

"There wasn't any money?"

"A few notes, folded. I remember that, too. Not many. Maybe two or three. Hundred-franc notes. I said to myself that those wouldn't take her far."

"Anything else?"

"No. I think that was all."

There was a knock on the door. It was Janvier, who had just arrived; the sight of the photographs on the desk startled him as much as it had Maigret.

"You've found some photos of her?" he asked in astonishment.

Then he frowned, took a closer look.

"They were done upstairs?"

Finally, he murmured:

"Queer girl, wasn't she?"

They still knew nothing about her, except that no one, apart from a hired-dress shopkeeper, appeared to know her.

"What do we do now?"

Maigret could only shrug his shoulders and reply:

"Wait!"

CHAPTER THREE

MAIGRET, feeling a bit glum, a bit disappointed, had stayed on at Headquarters till seven o'clock that evening, and taken the bus home to the Boulevard Richard Lénoir. An evening paper was spread out on a table, with a photograph of the unknown girl on the front page, and the fact that Chief-Inspector Maigret was handling the case must undoubtedly be mentioned somewhere in the article.

But his wife asked no questions. Nor did she make any attempt to take his mind off things, and once, towards the end of their *tête-à-tête* dinner, he found himself watching her attentively, surprised to find her as worried as he was himself.

He didn't wonder whether she was thinking of the same subject. Afterwards, he sat down in his arm-chair, lit his pipe and read the paper, while Madame Maigret cleared away and washed-up. Not until she sat down opposite him, with her mending-basket on her knee, did he cast two or three sidelong glances at her and finally mutter, as if he thought it unimportant:

"I'm wondering on what occasions a girl suddenly has to get hold of an evening dress."

What made him so certain that she had been thinking about this all along? Hearing her little sigh of satisfaction, he would even have sworn she had been waiting for him to say something about it.

"It may be for some quite simple reason," she observed.

"What do you mean?"

"I mean that a man probably wouldn't put on a dinner-jacket or tails without some definite purpose. It's different with girls. When I was thirteen I spent hours and hours, in secret, altering an old evening dress my mother had thrown away."

He looked at her, surprised, as though he had suddenly discovered an unknown side of his wife's character.

"In the evening sometimes, when I was supposed to be asleep, I'd get up and put that dress on and admire myself in the glass. And once when Father and Mother were out, I put it on, with a pair of Mother's shoes which were too big for me, and walked as far as the corner of our street."

He remained silent for over a minute, without noticing that she was blushing at this confession.

"You were thirteen," he said at last.

"One of my aunts, Aunt Cécile, whom you never met, but you've often heard me speak of her—she was the one who was very well off for a few years and then her husband suddenly lost all his money—she often used to shut herself up in her room and spend hours doing her hair and dressing-up as though she were going to the opera. If anyone knocked on the door, she'd call out that she had a headache. I peeped through the keyhole one day and found out what it really was. She was looking at herself in her wardrobe mirror, smiling and waving her fan."

"That was a long time ago."

"Do you suppose women have changed?"

"A girl would need a more serious reason than that to go knocking at Mademoiselle Irène's door at nine o'clock at night and asking for an evening dress, when she had only two or three hundred francs in her pocket, putting it on then and there, and walking out into the rain."

"I only mean it might not be what a man would call a serious reason."

He understood what she meant, but was not convinced by it. "Are you sleepy?"

He nodded. They went to bed early. Next morning was windy, with a showery sky, and Madame Maigret made him take his umbrella. At the Quai des Orfèvres he nearly missed the 'phone call. He was just leaving his office to go for the daily report when the telephone began to ring. He turned back from the door to answer it.

"Hello? Inspector Maigret here."

"Someone who won't give any name wants to speak to you personally," the operator told him.

"Put them through."

The moment the connection was made he heard a voice shouting, so shrilly that it made the instrument vibrate, the voice of someone who was unused to telephoning.

"Are you Inspector Maigret?"

"That's me, yes; who's speaking?"

There was no answer.

"Hello? Are you there?"

"I've something to tell you about the girl who's been murdered."

"The one in the Place Vintimille?"

Another pause. He began to wonder whether the caller was a child.

"Go on. Do you know her?"

"Yes. I know where she lived."

He felt sure it was because the telephone scared her, and not because she was reluctant to give her news, that the speaker made such long pauses. Instead of speaking naturally she shouted, with the mouthpiece too close. There was a wireless somewhere, playing music. He heard a baby crying.

"Where was it?"

"Rue de Clichy—No. 113b."

"Who are you?"

"If you want some information, just ask the old woman on the second floor—Madame Crêmieux, her name is."

He heard a second voice in the background, calling:

"Rose! . . . Rose! . . . What on earth. . . ."

Then, almost at once they had rung off.

He was only a few minutes in the Head's office, and as Janvier had just arrived, it was he whom he took with him.

39

The detective had combed Paris the evening before, without result. As for Lognon, who had been dealing with the night-clubs and taxi-drivers, he had as yet given no sign of life.

"She sounded like a young maid fresh from the country," said Maigret to Janvier. "She had an accent, but I couldn't place it."

No. 113b, Rue de Clichy was a middle-class house, like most of those in the neighbourhood. The two men first stopped at the concierge's, a woman of about forty, who looked suspiciously at them as they came in.

"Police Headquarters," said Maigret, showing his badge.

"What do you want?"

"I believe you have a Madame Crêmieux among your tenants?"

"Second floor left."

"Is she at home?"

"Unless she's gone out to do her shopping. I haven't seen her go past."

"She lives alone?"

The concierge did not seem to have an entirely easy conscience.

"She does and she doesn't."

"What do you mean?"

"From time to time she has someone with her."

"A relative?"

"No. After all, I don't see why I should make a mystery of things. Let her manage her own affairs. Every now and then she takes a lodger."

"Only for a short time?"

"Of course, she'd rather have someone permanent, but with a character like hers they soon get fed up and leave. The last one must have been the fifth, if not the sixth."

"Why didn't you say so at once?"

"Because the first time she had someone, a sales-girl at the Galeries, she asked me to say it was her niece."

"I suppose she gave you a tip?"

She shrugged her shoulders.

"First, the landlord won't allow any subletting. Secondly, anyone who lets a furnished room is supposed to inform them at the police-station and fill in papers. And third, I don't think she includes the rent in her income-tax return."

"Was that why you didn't report to us?"

She knew what he meant. In fact, a copy of the previous day's

40

paper was still lying on a chair, with the photograph of the unknown girl showing.

"Do you know her?"

"She's the latest."

"The latest what?"

"The latest lodger. The latest niece, as the old girl would say."

"When did you see her last?"

"I don't remember. I didn't pay attention."

"Do you know her name?"

"Madame Crêmieux called her Louise. She never had any letters while she was here, so I don't know her surname. I told you, I wasn't supposed to know she was a lodger. People have a perfect right to invite their relations to stay. And now, because of that, I'm in danger of losing my place. I suppose it'll all come out in the papers?"

"Possibly. What kind of person was she?"

"The girl? Just an ordinary kind of person. She'd nod when she went past the lodge, if she happened to think of it, but she never bothered to speak to me."

"Had she been here long?"

Janvier was making notes on a pad, and this intimidated the concierge, who pondered each question before answering it.

"If I remember rightly, she arrived just before New Year."

"She brought luggage?"

"Only one small blue suitcase."

"How had she come across Madame Crêmieux?"

"I ought to have known all this would lead to no good. I've never let myself be talked round before, and I promise you I shan't do it again, whatever happens. Madame Crêmieux was already living here before the death of her husband, who was assistant manager of a bank. In fact, they were here when I came."

"When did he die?"

"Five or six years ago. They had no children. She began to complain, saying that it was dreadful to be left alone in that big flat. Then she'd go on about money, how her pension stayed just the same although the cost of living was always going up."

"Is she wealthy?"

"She must be comfortably off. One day she let slip that she owned two houses somewhere in the twentieth *arrondissement*. The first time she had a lodger she tried to make me believe the girl was a relation up from the country, but I soon guessed the truth and tackled her about it. So then she offered me a quarter of the rent she was getting, and I was fool enough to accept. It's true that her flat is too big for one person."

"Did she put advertisements in the papers?"

"Yes. Without the address. Just the telephone number."

"What sort of people were her lodgers?"

"It's difficult to say. Nice girls, nearly always. Girls who had jobs and were glad to find a bigger room than they'd get in lodgings, for the same price or even less. Just once she had a girl who looked as respectable as the others, but who got up at night to let in men. That didn't last more than two days."

"Tell me about the last one."

"What do you want to know?"

"Everything."

The concierge glanced automatically at the newspaper photograph.

"I've told you: I only saw her when she passed. She used to go off in the morning about nine or half-past."

"You don't know where she worked?"

"No."

"Did she come back for lunch?"

"No. Madame Crêmieux never let them do any cooking in the flat."

"When did she get home?"

"In the evening. Sometimes at seven o'clock, sometimes not till ten or eleven."

"Did she go out a lot? Did men or women come to call for her?"

"Nobody ever called for her."

"You never saw her in evening dress?"

The woman shook her head.

"She was an ordinary girl, you know, and I hardly took any notice of her. Specially as I felt sure she wouldn't be here long."

"Why not?"

"I told you already. The old woman is keen enough on letting a room, but she doesn't expect to put herself out about it. She's used to going to bed at half-past ten, and if her lodger is unwise enough to get back later than that, there's a row. What she really wants is not so much a lodger as someone to keep her company and play cards with her."

She was puzzled by Maigret's smile. He was remembering Elisabeth Coumar, the dressmaker in the Rue de Douai, who took in homeless girls, perhaps out of pure kindness, perhaps partly because she was lonely; and as they owed everything

42

to her they became a sort of slave for a space of time.

Madame Crêmieux took in lodgers. It was really much the same thing. How many were there in Paris, widows and old maids, who tried to make sure of companionship in this way, preferably the company of someone young and carefree?

"If only I could give back what little money it brought me, and avoid losing my job. . . ."

"So you don't know who she was, where she came from, what she did or what friends she had?"

"No."

"You didn't like her?"

"I don't like people who are no richer than I am and think they're better."

"You think she was poor?"

"I always saw her in the same dress and coat."

"Are there any maids in the house?"

"Why do you ask me that? There are three. One in the first-floor flat, then one in the second on the right, and one——"

"Is one of them young and just up from the country?"

"You must mean Rose."

"Which is she?"

"The one on the second floor. The Larchers had two children already. Madame Larcher had another two months ago, and as she couldn't manage by herself, she got a girl from Normandy."

"Have the Larchers got the telephone?"

"Yes. The husband has a good job with an insurance company. They bought a car the other day."

"Thank you."

"If you could manage so the landlord doesn't find out——"

"One more question. Yesterday, when you saw the girl's photo in the paper, I suppose you recognized her?"

The woman hesitated, then lied.

"I wasn't sure. The first photo that came out, you know——"

"Madame Crêmieux came to you about it?"

She blushed.

"She stopped on her way back from shopping. She just said that the police were paid well enough without people doing their work for them. I knew what she meant. Since I saw the second photo, this one, I've had half a mind to ring you up, and on the whole I'm glad you've come, it takes a big weight off my mind."

Maigret and Janvier went up to the second floor in the lift. From beyond the right-hand door came the voices of children—and then another voice, which Maigret recognized, shouting:

43

"Jean-Paul! Jean-Paul! Will you stop teasing your little sister!"

He rang the left-hand doorbell. There were light, cautious footsteps and a voice behind the door asked:

"Who is that?"

"Madame Crêmieux?"

"What do you want?"

"Police."

After a longish pause the voice murmured:

"Just a minute."

The woman went away, no doubt to make herself presentable. When she came back her footsteps sounded different; she must have changed from bedroom slippers to shoes. She opened the door reluctantly, stared at the two men with little, piercing eyes.

"Come in. I haven't finished the housework."

All the same, she was wearing quite a smart black dress, and her hair was carefully done. She was about sixty-five or seventy years old, small, thin and amazingly lively for her age.

"Have you an identity paper?"

Maigret showed his badge, which she examined with care.

"So you are Chief-Inspector Maigret?"

She showed the men into a drawing-room which, though large, was so crammed with furniture and ornaments that there was hardly room to move.

"Sit down. What have you come about?"

She sat down with a certain dignity, though not able to keep her fingers from fidgeting nervously.

"About your lodger."

"I have no lodger. I may occasionally have a visitor and offer to put them up——"

"We know all about that, Madame Crêmieux."

She showed no sign of embarrassment, but gave a shrewd glance at the Chief-Inspector.

"All about what?"

"Everything. We don't come from the Inland Revenue, and the way you make out your income-tax return is none of our business."

There was no newspaper in the room. Maigret produced from his pocket a photo of the unknown girl.

"Do you recognize her?"

"She lived here for a few days."

"A few days?"

"Possibly a few weeks."

44

"Or still more possibly, two and a half months?"

"Perhaps. At my age, time is of so little importance! You would never believe how quickly the days pass!"

"What's her name?"

"Louise Laboine."

"Is that the name on her identity-card?"

"I never saw her identity-card. That is the name she gave me when she called here."

"You don't know if it was her real one?"

"I had no reason to suspect the contrary."

"She answered your advertisement?"

"Did the concierge tell you?"

"Never mind that, Madame Crêmieux. Don't let's waste time. And remember that I ask the questions."

"Very well—please continue," she replied, with dignity.

"Louise Laboine answered your advertisement?"

"She telephoned to ask the price. I told her. She asked whether I could not reduce it a little, and I advised her to come and see me."

"Did you make a reduction for her?"

"Yes."

"Why?"

"Because I am always taken in."

"By what?"

"When they come to call on me they always seem such nice girls, so modest and considerate. I asked this one whether she went out in the evenings, and she said no."

"Do you know where she worked?"

"In an office, so I understood, but I don't know which. It was several days before I realized what type of girl she was."

"What type . . . ?"

"Most unsociable; when she had decided to keep things to herself——"

"You know nothing about her? She didn't talk to you?"

"As little as possible. She treated the place like an hotel. Every day as soon as she was dressed she would go out, with no more than a vague 'Good morning' if she happened to meet me."

"Did she always leave at the same time?"

"Now that was what puzzled me. The first two or three days she went off at half-past eight, so I supposed she began work at nine o'clock. Then, for several days, she didn't leave till a quarter-past nine, and I asked her if she had changed jobs."

45

"What did she say?"

"Nothing at all. That was her way. When she didn't want to answer a question, she would pretend not to have heard it. In the evening she always tried to avoid me."

"Did she have to go through this room to get to her own?"

"Yes. I generally sit here. I used to ask her to sit down and have a cup of tea or coffee. Only once did she condescend to keep me company, and I'm certain she didn't open her mouth more than five times in the hour she stayed."

"What did you talk about?"

"All sorts of things. I was trying to find out."

"Find out what?"

"Who she was, where she came from, where she had lived before."

"Didn't you get anything out of her?"

"All I discovered was that she knew the South. I talked about Nice, where my husband and I used to spend a fortnight every year, and I could see she'd been there, too. When I asked her about her father and mother, she put on her far-away look. If you'd seen her with that look on her face you would have been infuriated, you would indeed."

"Where did she get her meals?"

"Outside; at least she was supposed to. I don't allow cooking in the bedroom, because of the danger of fire. Once they bring in a spirit-lamp one never knows what may happen, quite apart from the fact that all my furniture is old and valuable, family heirlooms. All the same, I found breadcrumbs lying about, and sometimes she had burnt pieces of greasy paper which had undoubtedly wrapped up some cold meat."

"She spent the evenings alone in her room?"

"Very often. She didn't go out more than two or three times a week."

"Did she dress up when she went out?"

"How could she dress up, when all she had in the world was one dress and one coat? Last month what I had been expecting happened."

"What had you been expecting?"

"That sooner or later she would be unable to pay her rent."

"She didn't pay it?"

"She gave me a hundred francs on account, and promised to pay the rest at the end of the week. At the end of the week she tried to dodge me. I waylaid her, and she told me she would have the money in a day or two. Don't imagine I'm grasping

46

and think of nothing but money. I need it, of course, like every-body else. But if only she'd have behaved like a human being, I would have been more patient."

"You gave her notice?"

"Three days ago—the day before she disappeared. I simply told her I had a relative coming up from the country and should need the room."

"How did she take it?"

"All she said was 'Very well.' "

"Will you show us her room?"

The old lady rose, still dignified.

"This way, please. As you will see, she would never have found such a room anywhere else."

And indeed it was a spacious room, with two large windows. Like the drawing-room, it was furnished in the style of the last century. There was a heavy mahogany bedstead, and between the windows stood an Empire writing-desk which must have belonged to Monsieur Crêmieux and been put there for lack of a better place. Heavy velvet curtains hung at the windows, and the walls were adorned with family photographs in black or gilt frames.

"The only slight inconvenience is that we have to share the bathroom. But I always let her have it first and never went in without knocking."

"You haven't removed anything since she left, I suppose?"

"Certainly not."

"When she failed to come back, you searched through her belongings?"

"There was not much to search. I merely came in to see whether she had taken them with her."

"She hadn't taken them?"

"No. You can see for yourself."

On the chest-of-drawers lay a comb, a hairbrush, a cheap manicure set and a box of face-powder of a popular brand. There was a tube of aspirin, too, and another which contained sleeping pills.

Opening the drawers, Maigret found nothing except a few underclothes and an electric iron wrapped up in a rayon slip.

"What did I tell you!" exclaimed Madame Crêmieux.

"What?"

"I had also warned her that I did not allow washing and ironing. So that was what she used to do in the evening, when

47

she locked herself in the bathroom for an hour at a time! That's why she used to lock her bedroom door, too!"

In another drawer they found a box of cheap writing-paper, two or three pencils and a fountain-pen.

A cotton dressing-gown was hanging in a wardrobe and a blue fibre suitcase stood in a corner of the room. The suitcase was locked. There was no key anywhere about, so Maigret prised up the catch with his pen-knife, as the old woman drew nearer. The suitcase was empty.

"Nobody's ever been round asking for her?"

"Nobody."

"You don't think anyone can have got into the flat while you were out?"

"I should have noticed. I know the exact position of everything in the place!"

"Did anyone ever ring her up?"

"Only once."

"When was that?"

"About a fortnight ago. No—longer. A month ago, perhaps. One evening about eight o'clock, when she was in her room, someone rang up and asked for her."

"A man?"

"A woman."

"Can you remember the exact words?"

"The voice said, 'Is Mademoiselle Laboine at home?' I said I thought she was, and went and knocked on her door, calling 'Telephone, Mademoiselle Louise.'

" 'For me?' she seemed astonished.

" 'Yes, for you.'

" 'Coming,' she said.

"That was the time I had the impression she'd been crying."

"Before or after the telephone call?"

"Before—when she came out of her room."

"Was she fully dressed?"

"No—she was in her dressing-gown and her feet were bare."

"Did you hear what she said?"

"She said hardly anything—only 'Yes . . . yes . . . all right . . . Who . . . perhaps. . . .' And she ended up with 'See you presently.' "

"She went out then?"

"Ten minutes later."

"What time did she get back that evening?"

"She was out all night. It wasn't till six o'clock next morning that I saw her come back. I was waiting for her—I'd made up my mind she'd have to leave. She told me she'd spent the night with a relative who was sick. She didn't look as though she'd been out enjoying herself. She went to bed and stayed there for two days. I took her in her meals and bought aspirin for her. She said she had 'flu.''

Did she realize that every word she uttered was helping to build up a picture in Maigret's mind, though he seemed to be hardly listening? He was gradually forming an impression of the life the two women had led in this dark, over-crowded apartment. It was easy enough with one of them: she stood there before him. But it was more difficult to imagine the girl's attitude, her voice and gestures, let alone what her thoughts could have been.

He knew her name now, assuming that it was her real one. He knew where she had slept during the last two months, where she had spent some of her evenings.

He knew also that, twice, she had gone to the Rue de Douai to hire or borrow an evening dress. The first time she had paid up. The second time she had had only two or three hundred francs on her, barely enough to pay for a taxi or a scanty meal.

Had her first visit to Mademoiselle Irène resulted from the telephone call? It seemed unlikely. She had appeared at the shop earlier on that occasion.

Besides, she had got back to the Rue de Clichy at six o'clock next morning, wearing her usual dress and coat. She could not already have returned the blue satin dress to Mademoiselle Irène, who was a late riser.

It seemed from all this that two months previously, about the first of January, she had not reached the end of her resources, for she had been able to rent a room. She had very little money. She had haggled to bring down the rent. She used to leave the house every morning at more or less the same time, first about half-past eight and then not till after nine o'clock.

What did she do all day? And during the evenings she didn't spend in her room?

She did not read. There were no books or magazines to be seen. If she did any sewing it could only have been mending, for in a drawer there were merely three reels of cotton, a thimble, a pair of scissors, some beige silk for darning stockings and a case with a few needles in it.

According to Dr. Paul she was about twenty years old.

"I can assure you I shall never take a lodger again!"

"She kept her room in order herself, I suppose?"

"You don't imagine I waited on her? Another girl tried that once, but I promise you she soon thought better of it!"

"How did she spend her Sundays?"

"In the morning she used to sleep late. The very first week I noticed she didn't go to Mass. I asked her whether she wasn't a Catholic. She said she was. Just for something to say, you understand? Sometimes she didn't go out till past one o'clock. I suppose she went to the cinema. I remember once picking up a cinema ticket in her room."

"You don't remember what cinema it was for?"

"I didn't notice. It was a pink ticket."

"Just the one?"

Maigret suddenly looked sternly at the old woman, as though to forbid her to lie:

"What did she have in her handbag?"

"However should I——"

"Answer my question. Some time or other you must have taken a look into it when she left it lying about."

"She hardly ever left it lying about."

"Once was enough. Did you see her identity-card?"

"No."

"Hadn't she got one?"

"Not in her bag. At any rate, it was not there on that occasion. It was only a week ago that I had the opportunity of looking in. I was beginning to have my suspicions."

"What about?"

"If she had been in regular employment she would have had something to pay her rent with. And it was the first time I had come across a girl of her age with only one dress to her name. Besides, I couldn't get her to give me any information about herself, or what she did, where she came from, where her family lived."

"What conclusion had you come to?"

"That . . . she might have run away from home. Or else——"

"What?"

"I don't know. I couldn't place her, you see. With some people one knows where one is at once. But not with her. She had no accent. She didn't seem like a country girl either. I think she had had some education. Except for her habit of not answering questions and keeping out of my way, she had quite good manners. Yes, I think she must have been well brought up."

"What was in her bag?"

50

"Lipstick, powder, a handkerchief and two keys."

"What keys?"

"A key to the front door of this flat, which I had given her, and the key of her suitcase. There was a shabby note-case, too, with money and a photograph in it."

"A man or a woman?"

"A man. But not what you think. The photo was at least fifteen years old, faded and dog-eared, and it showed a man of about forty."

"Can you describe him?"

"A handsome, distinguished-looking man. What particularly struck me was that he was wearing a very light-coloured suit, probably a linen one, such as I have often seen at Nice. I thought of Nice because there was a palm-tree behind him."

"Did you notice any likeness?"

"To her? No. The same idea occurred to me. If he was her father, she didn't take after him at all."

"Would you recognize him if you saw him?"

"If he hadn't altered too much."

"You didn't ask your lodger about him?"

"How could I have explained that I'd seen the photo? By opening her bag? All I did was to mention Nice—the Riviera. . . ."

"Bring all that along, will you, Janvier."

Maigret pointed to the contents of the drawers, the dressing-gown in the wardrobe and the blue suitcase. There was room for everything in the suitcase, and as the lock was broken they asked the old lady for a piece of string to fasten it.

"Do you think I shall get into trouble?"

"Not with us."

"With the income-tax people?"

"That's not our affair," growled Maigret with a shrug.

CHAPTER FOUR

THE old woman, through a crack in the door which she had taken care not to shut tight, saw them walk, not to the lift or the stairs, but to the flat at the other end of the landing. As they came out again, Maigret noticed that the door quivered slightly, and on the way down remarked to Janvier:

"She's jealous!"

Once, at the trial of a man he had sent to the High Court, a friend who was following the case had whispered:

"I wonder what he's thinking about!"

And Maigret had replied casually:

"What this evening's papers will say about him."

He held that murderers, at least until their condemnation, are less preoccupied by their crimes and much less by the thought of their victims, than by the impression they are making on the public. They have become celebrities overnight. Journalists and photographers swarm round them. People sometimes queue for hours to be allowed in to look at them. So it is not surprising if they develop a ham-actor's attitude.

Old Madame Crêmieux had certainly not been pleased when the police invaded her flat. Besides, Maigret had a way of putting questions which made it impossible to give the answers one would have preferred. She had been forced to confess certain not very pleasant things.

But all the same, she had been the centre of attention for nearly an hour, with even her slightest words being recorded in a notebook!

And then the Chief-Inspector went straight across to pay the same compliment to a rough little servant-girl!

"What do you say to a drink?"

It was after eleven o'clock. They went into a bar at the corner of the street and drank their *apéritif* in silence, as though chewing over what they had just discovered.

With Louise Laboine it was like a photographic plate put into the developer. Two days ago they had not known of her existence. Then she had become a blue shape, a profile against the wet pavement of the Place Vintimille, a white body on a marble slap at the Medico-Legal Institute. Now she had a name; and a picture was beginning to form, dim as it still was.

Rose's employer had been rather annoyed, in her turn, when Maigret had said to her:

"Do you mind looking after the children while we ask your maid a few questions?"

Rose was not yet sixteen and had not lost her dewy look.

"It was you who rang me up this morning, wasn't it?"

"Yes, sir."

"You knew Louise Laboine?"

"I didn't know her name."

"You used to pass her on the stairs?"

"Yes, sir."

"Did she speak to you?"

"She never spoke to me, but she used always to smile. I always thought she looked unhappy. She looked like a film actress."

"Did you ever seen her anywhere except on the stairs?"

"Several times."

"Where?"

"On a bench in the Trinité garden, where I go nearly every afternoon with the children."

"What was she doing there?"

"Nothing."

"Waiting for someone?"

"I never saw anyone with her."

"Did she read?"

"No. Once she ate a sandwich. Do you suppose she knew she was going to die?"

That was all they had found out from Rose. It proved that for some time, at any rate, the girl had had no regular work. She hadn't bothered to go far. She just used to walk down the Rue de Clichy, and without leaving the district, go and sit in the garden in front of the Trinité church.

It had occurred to Maigret to ask:

"Did you ever see her go into the church?"

"No, sir."

The Chief-Inspector paid, wiped his mouth, and got back into the little car, followed by Janvier. At the Quai des Orfèvres, he saw straightway a grey figure in the ante-room, and recognized Lognon, whose nose was more red than ever.

"You waiting for me, Lognon?"

"For an hour."

"Doesn't look as though you'd been to bed."

"That's of no importance."

"Come along to my office."

Those who had seen Lognon waiting for him must have taken him not for a policeman, but for someone who had come to relieve his conscience, his manner was so glum and preoccupied. He had a real cold by this time, his voice was hoarse, and he had to keep pulling his handkerchief out of his pocket. But he made no complaint, he assumed a resigned attitude, the attitude of a man who has suffered all his life and expects to do so till the end of his days.

Maigret sat down and filled a pipe, without the other, perched on the edge of a chair, uttering a word.

"Got some news for us, have you?"

53

"I've come to report on my work."

"Carry on, old man."

This cordiality was wasted on Old Grouch, who doubtless took it for some sort of sarcasm.

"Last night I made the same round as the night before, but more carefully. Until about three a.m.—four minutes past three, to be precise—it led to no results."

While speaking he took a piece of paper out of his pocket.

"At four minutes past three, outside a night-club called *Le Grelot*, I spoke to a taxi-driver called Léon Zirkt, aged fifty-three, who lives at Levallois-Perret."

These details were probably superfluous. But the Detective-Sergeant was deliberately dotting his i's to imply that it was not for a mere subordinate like himself to decide what might or might not be important.

He went on in an expressionless voice, without looking at the Chief-Inspector, who was unable to repress a smile:

"I showed him the photograph, or rather the photographs, and he recognized the one in evening dress."

He paused, like an actor. He did not yet know that Maigret had already discovered the girl's name and her last address.

"On Monday night, shortly before midnight, Léon Zirkt was waiting opposite the *Roméo*, a new night-club in the Rue Caumartin."

He had prepared everything beforehand, and now took another piece of paper out of his pocket; this time it was a newspaper cutting.

"That night, as an exception, the *Roméo* was not open to ordinary clients, because it had been hired for a wedding party."

Like counsel in court submitting a document to the judge, he put the newspaper cutting before Maigret and returned to his chair.

"As you will see, this was to celebrate the marriage of a certain Marco Santoni, the representative in France of a well-known brand of Italian vermouth, to Mademoiselle Jeanine Armenieu, no occupation, of Paris. There were a lot of guests, for it seems that Marco Santoni is popular in the smart world."

"Did you get these particulars from Zirkt?"

"No, I went to the *Roméo*. As I said before, the taxi-driver was waiting with a few others. It was drizzling. At about a quarter-past twelve a girl in a blue evening dress and a dark velvet cape came out of the place and began to walk away. Zirkt

54

called to her as usual, 'Taxi?' But she walked on with a shake of the head."

"He is certain she was our girl?"

"Yes. There's a neon sign lighting up the entrance to the *Roméo*. And Zirkt, who's accustomed to night work, noticed at once that the dress was pretty shabby. Besides, Gaston Rouget, the doorkeeper at the *Roméo*, recognized the photo as well."

"The taxi-driver doesn't know where she went, I suppose?"

Lognon had to blow his nose. He showed no self-satisfaction; on the contrary, he wore an expression of exaggerated humility, as though ashamed of having so little to contribute.

"At that moment—or rather, a few minutes later—a couple came out of the *Roméo* and asked to be driven to the Étoile. Going through the Place St. Augustin, Zirkt saw the girl crossing it on foot. She was walking quickly, towards the Boulevard Haussmann, as though making for the Champs-Élysées."

"Is that all?"

"He set down his clients, and later on, to his surprise, saw the girl again, at the corner of the Boulevard Haussmann and the Faubourg St. Honoré. She was still walking. He looked at his watch, wondering how long she had taken to go all that distance. It was getting on for one o'clock."

Now, Louise Laboine had been killed at about two o'clock and found dead in the Place Vintimille at three.

Lognon had done a good job. And his story was not yet finished. Maigret realized this on seeing that he kept his seat and was now producing a third scrap of paper from his pocket.

"Marco Santoni's flat is in the Rue de Berri."

"Have you seen him, too?"

"No. After the supper at the *Roméo* the bride and bridegroom caught a plane for Florence, where they are to stay for a few days. I spoke to his manservant, Joseph Ruchon."

Lognon had no car at his disposal. He had certainly not taken a taxi, knowing that his expense account would be closely scrutinized. He must have covered all this ground on foot during the night and by bus or Underground since morning.

"I also questioned the barman at *Fouquet's* in the Champs-Élysées, and the barmen of two other places. I was unable to interview the barman at *Maxim's* as he lives out of town and had not arrived yet."

The hoard in his pocket seemed inexhaustible. He kept fishing out one paper after another, each dealing with a new stage of his investigation.

"Santoni is forty-five years old. He is a good-looking man, a little stout, very well groomed, who patronizes night-clubs, bars and the best restaurants. He has had many mistresses, most of them models or dancers. About four or five months ago, so far as I can discover, he met Jeanine Armenieu."

"Was she a model?"

"No. She didn't belong to his circle. He never told anyone where he had found her."

"How old?"

"Twenty-two. Soon after making Santoni's acquaintance she went to live at the *Hôtel Washington* in the Rue Washington. Santoni often went to see her there and Jeanine sometimes spent a night at his flat."

"Is this the first time he's been married?"

"Yes."

"Did his manservant see the photograph of the dead girl?"

"I showed it to him. He declared positively that he didn't know her. I showed it to the three barmen, too, who all said the same."

"Was the valet in the flat during Monday night?"

"He was finishing the packing for the honeymoon trip. No one rang the bell. Santoni and his bride came in at five in the morning, very gay, changed in a great hurry and left for Orly airport."

There was another pause. Each time Lognon gave the impression that he had come to the end of his story, but his silence was such and his attitude so humble, that Maigret was not taken in.

"Do you know whether the girl stayed long at the *Roméo*?"

"As I told you, I questioned the doorkeeper."

"Did the guests have to show their invitation-cards at the door?"

"No. Some people showed them, others didn't. The doorkeeper remembers seeing the girl come in a little before midnight, when dancing had just begun. Precisely because she didn't look like the usual type of client, he let her in, thinking she must be a friend of the bride."

"So she stayed for about a quarter of an hour?"

"Yes. I asked the barman."

"Was he at the *Roméo* this morning?"

Lognon replied simply:

"No. I went to his home, at the Porte des Ternes. He was asleep."

Added together, all these comings and goings amounted to an impressive number of miles. Maigret could not help visualizing Lognon as he covered them on foot during the night and in the early hours of the morning, like an ant weighed down by a crushing load but undeterred by anything in its way.

There was hardly another detective in the whole Force capable of getting through so much work, without forgetting a single point, without leaving anything to chance; and yet, though poor Lognon's one ambition for the past twenty years had been to be promoted to Police Headquarters, he would never get there.

Partly due to his disposition. And then, because he lacked the basic requirements of education and failed every examination he sat for.

"What does the barman say?"

Out came another scrap of paper, bearing a name and address and a few notes. Lognon did not need the notes, he had the whole thing by heart.

"When he first noticed her she was standing just inside the door. The head waiter came up and said something to her in a low voice. She shook her head. He had probably asked her whose party she was to join. Then she slipped through the crowd. A lot of people were standing up, and couples were dancing between the tables as well as on the floor."

"Did she speak to the bride?"

"It took her some time, because the bride was dancing, too. Finally she managed to get to her, and they talked for some minutes. Twice Santoni grew impatient and interrupted them."

"Did the bride give her anything?"

"I asked that. The barman couldn't say."

"Did they seem to be quarrelling?"

"Apparently Madame Santoni's manner was reserved, not to say cold, and she shook her head several times. Then the barman lost sight of the girl in the blue dress."

"I suppose you haven't questioned the head waiter?"

This was turning into a game.

"He lives in the Rue Caulaincourt, right at the top end. He was asleep, too."

For Lognon had been there as well!

"He confirmed what the barman had told me. He had gone up to the girl to ask who she was looking for, and she replied that she was a friend of the bride and only wanted to have a word with her."

At this point Lognon got up, which showed he had nothing more to produce.

"You've done a wonderful job, old man."

"I've done what I had to do."

"And now get to bed. You ought to take care of yourself."

"This is only a cold."

"Yes, but if you don't look out it'll turn into bronchitis."

"I have bronchitis every winter, but I've never stayed in bed for it."

That was the trouble with Lognon. By the sweat of his brow—literally—he had collected a certain amount of probably valuable information. If one of his own detectives had collected that information, Maigret would at once have put several others on the job, so as to get the most he could out of it. One man alone cannot do everything.

But if the Chief-Inspector did that now, Old Grouch would feel that the bread was being snatched from his mouth.

He was dead beat, hoarse and tormented by his cold. He had not had more than seven or eight hours' sleep altogether in the past three nights. But he had to be allowed to carry on. And even then he looked upon himself as a victim, a poor fellow, left with the most thankless part of the work and robbed, at the last moment, of the credit for his success.

"What do you propose to do next?"

"Unless you're thinking of putting another man——"

"Of course not! I only meant it would be a good thing for you to get a bit of rest."

"I shall have plenty of time to rest when I'm pensioned off. I haven't had time to go to the Town Hall of the eighth *arrondissement*, where the marriage took place, or to the *Hôtel Washington*, where the new Madame Santoni had been staying. I might find out there where she used to live before, and that might help me to discover the dead girl's address."

"She had been lodging for the last two months in the Rue de Clichy with a certain Madame Crêmieux, a widow, who sub-let her a room in her flat."

Lognon's lips tightened.

"We don't know what she was doing before that. At Madame Crêmieux's she gave her name as Louise Laboine, but her landlady never saw her identity-card."

"May I go on with my enquiry?"

What would be the use of objecting?

"Of course, old chap, if you want to. But don't get knocked up."

"Thank you."

Maigret stayed for some time alone in his office gazing absently at the chair on which Old Grouch had been sitting just before.

Still as on a photographic plate, new features of Louise Laboine were gradually appearing; but the general impression remained vague.

Had she been trying to find Jeanine Armenieu during those last two months, when she had no regular work?

She might, for example, have suddenly seen in the paper that this girl was to marry Marco Santoni, and that a big wedding reception would be held at the *Roméo*.

If so, it must have been evening before she read the announcement, for it was after nine o'clock when she rushed to Mademoiselle Irène to get herself an evening dress.

She had left the shop in the Rue de Douai towards ten o'clock. What had she done between ten and midnight? She had only about twenty minutes' walk from the Rue de Douai to the Rue Caumartin. Could she have spent all that time in the streets, trying to make up her mind?

Dr. Paul's report was still lying on the desk. Maigret glanced over it again. It stated that the girl's stomach contained an appreciable quantity of alcohol.

According to the head waiter's statement, she had had no chance to drink during the fairly short time she spent in the *Roméo*.

So she must either have been drinking beforehand, to screw up her courage, or afterwards, between the time when she left the wedding reception and the time when she was found dead in the Place Vintimille.

He walked across to the door of the Duty Room, opened it and called Janvier.

"I've got a job for you. Go up to the Rue de Douai and walk down from there to the Rue Caumartin, stopping at every bar and café, and show them the photograph."

"The one in evening dress?"

"Yes. Try to find out whether anyone saw the girl on Monday night, between ten o'clock and midnight."

Just as Janvier was closing the door, Maigret called after him:
"If you meet Lognon, don't tell him what you're doing."

"Very well, Chief!"

59

The blue suitcase stood in a corner of Maigret's office, and it seemed to have no more to tell them. It was a cheap one, of a make on sale in all department stores and in the shops around railway stations. It was battered.

Maigret went out of his office, and, at the end of the passage, into the room occupied by his colleague Priollet, of the Society Division. Priollet was signing letters, and Maigret placidly puffed at his pipe as he watched him.

"Anything I can do for you?"

"Something you can tell me. Do you know a fellow called Santoni?"

"Marco?"

"Yes."

"He's just got married."

"What else do you know about him?"

"He makes a lot of money, and spends it as easily as he earns it. Handsome fellow, fond of women, good food and expensive cars."

"Anything against him?"

"Not a thing. He comes of a good family, from Milan. His father's some kind of vermouth magnate, and Marco runs the French side of the business. He hangs around the bars in the Champs-Élysées, the fashionable restaurants and the pretty girls. One of them got her hooks on to him a few months ago."

"Jeanine Armenieu."

"I didn't know her name. We have no reason to concern ourselves with him or his love-affairs. I happened to hear he was getting married, because he gave a terrific party in a night-club he hired for the occasion."

"I'd like you to make a few enquiries about his wife. She's been living at the *Hôtel Washington* for the last few months. I want to know where she came from, what she was doing before she met him, and who her friends were—men and women. Especially women."

Priollet made some pencil jottings on a pad.

"Is that all? Anything to do with the girl from the Place Vintimille?"

Maigret nodded.

"You don't happen to have anything in your files about a certain Louise Laboine?"

Priollet swung round towards an open door:

"Dauphin! Did you hear that name?"

"Yes, sir."

60

"Check up on it, will you?"

A few minutes later Sergeant Dauphin called from the next room:

"Nothing about her."

"Sorry, old man. I'll see about Madame Santoni. But I can't get at her for questioning just yet, because the papers say they are honeymooning in Italy."

"I don't want her questioned for the time being."

According to the clock on the mantelpiece—a black clock, identical in appearance with the one in Maigret's office and every Chief-Inspector's office—it was a few minutes before noon.

"Come and have a drink."

"Not just now," replied Priollet, "I'm expecting someone."

Maigret did not seem to know what to do with his huge self. He strolled down the corridor and looked, with a glum expression on his face, into the glass-partitioned waiting-room where two or three people were disconsolately waiting. A few minutes later he went up a narrow staircase which led to the attics, and pushed open the door of the laboratory. Moers was peering through a microscope.

"Have you had a look at those clothes I sent up?"

There was never any sign of excitement in this part of the building; men in grey smocks did their meticulous work, manipulating complicated apparatus in an atmosphere of perfect calm, and Moers himself looked like the personification of tranquillity.

"The black dress had never been to the cleaner's," he said, "but it had often had spots cleaned with benzine and been regularly brushed. All the same, there was some dust caught in the fibres. I analysed that. And I looked at some spots which the benzine hadn't digested. That's how I traced the green paint."

"Is that all?"

"Nearly. A few grains of sand."

"River sand?"

"Sea sand, the kind you get on the Normandy coast."

"Is that the same as Mediterranean sand?"

"No. Atlantic coast sand is different, too."

Maigret pottered about the laboratory for a little time, and knocked his pipe out against the heel of his shoe. When he went downstairs again it was after twelve o'clock and the plain-clothes men were going off to lunch.

"Lucas is looking for you!" said one of them, Jussieu, who worked under him.

61

He found Lucas with his hat already on.

"I was just going. I left a note on your desk. Féret asks you to ring him up as soon as possible. It's about the young girl, apparently."

Maigret went into his office and picked up the telephone.

"Get me through to the Flying Squad at Nice, please."

He had never known so few telephone calls after the publication of a photograph in the papers. So far there had been only one, that from Rose, the little servant in the Rue de Clichy.

And yet dozens, hundreds, of people must have seen the girl, who had been about in Paris for several months at the very least.

"Hello? Féret?"

"Is that you, Chief?"

Detective-Sergeant Féret had worked under Maigret before going to Nice, where he had asked to be transferred because of his wife's health.

"I had a 'phone call early this morning about that girl you're concerned with. Do you know her name now, by the way?"

"Apparently it was Louise Laboine."

"That's right. Would you like to have the particulars? They don't add up to much, I'm afraid. I thought I'd wait for your instructions before investigating any further. Anyhow, about half-past eight this morning I had a 'phone call from a woman fishmonger; Alice Feynerou, her name is. . . . Hello? . . ."

"Hello—yes?"

Maigret was jotting down the name on one of Lognon's papers on the off-chance.

"She said she'd recognized the photograph, which had just come out in the *Éclaireur*. But it went pretty far back—four or five years, it seems. The girl, who was only a kid at the time, was living with her mother in the house next door to the fish-shop."

"Was the woman able to tell you anything about them?"

"The mother used to run up bills, that's what she remembers best. She described them as 'the sort one should never give credit to.' "

"What else did she say?"

"The girl and her mother had quite a pleasant flat, not far from the Avenue Clémenceau. The mother was said to have been a beauty in her day. She was older than one would expect the mother of a fifteen- or sixteen-year-old girl to be. In those days she was already well past fifty."

"What did the two of them live on?"

62

"Goodness knows. The mother used to dress very smartly, usually went out after lunch and didn't get home till late at night."

"Is that all? No man in the story?"

"No man. If there'd been any gossip, the fish-woman would have been only too delighted to tell me about it."

"Did they leave the neighbourhood together?"

"Apparently. One fine day they vanished, and they seem to have left a few debts behind them."

"Have you checked the name Laboine in your records?"

"That was the first thing I did. There's nothing there. I've asked all the other chaps. One of them, who's been here a long time, says the name sounds familiar, but doesn't remember in what connection."

"Would you look into it?"

"I'll do my best. What do you mostly want to know?"

"Everything. When the girl left Nice. What's become of the mother. What they lived on. Who their friends were. By the way, if the girl was only fifteen or sixteen at that time, she was probably still at school. Would you check up with the schools in the town?"

"Right. I'll ring you back as soon as I've anything to report."

"Check the casino, too, about the mother."

"That's just occurred to me."

A few more lines added to the picture. It was a little girl, now, that telephone call had conjured up, a little girl who used to be sent for fish to a shop where her mother owed money and where she had a cool reception.

Maigret put on his coat and hat and went downstairs, passing, without a glance, a man who was being led up by two policemen. Before crossing the courtyard he went into the office of the Hotels Section. He had written the names Louise Laboine and Jeanine Armenieu on a piece of paper.

"Would you ask your fellows to look for these two names in the registration forms? More likely to be last year than this."

It was best that poor Lognon shouldn't find out that some of his work was being done for him in this way.

There had been a shower a few minutes earlier, and now the sun had come out and the rain was already drying off the cobblestones. Maigret nearly hailed a passing taxi, but changed his mind and walked slowly to the *Brasserie Dauphine*, where he remained standing at the bar. He couldn't decide what he wanted to drink. Two detectives from another department were discussing the retirement age.

"What'll you have, Monsieur Maigret?"

He might have been thought to be in a bad temper, but those who were used to him knew it was not that. Only, he was everywhere at once, at the widow's flat in the Rue de Clichy, at the dress-shop in the Rue de Douai, on the bench in the Trinité garden, and now in Nice, imagining a little girl in a fish-shop.

All these pictures, still dim, mingled together, but something was bound to emerge. There was one, in particular, which he could not blot out of his mind, that of a body lying naked under the harsh electric-light with the figure of Dr. Paul, in his white overall, pulling on a pair of rubber gloves.

"A Pernod!" he said without thinking.

Hadn't Paul said that, before she was knocked on the head, the girl had fallen to her knees?

A little before that she had called at the *Roméo* in the Rue Caumartin, where a taxi-driver had noticed her shabby dress, where the barman had seen her making her way through the crowd of dancers, where she had spoken to the head waiter and afterwards to the bride.

Then she walked through the rain. She had been seen crossing the Place St. Augustin and glimpsed later on in the Boulevard Haussmann, at the corner of the Faubourg St. Honoré.

What was she thinking about, all that time? Where was she going? What was she hoping for?

She had practically no money left, scarcely enough for a meal. Old Madame Crémieux had turned her out.

She could not have gone very far, and then, somewhere, someone had slapped her or hit her with his fist, she had fallen to her knees, and someone had struck her on the head with a hard, heavy weapon.

That, if the post-mortem could be relied on, had been about two o'clock. What had she been doing between midnight and two in the morning?

After that there was nothing more that she had done; it was the murderer who had gone and deposited her dead body right in the middle of the Place Vintimille.

"Queer sort of a girl!" grunted Maigret.

"I beg your pardon?" said the waiter enquiringly.

"Nothing. What time is it?"

He went home to lunch.

"About that question you asked me last night," remarked

Madame Maigret during their meal: "I've been thinking about it all morning. There's another reason why a girl might put on an evening dress."

Not so tactful with her as with Lognon, he muttered absentmindedly, without giving her a chance to finish:

"I know. For a wedding."

Madame Maigret said no more.

CHAPTER FIVE

TWICE, or perhaps three times that afternoon, Maigret, raising his head from his papers, looked at the sky and, seeing that it was pale blue, with gold-tipped clouds and that the roof-tops were streaming with sunlight, stopped his task with a sigh and went over to open the window.

On each occasion he had hardly had time to return to his desk and draw in some breaths of spring air which made his pipe taste all the better, before the papers began to flutter about, then rose in a whirl and finally scattered over the room.

The clouds had already turned from white-and-gold to slate grey and rain was slanting down and splashing on the window-sill, while passers-by on the Pont St. Michel suddenly began to walk more quickly like people in the early silent films, the women holding their skirts.

After his second attempt it was not even rain that began to fall, but hailstones, which bounced on the sill like ping-pong balls, and after shutting the window he found some in the middle of the floor.

Was Lognon still out of doors, with doleful eyes and hanging head, like a game-dog following some unknown scent through the crowd? It was quite possible. It was rather likely. He had not telephoned. He never carried an umbrella. And he was not the kind of man to squeeze into a doorway with other people and wait for a shower to pass; in fact, he very likely got a bitter satisfaction from being soaked, from being the only one, at the height of the downpour, to walk along the pavement, a martyr to injustice and to his own conscientiousness.

As for Janvier, he had got back to the office at about three o'clock, slightly tipsy. He was seldom seen in this state, his eyes brighter and his voice more jocular than usual.

"I've got it, Chief!"

65

"Got what?"

To judge by Janvier's tone he might have found the girl alive.

"You were quite right."

"About what?"

"I did all the bars and all the cafés."

"So I see."

"She didn't stop till she got to the one at the corner of the Rue Caumartin and the Rue St. Lazare. The waiter who served her is called Eugène. He's bald, lives at Bécon-les-Bruyères, and has a daughter about the same age as the dead girl."

Janvier crushed out his cigarette in the ash-tray and lit another. "She came in about half-past ten and sat down in a corner, near the cash-desk. She looked cold and ordered a grog. When Eugène brought it, she asked him for a telephone-counter. She went into the telephone-box, but came out again almost at once. From that time until nearly midnight she made at least ten attempts to 'phone somebody."

"How many grogs did she drink?"

"Three. Every few minutes, she went back in the box and dialled a number."

"Did she finally get it?"

"Eugène doesn't know. Each time he thought she'd begin to cry; but she didn't. Once he tried to start a conversation, and she just stared at him without answering. You see, it all fits in. She left the shop in the Rue de Douai at a few minutes past ten. She had time to walk down to the Rue Caumartin. She stayed in the café, trying to get someone on the telephone, until she moved on to the *Roméo*. Three grogs isn't bad for a girl of that age. She must have been a bit high."

"And practically penniless," observed Maigret.

"I hadn't thought of that. It's true. What do I do now?"

"Are you free at the moment?"

"Except for some routine stuff."

Now he, too, was bent forward at his own desk, probably wishing that his round of the cafés had been a longer one.

Maigret glanced through some files, making notes as he went on, and now and then rang up some other department. It was nearly five o'clock when Priollet came in. Before sitting down he enquired:

"I'm not disturbing you?"

"Not a bit. I'm just getting rid of some old stuff."

"You know Lucien, one of my Inspectors? He lives not far from you."

66

Maigret vaguely remembered the man. He was short, fat and very dark, and his wife kept a herb shop in the Rue du Chemin-Vert. Maigret saw him chiefly in the summer, standing in the doorway of the shop, when he and his wife went past on their way to dine with Dr. Pardon.

"A quarter of an hour or so ago, I asked Lucien, on the off-chance, as I've asked all my other men."

"About Jeanine Armenieu?"

"Yes. He looked at me with a frown. 'That's queer,' he said. 'My wife was just talking about her at lunch. I didn't pay much attention. Wait a minute, I'm trying to remember what she said. Oh yes:

" ' *"You remember that pretty, busty, red-haired girl who used to live next door? She's just got married, to a rich man. They hired a whole night-club for the wedding party."* My wife mentioned the name, and I'm sure it was Armenieu. And she added: *"I suppose she won't be coming round to buy camomile from me any more."* ' "

Maigret himself might have come across the girl, and she had probably gone to the same shops as Mme. Maigret, who did nearly all her marketing in the Rue du Chemin-Vert.

"Lucien asked me whether he should make any enquiries. I said I thought you'd rather keep things in your own hands."

"Nothing fresh about Santoni?"

"Nothing of interest, except that his friends were surprised that he got married. None of his other affairs had lasted very long."

This was an interval between two showers. The sun had come out and the streets were drying. Maigret felt in need of fresh air, and was about to put on his hat and coat when the telephone rang.

"Hello? Chief-Inspector Maigret here."

It was Nice. Down there Féret must have made a discovery, for he was as excited as Janvier had just been.

"I've found the mother, Chief! I had to go to Monte Carlo to get hold of her."

It's nearly always like that. You mark time for hours, days, sometimes weeks, and then all the information pours in at once.

"Was she at the Casino?"

"She's still there. She informed me that she couldn't leave the roulette table before she'd won back her stake and earned her living for the day."

"She goes there every day?"

"Exactly as other people go to an office. She plays until she's won the few hundred francs she needs to live on. Then she leaves, without trying to win any more."

Maigret knew the system.

"What sort of weather are you having?"

"Glorious. The town's packed with foreigners who've come for the Carnival. To-morrow there's the *bataille de fleurs*, and they're putting up the stands now."

"Is her name Laboine?"

"Her identity-card says 'Germaine Laboine,' but she calls herself Liliane. The croupiers call her Lili. She's nearly sixty, heavily made-up and loaded with fake jewellery. You see the sort? I had a hell of a job to get her away from the roulette table, where she stuck like an old hand. To make her budge I had to tell her, straight out, 'Your daughter's dead.'"

"She hadn't seen it in the papers?" asked Maigret.

"She never reads the papers. These people are only interested in roulette. Every morning they buy a printed list of the winning numbers that came up the day before and during the night. Several of them take the same bus from Nice, and rush straight to the tables, like shop-girls to their counters."

"How did she take the news?"

"It's hard to say. Red had just come up for the fifth time, and she'd put her stake on black. First she pushed some chips across the table. Her lips moved, but I couldn't hear what she said. It wasn't until black at last came up and she'd scooped in her winnings, that she came away from the table."

"'How did it happen?' she asked me."

"'Won't you come outside with me?'"

"'I can't just now. I have to keep an eye on the table. We can quite well talk here. Where did it happen?'"

"'In Paris.'"

"'Did she die in hospital?'"

"'She was killed. She was found dead in the street.'"

"'An accident?'"

"'A murder.'"

"That seemed to surprise her; but she still cocked an ear as the croupier called out the numbers. At one time, she interrupted me by saying:

"'Excuse me. . . .'

"And she went and put some chips on a number. I wondered whether she drugged. But on the whole I think not. She's reached

68

a stage where she's not much more than a piece of clockwork, if you know what I mean."

Maigret agreed. He had seen others of her kind.

"It took a long time to get anything out of her. She kept saying: 'Why can't you wait till this evening, when I get back to Nice? I'll tell you all you want to know then. There's nothing to hide.'

"Are you there, Chief? Mind you, she had some excuse for claiming it was impossible for her to leave the Casino. It's almost a profession for those people. They have a small capital, enough to double their stake a certain number of times. As long as they can keep on doing that and their colour finally comes up, they're safe. But they have to be satisfied with small winnings, enough to live on and pay their bus fare every day. The management knows them. There are a few men among them, but most of them are elderly women. When there are a lot of people in the place and all the tables are full, the management gets rid of them by doling them out the sum they'd have won in a few hours anyhow. . . ."

"Does she live alone?"

"Yes. I'm to go round there when she gets home. She has a furnished room in the Rue Greuze, near the Boulevard Victor-Hugo. Her dress dated back at least ten years, and so did her hat. I asked her whether she'd been married, and she answered: 'That depends on what you mean by married.'

"She informed me that she'd been an artiste, that under her stage name of Lili France she'd toured for years in the Near East and in Asia Minor. I suppose you know what that means, too?"

In the old days there were agencies in Paris to recruit these artistes. They only had to learn a few dance steps or a few songs. Then off they were sent to Turkey, Egypt or Beirut, where they were employed as bar-girls in cabarets.

"Was that where her daughter was born?"

"No. She was born in France, when her mother was nearly forty."

"At Nice?"

"As far as I could make out. It isn't easy to question a woman whose eyes are riveted on a little roulette ball and whose fingers tighten every time it comes to a stop. In the end, she put her foot down. 'I've done nothing wrong, have I? Then leave me alone. I've told you I'll answer all your questions this evening.'"

"Is that all you got from her?"

"No. The daughter cleared out four years ago, leaving a letter to say she was going for good."

"She'd be about sixteen then?"

"Just sixteen. She left on her birthday, and her mother's not heard a word from her since."

"She didn't inform the police?"

"No. I think she was rather glad to be rid of her."

"And she never learnt what had become of her?"

"She got a letter a few months later from a Mademoiselle Poré, living in the Rue du Chemin-Vert, who said she'd do better to keep an eye on her daughter and that it would be as well not to leave her alone in Paris. I don't know the number of Mademoiselle Poré's house, but Madame Laboine promised to let me have it this evening."

"I can get hold of her."

"You know about that?"

"More or less."

Maigret glanced at Priollet, who was listening. The same information now was coming in from several different sources at once.

"What time are you to go and see her?"

"As soon as she gets back to Nice. That may be any time between seven o'clock and midnight. It depends on how the roulette goes."

"Ring me up at Boulevard Richard-Lénoir."

"Right, Chief."

Maigret rang off.

"From what Féret tells me from Nice," he said, "the person with whom Jeanine Armenieu stayed in the Rue du Chemin-Vert was a Mademoiselle Poré. And she knew Louise Laboine."

"You're going over there?"

Maigret opened the door.

"Coming with me, Janvier?"

A few minutes later they set off by car. In the Rue du Chemin-Vert they pulled up at the herbalist's, and found Lucien's wife behind the counter, in the half-light of the shop with its pleasant smell of dried herbs.

"What can I do for you, Monsieur Maigret?"

"It seems you know Jeanine Armenieu?"

"My husband told you? I was talking to him about her at midday to-day, because I'd just read an account of her wedding in the paper. She's a real beautiful girl."

"How long is it since you last saw her?"

70

"At least three years. Wait a minute. It was before my husband got his rise. That would be nearly three and a half years ago. She was very young then, but fully developed, very much a woman, and all the men used to stare after her in the street."

"She lived next door to you?"

"She was staying with her aunt, Mademoiselle Poré, a good customer of mine, who works at the telephone exchange. After a time I believe they didn't get on very well, and Jeanine decided to move to a place of her own."

"Do you think Mademoiselle Poré is at home now?"

"If I'm not mistaken, she's working from six in the morning till three in the afternoon this week. So the chances are you'll find her at home."

Maigret and Janvier went into the next-door house soon afterwards.

"Mademoiselle Poré?" they asked the concierge.

"Second floor left. There's someone with her already."

There was no lift. The stairs were dark. Instead of a press-button, there was a plush rope hanging which set a little bell jangling inside the apartment.

The door opened at once. A thin, sharp-featured woman with beady black eyes stood looking severely at them.

"What do you want?"

Maigret was about to reply when he caught sight of Lognon inside in the gloom.

"I'm sorry, Lognon. I didn't know you'd be here."

Old Grouch gazed at him with a resigned expression, while Mademoiselle Poré murmured, "You know each other?"

She moved to let them in. The flat was very clean and smelt of cooking. There were four of them now, standing awkwardly in the little dining-room.

"Have you been here long, Lognon?"

"Not more than five minutes."

This was not the moment to ask him how he had got hold of the address.

"Have you found out anything yet?"

It was Mademoiselle Poré who replied:

"I'd begun to tell him what I know and I haven't finished. My only reason for not going to the police when I saw the photograph was that I couldn't be sure of recognizing her. People change in three and a half years, especially at that age. Besides, I don't like interfering when it's none of my business."

"Jeanine Armenieu is your niece, isn't she?"

71

"I was not referring to her, but to her friend. As for Jeanine, yes, she is the daughter of my half-brother, and the way he brought her up is nothing to be proud of."

"Does she come from the South?"

"If you call Lyon the South. My poor brother works in a textile factory, and he's been a changed man since he lost his wife."

"When did his wife die?"

"Last year."

"Jeanine Armenieu came to live in Paris four years ago, I believe?"

"Yes—about four years ago. Lyon wasn't good enough for her any longer. She was seventeen years old and wanted a life of her own. They're all like that nowadays, I'm told. My brother wrote to tell me he couldn't keep her back any longer, she'd made up her mind to leave home; and he asked me whether I would find room for her. I said I could, and that I might even be able to find a job for her."

She pronounced each syllable distinctly, as though relating something of the utmost importance. Looking from one to another of the men, she suddenly asked:

"If you all belong to the police, how is it you arrived separately?"

What reply could they give? Lognon hung his head.

Maigret said:

"We belong to different departments."

Really putting her foot in it, she looked at Maigret's impressive bulk, and remarked:

"I suppose you're the most important. What are you?"

"Chief-Inspector."

"Are you Inspector Maigret?"

As he nodded, she drew forward a chair for him.

"Won't you sit down? I'll tell you the whole story. Where was I? Oh yes, my half-brother's letter. I can look it up if you like, I keep all the letters I receive, even family ones."

"It's not necessary. Thank you."

"Just as you like. Well, to cut a long story short, I received this letter, answered it, and my niece arrived one morning about half-past seven. That in itself is enough to give you an idea of her mentality. There are some very good trains during the day, but she had insisted on taking a night train. It sounds more romantic, you see? Luckily I was on the second shift that week. Well, to get on, I won't say anything about her clothes or her hair style. But I said a word to her about them, and explained squarely that if she didn't want to make herself a by-word in the district, she'd do well to alter them.

"I've been twenty-two years in this flat. It isn't big or luxurious, but it has got two bedrooms, one of which I gave to Jeanine. I made outings for a week to show her round Paris."

"What did she mean to do?"

"Need you ask? To find a rich man—that was what she meant to do. And according to the papers, she's succeeded. But I wouldn't like to go about it the way she did."

"Did she find work?"

"Behind the counter in a shop on the main boulevards. A leather-goods shop near the Place de l'Opéra."

"Did she stay there long?"

She was obviously determined to tell her story in her own way.

"If you keep asking me questions, you'll make me forget where I've got to. I shan't leave anything out, you may be sure. So there were the two of us living here. That is to say, I thought there were two of us living here. One week out of two I'm free in the morning, and the other week after three in the afternoon. Months went by. It was winter—a very cold winter. I went on doing my shopping in the neighbourhood as usual. And it was because of the food that I began to get suspicious, especially because of the butter, which was disappearing unusually fast. So was the bread. And sometimes I couldn't find in the larder the left-over meat or cake I was sure I had put away.

" 'Did you eat that cutlet?' 'Yes, Auntie; I felt a bit hungry yesterday evening.'

"To cut a long story short, it was a long while before I caught on. Do you know what? All that time, without my knowing it, there had been a third person in my flat.

"Not a man—never fear. A young girl. The one whose photo was in yesterday's paper—who was found dead in the Place Vintimille. Which proves, by the by, that I was right to get upset, for things like that don't happen to people like you and me."

She never had to pause for breath. She was standing up all this time, with her back to the window, her hands clasped over her flat stomach, and her words came pouring out, sentences one after another in a continuous stream.

"I've nearly finished—don't worry. I mustn't waste your time, for I expect you're a very busy man."

She was talking solely to Maigret, and Lognon she now considered as a mere extra.

"One morning, when I was doing the housework, I dropped a reel of cotton. It rolled under Jeanine's bed and I bent down to pick it up. I must confess I gave a shriek, and I think in my place you would have done the same. There was someone under the bed, someone staring at me with eyes like a cat's.

"Luckily it was a woman. That made it less frightening. To be on the safe side, I went and fetched the poker, and then I said:

" 'You come out of there.'

"She wasn't even as old as Jeanine, she can't have been more than sixteen. But do you suppose she burst into tears or begged my pardon? Not a bit of it. She went on staring at me as though I was the one who was behaving outrageously.

" 'Who let you in here?' I asked.

" 'I'm a friend of Jeanine's.'

" 'Is that a reason for hiding under the bed? What were you doing there, under the bed?'

" 'Waiting for you to go out.'

" 'Why?'

" 'So I could get out myself.'

"Would you believe it, Inspector? This had been going on for weeks, for months. She'd arrived in Paris at the same time as my niece. The two of them had struck up an acquaintance in the train. They were travelling third class, and as they couldn't sleep they had spent the night telling each other their life-stories. This girl—Louise, her name was—had just enough money to last for two or three weeks.

"She found work, sticking stamps on envelopes in some office or other, but her employer soon began to make passes at her, it appears, and she slapped his face.

"At least that's what she told me, but it isn't necessarily so.

"When her money was all gone and she'd been thrown out of the cheap hotel where she was staying, she got in touch with Jeanine, who offered to let her sleep here for a few nights, till she found other work.

"Jeanine had not dared to say anything to me about it. She used to let Louise into the flat while I was out, and the child hid under my niece's bed until I was asleep.

"During my weeks on the second shift, she had to stay under the bed till half-past two, as I don't begin work till three o'clock."

All this time Maigret had been trying hard to keep a straight face, for Mademoiselle Poré never took her eyes off him, and would not have appreciated the least sign of amusement.

"To cut a long story short . . ." she repeated.

74

It was at least the third time she had used this phrase, and Maigret could not restrain a glance at his watch.

"If I am boring you——"

"Not at all."

"You have an appointment?"

"I still have some time."

"I am coming to the end. But I want to make it clear that for several months every word I said was overheard by a third person, an adventuress whom I had never even met and who was spying on all my movements. I was going on with my quiet, orderly life, thinking I was on my own, never suspecting——"

"You wrote to her mother, I believe?"

"How do you know? She told you?"

Lognon looked very sour. He had discovered the Poré clue, which had probably cost him some long, tedious foot-slogging around Paris. How many showers had he been caught in, not bothering to take shelter?

But Maigret had not even needed to leave his office. Information came to him without his stirring a finger. So not only had he caught up with Mademoiselle Poré almost at the same moment as Lognon, but he even seemed to know more about her.

"I didn't write to her mother at once. I began by throwing the girl out and telling her she had better not come back. I suppose I could have sued her?"

"For trespass?"

"And for the food she stole during all those weeks. When my niece got home I didn't mince my words about what I thought of her and the company she kept. Jeanine wasn't much better herself, as I discovered when she left here in her turn a few weeks later and went to live in an hotel room. The young lady needed her freedom, you understand? To entertain men!"

"Are you sure she did?"

"Why else should she have wanted to move to an hotel, when she had board and lodging here? I asked her about her friend, and got the name and address of the girl's mother. After hesitating for nearly a week, I wrote her a letter of which I kept a copy. I don't know whether it had any effect, but she can't say I didn't warn her! Would you like to see it?"

"It isn't necessary. Did you keep in touch with your niece after she left here?"

"She never once came near me again, or thought to send me a card at New Year. I suppose all young people are the same

75

nowadays. What little I know of her I heard from my brother, who's got wool over his eyes. She twists him round her little finger. She writes to him every so often, tells him that she's well, that she's working hard, and always ends up by promising she'll soon be home to see him."

"Has she ever been back to Lyon?"

"Once, for Christmas."

"She hasn't any brothers or sisters?"

"She had a brother, but he died of tuberculosis. To cut a long story short——"

Maigret was beginning automatically to count the number of times she used the phrase.

"She's twenty-one now. I suppose she told my brother she was getting married, but he hasn't mentioned it to me. I learnt of it from the newspapers. Wasn't it a curious coincidence, her friend being killed on the night of the wedding?"

"Were they still in touch?"

"How should I know? But if you ask me, a girl like Louise didn't lose a friend that easily. People who live by sponging on others and hiding under beds take some shaking off. And that Santoni is a really rich man."

"So it's three years now since you last saw your niece?"

"A little more than three years. Once last summer, round about July, I caught sight of her in a train. It was at St. Lazare station. I was going to Mantes-la-Jolie for the day. It was very hot. It was my free day and I was longing to get out into the country. There was a train drawn up alongside ours, a Pullman train; someone told me it was going to Deauville. Just as we began to move out of the station, I saw Jeanine in the other train. She pointed me out to the person sitting next to her, and at the last moment she gave me a mocking little nod."

"She was with a woman?"

"I couldn't see. I got the impression she was well dressed, and there were only first-class carriages on that train."

Janvier, as usual, had been taking notes, not many, for all this chatter could be summed up in a few words.

"Did you know what friends your niece had while she was living here?"

"According to her, she had none at all. But one can hardly rely on the word of a girl who hides people under her bed."

"Well, thank you, Mademoiselle."

"Is that all you want to know?"

"Unless you have any further information?"

"I can't remember. . . . No. If anything occurs to me later on. . . ."

She hated to see them go. She wished she had more to tell them. Lognon let Maigret and Janvier pass, and brought up the rear as they went downstairs.

Outside on the pavement, the Chief-Inspector was rather at a loss for words.

"I'm sorry, old man. If I'd known you were there. . . ."

"It doesn't matter."

"You've done a good job. Things will probably move fast now."

"Does that mean you don't need me any more?"

"Of course I didn't mean that!"

Lucien's wife was watching them through the window of her shop.

"I've nothing particular for you to do at the moment. Perhaps you ought to rest a bit now and look after that bronchitis."

"It's only a cold. Thank you, all the same."

"Can I drop you somewhere?"

"No. I'll take the Underground."

He was determined to stress the difference between those who left by cars and himself who was walking to the Underground where, as it was now six o'clock, he would be caught in the crowds.

"Congratulations. If you find out anything fresh, ring me up. I'll keep you informed about my end of things."

When he was alone again in the car with Janvier, Maigret sighed.

"Poor Lognon! I'd have given a lot to have arrived after he'd left."

"Are you going back to Headquarters?"

"No. Drop me at home."

It was just round the corner. They had no time to discuss what they had just learned. No doubt both of them were thinking of the child of sixteen who had run away from her mother and who, for months, had been obliged every day to hide under a bed.

Old Madame Crêmieux had said the girl was stand-offish, not deigning to speak to anyone. Rose, the Larchers' little servant, had seen her sitting all alone, for hours, on a bench in the Trinité garden. All alone she had paid her two visits to Mademoiselle Irène's shop. She had gone alone to the *Roméo*, and been alone

77

at the last, when she left there, refusing the offer of the taxi-driver who had seen her later, in the rain, first as she walked across the Place St. Augustin and then as she came to the Faubourg St. Honoré.

After that there was nothing, but a body stretched out on the wet cobbles of the Place Vintimille.

She no longer had the velvet cape or the silver brocade hand-bag she had borrowed, and one of her high-heeled shoes was missing.

"See you to-morrow, Chief."

"See you to-morrow, Janvier, my boy."

"Any instructions?"

It was impossible to question Jeanine Armenieu, now Madame Santoni, who was honeymooning at Florence.

"I'm expecting a call from Nice this evening."

There were still a lot of gaps to fill in.

And somewhere there was someone who had killed the young girl and brought her to the Place Vintimille.

CHAPTER SIX

At DINNER, Madame Maigret began to talk about their neighbour's little girl, who had paid her first visit to the dentist that day, and had said. . . . What was it she had said? Maigret, without realizing that he was not listening properly, sat watching his wife, whose voice flowed on with a pleasant musical sound, and finally she broke off to ask him:

"Aren't you amused?"

"Oh yes—it's very funny."

His mind had been far away. It happened to him now and then. At such times he would look at people, with heavy, staring eyes, and those who didn't know him well couldn't tell that in his eyes they were only a kind of wall or backcloth.

Madame Maigret did not try again, and set about doing the dishes, while he sank into his arm-chair and opened the evening paper. Once the washing-up was finished, silence descended on the apartment, broken only by the sound of crackling paper as a page was turned, and twice the rain could be heard falling outside.

About ten o'clock, seeing him carefully fold the paper, she hoped for a moment they were going to bed; but he only took a magazine from a pile nearby, and began reading that. So she went on sewing, making a remark now and again, not to let the silence seem too empty. It didn't matter whether he answered or not, or merely grunted: it was more homely.

The people in the flat above had switched off the wireless and gone to bed.

"You're waiting for something?"

"I may get a telephone call."

Féret had promised to look up Louise's mother as soon as she got back from Monte Carlo and ask her some more questions. He might be delayed by another job. The evening before the Battle of Flowers, they would be pretty busy down there.

After a time Madame Maigret noticed that her husband was no longer turning the pages. His eyes were still open, however. She waited a long time before suggesting:

"What about going to bed, all the same?"

It was after eleven o'clock. Maigret made no objection, carried the telephone into the bedroom, plugged it in and stood it on his bedside table.

They undressed and took turns in the bathroom, going through their usual nightly routine. When they were in bed, Maigret put out the light and turned to kiss his wife.

"Good-night."

"Good-night. Do try to get to sleep."

His thoughts were still revolving around Louise Laboine and the other people who had emerged, one by one, from the background, to form a kind of procession escorting her. The only difference was that now all these people were becoming indistinct and fantastic, and that in the end they got mixed up and began to play one another's parts.

Later still, Maigret dreamt he was playing chess. But he was so tired, and the game had been going on so long, that he began to confuse the various pieces, mistaking queen for king, bishops for knights, and forgetting where he had moved his castles. This was all very distressing, because the Chief was watching him. The game was of the utmost importance to Police Headquarters. His opponent, in fact, was none other than Lognon, whose face wore a sardonic smile as he waited confidently for the moment when he would checkmate Maigret.

That must not happen. The prestige of Headquarters was at stake. That was why they were all standing behind him, watching—Lucas, Janvier, young Lapointe, Torrence, and others whose faces he could not distinguish.

"You whispered to him!" said Lognon to someone who was standing by the Chief-Inspector's shoulder. "But it doesn't matter."

He, Lognon, was all alone. He had nobody to help him. If he won, what on earth would people say?

"Whisper as much as you like. All I ask is that there's no cheating."

Why should Lognon suspect that Maigret had been intending to cheat? Was he in the habit of cheating? Had he ever cheated in his life?

If only he could find his queen, he'd be all right—everything depended on her. The best thing would be to have another look at all the squares, one by one. The queen could not have been lost.

The telephone began to ring. He stretched out an arm, and took a moment to find the electric switch.

"A call for you from Nice."

The alarm-clock said ten minutes past one.

"Is that you, Chief?"

"Just a minute, Féret."

"Perhaps I was wrong to wake you up?"

"No. I'm glad you did."

He took a sip of water. Then, as his pipe was lying on the bedside table with some tobacco left in it, he lit it.

"Good! Now go ahead."

"I wasn't sure what to do. I don't know anything about the case except what's been in the papers, so it's difficult for me to tell what's important and what isn't."

"Have you seen the Laboine woman?"

"I've just left her. She didn't get back from Monte Carlo till half-past eleven. I went round at once. She lives in a kind of boarding-house, which seems to cater mostly for crazy old women like herself. The funny thing is that most of them are retired actresses. There's one who used to be a trick rider in a circus, and the landlady was once a singer at the opera, or so she says. It's difficult to describe the impression one gets in the place. None of them had gone to bed. In the evening, those who aren't at the Casino play cards in the drawing-room, which looks straight out of the last century. It's rather like an old-fashioned waxwork show. But I'm boring you!"

"No."

"I tell you all this because I know you like to form your own impression. Since you haven't been able to come down here——"

"Go on."

"First of all I've discovered her background. Her father was a village schoolmaster, in the Haute-Loire. When she was eighteen she went to Paris, and for the next two years she had walking-on parts at the Châtelet. Towards the end she'd be given a little dancing to do in *Round the World in Eighty Days* and in *Michel Strogoff*. Then she went to the Folies-Bergère. And after that she made her first tour, with a company in South America, where she stayed several years. It's impossible to get any precise dates out of her, she's always in a muddle.

"Are you there? I began to wonder again whether she didn't take drugs. But watching her closely, I realized it wasn't that. It's just that she isn't very intelligent, perhaps not quite all there, in fact."

"She never married?"

"I'm just coming to that. She was about thirty when she began her round of the night-clubs in the Near East. It was before the war. She trailed around Bucharest, Sofia, Alexandria. She spent several years at Cairo, and apparently even got as far as Abyssinia.

"I had to worm all this out of her bit by bit. She slumped in an arm-chair, rubbing her swollen ankles, and at one point she asked whether I'd mind if she took off her corset. To cut a long story short——"

The phrase reminded Maigret of Mademoiselle Poré, Jeanine Armenieu's aunt, and her interminable monologue.

Madame Maigret had opened one eye and was watching him.

"At Istanbul, when she was thirty-eight years old, she met a man called Van Cram."

"A man called what?"

"Julius Van Cram—a Dutchman, apparently. According to her, he looked like a real gentleman, and he was staying at the Pera Palace."

Maigret frowned, trying to remember what the name reminded him of. He felt certain he had heard it before.

"How old is Van Cram, do you know?"

"He was a lot older than she was. He must have been over fifty then, so he'd be about seventy by now."

"Is he dead?"

"I don't know. Let me think. I'm trying to tell you everything in the order it came out, so as not to forget any points. She showed me a photo of herself at that time, and I must say she was still a good-looking woman—not young, but an attractive middle-age."

"What did Van Cram do?"

"She doesn't seem to have enquired into that. He spoke several languages fluently, specially English and French. German, too. And he used to go to parties at the various Embassies. She says he fell in love with her and they lived together for a time."

"At the Pera Palace?"

"No. He took a flat for her, not far from the hotel. You must excuse me, Chief, if this is all a bit vague. You can't imagine what a job I had getting even this much out of her! She was always breaking off to tell me about some woman she'd met in one night-club or another and give me all her life story; and she'd begin lamenting and saying 'I know you think I've been a bad mother. . . .'

"After a time she offered me a liqueur. She doesn't drug, but I've an idea she's fond of the bottle.

"'Never a drop before I go to the Casino,' she assured me. 'And I don't drink while I'm playing. Just a glass afterwards, to help me relax.'

"She informed me that gambling was the most strenuous of all human activities.

"To get back to Van Cram. After a few months she found she was pregnant. It had never happened to her before, and she could hardly believe it.

"She told her lover about it, thinking he'd advise her to be rid of the child."

"Would she have agreed to that?"

"She doesn't know. She talks as though the whole thing was a bad joke that fate played against her.

"'I ought to have been pregnant scores of times, and it had to happen when I was over thirty-eight!'

"Those were her words. Van Cram didn't turn a hair. A few weeks later he asked her to marry him."

"Where were they married?"

"At Istanbul. That's what complicates things. I think she was genuinely in love with him. He took her to an office, she doesn't know exactly where, and she signed some papers and took an oath. As long as he said they were married, she believed him.

"A few days after that, he suggested she should come back to France to live."

"With him?"

82

"Yes. They took an Italian boat to Marseilles."

"Did she have a passport in the name of Van Cram?"

"No. I asked her that. It seems they didn't have time to get a new passport for her. They stayed at Marseilles for a couple of weeks and then moved to Nice. That's where the baby was born."

"Were they staying at an hotel?"

"They'd taken a comfortable flat somewhere off the Promenade des Anglais. Two months later, Van Cram went out to buy cigarettes and didn't come back, and she's never seen him since."

"She never had any news of him?"

"He's written to her several times, from all sorts of places—London, Copenhagen, Hamburg, New York, and sent her money each time."

"Large sums?"

"Sometimes, yes. Other times it was next to nothing. He always asked her for news of herself, and especially of the child."

"And did she reply?"

"Yes."

"*Poste restante*, I suppose?"

"Yes. It is since then that she's been gambling. The girl grew up, went to school."

"Did she ever see her father?"

"She was only two months old when he went away, and so far as his wife knows he's never been back to France since then. The last money-order she had was a year ago; it was a pretty big one, but she lost the whole sum in one evening."

"Did Van Cram ever ask where the girl was? Does he know she's left home and gone to Paris?"

"Yes. But the mother didn't know the girl's address."

"Is that the lot, old chap?"

"Just about. I didn't feel she was being quite truthful when she claimed she had no notion where her husband's money came from. . . . Oh, I nearly forgot the most important point. . . . A few years ago she had to renew her identity-card and decided to get one in the name of Van Cram. She was asked for her marriage certificate. She showed the only paper she had, which was made out in Turkish. They examined it carefully, even sent it to the Turkish Consulate. In the end they told her the paper was worthless and she'd never been married at all."

"Was she upset?"

"No. Nothing could upset her, except perhaps seeing red

83

come up twelve times running when she's pinned her faith to black. Listening to her talk, one somehow feels she isn't quite real. She doesn't live in the same world as us. When I spoke about her daughter she didn't show the slightest sign of grief. All she said was:

" 'I hope she didn't suffer too much.' "

"You're off to bed now, I suppose?"

"No such luck! I've got to dash over to Juan-les-Pins, where they've just caught someone cheating in the Casino. . . . Anything else you want me to do, Chief?"

"Not at present. Half a second! Did she show you a photo of her ex-husband?"

"I asked to see one. She said she'd only had one, which she'd taken without his knowledge because he avoided photographers like the plague. Her daughter must have taken it to Paris with her, because it disappeared when she left."

"Thank you."

A moment later, Maigret rang off. But instead of putting out the light and going to sleep again, he got up and filled another pipe.

Old Madame Crêmieux had mentioned having seen a photo in Louise's note-case, but he had been concentrating so hard on the girl herself that he had not taken much notice.

He stood there in his pyjamas, with bare feet in bedroom slippers. His wife refrained from questioning him. Perhaps because of his dream, he suddenly remembered Lognon. Hadn't he said rather casually to him, not long ago, "I'll keep you informed."

The news about Julius Van Cram might affect the whole course of the investigation.

"I'll ring him up in the morning," he muttered.

"What did you say?"

"Nothing. I was talking to myself."

But he looked up Old Grouch's home telephone number in the Place Constantin Pecqueur. That way, he would be above reproach.

"Hello? . . . Could I speak to your husband, please? I'm sorry to have woken you, but——"

"I wasn't asleep. I never get more than an hour or two of sleep in the night."

It was Madame Lognon, at once querulous and mournful.

"This is Chief-Inspector Maigret."

"I recognized your voice."

84

"Might I have a word with your husband?"

"I thought he was with you. At least, he told me he was working for you."

"What time did he go out?"

"Directly after dinner. He hurried over his food and went off, saying he'd probably be out all night."

"Did he tell you where he was going?"

"He never tells me that."

"Thank you very much."

"Isn't it true that he's working for you?"

"Oh yes."

"Then how is it that you don't know——"

"I don't necessarily know of every single thing he does."

She was not convinced; she suspected him of lying, to shield her husband, and would doubtless have asked further questions if he had not rung off. He immediately telephoned to the Second District Station, where the telephone was answered by a detective called Ledent.

"Is Lognon there?"

"He hasn't been in at all to-night."

"Thank you. If he comes in, ask him to ring me at my home."

"Very well, Monsieur Maigret."

Then an unpleasant idea struck him, an echo of his dream. Knowing that Lognon was out and about, without the slightest idea what he was doing, he suddenly felt uneasy. There was no more need to visit night-clubs or question taxi-drivers, and everything possible seemed to have been squeezed out of the *Roméo*.

Yet Lognon was off on some all-night chase. Could he have got hold of a clue?

Maigret was not jealous of his colleagues, least of all of his plain-clothes men. When a case was satisfactorily concluded, he nearly always gave them the credit for it. He seldom made statements to the Press. That very afternoon he had left Lucas to talk to the journalists assigned to cover Headquarters.

At the moment, however, he felt irritated. For it was true that, as in the game of chess in his dream, Lognon was alone while Maigret himself could call on the entire Headquarters organization, not to mention the flying squads and the whole police system.

He was ashamed of this feeling, but all the same he felt tempted to dress and go to the Quai des Orfèvres. There was work for him to do there, now he knew the name of the man

85

whose photo Louise Laboine had stolen from her mother and kept so carefully.

His wife watched him go into the dining-room, where he opened the sideboard cupboard and poured himself a small glass of plum brandy.

"Aren't you coming back to bed?"

The logical thing would be to go to the Quai, and he felt that instinctively. If he did not do so, it was to give Lognon his chance and punish himself for his ungenerous thought.

"This case is worrying you, isn't it?"

"It's rather complicated."

It was strange, too, that until now he hadn't been thinking about the murderer, only about the victim; the whole enquiry had been concentrated on her. But now that at last they knew a bit more about her, they could begin to wonder who had killed her.

What on earth could Lognon be up to? He went over to the window and looked out. There was a full moon and a clear sky. The rain had stopped, the roofs were gleaming.

He knocked out his pipe, climbed heavily into bed and kissed his wife.

"Wake me at the usual time," he said.

He had no more dreams that night. When he sat up in bed to drink his morning coffee, the sun was shining. Lognon had not telephoned, which suggested that he had neither called in at the station nor gone home.

At the Quai des Orfèvres Maigret listened to the report without taking part in the discussion, and as soon as it was over went upstairs to the Records Office. There, covering several miles of shelves, were the files of all those who had ever been in trouble with the law. The clerk on duty wore a grey overall, which gave him the air of a warehouse attendant, and the place smelt of musty paper, like a public library.

"Will you see if you have anything about a man called Van Cram, Julius Van Cram?"

"Would it be lately?"

"It might be twenty years ago, or even more."

"Will you wait?"

Maigret sat down. Ten minutes later the clerk brought him a file labelled Van Cram; but it referred to a Joseph Van Cram, who worked for an insurance company in the Rue de Grenelle, Paris, had been convicted of forgery two years previously, and was then only twenty-eight years old.

86

"Is this your only Van Cram?"

"Except for a Von Kramm, with a K and two m's, and he died at Cologne twenty-four years ago."

On a lower floor of the building there were other files, dealing not only with convicted criminals, but with everyone the police had at any time been called upon to investigate. Van Cram the insurance clerk and Von Kramm of Cologne were both here, too.

By going through the list of international crooks and eliminating such of them as had never been in the Near East and whose ages did not tally with that of Madame Laboine's husband, Maigret found himself left with a mere handful of file-cards, one of which ran:

"Hans Ziegler, *alias* Ernst Marek, *alias* John Donley, *alias* Joey Hogan, *alias* Jean Lemke (real name and nationality unknown). Confidence trickster. Specialized con-man. Speaks fluent French, English, German, Dutch, Italian and Spanish, and a little Polish."

It was the Prague police who, thirty years ago, had circulated to all countries the photograph of this Hans Ziegler, who with the help of an accomplice, had swindled a large sum of money. Ziegler had said he was born at Munich, and had worn a blond moustache.

London soon made his acquaintance, as John Donley, a native of San Francisco; and he had been arrested at Copenhagen under the name of Ernst Marek.

He had cropped up in other places as Joey Hogan, Jules Stieb and Carl Spangler.

His appearance, too, changed as the years went by. At first he was tall and thin, though broad-shouldered. He had gradually put on weight and acquired a certain dignity.

He was a good-looking man and dressed well. In Paris he had stayed at a big hotel in the Champs-Élysées, in London at the Savoy. He went to the best places everywhere, and everywhere his method was the same—he followed a system which others had perfected long before, but which had seldom found such a brilliant exponent.

He always worked with another man; but nothing was known about this accomplice, except that he was younger and spoke with a Central European accent.

They would go into some smart bar and single out a victim, a prosperous-looking man, preferably an industrialist or business man up from the provinces.

87

After taking a few drinks with this selected victim, Jean Lemke, Jules Stieb or John Donley, as the case might be, would begin to regret that he didn't know the country well.

"I shall have to find some absolutely trustworthy person," he would say. "I have a very awkward job to put through, and I really don't know how to set about it. I'm so afraid of being swindled!"

After that the details varied, but the main story was always the same. A very wealthy old lady—if this was taking place in Europe she would usually be an American—had entrusted him with a lot of money, to be divided among a certain number of deserving cases. He had the money, in notes, upstairs in his hotel room. But how, being a complete stranger to the country, could he decide what cases were deserving?

Oh! And the old lady had said that part of the money—a third, say, or a quarter—could be used to meet expenses.

Would his new friend—for they were friends, weren't they?—who was obviously an honest man, be kind enough to help him? Naturally they would share the expense-money. . . . It made quite a tidy sum.

He was obliged to be cautious, and felt bound to ask for some security. . . . Suppose his friend paid such-and-such a sum into a bank, just to prove his good faith. . . .

"Wait for me here a moment. . . . Or—no, why don't you come up to my suite?"

The bank-notes were there. There would be a whole despatch-case of them, done up in impressive wads.

"We'll take these with us, and look in at your bank so you can draw the money. . . ."

The amount varied according to the country.

"We'll deposit the whole sum into my account and I'll hand you the despatch-case. All you'll have to do is to distribute the notes, after deducting your share."

In the taxi the despatch-case was placed between them. The victim cashed his cheque. Outside his own bank, which was generally a big one in a central part of the town, Lemke, *alias* Stieb, *alias* Ziegler, etc., would leave the brief-case with his companion.

"I won't be a minute. . . ." He dashed off, and the victim, who would never see his own money again, soon discovered that the wads of notes, except the top ones, consisted of strips of newspaper.

On most of the occasions when the man had been arrested,

88

he had nothing compromising in his possession. The stolen money had vanished, carried off by an accomplice to whom he had passed it, unperceived, in the crowd thronging the bank.

One and only one of the records, supplied by the Danish police, added:

"According to statements which we have been unable to verify, this man would actually be of Dutch origin, named Julius Van Cram and born in Gröningen. The son of a good family, he began work at the age of about twenty-two in an Amsterdam bank of which his father was director. At that time he already spoke several languages, had received an excellent education, and was a member of the Amsterdam Yacht Club.

"Two years later he disappeared, and a few weeks afterwards it was discovered that he had absconded with part of the bank's funds."

Unfortunately it had been impossible to obtain any photographs of this Van Cram, whose finger-prints had not been recorded.

A comparison of dates brought Maigret another interesting discovery. Unlike most crooks and swindlers, this man seldom did two jobs in succession. He would take weeks, sometimes months, to perfect his plans, and the sum involved was always a large one.

After which, several years would generally go by before he turned up again, in a completely different part of the world, playing the same game with just as much skill and attention to detail as before.

Didn't this imply that he did not operate again until his funds were running low? Did he keep an iron reserve? Had he a hoard concealed somewhere?

His last exploit had taken place six years ago, in Mexico.

"Come here a minute, will you, Lucas?"

Lucas stared in astonishment at the files heaped up on the desk.

"I want you to send a few telegrams. But first of all, send someone to see Madame Crêmieux, in the Rue de Clichy, and make sure that this man is the one whose photo she found in her lodger's handbag."

He gave Lucas a list of the countries where the man had worked and the names he had gone by in each of them.

"And ring up Féret at Nice, too. Ask him to go and see Madame Laboine again and try to find out where her money-orders were sent from, and on what dates. I don't expect she'll have kept the counterfoils, but it's worth while enquiring."

He broke off suddenly:

"Any news of Lognon?"

"Was he going to ring you up?"

"I don't know. Will you call up his flat?"

He got Madame Lognon at the other end.

"Is your husband back?" asked Maigret.

"Not yet. Do you still not know where he is?"

She was worried, and he was beginning to be worried, too.

"I expect he's trailing someone and it's taken him out of town," he said to reassure her.

He had spoken of trailing on the spur of the moment, and then had to listen to the lamentations of Madame Lognon, who complained that her husband was always given the most thankless and dangerous tasks.

Could he very well explain that whenever Lognon had got into a tight corner, he had done it on his own initiative, and usually in defiance of orders he had been given?

He was so anxious to do well, wanted so much to distinguish himself, that he went blindly ahead, convinced each time that at last he was about to prove his value.

His value was recognized by everyone. He was the only one who failed to know this.

Maigret rang up the Second District Station, but there was no news of Old Grouch to be had there either.

"Has he been seen in the neighbourhood?"

"Not that I've heard."

In the next room Lucas, who had sent a plain-clothes man to the Rue de Clichy, was dictating his telegrams over the 'phone. Janvier stood in the doorway, waiting for Maigret to ring off so he could ask for instructions.

"I think Monsieur Priollet wants to see you. He came in just now, but you weren't in your office."

"I was upstairs."

Maigret went along to Priollet's office and found him questioning a drug-pedlar, with pinched nostrils and red-rimmed eyes.

"I don't know if you're still interested, and you may have heard this from someone else; but I've been told this morning that Jeanine Armenieu lived for some time in a flat in the Rue de Ponthieu."

"Do you know the number?"

"No, but it's not far from the corner of the Rue de Berri, and there's a bar on the ground floor."

"Thank you, old man. Anything about Santoni?"

"Nothing. I don't think we have anything against him and he's probably plunged in wedded bliss at Florence."

Maigret found Janvier still in his own office.

"Get your coat and hat."

"Where are we going?"

"Rue de Ponthieu."

He would probably find out a bit more about the dead girl there. She was still his chief concern. But that wretched Lognon was beginning to play an important role. And, unfortunately, nothing was known about that role.

"The first man who said 'Too many cooks spoil the broth' was darn well right," grumbled Maigret as he got into his overcoat.

It was hardly probable that Old Grouch would still be roaming the streets from one address to another. At five o'clock on the previous afternoon, to all appearances—though with him it was never easy to tell—he had had nothing definite to go on.

He'd been home to dinner, and set out again directly after.

Before leaving the building, Maigret put his head into the Duty Room.

"I'd like one of you to ring up the railway stations, just on the off-chance, to make sure Lognon hasn't gone off by train."

Trailing someone, for instance. It was possible. And if so he might not have been able to telephone to Headquarters or his own office.

If so, too, he would have information that nobody else had got.

"Ready, Chief?"

"Ready."

Maigret, in ill-humour, had the car stopped in the Place Dauphine for a drink.

He was not jealous of Lognon, of course. If Lognon could find out who had murdered Louise Laboine, so much the better. If he made an arrest, good for him.

But damn it all, he might at least keep in touch, like everybody else.

CHAPTER SEVEN

WHILE Janvier went into the building to ask for information, Maigret stood waiting on the kerb, with his hands in his pockets, thinking that the Rue de Ponthieu was something like the wings, or perhaps the back stairs, of the Champs-Élysées. Each of the main thoroughfares of Paris is partnered in this way by a narrow, lively street, usually running parallel to it, where there are small bars and provision shops, restaurants for drivers, cheap hotels, barbers' shops, and every kind of small trader's.

Here, there was a wine-shop which tempted him, and he was probably going to enter it when Janvier reappeared.

"It's here, Chief."

They had struck lucky at the very first building. The lodge was as dark as such rooms usually are in Paris, but the concierge was young and attractive, and a baby was kicking about in a play-pen.

"You belong to the police, too, don't you?"

"What makes you say 'too'?"

"Because someone from the police has already been here—last night. I was just going to bed. He was a little man who looked so miserable that until I noticed he had a cold, I thought his wife must have died and he was crying."

One could hardly help smiling at this description of Old Grouch.

"What time was this?"

"About ten o'clock. I was undressing behind the screen, and I had to keep him waiting. Have you come about the same thing?"

"I suppose he asked you about Mademoiselle Armenieu?"

"Yes, and about her friend, the girl who was murdered."

"Did you recognize her photo in the paper?"

"I thought so, but I wasn't quite sure."

"Was she a tenant of yours?"

"Won't you gentlemen sit down? You don't mind if I go on getting the baby's feed ready? If you're too hot please take your coats off and make yourselves comfortable."

In her turn she asked:

"You're not from the same department as the one who came yesterday? But I don't know why I ask that, it's none of my business. As I told your colleague, the real tenant, the one who had the lease, was Mademoiselle Armenieu, Mademoiselle Jeanine, as I used to call her. She's married now. It was in the papers. Did you know?"

Maigret nodded.

"Did she live here long?"

"For about two years. When she first arrived she was still very young and inexperienced, and she often came to ask my advice."

"She was working?"

"At that time she was a typist, in an office not far from here—I don't know exactly where. She took the little flat on the third floor; it looks on to the courtyard, but it's very nice."

"Her friend didn't share it with her?"

"Yes. But as I said, she was the one who paid the rent, and the lease was in her name."

She showed no reluctance to talk. It came all the more easily to her because she had already given the same information the day before.

"I know what you're going to ask next. They left about six months ago. To be quite exact, Mademoiselle Jeanine left first."

"I thought the flat was in her name?"

"Yes. It was nearly the end of the month. There were three or four days to go. One evening Mademoiselle Jeanine came in, sat down where you're sitting now, and said to me:

" 'Madame Marcelle, I'm fed up. This time I'm through for keeps.' "

"Through with what?" enquired Maigret.

"With the other girl, her friend, Louise."

"Didn't they get on together?"

"That's what I want to try to explain. Mademoiselle Louise never stopped to chat, and I hardly know anything about her except from her friend, so that I heard only one side of the story. At the beginning I took them for sisters, or cousins, or childhood friends. Then Mademoiselle Jeanine told me they'd only met in the train, two or three months before."

"Didn't they like each other?"

"Yes and no. It's difficult to explain. We get quite a number of girls of that age in this house, off and on. There are two here now who dance at the *Lido*, and one who's a manicurist at the *Claridge*. Most of them tell me all about themselves. So did Mademoiselle Jeanine, after a few days. But Louise, the other one, kept herself to herself. For a long time I thought she was stuck-up, but then I began to wonder whether it wasn't just shyness, and I'm still inclined to believe it was that.

"You see, when these youngsters first come up to Paris and feel lost among the millions of people, they either bluff, boast, throw their weight about or else they shrink back into their shells.

"Mademoiselle Jeanine was one of the first kind. She wasn't afraid of anything. She went out nearly every evening. After a few weeks she'd be out till two or three in the morning, and

93

she'd learnt how to dress. And she hadn't been here three months when I heard her come in at night, with a man.

"That was no business of mine. She was in her own place. This isn't a family hotel."

"Each of them had a separate room?"

"Yes. But still! Louise must have heard everything, and in the morning she had to wait till the man left before she could get into the bathroom or the kitchen."

"Was that what they quarrelled about?"

"I'm not sure. A lot of things can happen in two years, and there are twenty-two tenants in this building. I couldn't guess that one of those girls was going to be murdered."

"What does your husband do?"

"He's head waiter in a restaurant in the Place des Ternes. You don't mind if I give the baby his food?"

She put the child into its high-chair and began feeding it, a spoonful at a time, without losing the thread of her story.

"I told all this to your colleague yesterday and he made notes. If you want my opinion, I'd say Mademoiselle Jeanine knew what she wanted and would stick at nothing to get it. She didn't go about with just anybody. Most of the men she brought here had their own cars, which I used to see in front of the house when I put out the dustbins first thing in the morning. They weren't all necessarily young, but they weren't old either. What I'm trying to make you understand is, it wasn't simply for fun.

"She used to ask me questions that showed what she was after. For instance, if she'd been asked to meet someone at a restaurant where she'd never been before, she'd want to know whether it was a smart place or not, how she ought to dress to go there, and so on.

"It took her less than six months to know Paris, in some ways, inside out."

"Her friend never went with her?"

"Only when they went to the cinema."

"How did Louise spend her evenings?"

"Mostly she'd stay up above. Sometimes she'd go for a stroll, but never far, as though she were afraid.

"They were about the same age, but Mademoiselle Louise was like a little girl, compared with her friend.

"That was what used to annoy Mademoiselle Jeanine at times. She said to me once:

" 'If only I'd had the sense to go to sleep in the train, instead of chattering with her!'

94

"But I'm sure she liked having someone to talk to, especially at the beginning. You may have noticed that girls who come up to Paris to look for work nearly always join up in pairs.

"Later on, little by little, they begin to hate each other.

"That's what happened, all the more quickly because Mademoiselle Louise couldn't adapt herself and never kept a job for more than a few weeks.

"She hadn't had much education. It seems her spelling was bad, so she couldn't do office work. And when she got a job in some shop or other, something always went wrong. The boss maybe, or the head of a department, who tried to go to bed with her.

"Instead of using a little tact to make them see she wasn't that kind of girl, she'd get on her high horse and slap their faces, or fling out and slam the door behind her. Once there were some thefts in the shop, and she came under suspicion, although she was certainly innocent.

"Of course it was her friend who told me these things. All I know for myself is that there were times when Mademoiselle Louise had no work, and went out later than usual to do the round of the addresses she'd picked out of the 'Situations Vacant' columns."

"Did they have their meals in the flat?"

"Nearly always. Except when Mademoiselle Jeanine went out with friends. Last year they went to Deauville together for a week. That is, they went off together, but the little one—I mean Louise—came back first and Jeanine was away several days longer. I don't know what had happened. For quite a time they weren't on speaking terms, though they still shared the flat."

"Did Louise get any letters?"

"Never any private ones. I thought she must be an orphan. Her friend told me she did have a mother down in the South, a half-wit who did nothing for her daughter. Now and then, when Mademoiselle Louise had written to apply for a job, she'd get a few letters with printed addresses on the envelopes, and I'd know what that meant."

"And Jeanine?"

"A letter from Lyon every two or three weeks. From her father, who's a widower down there. Apart from that, she mostly had notes that came by messenger, to make dates."

"How long ago did Jeanine talk to you about wanting to get rid of her friend?"

"She began talking about it more than a year ago, maybe

95

eighteen months; but it was always when they'd quarrelled or the other one had just lost her job again. Jeanine would groan:

" 'To think I left home to be free, and now I've saddled myself with that idiot!'

"But a day or two later she'd be glad to find her at home, I'm sure. It's rather the same as with married couples. I expect you're both married?"

"So it's six months since Jeanine Armenieu left here?"

"Yes. She'd changed a great deal in those last months. She dressed better, more expensively, I mean, and went to places that were a cut above those she'd been used to before. Sometimes she'd stay away for two or three days on end. And flowers used to arrive for her, and boxes of chocolates from the *Marquise de Sévigné*. I caught on.

"Anyhow, one evening she came in here, sat down, and said:

" 'This time I'm going for good, Madame Marcelle. I've nothing against this place, but I can't share a flat with that girl for the rest of my life.'

" 'You're not getting married?' I joked.

"She didn't laugh, and said quietly:

" 'Not at once. When I do, you'll read about it in the papers.'

"She'd already met Monsieur Santoni, no doubt. She was quite sure of herself, and her little smile gave the show away.

"Still joking, I said:

" 'You'll invite me to the wedding?'

" 'I don't promise to invite you, but I'll send you a nice present.' "

"And has she?" asked Maigret.

"Not yet. She probably will. Anyhow, she's got what she wanted, and now she's honeymooning in Italy. To get back to that evening, she admitted to me that she was leaving without a word to her friend, and would take care the girl didn't find out where she'd gone.

" 'If she did, I should be landed with her again!'

"She did just as she'd said she would. She went off, with her two suitcases, while Louise was out, and didn't even leave her address with me, to be on the safe side.

" 'I'll look in now and then to see if there are any letters for me.' "

"Did you see her again?"

"Three or four times. Well, there were a few days left before the next month's rent was due. On the last morning, Mademoiselle Louise came and told me she had to leave. I must say I was sorry for her. She didn't cry, but her lips were trembling as she talked to me, and I could see she felt completely lost. Her only luggage was a little blue suitcase. I asked her where she was going, and she said she didn't know.

" 'If you'd like to stay on for a few days,' I suggested, 'until I find another tenant. . . .'

" 'Thank you very much, but I'd rather not. . . .'

"That was just like her. I watched her walk away down the street, carrying her suitcase, and as she turned the corner I felt like calling her back to give her a little money."

"Did she come back to see you, too?"

"She came back, but not to see me. It was to ask me for her friend's address. I told her I hadn't got it. I don't suppose she believed me."

"Why did she want to get in touch with her?"

"Probably to get in with her again, or ask for money. By the state of her clothes it was easy to see that things were rough."

"When was the last time she came?"

"Just over a month ago. I'd been reading the paper, and it was lying on the table. I suppose I ought not to have done it, but I said:

" 'I don't know where she lives, but there's something about her in the gossip column to-day.'

"And there was. It went more or less like this:

" '*Marco Santoni, of the well-known vermouth firm, has been seen every evening at Maxim's with a beautiful model, Jeanine Armenieu.*' "

Maigret looked at Janvier, who saw the point. It was just over a month since Louise Laboine had gone for the first time to the Rue de Douai to hire an evening dress from Mademoiselle Irène. Wasn't that in order to go to *Maxim's* and look for her friend?

"You don't know whether she saw her?"

"She didn't see her. Mademoiselle Jeanine came round a few days after that, and when I asked her, she laughed and said:

" 'We go to *Maxim's* very often, but not every evening, all the same. Besides, I don't think they'd let poor Louise inside the place.' "

"Did you tell all this to the detective who called yesterday evening?" enquired Maigret.

"Not with so many details, perhaps, because there are some things I have remembered since."

"You didn't tell him anything else?"

Maigret was trying to think what Lognon could have found

to work on in the story he had just heard. At ten o'clock the previous evening he had been in this very concierge's lodge. And since then there had been no news of him whatsoever.

"Do you mind waiting a minute while I put the baby to bed?"

She wiped his hands and face, laid him on the table to change him, and carried him off into a kind of recess, where they could hear her whispering tenderly to him.

When she came back she looked rather worried.

"I wonder now whether I'm not to blame for what's happened. If only these girls wouldn't make such a mystery of things, it would be so easy! I can understand Mademoiselle Jeanine not leaving me an address, because she didn't want to be bothered by her friend. But Mademoiselle Louise really might have given me hers.

"About ten days ago, perhaps a little more, I'm not certain, a man came in and asked me if a Louise Laboine lived here.

"I told him she didn't, she'd left several months ago, that she was still in Paris but I didn't know her address, though she came to see me now and again."

"What kind of a man?"

"A foreigner. Judging by his accent, I should say he was English or American. Not rich or smartly dressed. A little, thin fellow. Why, he was a bit like that detective who came yesterday. I don't know why, but he reminded me of a clown.

"He seemed taken aback, and asked anxiously whether I thought I should be seeing her soon.

" 'It might be to-morrow or it might not be for a month,' I said.

" 'I'll leave a note for her.'

"He sat down at the table, asked me for a piece of paper and an envelope, and began writing in pencil. I put the letter into an empty pigeon-hole and thought no more about it.

"When he came back, three days later, the letter was still there, and he seemed even more discouraged.

" 'I can't wait long,' he said, 'I shall soon have to be going.'

"I asked him if it was important, and he said:

" 'For her, yes. Very important.'

"He took back the letter and wrote another, taking longer over it this time, as though he had to make up his mind about something. In the end he held it out to me, with a sigh."

"You didn't see him again?"

"Only on the next day. Three days later Mademoiselle Jeanine called in. That was when she told me, in great excitement:

" 'You'll soon be reading about me in the papers.'

"She'd been shopping in the neighbourhood, and was carrying all sorts of little parcels from the best shops.

"I told her about the letter for Mademoiselle Louise and the little thin man's visits.

" 'If only I knew where to find her,' I added.

"She thought for a moment.

" 'Perhaps you'd better give it to me,' she said in the end. 'If I know Louise she won't lose much time in coming to see me, as soon as she finds out from the papers where I am. . . .'

"I hesitated. I decided she was probably right."

"You gave her the letter?"

"Yes. She glanced at the envelope and stuffed it into her bag. As she was leaving, she said to me:

" 'It won't be long now before you get your present, Madame Marcelle!' "

Maigret sat silent, looking down at the floor.

"Is that all you told the Detective-Sergeant?"

"I think so. Yes. I'm trying to remember. I don't see what else I could have said."

"Louise never came round after that?"

"No."

"So she didn't know her ex-girl-friend had a letter for her?"

"I suppose not. Anyhow, she didn't hear of it from me."

In the last fifteen minutes Maigret had found out much more than he had hoped for. But the trail came to a full stop at this point.

He was now thinking even more of Lognon than of Louise Laboine—as though Old Grouch had suddenly stepped into the leading role.

He had come here and had heard the same story. Whereupon he had vanished without trace.

Any other man, after learning what he had learnt the evening before, would have rung up Maigret to pass on the information and ask for instructions. Not Lognon! He had been determined to see the thing through by himself.

"You look worried," remarked the concierge.

"I suppose the Sergeant didn't say anything to you or make any comment?"

"No. He just thanked me and went out, and turned to the right when he got into the street."

What could they do but thank her in their turn, and leave? Without consulting Janvier, Maigret led him across to the *bistro* he had noticed before, ordered two Pernods and drank his in silence.

"Would you ring up Second District and find out if they have any news of him? Then ring his wife in case the office knows nothing. And failing that, make sure he hasn't been in touch with Headquarters."

When Janvier emerged from the telephone-box, Maigret was slowly emptying a second glass.

"Not a thing!"

"I can only think of one explanation, that he telephoned to Italy."

"Are you going to do that?"

"Yes. We shall get through more quickly from the office."

By the time they got back there, nearly everyone had gone out for lunch. Maigret sent for a list of Florence hotels, picked out the most expensive and, at his third call, was told that the Santonis were indeed staying there. They were not in their suite, having gone down about half an hour earlier to lunch at the restaurant.

There, after a few minutes, he was able to get into touch with them, and by a lucky chance the head waiter had worked in Paris and spoke a little French.

"Will you ask Madame Santoni to come to the telephone?"

When the head waiter had delivered the message, it was a man's aggressive voice that Maigret heard next.

"Will you kindly tell me what is the meaning of this?"

"Who is speaking?"

"Marco Santoni. Last night we were woken up to be told that the Paris police urgently needed some information. To-day you start pestering us in the restaurant."

"I'm sorry, Monsieur Santoni. I am Chief-Inspector Maigret, of the Police Headquarters."

"That doesn't explain why my wife is being pursued by——"

"It is not with her that we are concerned. But it so happens a former girl-friend of hers has been murdered. . . ."

"That's what the fellow told us last night. And so what? Is that any reason for——"

"A letter had been entrusted to your wife. That letter would probably enable us——"

"Does she have to be rung up twice for that? She told all she knew to the detective."

"The detective has disappeared."

"Ah!"

His anger subsided.

"In that case I'll call my wife. I hope after that you'll leave her in peace, and manage to keep her name out of the papers."

There was some whispering. Jeanine was probably in the telephone-box with her husband.

"Hello?" she said.

"I'm so sorry, Madame. You know already what this is about. The concierge in the Rue de Ponthieu gave you a letter for Louise."

"I wish I'd never offered to take it!"

"What has become of that letter?"

There was a silence, and for a second Maigret wondered whether the line had been cut off.

"Did you give it to her on your wedding night, when she came to see you at the *Roméo*?"

"Of course not. I wasn't going to carry the letter about with me on my wedding night."

"Was it because of that letter that Louise came to look for you?"

Another silence, as if in hesitation.

"No. She hadn't even heard about it."

"What did she want?"

"To borrow money from me, of course. She told me she hadn't a *sou* left, that her landlady had thrown her out, and she hinted that she had no choice but to kill herself. Not as clearly as that. With Louise, nothing was ever clear."

"Did you give her any money?"

"Three or four thousand-franc notes. I didn't count them."

"You told her about the letter?"

"Yes."

"What exactly did you tell her?"

"What it said."

"You read it?"

"Yes."

Another silence.

"You may not believe me, but I didn't do it out of curiosity. It wasn't even I who opened it. Marco found it in my bag. I told him the story and he didn't believe it, so I said, "Open it then, and see for yourself.' "

In an undertone she spoke to her companion, who had stayed in the telephone-box:

"Hush," she told him. "It's best to tell them the truth. They'll find it out sooner or later, anyhow."

"Do you remember what it said?"

"Not word for word. It was badly written, in bad French, full of spelling mistakes. It went more or less like this:

" 'I have a very important message for you, and I must see you as soon as possible. Ask for Jimmy, at *Pickwick's Bar* in the Rue de l'Étoile. That's me. If I'm not there, the barman will tell you where to find me.'

"Are you still there, Inspector?"

Maigret was making notes. "Go on," he grunted.

"The letter said after that: 'I may not be able to stay long enough in France. If I can't, I'll leave the paper with the barman. He'll ask you to prove your identity. You'll understand why afterwards.' "

"Was that all?"

"Yes."

"Did you give this message to Louise?"

"Yes."

"Did she seem to understand?"

"Not at first. Then she seemed to think of something, thanked me and went away."

"You didn't hear any more from her during the night?"

"No. How could I have done? It wasn't until two days later that I happened to pick up a paper and saw she was dead."

"Do you think she went to *Pickwick's Bar?*"

"It's very likely, isn't it? What would you have done in her place?"

"Did anyone know about this, except you and your husband?"

"I don't know. The letter was in my bag for two or three days."

"You were staying at the *Hôtel Washington* then?"

"Yes."

"Did you have any visitors?"

"Only Marco."

"Where is the letter now?"

"I must have put it away with other papers."

"Are your things still at the hotel?"

"Certainly not. I took them to Marco's flat the day before the wedding, except for my toilet things and a few clothes, which the valet went to fetch next day. Do you suppose it was because of that message that she was killed?"

"Quite possibly. She didn't say anything about it?"

"Nothing at all."

"She'd never spoken to you of her father?"

"I asked her one day whose photo it was that she kept in her note-case, and she said it was her father's picture. 'Is he still alive?' I asked again. She looked at me as though she didn't want to answer and was being hush-hush about it. So I shut up. Another time, when we were discussing our parents, I asked her: 'What does your father do?' She stared at me in the same way, without a word; she was like that. I don't want to sound unkind about her now she's dead, but——"

Her husband must have intervened, for she broke off with: "I've told you everything I know."

"Thank you very much. When do you expect to be back in Paris?"

"In a week's time."

Janvier had been listening to the conversation through the second ear-piece.

"It seems to me we've picked up Lognon's trail again," he said with a wry smile.

"Do you know *Pickwick's Bar*?"

"I've passed it now and again, but I've never been inside."

"Neither have I. Are you hungry?"

"I'm still more anxious to find out——"

Maigret opened the door of the next office and called to Lucas:

"No news of Lognon?"

"No, sir."

"If he rings up, you can reach me at *Pickwick's Bar* in the Rue de l'Étoile."

"A woman came to see me just now, sir, the manageress of a small hotel in the Rue d'Aboukir. She took long enough to make up her mind. She said she'd been so busy for the last few days that she hadn't even read the papers. Anyhow, she came to say that Louise Laboine had spent four months at her hotel."

"When?"

"Quite lately. She left two months ago."

"So she must have gone from there straight to the Rue de Clichy."

"Yes. She'd been working in a shop in the Boulevard Magenta. It's one of those places with an outside stall for cut-price goods. The girl spent part of the winter out there, got a cold on her chest in the end, and had to stay in bed for a week."

"Who looked after her?"

"Nobody. Her room was on the top floor, a kind of garret. It's the lowest possible sort of place, and most of the clients are Algerians."

The gaps were nearly all filled in now. It was possible to reconstruct the girl's story from the moment she left her mother at Nice to the evening she found Jeanine at the *Roméo*.

"Coming, Janvier?"

All that remained was to discover how she had spent a period of about two hours on the night of her death.

The taxi-driver had seen her in the Place St. Augustin and then, still walking in the direction of the Arc de Triomphe, at the corner of the Boulevard Haussmann and the Faubourg St. Honoré.

That was the way to go to reach the Rue de l'Étoile.

Louise, who had never known how to organize her life, who had found, to depend on, only a girl she had met in a train, had been walking fast all alone in the drizzle, as though she were eager to meet her fate.

CHAPTER EIGHT

THE façade, between a cobbler's booth and a laundry where women could be seen ironing, was so narrow that most people probably went by without thinking there was a bar there at all. It was impossible to see anything inside because of the greenish bottle-glass windows. Above the door, which was screened by a dark red curtain, was a sham-antique lantern on which the words *Pickwick's Bar* were painted in an attempt at Gothic lettering.

Once inside, a change came over Maigret, who seemed to harden, to become more aloof in manner, and a similar change automatically took place in Janvier's attitude.

The long, narrow bar-room was apparently deserted. Because of the bottle-glass windows and narrow front, the room was dark, with here and there a gleam of light on polished wood.

A man in shirt-sleeves, who stood up as they came in, put down something—probably the sandwich he had been eating, sitting behind the bar, out of sight, when the door opened.

With his mouth still full, he watched them come towards him, without saying a word, without betraying any expression on his face. His hair was very black, almost blue; he had heavy eyebrows, giving him an obstinate appearance, and there was a cleft in the middle of his chin as deep as a scar.

Maigret seemed hardly to glance at him, but it was evident that they had recognized each other and that it was not their first encounter. He walked slowly to one of the tall stools and sat down, unbuttoning his overcoat and pushing his hat to the back of his head. Janvier did the same.

After a silence, the barman asked:

"Will you have a drink?"

Maigret hesitated and looked at Janvier.

"What about you?"

"I'll join you."

"Two Pernods, if you have any."

The barman served them, put a jug of iced water on the mahogany bar-top, waited, and for a moment it seemed they would play at seeing who could keep the silence for the longest time.

It was the Chief-Inspector who broke it.

"What time did Lognon get here?"

"I didn't know his name was Lognon. I've always heard him called Old Grouch."

"What time?"

"Eleven, perhaps. I didn't look at the clock."

"Where did you send him?"

"Nowhere."

"What did you say to him?"

"I answered his questions."

Maigret was picking olives from a bowl that stood on the bar and eating them one by one, without appearing to notice what he was doing.

The moment they had come in and the barman had stood up behind the counter, Maigret had recognized him as a certain Albert Falconi, a Corsican, whom he had sent to prison at least twice for running an unlicensed gaming-house, and once for trafficking in gold with Belgians. On another occasion Falconi had been arrested under the suspicion of having murdered a member of the Marseille gang in Montmartre; but they had been able to prove nothing against him, and he had been released.

He was about thirty-five years old.

No words were wasted on either side. Both were professionals, as it were, and every sentence uttered by either of them carried the full weight of its significance.

"When you saw the papers on Tuesday morning, you recognized the girl?"

Albert didn't deny it, he admitted nothing, but continued to gaze at the Chief-Inspector with impassive eyes.

"How many customers were here when she came on Monday night?"

Maigret looked up and down the room. There are a good many such bars in Paris, and the passer-by who comes into one on the off-chance, when it is empty, may wonder how it pays its way. The explanation is that these places have their regular customers, all belonging to much the same circle, who meet there regularly at certain times of the day.

In the mornings, Albert probably didn't open. He had very likely only just arrived and had not finished arranging his bottles. But in the evening all the stools would be taken, leaving just enough room to move along the wall. At the far end a steep flight of stairs led down to the basement.

The barman, too, seemed to be counting the stools.

"It was about full," he said at last.

"That was between midnight and one o'clock?"

"Much nearer one than midnight."

"Ever seen her before?"

"That was the first time."

Everybody must surely have turned to Louise and stared at her curiously. Any women who came to the bar would be professionals, of a very different type from the girl. Her faded evening dress and the ill-fitting velvet cape would be bound to cause a sort of sensation.

"What did she do?"

Albert frowned, as though searching his memory.

"She sat down."

"Where?"

He looked again at the stools.

"About where you're sitting now. It was the only empty stool near the door."

"What did she have to drink?"

"A martini."

"She ordered a martini right away?"

"When I asked her what she'd take."

"And then?"

"She sat there for quite a time without saying anything."

"She had a handbag?"

"She'd put it down on the bar. A silvery bag."

"Lognon asked you these questions?"

"Not in the same order."

"Go on."

"I like answering better."

"She asked you if you had a letter for her?"

He nodded.

"Where was the letter?"

The man turned, as if in slow motion, and pointed to a place where two or three envelopes intended for customers were pushed in between two bottles which could not often be brought into use.

"Here."

"You gave it to her?"

"I asked to see her identity-card."

"Why?"

"Because I'd been told to do so."

"Who by?"

"The bloke."

He never said more than was necessary, and obviously spent each pause in trying to guess the next question.

"Jimmy?"

"Yes."

"Do you know his surname?"

"No. People don't usually give their surnames in a bar."

"It depends in what bars."

Albert shrugged, as though to indicate he wasn't taking offence.

"Did he speak French?"

"Rather well, for an American."

"What kind of a bloke?"

"You know better than I do, don't you?"

"Tell me, anyhow."

"I got the impression that he'd probably spent a good many years in the cooler."

"A small, thin, sickly-looking fellow?"

"Yes."

"He was in here on Monday?"

"He'd left Paris four or five days before."

"Before that, he came every day?"

Albert nodded patiently, and as the glasses were empty by now, he reached for the Pernod bottle.

"He spent most of his time here."

"Do you know where he was living?"

"Probably in some hotel nearby; I don't know which."

"Had he already given you the envelope?"

"No. He'd only said that if the young lady came and asked for him, I was to tell her what time she would find him here."

"What times did he say?"

"In the afternoon, after four o'clock, and practically the whole evening, until very late."

"What time do you close?"

"About two or three o'clock in the morning. It depends."

"Did he ever talk to you?"

"Sometimes."

"About himself?"

"About all sorts of things."

"Did he tell you he'd done time?"

"He kind of hinted it."

"Sing Sing?"

"I think so. If Sing Sing is in New York State on the Hudson River, that's the place."

"He didn't tell you what was in the envelope?"

"No. Only that it was important. He was in a hurry to get away."

"Because of the police?"

"Because of his daughter. She's getting married next week, at Baltimore. That's why he had to leave without waiting any longer."

"Did he describe the young lady who would come?"

"No. He only told me to make sure it was really her. That's why I asked to see her identity-card."

"She read the letter in the bar?"

"She went down below."

"What is there, down below?"

"The toilets and the telephone-boxes."

"You think she went down there to read her letter?"

"I suppose so."

"Did she take her handbag with her?"

"Yes."

"How did she look when she came up again?"

"She wasn't as depressed as before."

"Had she been drinking before she got here?"

"I don't know. Perhaps."

"What did she do after that?"

"Went back to her place at the bar."

"And ordered another martini?"

108

"Not her. The other American."

"What other American?"

"A tall fellow with a scar on his face and cauliflower ears."

"You don't know him?"

"That chap, not even his first name."

"When did he begin coming here?"

"About the same time as Jimmy."

"Did they know each other?"

"Jimmy certainly didn't know him."

"And what about the other chap?"

"I had the impression he was following Jimmy."

"Did he come at the same times?"

"Just about—in a big grey car that he used to park right outside."

"Jimmy never talked to you about him?"

"He asked whether I knew him."

"You told him you didn't?"

"Yes. That seemed to worry him. Then he said it must be the F.B.I. that was wondering what he was up to in France, and having him shadowed."

"Do you believe that was it?"

"I stopped believing anything a long time ago."

"When Jimmy left for the States, the second fellow kept on coming?"

"Regularly."

"Was there any name on the envelope?"

"Just 'Louise Laboine—Paris.' "

"Could customers read it from their seats?"

"Certainly not."

"You never leave the bar for a moment?"

"Not when there are people here. I don't trust anyone."

"Did he speak to the young lady?"

"He asked her if he might offer her a drink."

"She accepted?"

"She looked at me, as if she wanted advice. One could see she wasn't used to that kind of thing."

"You nodded to her to accept?"

"I didn't make any sign at all. I simply served two martinis. Then I went to the other end of the bar and paid no more attention."

"Did the girl and the American go off together?"

"I think so."

"In his car?"

"I heard the sound of an engine."

"Is that all you told Lognon?"

"No. He asked me some other questions."

"What questions?"

"If the chap had been down to telephone. I said he hadn't. If I knew where he lived. I said I didn't. And whether I had any idea where he'd gone."

Here Albert looked significantly at Maigret and waited.

"Well?"

"I'll tell you exactly what I told Old Grouch. The day before, the Yank had asked me the best way to get to Brussels. I advised him to leave Paris by way of Saint-Denis, go through Compiègne, and then——"

"Is that all?"

"No. An hour, maybe, before the kid came in, he began talking again about Brussels. This time he wanted to know which was the best hotel. I told him I always stayed at the *Palace* myself, opposite the Gare du Nord."

"What time was it when you told Lognon this?"

"About one in the morning. It took longer than with you, because I had to keep attending to clients."

"Have you got a railway time-table?"

"If you want the Brussels train, I'll save you the trouble. The Sergeant went down and rang up the station. There were no more trains that night. The next was at half-past five in the morning."

"He told you he would take it?"

"He didn't need to tell me."

"What do you think he did till five o'clock?"

"What would you have done?"

Maigret reflected. The investigation had just led to two foreigners, both of whom had apparently lived in this district and both of whom had discovered *Pickwick's Bar*.

"You think Lognon went on a tour of the hotels around here?"

"It's your case, isn't it? I'm not responsible for Old Grouch."

"Janvier, will you go down and telephone to Brussels. Ask at the *Palace* if they've seen Lognon. He should have got there about half-past nine this morning. He may still be waiting for the American to arrive by car."

During the plain-clothes man's absence, he didn't say a word, and Albert, as if he also considered the conversation to be finished, sat down again behind the bar and went on eating.

Maigret had left his second Pernod untouched, but he had

emptied the plate of olives. He was gazing fixedly down the length of the room, at the row of stools, at the narrow staircase at the far end, and he might have been imagining the scene crowded with the people who were there on Monday night when Louise Laboine had come in, wearing the blue evening dress and the velvet cape and carrying the silver brocade handbag.

He was frowning heavily. Twice he opened his mouth as though to speak, but both times he changed his mind.

More than ten minutes went by, and the barman had time to finish his lunch, sweep the crumbs off the bar and drink a cup of coffee. He had just picked up a grubby rag and begun to dust the bottles on the shelf when Janvier reappeared.

"He's on the line, sir. Do you want to speak to him?"

"There's no need. Tell him he can come back."

Janvier hesitated, unable to conceal his surprise, wondering whether he had heard correctly, whether Maigret had meant it. Finally, accustomed to obeying orders, he turned back to the stairs with a murmured:

"Very well!"

Albert, for his part, had shown no surprise, but his face had hardened. He went on mechanically dusting his bottles, one by one, and he could see the Chief-Inspector, on whom he had turned his back, in the mirror behind the shelves.

Janvier came back. Maigret asked:

"Did he make any fuss?"

"He began to say something and then stopped. In the end he only said: 'As long as it's an order!'"

Maigret got up from his stool, buttoned his coat and straightened his hat.

"Get your coat on, Albert," he said simply.

"What?"

"I said, get your coat on. We're going round to the Quai des Orfèvres."

The man did not seem to understand.

"I can't leave the bar——"

"You've a key, haven't you?"

"What exactly do you want from me? I've told you what I know."

"D'you want us to take you away by force?"

"I'm coming. But——"

He sat by himself in the back of the little car, and didn't say a word all the way to Headquarters. He stared stubbornly ahead of him, the picture of a man trying to understand. Janvier said nothing either. Maigret smoked his pipe without a word.

"Upstairs!"

He made him go first into his office. In front of him, he asked Janvier:

"What time is it at Washington?"

"It must be about eight o'clock in the morning."

"By the time you can get through, even as a priority call, it'll be nearly nine. Ask for the F.B.I. If Clark's there, try to get him on the line. I'd like to speak to him."

Deliberately he took off his coat and hat and hung them up in the cupboard.

"You can take your coat off. This will take quite a while."

"You still haven't told me why——"

"How many hours were you in this office the day we talked about the gold bars?"

Albert had no need to search his memory.

"Four."

"You didn't notice anything in Tuesday morning's paper?"

"The photo of the girl."

"There was another photo, three men, tough chaps; they've been called the wall-borers. It was three o'clock that morning when they confessed. They'd been in this office a long time: eighteen hours."

Maigret went and sat down at the desk and began to arrange his pipes, as though looking for the best one.

"You, you'd had enough after four hours. It's all the same to me. There are several of us here to take it in shifts, and we have all the time in the world."

On the telephone he dialled the number of the *Brasserie Dauphine.*

"Maigret here. Would you send me up some sandwiches and beer? For how many people?"

He remembered that Janvier had had no lunch either.

"For two. Straight away, yes. Four pints—right."

He lit his pipe, walked across to the window, and stood for a moment watching the cars and pedestrians crossing the Pont St. Michel.

Albert, behind him, was lighting a cigarette, trying to keep his hand from shaking, with the preoccupied air of a man carefully weighing pros and cons.

"What do you want to know?" he asked at last, still undecided.

"Everything."

"I told you the truth."

"No."

Maigret did not turn round to look at him. Seen like this, from the back he really gave the impression of a man who has nothing else to do but to wait, smoking his pipe and watching the bustling crowd in the street.

Albert fell silent again. He remained silent so long that the waiter had time to come in from the *brasserie* with a tray, which he put down on the desk.

Maigret went over to the door into the Duty Room.

"Janvier!" he called.

The plain-clothes man appeared.

"I expect to get through in about twenty minutes."

"Help yourself. This is for both of us."

Saying this, he signed to him to go and eat his sandwiches and drink his beer in the next room.

Maigret sat down comfortably and began to eat. The parts were reversed. In *Pickwick's*, it was Albert who had sat eating behind his counter.

The Chief-Inspector seemed to have forgotten the other's presence, and to all appearances he was thinking of nothing, just slowly chewing and drinking an occasional draught of beer. His gaze wandered idly over the papers scattered on the desk.

"You're sure of yourself, aren't you?"

He nodded; his mouth full.

"You think I'm going to start talking, I suppose?"

He shrugged with an air of complete indifference.

"Why did you make Old Grouch come back?"

Maigret smiled.

And right then Albert, viciously, tore up his cigarette between his fingers, probably burnt himself, and growled:

"Damn!"

He was too tense to remain seated and got up, strode over to the window, pressed his forehead against the pane, staring down in his turn at the traffic on the bridge.

When he looked round again he had made up his mind and his agitation had subsided, his muscles relaxed. Uninvited, he took a drink from one of the two glasses of beer that remained on the tray, wiped his mouth and went back to his seat. This had been a last gesture of defiance to save his face.

"How did you guess?" he asked.

Maigret replied calmly:

"I didn't guess. I *knew* at once."

CHAPTER NINE

MAIGRET puffed at his pipe and gazed silently at the other man. It might have been supposed that if he was pausing, he did so like an actor, to give added weight to what he was about to say. But this was no studied effect. He hardly saw the barman's face opposite him. It was Louise Laboine he was thinking of. All the time he had been sitting silently in the bar in the Rue de l'Étoile while Janvier was down in the basement telephoning, he had tried to picture the girl as she came into the bar full of customers, wearing her shabby evening dress and the velvet cape that did not fit.

"You see," he said at last in a low voice, "at the first glance your story is perfect, almost too perfect, and I'd have swallowed it if I hadn't known the girl."

Albert in his astonishment exclaimed in spite of himself:

"You knew her?"

"I came to know her quite well."

Even now, still, as he spoke he could see her hiding under the bed in Mademoiselle Poré's; then, later on, quarrelling with Jeanine Armenieu in their rooms in the Rue de Ponthieu. He imagined her in the squalid hotel in the Rue d'Aboukir, and outside the shop in the Boulevard Magenta where she had worked out in the cold wind.

He could have repeated every word people had said about her, from the concierge to Madame Crêmieux.

He saw her going into *Maxim's*, and saw her, a month later, making her way through the crowd of wedding guests at the *Roméo*.

"To begin with, it's very unlikely she'd have sat down at the bar."

Because she would have felt that she was a fish out of water, that everyone was staring at her and noticing at once that she wore a second-hand dress.

"Even if she had sat down she wouldn't have ordered a martini. Your mistake was to think her like all the rest of the women who come to your place, and when I asked you what she drank you said automatically, 'A martini.' "

"She didn't drink anything," admitted Albert.

"She didn't go down to the basement to read her letter either. As usual in bars like yours with steady customers, there's no notice at the top of the stairs. Even if there were I doubt if she'd have had the pluck to thread her way behind the backs of twenty

114

or more clients, who were most of them probably pretty drunk.

"Besides, the papers didn't give the *full* results of the post-mortem. They said there was alcohol in her stomach, but what they didn't mention was that it was rum. And martinis are a mixture of gin and vermouth."

Maigret showed no sign of triumph, possibly because he was still thinking about Louise. He talked in a low voice, as though to himself:

"Did you really give her the letter?"

"I gave her a letter."

"You mean an envelope?"

"Yes."

"Containing a blank sheet of paper?"

"Yes."

"When did you open the real letter?"

"As soon as I knew Jimmy had taken the 'plane for the States."

"You had him followed to Orly?"

"Yes."

"Why? You still didn't know what it was all about."

"When a chap straight out of prison takes the trouble to cross the Atlantic to give a message to a girl, it's likely to be something important."

"Have you kept the letter?"

"I destroyed it."

Maigret believed this, convinced that Albert would not bother to lie any more.

"What did it say?"

"Something like this: 'I may not have taken much notice of you up till now, but you will understand one day that it was better for you. Whatever you may be told, don't think too harshly of me. We each of us choose our own path in life, often at an age when we lack judgment, and afterwards it's too late.

" 'You can trust the person who will give you this letter. By the time it reaches you I shall be dead Don't be unhappy about that, I'm old enough to go.

" 'It comforts me to know that from now on you will be well provided for. As soon as you can, get a passport and go to the United States. Brooklyn is a suburb of New York, which you may have heard of at school. At the address below you will find a little Polish tailor whose name is . . . !"

Albert stopped. Maigret signed to him to go on.

"I don't remember. . . ."

"You do."

"All right! '. . .whose name is Lukasek. Go and find him. Show him your passport and he'll give you a sum of money, in notes. . . .'"

"Is that all?"

"There were three or four more sentimental sentences that I can't remember."

"You remembered the address?"

"Yes. 1214, 37th Street."

"Who did you get to help you?"

Albert was again tempted not to answer. But Maigret's glance rested heavily upon him and he gave in:

"I showed the letter to a pal."

"Who?"

"Bianchi."

"Is he still with Big Jeanne?"

The fellow was suspected of being the leader of the Corsican gang, and Maigret had arrested him at least ten times, but had only once succeeded in getting him jailed. That, however, had been for five years.

The Chief-Inspector got up and opened the door into the next office.

"Is Torrence there?"

Someone fetched him.

"Take two or three men along with you. Make sure that Big Jeanne is still living in the Rue Lepic. You'll probably find Bianchi in her flat. If not, get her to tell you where to find him. Be careful, he may make a fight for it."

Albert listened, expressionless.

"Go on."

"What more do you want?"

"Bianchi couldn't send just anybody to the States to turn up at Lukasek's and ask for the cash. He'd guess the Pole would have instructions and demand proof of the girl's identity."

This was so obvious that he did not pause for a reply.

"So you waited till she came to *Pickwick's.*"

"We didn't mean to kill her."

To Albert's surprise Maigret answered:

"I'm convinced of that."

They were professionals, who ran no unnecessary risks. All they needed was the girl's identity-card. Once they had secured that, they would manage to get a passport for some girl accomplice, who would take the place of Louise.

116

"Bianchi was in your bar?"

"Yes."

"She left without opening the letter?"

"Yes."

"Your boss had a car outside?"

"Yes, with Tattoo Jack at the wheel. Now I've begun I may as well go on."

"They followed her?"

"I wasn't with them. I only know what they told me later. Don't bother to hunt for Tattoo Jack in Paris. He got scared after what happened and he's bolted."

"To Marseille?"

"Most likely."

"I suppose they intended to grab her handbag?"

"Yes. They drove past her first. Bianchi got out of the car just as she came level with them. The street was deserted. He caught hold of the bag, not realizing that it had a chain which was twisted round the kid's wrist. She fell on her knees. Seeing her open her mouth to scream, he hit her in the face. Apparently she clung to him, trying to call for help. It was then he took a cosh out of his pocket and clubbed her."

"You made up that story about the second American, just to get rid of Lognon?"

"What would you have done if you'd been in my shoes? Old Grouch fell for it."

All the same, during the greater part of the enquiry Lognon had been nearly always ahead of Police Headquarters. If only he had given more thought to Louise's mentality, he would have had his triumph, for which he had been waiting so long that he had ceased to believe in it.

What could he be thinking now, in the train that was bringing him back from Brussels? He was probably cursing his bad luck, feeling more than ever convinced that the whole world was leagued against him. He had not made a single technical error, and no training-course teaches policemen how to put themselves in the place of a girl brought up at Nice by a half-crazy mother.

For years Louise had stubbornly sought her place in life without success. Lost in a world that bewildered her, she had held on desperately to the first person she met, and that person had finally left her in the lurch.

Once alone, she had braced herself to face a hostile world, trying in vain to learn the rules of the game.

She probably knew nothing of her father. When she was still

quite small she must have wondered why her mother was not like others, why the two of them lived differently from their neighbours.

With all her might she had tried to fit in. She had run away from home. She had answered advertisements. And whereas Jeanine Armenieu easily found a job, she was soon driven out wherever she tried.

Had she finally come to believe, like Lognon, that there was a kind of conspiracy against her?

What made her so different from others? Why did everything have to happen to her?

Even her death was like a cruel joke played by fate. If the little chain on the silver bag had not been twisted round her wrist, Bianchi would simply have snatched the bag and the car would have driven away at top speed.

Had she then gone to the police no one would have believed her story.

"Why did they take the body to the Place Vintimille?"

"First, they couldn't leave it anywhere near my bar. Then, dressed as she was, she seemed more likely in Montmartre. So they chose the first deserted place they came to up there."

"Have they already sent anyone to the American Consulate?"

"Of course not. They're waiting."

"Inspector Clark is on the line, Chief."

"You may put him through to me here."

All that remained was to check for certain, and Maigret's few questions to the F.B.I. man were inspired chiefly by personal curiosity.

As usual, when he talked to Clark, the conversation was conducted half in Maigret's bad English and half in the American's bad French, each of them applying himself to speak the other's language.

Before Clark understood what the call was about, Maigret had to run through the whole list of names used by Julius Van Cram, *alias* Lemke, *alias* Stieb, *alias* Ziegler, Marek, Spangler, Donley. . . .

It was under the name of Donley that he had been buried, a month previously, in Sing Sing Penitentiary where he had been serving an eight-year sentence for fraud.

"Was the money found?"

"Only a little of it."

"Was it a large sum?"

"Around a hundred thousand dollars."

"His partner's name was Jimmy?"

"Jimmy O'Malley. He only got three years, and was released two months ago."

"He paid a visit to France."

"I thought his daughter was getting married some time soon."

"He went back home in time for the wedding. The money's in Brooklyn with a Polish tailor called Lukasek."

There was, after all, a small note of triumph in Maigret's voice.

"Lukasek, who may not realize what he's holding, has been instructed to give the parcel to a young girl called Louise Laboine."

"Will she be coming for it?"

"Unfortunately not."

The word had slipped out inadvertently. To make up for it, he went on hastily:

"She died in Paris this week."

Then he exchanged some greetings and even a bit of banter with Clark, whom he had not seen for several years. When he rang off he seemed surprised to see Albert still in his seat, smoking a cigarette.

The F.B.I. would almost certainly find the dollars and return them to some banker to whom they belonged, or perhaps to an insurance company, as the banker had probably been insured against theft. The little Polish tailor would go to jail. Probably for acting as a go-between, Jimmy O'Malley would be sent back to Sing Sing instead of giving away his daughter at Baltimore.

Louise's fate had depended on very little, on a thin chain wound round her wrist. If Mademoiselle Irène, in the Rue de Douai, had lent a different type of bag to the girl who came one evening to borrow a dress. . . .

And if she had called in at the Rue de Ponthieu in time for the letter to be delivered into her own hands. . . .

Would Louise Laboine have gone to America?

What would she have done afterwards, with the hundred thousand dollars?

Maigret finished his beer. It was tepid by this time. He emptied his pipe, not into the ash-tray, but into the coal-scuttle, by knocking it against the heel of his shoe.

"Will you come here, Janvier?"

He pointed to the barman, who knew at once what was happening. He was beginning to know the ropes.

"Take him into your office, write down his statement, make him sign it, and take him round to the cells. I'll ring up the magistrate, Coméliau."

It was mere routine. It no longer interested him. Just as Albert was going out, he called him back:

"I'd forgotten the three Pernods."

"They're on the house."

"Certainly not!"

Maigret handed over the notes, and just as he would have done at the bar in the Rue de l'Étoile, he murmured:

"Keep the change."

And as though he, too, were still behind his counter, the barman replied mechanically:

"Thanks."

DANGER AHEAD

comprising

RED LIGHTS (*Feux Rouges*)

and

THE WATCHMAKER OF EVERTON
(*L'Horloger d'Everton*)

both translated from the French by
NORMAN DENNY

RED LIGHTS

TO
MARIE-GEORGES SIMENON

CHAPTER ONE

HE CALLED it "going into the tunnel," an expression of his own, for his private use, which he never used in talking to anyone else, least of all to his wife. He knew exactly what it meant, and what it was like to be in the tunnel; yet, curiously, when he was there he never allowed himself to admit the fact, except for occasional brief instances, and always too late. As for determining the precise moment when he entered it, he had often tried to do this afterwards, but never with success.

To-day, for example, he had started Labour Day week-end in the best of spirits. The same thing had happened on other occasions. It had also happened that the week-end had nevertheless finished badly. But there was no reason why this should be inevitable.

He left his office on Madison Avenue at five o'clock, and three minutes later had joined his wife at their little bar on Forty-Fifth Street, where she had arrived first and had ordered a martini without waiting for him. There were not many regular customers in the dimly-lit room. In fact, he did not see a single face he knew, because everyone was rushing, even more hurriedly than on other Fridays, for the cars and trains which would take them to the sea or into the country. Within an hour New York would be empty except, in the quiet districts, for men in their shirtsleeves and bare-legged women seated in their doorways.

It was not yet raining. Since first thing that morning, and indeed for the past three days, the sky had been overcast, the air so laden with moisture that one could gaze steadily at the yellow splash of the sun as though looking at it through a pane of frosted glass. The weather forecasts were now predicting local storms and holding out hopes of a cooler night.

"Tired?"

"Not very."

They met there at the same time every evening in the summer, when the children were away in camp, always sitting on the same stools, and Louis, the barman, would greet them with a wink and start mixing their drinks without waiting for the order. They felt no need to start talking at once. One would offer the other a cigarette. Sometimes Nancy would push the dish of peanuts towards him, or he would pass her the olives, while they gazed absently at the small, pallid rectangle of the television receiver set high in the right-hand corner of the bar. Images flickered across it. A voice poured out a commentary on a baseball game, or a woman sang. It was quite unimportant.

"You'll be able to take a shower before we start."

It was her way of looking after him. She never failed to ask if he was tired, darting at him the sort of look one gives a delicate child or one that seems to be sickening for something. It ruffled him slightly. He knew he did not look his best at that time, with his shirt sticking to his body and his beard beginning to show, seeming darker against the skin softened by the heat. She was bound to have noticed the damp circles under his armpits.

It was the more irritating since she herself was as fresh as she had been when she left the house that morning, without a crease in her lightly starched linen suit, so that no one would have supposed, from the look of her, that she had spent the day in an office. She might have been taken for one of those women who don't get up before four in the afternoon, and make their first appearance at cocktail-time.

Louis asked:

"You going to get the kids?"

Steve nodded.

"New Hampshire?"

"Maine."

How many parents were there, in New York and the suburbs, who that evening would be setting off along the roads to fetch their children home from the camps up North? A hundred thousand? Two hundred thousand? Probably more. The figure must be tucked away in some corner of the newspaper. And then there were the children who had spent the summer with an aunt or grandmother in the country or by the sea. And it was the same everywhere, from one seaboard to the other, from the Canadian frontier right down to Mexico.

From the television screen a man in shirtsleeves, wearing thickly-rimmed glasses which seemed to make him feel hot, announced in a tone of gloomy conviction:

"*The National Safety Council predicts that this evening between forty and forty-five million motorists will be on the roads, and it estimates that between now and Monday evening four hundred and thirty-five people will have lost their lives in road accidents.*"

He finished lugubriously, before making way for a beer advertisement:

125

"Don't be one of them. Drive carefully."

Why four hundred and thirty-five, and not four hundred and thirty or four hundred and forty? Sandwiched between the regular programmes, these predictions would be repeated all that night, and to-morrow and the next day, until towards the end they acquired the suspense of a race-commentary. Steve recalled the voice of a speaker last year, when they were bringing the children back from Maine on the Sunday evening:

"Up to now the number of deaths is considerably lower than the official forecast, despite the collision of two air-liners over Washington airport, in which thirty-two people lost their lives. But watch out! The week-end isn't over yet!"

"Myself," said Louis, talking as usual in an undertone and fetching a fresh supply of peanuts, "my wife and kid are with my mother-in-law, near Quebec. They're coming back by train to-morrow."

Had Steve meant to order another martini? As a rule Nancy and he had only one, except occasionally when they dined in town before going to the theatre.

Perhaps he had wanted to, not necessarily to give himself a lift or because of the heat. In fact, for no special reason. Or rather, because this was not an ordinary week-end. When they got back from Maine there would be no more thought of summer, or of vacations; it would be winter setting in, the days growing shorter and the children at home, obliging them to come straight back from the office; a more complicated life altogether, without any let-up.

Didn't that rate another drink? He had not said anything, had made no movement, no sign to Louis. But Nancy guessed what was in his mind, and at once slipped down from her stool.

"You'd better pay. It's time we were going."

He wasn't really angry about it. A bit disappointed perhaps, slightly put out. What did irritate him was that Louis had known perfectly well what was going on.

They had to cross two streets to reach the car-park where they left their car for the day, and once past Third Avenue one might have thought it was a Sunday.

"Do you want me to drive?" said Nancy.

He said no, took his place at the wheel, drove towards Queensboro Bridge where the procession of cars was moving at a snail's pace. Two hundred yards further on a car had already turned over at the edge of the sidewalk, and a woman was seated on the ground with people crowding round her and a policeman trying to keep traffic moving along until the arrival of an ambulance.

"There's no point in leaving too soon," said Nancy, feeling in her handbag for cigarettes. "In an hour or two the worst of the crush will be over."

A few drops rolled down the windscreen as they drove through Brooklyn, but the rain which had been forecast had not yet really started.

He was in a good mood at that moment, and still was when they reached their home in Scottville, a new building-lot in the middle of Long Island.

"Do you mind if we just have something cold?"

"I'd prefer it."

The house, too, would be different once the children were back. During the summer he always had a feeling of aimlessness, as though the two of them had no reason for being there, or for being in one room more than another, and they were constantly at a loss to know what to do with their evenings.

"While you're making sandwiches I'll slip out and get some cigarettes."

"There are some in the cupboard."

"Well, it'll save time if I fill up with gas and oil."

She made no objection to this, which surprised him. And he did in fact go to the garage. While they were checking the tyres he darted into the Italian restaurant to have a whisky at the bar.

"Scotch?"

"Rye."

Yet he didn't really like rye. He had chosen the stronger of the two because he would probably not have another chance of a drink that night, and they'd be driving for hours along the highway.

Could one say that he had entered the tunnel? He had had only two drinks, no more than when they went to the theatre and Nancy drank the same as he did. . . .

"Did you get cigarettes?"

"You said there were some in the cupboard. I filled up with gas and had the tyres checked."

"We'll get some as we go."

There weren't any cigarettes in the house. Either she had made a mistake or she had deliberately told him otherwise.

She stopped him as he was on his way to the bathroom.

"You can have your shower after we've eaten, while I'm stacking the dishes."

She didn't order him about, actually, but she arranged their life in her own way, as though it were the natural thing to do. He was wrong. He knew he was wrong. Whenever he had had a drink or two he saw her differently, becoming annoyed by things which ordinarily he took for granted.

"You'd better take your tweed jacket and your raincoat."

A breeze was getting up outside, stirring the leaves of the still-slender trees which had been planted five years before, when the houses had been built and the streets laid out. Some had never taken root, and two or three attempts to replace them had been equally fruitless.

Across the way one of their neighbours was attaching a trailer with a canoe on it to his car, while his wife, flushed with recent sunburn, her fat thighs filling pale blue shorts, stood at the edge of the sidewalk holding the fishing-rods.

"What are you thinking about?"

"Nothing special."

"I wonder if Dana's grown any more. Last month I thought he was taller, and his legs looked thinner."

"It's normal at his age."

Nothing special happened. He had his shower, got dressed, and then his wife reminded him to go and switch off the electricity meter in the garage while she went round to see that all the windows were closed.

"Shall I take the bags?"

"Make sure they're properly shut."

Despite the breeze and the lowering sky, his clean shirt was damp by the time he got in behind the wheel.

"Shall we go the same way as last time?"

"We swore we'd never go that way again."

"Just the same, it's the best."

Less than a quarter of an hour later they were wedged in among thousands of other cars moving in the same direction, with inexplicable hold-ups and occasional, momentary bursts of almost frantic speed.

It was at the beginning of Merrit Parkway that they ran into their first thunderstorm, when darkness had not quite fallen and the cars had only switched on their side-lights. There were three lanes of traffic between the white lines heading north but many fewer, of course, coming the opposite way, and one could hear the rain drumming on the steel roofs, the monotonous swish of the wheels throwing up a spray of water, the irritating sweep-sweep of the windscreen wiper.

"Sure you aren't tired?"

"Certain."

Sometimes one file got ahead of the others and sometimes one had a sense of losing ground.

"You should have gotten into the third line."

"I'm trying."

"Not now. There's a fool behind us."

At every lightning-flash one had a glimpse of faces in the darkened interiors of the adjacent cars, all with the same strained expression.

"Cigarette?"

"Thanks, I'd like one."

She always passed them to him lighted when he was driving.

"Like the radio on?"

"I don't mind."

But she had to switch it off again because of the static caused by the storm.

It was not worth the effort of talking, either. The constant hubbub made it necessary to raise one's voice, which soon became tiring. Gazing straight ahead he had a sidelong vision of Nancy's profile, palely shining in the half-light, and he asked her several times:

"What are you thinking about?"

"Nothing special."

Once she added:

"And you?"

He said:

"About the children."

It was not true. In fact he was not thinking about anything special either. To be precise, he was sorry he had managed to slide into the third traffic-lane, because it would be difficult to change without his wife asking why. Yet in a little while, when they had left the Parkway, there would be bars along the side of the road.

Had they ever driven the children to or from the camp without his pulling in a few times for a drink? Only once, three years ago, when he had had a terrible scene with Nancy the night before, and, both deeply shaken, they had made the week-end into a second honeymoon.

"We seem to have left the storm behind."

She switched off the windscreen wiper, but had to switch it on again for a few minutes because big, isolated drops continued to splash against the screen.

"You're not cold?"

"No."

The air had grown cool. With one elbow thrust out of the window, Steve could feel the wind blowing under his shirt-sleeve.

"And you?"

"Not yet. I'll put on my coat in a little while."

Why did they feel an obscure need to exchange remarks of this sort? Was it to reassure themselves? If so, what were they afraid of?

"Now the storm's over I'll try the radio again."

There was music. Nancy gave him another cigarette, and lighting one herself lay back in her seat, blowing the smoke above her head.

"*Special report of the Connecticut Automobile Club. . . .*"

They were already in Connecticut, fifty miles from New London.

"*Labour Day week-end claimed its first victim in Connecticut at 7.45 this evening, when at the intersection of Highways 1 and 118, at Darrien, a private car driven by Mr. MacKillian, of New York, collided with a truck driven by Robert Ostling. MacKillian and his passenger, John Roe, were killed instantly. The truck driver was uninjured. Ten minutes later, thirty miles from there, a car driven by. . . .*"

He switched off. His wife opened her mouth to say something and then stopped. Had she noticed that, perhaps uncon-sciously, he had slowed down a little?

She finally said : "Past Providence there'll be less traffic."

"Until we run into the Boston mob."

He was not shaken by the accident reports, not alarmed. What got on his nerves was the incessant hum of wheels on either side of him, the headlights rushing to meet him every hundred yards, and also the sensation of being caught in a tide, with no way of escaping either to right or to left or even of driving more slowly, because his mirror showed a triple-string of lights following bumper to bumper behind him.

Neon signs had begun to flash by on the right, where, with the gasoline-pumps, they were the only manifestation of life. Except for them one might have thought that the highroad was suspended in space, and that nothing existed beyond it but night and silence. The towns, the villages, were set further back, and only rarely did a vague, reddish glow in the sky give a hint of their existence.

The only immediate reality was that of the restaurants and bars which sprang out of the darkness every few miles, their signs advertising in red, green and blue letters brands of beer or whisky.

He was now in the second traffic-lane. He had edged gradually into it without his wife's noticing, and suddenly, seeing a gap, he slid into the first.

"What are you doing?"

He nearly overshot a bar whose neon sign announced, "The Little Cottage", braked just in time, so abruptly that the car behind had to make a sudden swerve and a flood of abuse poured from it. The driver even shook his fist out of the window.

"I have to go to the men's room," he said, keeping his voice as natural as possible while he pulled up at the side of the road. "You aren't thirsty?"

"No."

It often happened. She would wait for him in the car. In another car parked in front of the bar, a couple were so closely embraced that for a moment he wondered whether they were one person or two.

A moment later, pushing open the door, he felt a different man, and he paused for an instant to survey the room bathed in a dim orange light. This bar was like all the others along the road, and not so very different from Louis' place on Forty-Fifth Street, with the same television set in the corner, the same smells, the same lights.

"Dry Martini with lemon peel," he said as the barman turned to him.

"Single?"

"Double."

If he hadn't been asked he would have made do with a single, but a double was better, because his wife probably wouldn't allow him to stop again.

He hesitated, glancing towards the door of the toilet, and then dutifully started for it from a sort of honesty, passing a man with very dark hair who was telephoning with a hand curved round the side of his mouth. His voice was harsh.

"Yes. Just tell him what I told you. Nothing else. He'll understand. I tell you, he'll understand, see?"

Steve would have liked to hear more, but the man glanced at him as he spoke with a far from encouraging look. What was it all about? Who was at the other end of the line?

He came back to the bar and emptied his glass in two gulps,

feeling in his pocket for the money. Would Nancy hold her tongue? Wasn't it bad enough that just because of her he couldn't stay there a few minutes simply to look at people and relax his nerves?

Perhaps he had now entered the tunnel. Perhaps he had been in it ever since they left Long Island. If so, he was not aware of the fact and thought himself the most normal man on earth, not in the least affected by the one or two drinks he had had.

Why did he feel uncomfortable, even guilty, as he went towards the car and got in without looking at his wife? She asked no questions, made no comment.

"That's better!" he murmured as though to himself, starting the engine.

It seemed to him now that there were fewer cars on the road, that the pace had slackened, so much so that he passed three or four that were really going too slowly. An ambulance coming the other way left him unmoved, his attention being occupied at that moment by strange lights, then by a white barrier which suddenly loomed in front of them.

"Detour," said Nancy's calm voice, a little too expressionless.

"I can see."

"On the left."

This made him blush, because he had nearly turned right.

He grumbled:

"We've never once come this way without having to turn off somewhere! Why can't they repair the road in winter?"

"In the snow?" she asked, in the same voice.

"Well, in the fall—anyway, some time when there aren't forty million motorists on the roads."

"You've passed the intersection."

"What intersection?"

"The one marked with an arrow showing the way back to the Highway."

"What about the people behind us?" he asked sarcastically.

There were still cars following, fewer than there had been, however.

"Everybody isn't going to Maine."

"Don't you worry. I'll get you to Maine all right."

A moment later he seemed to have triumphed, because they were emerging on to a major road.

"Well? What about your arrow now?"

"This isn't Highway Number One."

"We'll soon know."

What set his nerves on edge was her self-confidence, the calm with which she answered him.

He persisted: "I suppose you can't be wrong, can you?"

She said nothing, and this irritated him still more.

"Go on! Say what you want to say!"

"Do you remember the time when we made a detour of sixty miles?"

"And dodged the worst of the traffic!"

"But without meaning to!"

"Listen, Nancy, if you want to start a quarrel why not say so?"

"I'm not trying to quarrel. I'm trying to find out where we are."

"Well, as I'm driving, do me a favour and don't fuss!"

She remained silent. He did not recognize the road, either. It was narrower and not so good, without a single filling-station since they had entered it; and another storm was rumbling in the sky.

Nancy quietly took the roadmap out of the glove compartment and switched on the light on the dashboard.

"We must be between One and Eighty-two, on a road going to Norwich, but I can't find the number."

She tried, too late, to catch the name of a village that sprang up out of the darkness and then they had left its few lights behind and were passing through woods.

"Don't you really think we should turn back?"

"No."

With the map still on her knees she lit a cigarette, without offering him one.

"Furious?" he said.

"Me?"

"Yes, you! Why not admit you're furious? Just because I happened to miss the highway and we have to go a few extra miles! I seem to remember that not long ago you were saying we had any amount of time."

"Watch out!"

"What for?"

"You nearly went off the road."

"So now I don't know how to drive?"

"I didn't say that."

And then the words burst from him, for no precise reason.

"No, you didn't say it, but now I'm going to say something, my pet, and you might as well get it into your head, once and for all. . . ."

The strangest thing was that he had no notion what he was going to say. He groped round for something strong, decisive; something to give his wife a good dose of the humility she so badly needed.

"You see, Nancy, maybe you're the only person who doesn't know it, but you're a pest!"

"Watch the road, will you!"

"Sure I'll watch the road! And I'll drive nice and carefully, so as not to go off the tracks. Do you know what tracks I'm talking about?"

It seemed to him extremely subtle, and dazzling in its truth. Almost as though he had made a new discovery. What was wrong with Nancy, finally, was that she always stayed on the rails, never allowed herself the least diversion.

"You don't understand, do you?"

"Do I have to?"

"What? Do you have to know what I think? God almighty, it might at least help you to try and understand other people and make life a bit more pleasant for them. For me, in particular. Only I doubt if you care."

"Wouldn't you let me drive?"

"No, I wouldn't. Just for the sake of argument, suppose instead of always thinking of yourself and being so darned sure you're right, you took a good look at yourself in the mirror and asked yourself. . . ."

He was laboriously struggling to express something he felt, which he was convinced he had felt every day of his life throughout the eleven years they had been married. It was not the first time it had happened, but now he was sure he had made a discovery which would enable him to explain everything. She would have to understand some time, wouldn't she? And the day she understood, maybe she'd try and treat him like a grown man.

"Can you think of anything more senseless than to be like a train, always following the same route? along the same tracks? Well, just now on the Parkway I had the feeling I was like a train. Other cars were pulling up and men were getting out without having to ask anyone's leave to go and have a glass of beer."

"Did you have a beer?"

He hesitated, decided upon frankness.

"No."

"A martini?"

"Yes."

"A double?"

It infuriated him to have to answer:

"Yes."

"And before that?" she was unkind enough to insist.

"Before what?"

"Before we left."

"I don't understand."

"What did you drink when you went to fill up with gas?"

This time he lied.

"Nothing."

"Oh?"

"You don't believe me?"

"If it's true, a double martini hit you harder than usual."

"You think I'm drunk?"

"You're certainly talking the way you do when you've been drinking."

"Meaning, I'm not making sense?"

"I don't know if it's sense or not, but I know you hate me."

"Why won't you try to understand?"

"Understand what?"

"That I don't hate you, that I love you, in fact, that I'd be perfectly happy with you if only you'd treat me as a grown man."

"By letting you drink at every bar along the way?"

"You see!"

"What am I supposed to see?"

"You have to put it in the most humiliating way you can. You deliberately exaggerate everything. Am I a drunk?"

"Of course not. I'd never have married a drunk."

"Do I often have too much?"

"Not very."

"Not even once a month. Perhaps once in three months."

"Well then, what's the matter with you?"

"There wouldn't be anything the matter with me if you didn't treat me like a worm. Just because for one evening I'd like to get a little outside everyday life!"

"Does it cramp you so much?"

"I didn't say that. You take Dick, for instance. I don't suppose he ever goes to bed less than half-tight. But that doesn't stop you thinking how interesting he is, and you talk seriously to him by the hour, even when he's been drinking."

"For one thing, he isn't my husband."

"And what else?"

135

"There's a truck ahead of us."

"I can see."

"Be quiet a minute. We're coming to a cross-road and I want to see what's on the road-sign."

"You don't like me talking about Dick?"

"I don't mind."

"You're sorry you didn't marry him instead of me?"

"No."

They were again on the highway, with two lines of cars travelling very much faster than in the outskirts of New York, and overtaking furiously. Perhaps in the hope of silencing him, Nancy switched on the radio, which was giving out the eleven o'clock news.

". . . *The police have reason to believe that Sid Halligan, who escaped last night from Sing Sing Penitentiary, and has so far evaded his pursuers——*"

She turned it off again.

"Why did you switch off?"

"I didn't think you were interested."

He wasn't interested. He had never heard of Sid Halligan, did not even know that a prisoner had escaped from Sing Sing the night before. He had merely thought, as he heard the words, of the man telephoning in the bar, with his hand cupped round his mouth and a fierce glare in his eyes. There was nothing to it, except for her switching off without asking him, but it is trifles such as these. . . .

Where had they got to when she had broken off the argument? They had been talking about Dick Lowell, who had married a friend of Nancy's, and with whom they sometimes spent an evening.

Hell, what was the good of arguing? Did Dick care what his wife thought? The mistake he made was that he was always worrying about what Nancy thought, and always trying to win her approval.

"What are you doing?"

"Stopping, that's what."

"Listen. . . ."

This bar had a shabby look, with nothing but a few half-broken-down cars outside, and that made him all the more anxious to go in.

"If you stop," Nancy was saying, carefully pronouncing each syllable, "I warn you I shall go on alone."

It gave him a shock. For an instant he stared at her incredulously, and she met his gaze steadily. She was as trim and neat as when they had left New York—cool as a cucumber, he thought.

Perhaps nothing would have happened and he would have given way, if she had not added:

"You can always come on to the camp by bus."

He felt his lip twist in a queer sort of smile and, as calm as she was herself, he reached for the ignition-key, which he took out and put in his pocket.

Nothing of the kind had ever happened to them before. He could not turn back now. He was convinced that she needed a lesson.

He got out of the car and shut the door without looking at her, and made himself walk with a steady stride towards the entrance of the bar. When he looked round from the doorway she had not moved and he could see her pale profile through the glass.

He went in. Faces turned towards him, transformed by the smoke as though in the trick-mirrors at a fair, and when he put his hand on the counter he felt it sticky with alcohol.

CHAPTER TWO

DURING the time it had taken him to cross from the door to the bar the conversation ceased, the hubbub of voices that had filled the room an instant before stopped with the abruptness of an orchestral ending. Everyone had stayed motionless, their eyes following him without hostility, without interest, it seemed, and without its being possible to discern any expression on their faces.

After he had laid his hand on the counter, and the barman had reached out a hairy arm to wipe it with a dirty cloth, life had been resumed and no one seemed to pay him any further attention.

He had been struck by this. The bar was very different from the usual roadside places. There must be a village quite near, or a small town, probably a factory, because the people were talking with different accents and two negroes were leaning against the bar near him.

"What'll it be, stranger?" asked the man behind the counter.

He had not used the word facetiously. His voice was friendly.

"Rye," murmured Steve.

He ordered it this time, not because it was stronger but because here he would have attracted notice by ordering Scotch. He did not want to leave Nancy alone too long. On the other hand, he must not return to the car too soon, or his gesture would be wasted.

He was dismayed by the firm line he had taken. And half-inclined to be ashamed, although in his heart he was convinced that he was within his rights and that his wife deserved a lesson.

Thanks to her he scarcely knew places like this, and he breathed in the heavy atmosphere with relish, contemplating the dark-green painted walls adorned with old lithographs and gazing through an open doorway into an untidy kitchen where a woman with grey hair falling over her face was drinking with two other women and a man.

A very large, old-type television screen was fixed above the bar. The streaked pictures quivered, splintering in a way that reminded one of very old films, and no one bothered to look at them; nearly everyone was talking loudly, one of the negroes standing next to him kept joustling him as he stepped back to gesticulate, and each time apologized with a loud laugh. At a corner table two middle-aged lovers sat with their arms round each other's waist, cheeks pressed together, motionless as in a photograph, silent, their gaze lost in space.

Nancy would never understand all this, even he would have found it difficult to explain to her what there was to understand. She thought he had stopped simply for the sake of having a drink and it wasn't true; it was precisely her kind of truth, which made her seem to be invariably in the right.

He was not angry with her. He wondered if she was crying, out there alone in the car, and he got a dollar bill out of his pocket and laid it on the counter. It was time to be going. He had been there about five minutes. A "still" suddenly appeared on the television screen, the photograph of a little girl aged about four, huddled in a closet with brooms and buckets; he did not listen to the commentary, and the picture was replaced by one of a shopfront with a smashed window-pane.

He was picking up his change, just about to turn away, when he felt a hand on his shoulder and heard a voice say, pronouncing the words with care:

"Have one on me, brother!"

It was the man on his right, whom he had scarcely noticed. He was by himself, leaning on the counter, and when Steve looked at him he stared back with an uncomfortable fixity. He must have had a lot to drink. His voice was thick, his movements studied, as though he knew his balance was uncertain.

Steve was inclined to refuse, saying that his wife was waiting for him. The man, guessing what was in his mind, turned to the barman and pointed to their two empty glasses, and the barman gave Steve a slight nod which meant "You can accept it."

Or perhaps he was really saying: "You'd better accept it."

The man wasn't a noisy drunk. Indeed, was he an habitual drunkard at all? His white shirt was as clean as Steve's, his fair hair newly cut, and his sun-tanned skin brought out the pale blue of his eyes.

With his eyes fixed upon Steve he raised his glass, and Steve raised his own and emptied it at a gulp.

"Thanks. My wife. . . ."

He broke off because of the smile that spread over the other's face. It was as though this man who continued to stare steadily at him and said nothing knew everything, knew him like a brother, read his thoughts in his eyes.

He was drunk certainly, but in his drunkenness there was the bitter and smiling serenity of a being who has achieved Lord knows what superior wisdom.

Steve was in a hurry to get back to Nancy, and at the same time he feared to disappoint this man he did not know, who must be about his own age.

Turning to the barman, he said:

"The same!"

He would have liked to talk but could think of nothing to say. Silence, however, did not trouble the man and he continued to gaze at Steve with satisfaction, as though they were friends of long standing who had no need to talk.

Only when he tried to light a cigarette with a shaking hand did the degree of his intoxication become apparent, and he realized it, and his look, and the twist of his lip, seemed to say:

"Sure I've had a lot to drink! I'm drunk. So what?"

That gaze expressed so many things that Steve felt as uncomfortable as if he had been undressed in public.

"I know. Your wife's waiting for you in the car. She's going to make a scene. So what?"

Had he also guessed that he had children at a holiday-camp in Maine? And a fifteen-thousand dollar house on Long Island, payable in twelve years?

There must be an affinity between them, things in common which Steve would have liked to find out. But the thought that

Nancy had now been waiting over ten minutes, perhaps a quarter of an hour, put him in a sort of panic.

He paid his round, awkwardly held out his hand, which the other man clasped, gazing into his eyes with so much insistence that he seemed to be trying to convey to him some mysterious message.

The same silence as when he entered accompanied him on his way out, and he did not venture to look round, opened the door, found that it had started to rain again. He noticed that a good many of the parked vehicles were delivery vans, picked his way to his car, then stopped dead when he saw that his wife was not there.

At first he looked about him, thinking she had got out to stretch her legs. The rain was no longer heavy, but a fine, gentle drizzle with a pleasant coolness.

"Nancy!" he called in a low voice.

But there was not a pedestrian in sight on either side of the road. He was about to go back into the bar, to explain what had happened and perhaps telephone the police, when, as he leaned in through the car window, he saw a scrap of paper on the seat. Nancy had torn it out of her diary and written:

"I'm going on by coach. Have a good trip!"

For the second time he was tempted to go back into the bar, this time to get drunk with the unknown friend. What caused him to change his mind was the sight of a cluster of lights about five hundred yards further on. It was a cross-road where the long-distance coaches probably stopped, and his wife must have walked in that direction. Perhaps he could still manage to catch her.

He started the engine, and as he drove he peered out at the sides of the road, which, so far as he could tell in the darkness, was bordered by fields or open country.

He did not see anyone, reached the cross-road, pulled up in front of a cafeteria from outside which one could see its gleaming white walls, its chrome-nickel counter, two or three customers busy eating.

He ran in and asked:

"Do the buses stop here?"

A dark-haired, peaceful-looking woman engaged in making hot-dogs answered:

"If you want the one for Providence, you've missed it. It went by five minutes ago."

"You haven't seen a fairly young woman in a light-coloured

suit? Or rather, she should have been wearing a gabardine coat. . . ."

He suddenly remembered that he hadn't seen the coat in the car.

"She didn't come in here."

Without stopping to think he dashed out again, still agitated, conscious that he must look like a lunatic. A road went off to the right, the main street of a village, with the lighted window of a furniture-store displaying a bed covered in blue satin. He did not trouble to ask where he was or to look at the map, but jumped into the car, started off jerkily and drove straight along the wet road.

The coaches seldom went at more than fifty miles an hour, and his idea was to overtake the one she was in, follow it to the next stopping-place, where he would ask her to get back into the car; and she could drive if she wanted to.

He had been in the wrong. She was in the wrong, too, but she would not admit it, and so, as usual, it was he who would end by apologizing. He started the windscreen wipers, trod hard on the accelerator, and since both windows were open the wind ruffled his hair and, almost icily, blew down his neck.

Perhaps he talked to himself during those minutes, while he stared ahead searching for the rear-lights of the coach. He overtook ten, fifteen cars, of which two at least swerved abruptly at his passing. The sight of the speedometer needle touching seventy caused him a certain feverish excitement, and he almost wished a speed-cop would come after him; he made up a story about it, about having to catch his wife at all costs, about the children waiting for them in Maine. Surely, in the circumstances, one was justified in breaking the rules?

He came to another lighted crossing, surrounded by gasoline-pumps, where the road forked. At first glance one fork looked as good as the other. He did not slow up to choose, and not until he had covered another fifteen miles did he realize that he had gone wrong again.

He could have sworn just now that he was in Rhode Island State. How and when had he come to turn back? He could not understand it, but the fact remained that he had been travelling away from his destination and that the road signs announced the town of Putman, in Connecticut.

It was no longer any use trying to overtake the coach. From now on Steve's time was all his own. Too bad for Nancy if she was furious. Too bad for him, too. Too bad for both of them!

He thought of trying to find the bar he had come from, but it would have been almost impossible. There would be others further on, as many as he wanted, where, now that he was so to speak a bachelor, he could stop without having to make excuses.

The thing he was sorry about was not having had a chance to talk to the man who had laid a hand on his shoulder and offered him a rye. He remained convinced that they would have understood one another. It wasn't just that they were the same age, but they were of the same build, the same light colouring, the same fair hair—like one another right down to their long, bony, square-tipped fingers.

He would have liked to know whether the man, too, had been brought up in a town, as he had, or whether he'd been born in the country.

He was more experienced than himself, he admitted. Very likely he wasn't married, or, if he was, he didn't bother about his wife. Who knows? Steve wouldn't have been surprised to learn that he had children, too, but had walked out on them and their mother.

Something of that sort must have happened to him. Anyway, he didn't worry about being at the office at nine o'clock sharp, and getting back in good time so that the baby-sitter could go home.

For when Bonnie and Dan weren't in camp, that is to say, during the greater part of the year, it was not Nancy who got home early to look after them, it was he. Because in her office she was a person of importance, the right-hand of Mr. Schwartz, head of the firm of Schwartz and Taylor, who came between ten and eleven in the morning and had a business lunch nearly every day, after which he worked till six or seven in the evening.

Had the man in the bar guessed? Did it show on his face? He wouldn't be surprised. After years of that sort of life it would be bound to show in one's expression.

And the car? It was registered in his name, granted, but his wife was the one who used it in the evening to drive back to Scottville. And always with good reason! Because of her important position with Mr. Schwartz, so important that when, after the children were born, Steve had wanted her to stay at home, Mr. Schwartz had taken the trouble to come personally to persuade Nancy to go back to work.

On the stroke of five he, Steve, was free. He could make a dash for the Lexington Avenue subway station, get wedged in the crush, and at Brooklyn sprint for the bus which stopped at the end of their lot.

Altogether it didn't take more than three-quarters of an hour, and he would find Ida, the coloured girl who minded the children when they got back from school, with her hat on already. Her time must be valuable, too. Everybody's time was valuable. Everybody's except his own. . . .

"Hello, is that you? I'm going to be late again to-night. Don't expect me before seven, maybe half-past. Will you give the children their supper and put them to bed?"

He was on Highway Six, less than ten miles from Providence, and he had had to slow down because he was caught in the stream of traffic again. What were they all thinking, the other men he could see seated at the wheels of cars? Most of them had a woman beside them. Some had children asleep on the back seat. He seemed to feel all round him the dismal weariness of waiting-rooms and occasionally he heard a burst of music, or the officious voice of an announcer.

For some time now the windscreen wiper had been working unnecessarily, and on both sides of the road the restaurants and filling-stations were becoming more numerous, drawing closer together to form an almost unbroken chain of lights, with a patch of darkness only every mile or so.

He longed for a glass of iced beer, but precisely because there was nothing to hold him back he was determined to choose the right place to stop. The last bar had left him with a sort of nostalgia and he would have liked to find another of the same kind; so he went past the places that looked too new, past the too showy signs.

A police-car passed him with its siren going, then an ambulance, then another and a little further on he had to slow to a walking pace in a line of traffic that moved round two cars one of which had literally climbed on top of the other.

He had time to see a man in a white shirt like himself, like his friend in the bar, with his hair dishevelled and blood on his face, who was explaining something to the police with one arm pointing towards a point in space.

How many dead had the experts predicted for the week-end? Four hundred and thirty-five. He remembered the exact figure. Therefore he wasn't drunk. The proof was that he had driven at seventy miles an hour without the least mishap.

Nancy, in the stifling half-darkness of the motor-coach, with the other passengers sound asleep all round her, must be regretting her decision. She was fastidious about rubbing shoulders with the crowd. The smell of humanity pervading the coach must certainly be bothering her as much as the familiarities of her neighbours. She would have been thoroughly unhappy in that last bar. Was she a bit of a snob?

He preferred to go on a mile or two after the bottleneck created by the accident, and at the point where he eventually pulled into the side of the road there were two places almost next door to one another, a pretentious establishment with a mauve neon sign, and then, beyond a gap which served as a car-park, a one-storey wooden building with the look of a log cabin.

This was the one he chose. Another proof that he wasn't drunk was that he remembered to take out the ignition key and to switch off the lights of the car.

At first glance this bar was less shabby than the other and the interior really was that of a log cabin, with wooden walls blackened by the years, big beams running across the ceiling, pewter and earthenware tankards on the shelves and a panoply of rifles dating from the time of the Civil War.

The owner, short and plump in a white apron, his head bald, had retained a slight German accent. There was a beer-pump, and the beer was served in huge glass tankards.

He took a moment to find room for himself at the counter, nodded towards the beer-pump without speaking and then gazed round at the people in the room as though looking for someone.

And perhaps he really was looking for someone, without realizing it. There was no television set here but a lighted juke-box, red and yellow, whose gleaming mechanism manipulated the records with a fascinating deliberation. In addition to the music that poured from it a small, brown radio behind the bar was also playing, solely, it seemed, for the benefit of the proprietor, who bent down to listen to it whenever he had a moment to spare.

Steve drank his beer in big, thirsty gulps, wiped his mouth with the back of his hand, and said without an instant's pause:
"A rye!"

The beer had no taste. He wanted to recapture the oily flavour of Irish whiskey, which made him gasp a little whenever he drank it. He perched himself with one buttock on a stool, his elbows on the counter, in exactly the attitude of the stranger at the last bar.

His eyes were also blue, a slightly darker shade, and his

shoulders certainly as broad, with the same swelling of the shirt-sleeves over the biceps.

He drank more slowly now, listening with one ear to what the two men on his right were saying. They were drunk. Everybody in the place was more or less drunk and from time to time one heard a great burst of laughter or the smashing of a glass on the floor.

". . . so I asked him what kind of a sucker he took me for—twelve bucks a ton!—and when he saw I wasn't kidding he looked me right in the eyes, like this, and . . ."

Tons of what? Steve never found out. The conversation afforded no clue, and the man who was listening didn't seem to care, being more interested in trying to catch what was being said by the radio. Another news-bulletin. The announcer was giving a list of accidents, one of which had been caused by a tree struck by lightning, which had fallen on to the roof of a car.

Then there was political news, but Steve did not listen, seized by a sudden desire to put a hand on the shoulder of his neighbour on the left, just as the stranger had done to him, and to say as nearly as possible in the same tone of voice, with the same impenetrable expression:

"Have one on me, brother."

Because the man on this side of him was also alone. But, unlike the other, he did not seem to be drunk and the glass of beer in front of him was three-quarters full.

He was a different type. Dark-haired, with a long face, sallow skin, dark eyes, and thin, extraordinarily flexible fingers which he used from time to time to take the cigarette out of his mouth.

He had glanced at Steve as he entered, and had immediately looked away. Pulling a cigarette-pack from his pocket, he found it empty and left the bar for a moment to go to the automatic machine.

This was when Steve noticed his boots. They were muddy and too large—big, farmer's boots which did not go with the rest of him. He was wearing no jacket or tie, simply a blue cotton shirt and dark trousers kept up by a wide belt.

Despite his cumbersome footgear he moved like a cat, contrived to come and go without touching anyone, returned to his stool with a cigarette between his lips, glanced quickly at Steve who opened his mouth to speak to him.

He had to talk to someone. Since Nancy had wanted it this way this was his night, a chance that perhaps would never come again. So far as Nancy was concerned, all he had to do was to impress upon his mind, while it was still clear, that he must telephone the Keanes between five and six in the morning. By that time his wife would have reached the camp. As in the two previous years, the Keanes had kept a room for them in one of the bungalows, or at the very least a bed, because during Labour Day week-end it would have been hopeless to try and find anything elsewhere. It was the same everywhere, from one end to the other of the United States.

"Forty-five million motorists!" he jeered in an undertone.

He had spoken deliberately to catch his neighbour's ear.

"Forty-five million men and women loose on the roads!"

This suddenly looked to him like a discovery and he thought seriously about it while he gazed at the dark-haired young man on his left.

"That's a thing you won't see in any other country on earth! Four hundred and thirty-five deaths by Monday evening!"

At last he made the gesture he so longed to make, and tapped the man lightly on the shoulder.

"Have one on me?"

The other looked round at him without troubling to answer, but Steve let it go and called to the proprietor, bent over his tiny radio.

"Two!" he said, holding up two fingers.

"Two what?"

"Ask him what he wants."

The young man shook his head.

"Two ryes," said Steve obstinately.

He wasn't offended. He hadn't responded to the man in the other bar, either.

"You married?" he asked.

The young man wore no wedding-ring, but that didn't prove anything.

"Well, I've got a wife and two kids, a daughter of ten and a boy of eight. They're both in camp."

His neighbour was too young to have children that age. He wasn't more than twenty-three or four. He probably wasn't even married.

"New York?"

He got an answer of sorts, since the other shook his head.

"You're from round these parts? Providence? Boston?"

A vague gesture, which wasn't affirmative either.

"The funny thing is, I don't really like rye. Do you like rye? I wonder if there's anybody who really likes rye!"

146

He emptied his glass and pointed to the one his companion had not touched.

"You don't want it? Well, O.K.—it's a free country. No offence. Another night maybe I wouldn't drink the stuff for a million dollars. To-night it happens I'm on rye. That's the way it is. And if you want to know, it's my wife's fault."

At any other time he would have shied away from a man who talked as he was doing now. This he perceived in a momentary flash, and it mortified him.

But the next instant he had swung back to the conviction that this was the night of his life and that it was vitally important to explain this to his haggard-faced companion.

Perhaps the reason why he wasn't drinking was because he was sick? His face was grey, his lower lip had a sort of tic which now and then caused the cigarette to quiver. Steve even wondered if he doped.

That would have disappointed him. Any kind of drug frightened him, marihuana, heroin, or whatever, and he always watched with mingled terror and embarrassment a customer at Louis' Bar, a pretty woman, still very young, who worked as a model and was said to be an addict.

"If you aren't married, maybe you've never asked yourself the question. And yet it's a vital question. People talk about all kinds of things that they think are important, but they're scared to talk about this. Take my wife. Am I right, or am I wrong?"

He had started badly and could not pick up the thread of his thought. In any case, that was not the root of the matter. It had to do with women certainly, but indirectly. What he was trying to explain was something complicated, so subtle that he did not hope to get back to it.

At moments he seemed to have ten phrases on his lips at once, ten thoughts, all of which had their place in his chain of reasoning; but no sooner had he uttered a few words than he felt his task to be virtually impossible.

This depressed him.

"Same thing, boss!"

He nearly lost his temper when he saw the proprietor hesitate before serving him.

"Do I look like a drunk? Am I the kind of man to start a ruckus? I'm talking quietly to this boy here without even raising my voice. . . ."

The drink was served, and he gave a chuckle of satisfaction.

"That's better. . . . What was I saying? I was talking about

women, and about the highways. That's the whole point.
Remember that. Women against highways, see? Women follow
the tracks. Fine! They know where they're going. Even when
they're still kids they know where they're heading for, and
when you kiss them good-night after a party they smell the
orange-blossom! Right?

"Mind you, I've got nothing against them! I'm just stating
one of the facts of Nature. . . ."

Women and railroad tracks.

Men and highways.

Because whatever they do, men have got something in here. . . .

He thumped his chest with conviction, and in doing so again
lost the thread of his argument. The words just wouldn't come.

"Men. . . ." he repeated, making an effort.

He would have liked to explain what men need, what they are
deprived of through lack of understanding. That was where the
difficulty lay. It wasn't a matter of drinking a certain number of
ryes, as Nancy would have said sarcastically. The rye had
nothing to do with it. What mattered on a night like this, for
instance, a memorable night, when forty-five million motorists
were loose on the roads, was to understand, and to understand
it was necessary to go off the tracks.

Just as when he had gone into that other bar! Where else
would he have met a man like the one he had got to know without
any need to say anything? Certainly not at the office. His firm,
"World Travellers," also sold mileage: air-mileage—trips in
luxury-aircraft to London, Paris, Rome or Cairo. To anywhere
on earth. Every customer was in a hurry. It was indispensable,
it was vitally important for each and every one to leave
immediately. Not at Schwartz & Taylor, either, who sold
publicity space—magazine pages, radio and television time,
poster-hoardings along the roads.

Not even at Louis' Bar, where at five o'clock customers such
as he came to the trough to restore themselves with a dry martini.

He suddenly wanted a martini, but he was sure the proprietor
would not let him have it, and he did not want to risk a rebuff
in the presence of his new friend.

"You see, there are those that go off and those that don't.
And that's that!"

He was still talking about the rails. He was no longer precise.
He even skipped unnecessary words, perhaps because they were
difficult to pronounce.

"Take me. To-night I've gone off. . . ."

His earlier friend had very likely gone off the rails for good. So, too, perhaps, the man who, in the first bar, had been telephoning a mysterious message, a hand cupped round his mouth.

And what about this one? Steve was dying to ask; he kept winking at him to encourage him to talk about himself. He didn't work in an office, or on a farm either: that was obvious, in spite of his heavy boots. Perhaps he tramped along the roads, his pockets empty, hitch-hiking when he could? Didn't he realize that it was nothing to be ashamed of? Far from it!

"To-morrow I'll be with the kids. . . ."

At the thought he was overtaken by a wave of sentimentality which brought a lump to his throat, and it seemed to him suddenly that he was betraying Bonnie and Dan; he tried to picture them in his mind's eye, was unable to conjure up more than a hazy image and got out his wallet to look at the snapshots he always carried with him.

He had not really meant to say that. He loved his children well enough and had no regrets for all he did for them; but the thing he was trying desperately to explain was that he was a man, and that. . . .

He inserted his fingers under his driving-licence to get out the snapshots, and his head was turned away when his companion laid a coin on the counter and started for the door. It was done so quickly, like the gliding away of a snake, that it was a moment before he realized what had happened.

"He's gone?" he asked, turning towards the proprietor.

"And good riddance!"

"You know him?"

"I don't want to know him."

He was rather shocked that the owner of a place such as this should be sticking to the rails, too. Steve was the one who had been drinking, not the young man—he hadn't even finished his beer—yet it was Steve who was being treated with a certain consideration, probably because his face showed that he was a respectable, well-bred man.

"Those your children?" asked the proprietor.

"My son and daughter."

"You driving to the country for them?"

"To Walla-Walla camp, in Maine. There are two camps alongside one another, one for boys and the other for girls. Mrs. Keane has charge of the girls, while her husband, Hector, who looks like an old boy scout. . . ."

The proprietor was listening with care not to him but to his radio, his heavy eyebrows knitted, and fiddling with the knobs to try and get better reception, glaring at the juke-box, the noise of which drowned the other sound.

". . . has managed, it is not known how, to slip through three successive police roadblocks, and at about eleven o'clock was reported seen on Highway Number Two, driving north in a stolen car. . . ."

"Who's that?" asked Steve.

The radio continued: *"Be careful! He is armed."*

Then:

"Our next news bulletin will be broadcast at two o'clock."

Music followed.

"Who's that?"

Steve was being insistent for no reason.

"The guy who escaped from Sing Sing and shut the little girl in a closet with a chocolate bar."

"What little girl?"

"Farmer's daughter, at Croton Lake."

Preoccupied, the proprietor paid no further attention to him, looking round for someone more or less sober to talk to. He went towards a corner table where two men and two women sat drinking beer, elderly people, who looked as if they might be building contractors and their wives.

The music prevented Steve from hearing what was said. The proprietor pointed to the vacant stool beside him, and one of the women, the one nearest the cigarette machine, seemed suddenly to remember something. The proprietor listened, nodding his head; he gazed uncertainly at the telephone on the wall, and finally came back to Steve Hogan.

"You didn't notice anything?"

"Notice what?"

"You didn't see if he was tattooed on one wrist?"

Steve didn't follow, was doing his best to grasp what was wanted of him.

"Who?"

"The man you wanted to treat to a drink."

"He didn't accept. No offence."

At this the proprietor shrugged his shoulders and looked at him in a way he disliked. Now that he probably wouldn't be served with any more drink, and since there was no one to talk to, he might as well go.

He put a five-dollar bill on the counter, right in the wettest place, climbed off his stool unsteadily, and said:

"Keep the change!"

At the same time he made sure no one was giving him any dirty looks. He wouldn't have stood for it.

CHAPTER THREE

As he went towards the door, walking nonchalantly, as though in slow-motion, his lips wore the benevolent, protective smile of a strong man fallen among weaklings. He felt like a giant. Two men talking with their backs to him and their heads close together stood in his way so he swept them aside with a grand gesture, and though they were both as tall as he was, he had the impression of overtopping them by a head. In any case, the men made no protest. Steve was not looking for a fight, with them or with anyone, and if, when he reached the door, he turned and stood motionless, looking back into the room, he did not do so as a challenge.

He took time to light a cigarette and he felt fine. The air outside was fine, too, pleasantly cool, the pretentious roadhouse next door, with the row of lights outlining its gable, was ridiculous; the cars passed along the smooth surface of the road, all making the same sound. He went to his own car, which he had left in the darker part of the car-park, and opened the door; and all his movements, which were of a surprising largeness, everything he saw, everything he did, gave him an inward satisfaction.

As he slid behind the wheel he saw the man, sitting where Nancy should have been. Despite the darkness he instantly recognized the long oval of the face, the deep-set eyes, and he was dismayed neither by finding him there nor by all that his presence implied.

Instead of drawing back, hesitating, perhaps adopting a defensive attitude, he arranged himself comfortably, pulling up his trousers as he ordinarily did, then reached out to slam the door and turned the safety-catch.

He did not wait for the man to speak, but said, more in a conversational tone than as though he were asking a question:

"It's you?"

The words had not their ordinary meaning. He was living several layers above everyday reality, in a sort of super-reality, and he expressed himself in abbreviations, sure of himself and sure of being understood.

151

In saying, "It's you?" he was not simply asking if this was the man to whom he had offered a drink in the bar, and the other made no mistake about it. The question really meant: "It's you they're looking for?"

In his own mind it comprised even more. He could not have explained it, but in the few words he gathered together the scattered images collected almost unconsciously in the course of the evening, and assembled them in a coherent whole luminous with simplicity.

He was proud of his subtlety, proud of his calm, of the way he thrust the ignition-key into its slot without a tremor of his hand, awaiting, before he turned it, his companion's reply.

No humility. He did not want to appear humble. No indignation either, such as the proprietor of the bar might have shown, or a woman of Nancy's type. And no panic. He wasn't afraid. He understood. The proof that the other also understood and respected him in his turn was that he answered simply, without protest, without denial, without evasion:

"They recognized me?"

This was the way he had always imagined a dialogue between two men, real men, coming together on the highways. No unnecessary words. Every sentence meaning as much as a long speech. Nearly everyone talks too much. Had Steve needed to make any speeches earlier in the evening, to get the man in the first bar to see that he was something more than the commonplace office-worker he might have looked?

And now another stranger had chosen to take refuge in his car. He was armed, the radio had just said. But did he feel the need to point his gun at him? Did he seem threatening?

"I think the owner's suspicious," Steve told him.

It was queer the way things that he hadn't registered were coming back to him. He knew perfectly well that this was a man who had escaped from Sing Sing. He didn't remember the name, but then he could never remember names, only figures, and above all telephone numbers. A name ending in "gan," like his own.

There had been something about a farmer's wife near a lake, and a little girl locked in a closet with a slab of chocolate. He could recall the little girl's picture clearly, and so far as he could remember it was the first time he had ever seen a still photograph projected on to a television screen.

Then there had been a picture of a smashed shop-window, and some talk of Highway Two. Right?

If he'd been drunk, how could he have remembered all that?

"What description did they give?"

"They said something about tattoo marks."

He went on waiting, without impatience, for the signal to start his engine and it was as though he had known all his life that this hour would come. He was pleased, not only with the trust placed in him, but with the way he was bearing himself.

Hadn't he said earlier that this was his night?

"Are you able to drive?"

By way of reply he started off, asking:

"Shall I pass Providence on the country roads?"

"Stick to the highway."

"And suppose the police. . . ."

The young man reached over into the back of the car, picked up Steve's brown check sports coat and straw hat which were on the seat. The jacket was too wide at the shoulders, but he huddled in his corner like a traveller asleep, with the hat pulled over his eyes.

"Don't exceed the speed-limit."

"Check."

"And don't try to go through red lights."

So as not to have the cops after them, of course.

He was the one who asked:

"What is your name again?"

"Sid Halligan. They've given it out often enough over the air."

"Well, Sid, suppose we come to a road-block . . . ?"

He drove at forty-five, like the family cars they could see, piled high with baggage.

"Follow the others."

He had never been in a situation like this before, and yet he had no need of explanations. He felt as clear-headed as that first stranger, the one with blue eyes who resembled him.

First, on a night like this they couldn't stop all the cars on all the roads in New England and examine the passengers one by one, without causing the biggest bottle-neck of all time. Probably all they were doing was to have a quick glance inside the cars, more especially the ones occupied by a man alone.

In his car they were two.

"It's a laugh!" he thought.

Later on, past Providence, he'd strike up a conversation again. He had been right, after all, not to be annoyed by his companion's silence in the bar. Didn't he talk to Steve naturally like an old friend?

He had to watch the road. The cars coming the other way were more numerous. Cross-roads were now beginning to appear frequently and on a lower level could be seen the lights of a big town.

"Sure you know the way?" said the voice in the shadow.

"I've done it at least ten times."

"If there's a road-block . . ."

"I know. You told me."

"I suppose you can guess what would happen if you took it into your head to . . ."

Why did he have to say that? He didn't have to keep his hand in his pocket either, probably resting on the butt of his gun.

"I won't talk."

"Fine."

He would have been disappointed if there had been no road-block. Every time he saw stationary lights he thought it had happened, but in the end it turned out to be quite different from what he had imagined. The cars began to close up on one another until they were touching, and finally they came to a stop. There were stopped cars as far ahead as one could see, and they'd move forward a few yards only to stop again, as in a queue.

"This is it!"

"Yeah."

"Nervous?"

He regretted the word, which brought forth no reply. Once when they stopped opposite a bar he was tempted to dash in and have a quick one, but he dared not suggest it.

Despite the coolness of the evening he began to sweat unpleasantly, and his fingers drummed on the steering-wheel. Sometimes Halligan was buried in darkness, then, because of the lights of filling-stations, he would be glowingly visible, motionless in his corner like a man asleep. Despite his long, narrow face his head must be bigger than it looked for the straw hat was not too large for him and Steve had a big head himself.

"Cigarette?"

"No."

Steve lit one. His hand trembled like that of the man in the first bar when he had lit his, but with him he was sure it was just nervousness, or rather, impatience. He wasn't scared. Just in a hurry to get it over.

He could now see the way the road-block was organized. White-painted hurdles set up across the road allowed only a single file of cars to pass in either direction, and this caused a bottle-neck, but the cars did not actually stop at the barrier; they just slowed right down while uniformed police had a quick look inside.

Past Providence it would no doubt be over because they probably didn't search so far.

"What was that about the little girl?"

The radio was going in the car in front of them, and a woman had her head on the driver's shoulder.

Halligan made no reply. Not the right time to ask. Steve would broach the subject later. He also intended to go on with what he had been saying in the log cabin. If a man like Sid couldn't understand, no one could.

Had Sid always been like this? Had it come to him naturally, without any effort? Most likely he'd been very poor. If you were raised in a crowded slum, the whole family living in one room, and were a member of a gang by the time you were ten, it was bound to be easier.

Maybe he didn't even realize?

"Keep going."

And as they stopped again:

"How much gas in the tank?"

"Half full."

"How many miles does that mean?"

"About a hundred and fifty."

This was when he could have done with a rye to keep him on the level he had attained. Every now and then the well-being, the assurance, threatened to vanish. Stark, unpleasant thoughts occurred to him like the notion, for instance, that if they were arrested together the police would not believe in his innocence, and relays of detectives would grill him for hours without allowing him a glass of water or a cigarette. They'd take away his necktie and his shoe-laces. They'd fetch Nancy to identify him.

When there were only three cars left ahead, his legs became so weak that it took him a moment to find the accelerator when they had to move on.

"See you don't let them smell your breath!"

Halligan spoke out of the corner of his mouth without moving, still looking like a man asleep.

Their car reached the barrier, and as Steve was about to pull up a policeman signed to him to keep moving, to go faster, merely giving a vague glance inside. It was all over. It was over. The highway was clear ahead of them, or rather, the road leading down to the town through which they had to pass.

"Done it!" exclaimed Steve with relief, accelerating to forty.

"Done what?"

"We got through."

"The sign said thirty-five an hour. Direction Boston. You know the way?"

"It's the way I always go."

They passed a road-house festooned with red lights, and it made him thirsty; once again, however, he didn't mention it and lit a cigarette instead.

"Hey, what are you doing?"

"Why?"

"You're driving, aren't you? Can't you keep to the right?"

"Sorry!"

It was true that all of a sudden he was driving a little wildly, he couldn't tell why. Up to the time when they had passed the barrier he had felt well under control, as steady and sure of himself as when he'd left the log cabin. But now his body was inclined to sag, and the road ahead of him seemed to lack substance. At one turning he nearly went on to the sidewalk.

His thoughts had also grown confused, and he resolved that when they got back on the highway he would ask Sid's permission to stop for a drink. Would Sid mistrust him? Hadn't he just proved himself?

"Are you sure you're on the right road?"

"I saw an arrow marked Boston a little way back."

Then with a sudden disquiet:

"Where are you going?"

"Further on. Don't worry."

"I'm on my way to Maine. My wife's waiting for me with the children."

"Keep going."

They had left the outer districts behind, and now there was nothing but darkness on either side of the highway along which the cars, few and far between, travelled at an increasing speed.

"You'll have to fill her up before the gas-stations close."

Steve assented. He wanted to ask his companion a question, just one:

"Do you trust me?" He would have liked Sid to trust him, to know that Steve would never let him down.

Instead of this he said: "Most men are scared."

"Of what?" the other muttered. He had pulled off the hat and was lighting a cigarette.

Steve groped round for an answer. He ought to have been able to find one in a single word, because those are the only real answers. The thing seemed to him so clear that he was enraged by his inability to explain himself.

"I don't know," he confessed finally.

But he added instantly, feeling that it was a stroke of genius: "They don't know either!"

Sid Halligan wasn't scared. Perhaps he had never been scared, and that was why Steve respected him.

This guy, not even well-built, was alone on the highway, most likely without a cent in his pocket, and the police of three States had been chasing him for the last forty-eight hours. . . . He had no wife or children or home, probably no friends either, and he went his way in the night, when he needed a gun he smashed a shop-window to get one.

Did he ever wonder what people thought of him? He had leaned with his elbows on the bar, not drinking the glass of beer in front of him, waiting for the chance to move on, ready to clear out in an instant if the radio broadcast his description again and people started to look suspiciously at him.

"How long were you in for, at Sing Sing?"

Halligan started, not at the question, but because he had been on the verge of falling asleep and Steve's voice had aroused him.

"Ten years."

"How many had you done?"

"Four."

"You must have gone in pretty young!"

"Nineteen."

"And before that?"

"Three years in a reform school."

"What for?"

"Stolen cars."

"And the ten-year stretch?"

"A car and a hold-up."

"In New York?"

"On the road."

"Where were you coming from?"

"Missouri."

"Did you use your gun?"

"If I'd fired they'd have sent me to the chair."

Once, a year before, Steve had very nearly witnessed a hold-up, in broad daylight on Madison Avenue. To be precise, he had seen the epilogue. Opposite his office there was a bank with an imposing doorway. Shortly after nine in the morning, when he was putting through his first phone calls to the airports, the clangorous ringing of a bell had sounded outside, the bank's alarm-bell; and the people in the street had stood stock-still, most of the traffic had stopped, a policeman in uniform had run towards the doorway, pulling his revolver out of its holster.

After an absurdly short time he had reappeared, accompanied by one of the uniformed bank-police, and they were pushing in front of them two men so young that they were almost children, whose wrists were handcuffed and who held their arms in front of their faces. Someone had dashed out of a photographer's shop and started taking snapshots, and as though by magic, as though the whole thing had been rehearsed, a police-car had pulled up at the edge of the sidewalk, its siren going full blast.

For about two minutes the two youths had stayed there, isolated from the crowd, alone in the middle of a cleared space, motionless, in the same attitude, with the solemn doorway of the bank for a background: and when at length they were taken away Steve had reflected that it would be at least ten years before they again saw a city street, a sidewalk. What had most struck him, he remembered, was the thought that during all that time they would be deprived of women.

The picture of the little girl in the closet troubled him because she made him think of Bonnie, although Bonnie was ten years old.

"Why did you shut her in there?"

"Because she was yelling and she'd have roused the neighbours. I had to give myself time to get away from the village. I didn't want to tie her up like her mother, in case I hurt her. I found a chocolate bar in the drawer and I gave it to her, then I pushed her in the closet and told her not to be scared and locked her in. I wasn't rough with her. I did my best not to scare her."

"What about her mother?"

"There's a garage that's still open. You'd better stop and fill up."

Automatically Halligan thrust his hand in his pocket after putting the hat back on his head and huddling in his corner.

"Got enough dough?"

"Yes."

"Well, hurry up."

Without looking at them the garage hand started to unscrew the cap on the tank.

"How much?"

"Fill her up."

They sat silent and motionless. Then Steve held out a ten-dollar bill.

"You wouldn't happen to have any cold beer?"

Sid, in his corner, could say nothing.

"No beer. But I might hunt up a pint of hooch."

As his hand grasped the flat bottle Steve was so terrified in case Sid should prevent him drinking that he uncorked it instantly, and gulped down as much of the liquid as he could manage at a single breath.

"Thanks, pal. Keep the change."

"You going far?"

"Maine."

"The traffic begins to ease up at this time of night."

They started off again. After a moment Steve said:

"You want some?"

And his voice, as he asked the question, was the same as if he had been speaking to Nancy; as if he felt guilty, or thought it necessary to apologize. Halligan did not answer. He probably didn't drink. For one thing, it would have been dangerous for him to get drunk. Besides, he didn't need to.

Why not explain this to him? Steve felt no self-consciousness. They had time enough. The road stretched far ahead of them, bordered, so far as one could judge, by forests.

"Don't you ever get drunk?"

"No."

"Does it make you feel bad?"

"I just don't feel like it."

"Because you don't feel the need," said Steve.

He glanced at his companion and saw that he did not understand. He must be overwhelmed with fatigue. Here in the car he looked even paler than he had done in the log cabin, and he must be keeping a tight hold on himself so as not to fall asleep. Had he so much as closed his eyes since he broke out of the prison?

"Have you slept?"

"No."

"Are you sleepy?"

"I'll sleep later."

"Generally I don't drink either. Just one with my wife at

the end of the day, whenever we go home together. Other evenings I don't have the time, on account of the children."

He had a notion he had already told about the children waiting for him, and Ida, the coloured girl, standing by the door with her hat already on her head, looking as though she thought he'd got home late on purpose. Or was it something he had just thought about? Now he had a bottle handy he felt fine.

He groped for it on the seat with one hand, not to have a drink but just to make sure it was still there; and his companion's voice, out of the darkness, said sharply: "No!"

Sid was even more emphatic than Nancy.

"Keep your eyes on the road!"

"I'm watching it."

"You're driving all over the place."

"Do you want me to go faster?"

"I want you to drive straight."

"You don't trust me? I drive best when I've had a drink."

"One, maybe."

"I'm not drunk."

Sid shrugged his shoulders, sighed in the manner of a man not disposed to argue. Steve fumed silently. This attitude humiliated him, and he began to wonder whether Sid was intelligent.

Why did he let him drive instead of taking the wheel himself, if he didn't trust him? The answer occurred to him instantly, which proved that the mouthful of whisky he had gulped at the garage had not impaired his reasoning powers.

Even if they didn't run into another road-block, there was always a chance that a patrol would hold them up to inspect their papers. The police automatically go to the driver's side, so they would take no more notice of the man asleep in the other corner than they had done outside Providence.

It was beginning to get cold. The air was damp. The dash-board clock had not gone for months, and for some reason Steve did not like to get his watch out of his pocket. He had no idea of the time. When he tried to work out how much time had passed he became muddled, opened his mouth to say something and then closed it again.

He didn't know what he had been going to say. If he could stop a minute he'd get his raincoat, which must be either in the back of the car or in the baggage compartment, because he was beginning to shiver with only his shirt on, and he could not very well ask for his jacket.

"Where are you heading for?"

He shouldn't have asked that question, which might arouse Halligan's distrust. Luckily, Sid did not hear, for despite his efforts he had fallen asleep at last, and from his half-open mouth came a sound of regular breathing, with a slight wheeze.

Groping on the seat with his right hand, Steve found the bottle and cautiously pulled out the cork with his teeth. Since it was pretty certain that he would not be allowed to drink again he drained it to the last drop, in three gulps, holding his breath, while a sudden heat rose to his temples and misted his eyes.

He took care to put back the cork and replace the bottle, and he was just raising his hand from the seat when the car skidded violently, then gave several lurches. He straightened it up in time, took his foot off the accelerator, steadily thrust home the brake and after a few more jerks pulled up at the side of the road.

He was so taken aback, the thing had been so unexpected and so quick, that he had not paid any attention to Sid, and was dumbfounded to find that he was pointing his gun at him. Sid's face was expressionless, save for the look of an animal recoiling to meet a threat.

"A tyre . . ." stammered Steve, while a sweat broke out on his forehead.

It was not so much because of the revolver. It was because he could scarcely speak. His tongue had become so thick that the word was distorted as it issued from his lips. He tried again.

"A blow-out . . . not on purpose. . . ."

Without saying anything or lowering his weapon, Halligan lit up the dashboard, picked up the bottle which he held against the light with a look of disgust, and tossed it out of the window.

"Get out."

"O.K."

He would never have believed that alcohol could have such a devastating effect on him. Having got the door open, he was obliged to hang on to it while he got out.

"Do you have a spare?"

"In the boot."

"Well, make it fast."

With legs at once stiff and wobbling he worked his way along to the back of the car, but he was now certain that if he tried to go on standing he would end by collapsing altogether. It was particularly dangerous to bend down, because of giddiness. Even the handle of the baggage compartment was too difficult, too complicated for him, and it was Halligan who came and opened it.

"Got a jack?"

"I should have."

"Where?"

He didn't know. He didn't know anything any more. Something had given way inside him. He wanted to sit down on the grass at the edge of the road and start to cry.

"Well?"

He had to keep going whatever happened. If he didn't show good-will Halligan was quite capable of killing him. A car passed every two or three minutes, but the rest of the time they were alone in space, with the branches of trees rustling softly above their heads.

The people who went by, nearly all driving flat out, took no notice of the car pulled up at the side of the road, or of the two figures of which they caught a momentary glimpse in the beam of their headlights.

Halligan could shoot him if he felt like doing so, and drag his body into the woods, where it might not be found for days, particularly if they were at some distance from the nearest village. Would he hesitate to kill anyone? Probably not. Earlier, talking of the little girl, he had said that he had not hurt her and hadn't wanted to frighten her. But what had he done to the mother? Steve no longer dared put the question to him, or any question.

He had the jack in his hand. It was the right rear tyre that was flat, and Sid stood near him, holding his gun.

"You wondering where to put it?"

"I know."

To avoid bending over he went down on all fours, trying to put the jack in place, and suddenly he felt himself give way, he sprawled limply on the ground, arms outstretched, murmuring:

"Sorry."

He did not pass out. In fact, if Halligan hadn't been standing over him with the gun the sensation would not have been unpleasant. Everything in him had gone slack all at once, it was as though his body and head had emptied, and he didn't have to make any more effort, it was useless, he had nothing to do but let go and wait.

Perhaps he was going to sleep? It didn't matter. He had only once before been in this state, one night when they had had a party at home and he had drunk off all the heel-taps. When he and Nancy were alone he had let himself flop into an armchair, his legs thrust out in front of him, and he had sighed with intense relief, a blissful smile on his lips:

"Fin-ished!"

Although he knew what followed largely from what his wife had told him, he had a feeling he'd nonetheless retained certain hazy recollections. She had made him drink some coffee, most of which he had spilled, and then she had made him sniff ammonia. She had helped him to his feet, talking sharply in a commanding voice, and since he kept falling back she had ended by dragging him with his arms over her shoulders and his feet trailing on the carpet.

"I didn't want the children to find you sprawling in a chair in the living-room when they got up in the morning. . . ."

She had managed to undress him and put on his pyjamas.

"Lift yourself up, Steve. Do you hear me? Your hips, not your shoulders!"

Halligan was now dragging him on to the verge, where he let him slump on the long grass. Steve's eyes were not closed. He wasn't asleep. He knew what was going on, could hear Sid swearing as he wound up the jack, which squeaked.

There was no sense in worrying because in any case he was at his mercy. Defenceless as a new-born babe. The expression amused him. He repeated it to himself several times. Defenceless! It was all he could do to get himself seated upright when he realized that his head was resting on some nettles.

"Don't move!"

He made no attempt to answer. He knew he couldn't speak—and that was a laugh! He could still move his lips, with some effort, and no more sound came than out of a choked whistle.

Hadn't he said this was his night? Too bad Nancy wasn't there to see! True enough, she wouldn't have understood. Anyway, if she'd been there nothing would have happened. By this time they would have reached the camp.

He didn't know the time. He no longer needed to know. Nancy would have hesitated to wake Mrs. Keane. Her first name was Gertrude. You could hear Mr. Keane shouting to her right across the camp:

"Gertrude!"

His christian name was Hector. They had no children. It was impossible, he didn't know why, to imagine those two in the act of making a child.

Hector Keane wore khaki shorts which made him look like an overgrown boy, and he always carried a little trumpet slung round his neck for calling the children together. He joined in all their games, climbed trees, and one knew that it wasn't just to earn his living, or from a sense of duty, but because he really enjoyed it.

Sid was still working furiously on the wheel, and that was a laugh, too, because it made him mad and he kept on muttering things under his breath.

Did he want to kill Steve? Anyway, it wouldn't get him anywhere, only get him sent to the chair sooner or later, to use his own expression.

Perhaps he was going to leave him here. Steve wished he had put on his raincoat, because he was beginning to shiver.

If he could manage to stay awake perhaps he'd start getting some strength back. Despite the heaviness of his head, he refused to close his eyes and he wasn't losing consciousness. If his tongue hadn't felt so thick, as though paralysed, he'd have been capable of repeating everything he had said since the start of the evening. Maybe not in the same order. And that remained to be seen!

He was sure he had made sense. It might not seem that way at first, because he hadn't always bothered to use ordinary sentences. He had used short cuts. He had seemed to mix the subjects.

Actually, it all added up, and he didn't regret a thing. Only his raincoat. And also not having asked, when he might have done, what had happened to the mother of the little girl. He was sure Sid would have told him. The way things were, Sid had no reason to hide anything from him. Anyway, it had been given out over the radio.

Maybe Nancy was still in the bus? What would she do when she got to Hampton? There were still about twenty miles of bad road along the shore to reach the camp. If she couldn't get a cab, and if, as was probable, all the hotels in Hampton were full, what would she do?

In order to move more freely Sid had taken off the tweed jacket, and he was now screwing on the spare wheel. When he had finished the job he closed the baggage compartment without bothering to put in the wheel with the flat tyre. After all, it wasn't his car!

Steve was curious to see what he would do next. He seemed uncertain, worried; he put the jacket on again and came towards the verge. Standing over him, he stared down at Steve for some moments, then bending down he slapped him on either cheek, without anger, as though perfunctorily.

"Can you get up now?"

Steve had no wish to get up. The slaps had scarcely ruffled his blissful torpor, and he gazed upwards with an indifferent eye.

"Try!"

Gently he shook his head. And when he raised his arms to protect himself it was too late, two more slaps had stung his face.

"Now?"

He got on all fours, then to his knees, and his lips moved with the soundless words: "Don't beat me!"

Why did he think of the little girl and smile?

It was a laugh. With Halligan's help he staggered to the car and collapsed on the seat, but not behind the steering-wheel.

CHAPTER FOUR

BEFORE he opened his eyes he wondered at finding himself motionless. He did not yet remember the journey in the car, or the place where he might be, but some obscure instinct told him that this stillness was unnatural, even alarming.

Perhaps he made a slight movement and he felt an acute pain at the nape of the neck, like a thousand needles being driven into the flesh; and he thought he must have been injured, which would account for the heaviness of his head.

At the same time through his closed eyelids he perceived the glow of sunlight.

He could have sworn he had not slept; he was all the more baffled by the gap in his memory in that he had never lost the sense of the steady movement of the car.

Yet the movement had ceased. He was either injured or ill and he was afraid to learn the truth which could only be unpleasant; he postponed the moment of facing it, trying to plunge back into his torpor.

He was on the verge of succeeding, the torpor was creeping over him again, when a klaxon sounded close at hand, so piercing that he thought he had never heard anything like it, and a car went screaming past. Almost immediately there followed a truck with a hanging chain that bounced along the road with a sound of jingling bells.

He even thought he could hear real bells very far off, further away than the twittering of birds and the piping of a blackbird, but this must surely be an illusion, as no doubt was his imagining a sky of unreal blue in which two gleaming white clouds were suspended.

Was the scent of the sea and of pine trees also an illusion? And a rustling in the grass, which he took to be the movement of a squirrel?

His groping hand expected to feel smooth grass, but encountered instead the worn cloth upholstery of the car.

He opened his eyes suddenly, in defiance, and was dazzled by the light of the most brilliant morning he had ever known.

Except when cars passed, each setting up a scurry of cool air, there was no sound other than the singing of the birds and it moved him to discover that the squirrel really was there, now half-way up the bronze trunk of a pine tree and watching him with small, bright, round eyes.

The warmth of a summer's day rose up from the earth in a mist that caused the light to quiver, and the light so penetrated him through his eyes that he felt giddy and the sickening after-taste of whisky rose in his mouth!

There was no one in the car but himself, and he was not where he had been when he got in, but was seated at the wheel. The road was wide, smooth, splendid, built as though for the Triumph of an Emperor, with its white lines defining three lanes of traffic in either direction, pinewoods extending on either side as far as the eye could see, and the blue sky becoming mother-of-pearl over to the right, where perhaps, not very far away, the white fringe of the sea rolled up on to the beach.

When he tried to straighten his huddled body the same pain shot through the nape of his neck on the side nearest the open door, and he had no need to run his hands over the skin to know that he was not injured. He was simply stiff with cold. His shirt was still limp with the dampness of the night. He fished in his pocket for a cigarette, lighted it, and found the taste so unpleasant that he hesitated to smoke it. If he did so it was because the mere act of putting it to his lips, inhaling the smoke and blowing it out again in a familiar movement, gave him the feeling of having returned to life.

Before getting out he waited for a break between the cars which were passing at a steady rhythm, unlike that of the day before out of New York, and also unlike that of the night. These cars nearly all bore Massachusetts number-plates, and the people in them wore light-coloured clothes, the men in gaudy shirts and the women in shorts and some in swimsuits. He saw golf-bags, and canoes on the roofs.

They probably came from Boston and were heading for the nearby beaches. The radio was no doubt triumphantly heralding a perfect week-end, and predicting, as happened every year, that a million-and-a-half New Yorkers would crowd Coney Island beach during the afternoon.

Despite the mildness of the air he felt cold inside, and he searched fruitlessly for his tweed jacket or his raincoat. He had another, lighter jacket in his suitcase. Going round to the back of the car he opened the baggage compartment, and his expression became one of stupefaction and dismay.

He was filled with a vast sadness that morning, an almost cosmic sadness. The suitcase was gone; but before its removal Nancy's things had been taken out of it—underclothing, sandals and a swimsuit lay scattered among the tools. The toilet-kit which contained among other things his comb, toothbrush and razor was also gone.

He did not attempt to think. He was just sad, and would have given a great deal to have things turn out less squalidly.

Only when he had shut the baggage compartment did he notice that the right-hand rear tyre was flat. Until then he had not wondered why the car was drawn up on the verge.

There had been another blow-out, on the same wheel as before, which was not very surprising since the spare tyre was old and he never remembered to have it pumped up.

He had heard nothing. Halligan had not troubled to wake him, or else had tried and been unable to do so. Why should he have awakened him? He had gone off with the suitcase after ridding it of its feminine contents, and to make the look of the car pulled up at the side of the road seem natural, he had taken the precaution of placing Steve behind the wheel.

Perhaps there was a local line station somewhere near. Or else he could have thumbed a lift. The suitcase would have inspired confidence.

At the furthest point along the road, on the horizon, a red roof was visible in the sunshine, and the things gleaming below it must be a row of gasoline pumps. It was a long way off, half a mile or more. Feeling incapable of walking so far, Steve stationed himself beside the immobolized car, and turning leftwards extended his arm to every vehicle that passed.

Five or six went by without stopping. Then a red oil-truck

slowed, and the driver signed to him to jump on the running-board, opening the door without pulling up entirely.

"Flat?"

"Yes. Is that a garage down there?"

"Looks like it."

Steve felt himself grow pale. The jolting of the truck made him feel sick, his head hurt as though it had been hit with a hammer.

"Are we far from Boston?" he asked.

The huge, red-headed driver glanced at him with astonishment in which there was a hint of suspicion.

"You going to Boston?"

"Well no, I'm going to Maine."

"Boston's fifty miles back. Right now we're going through New Hampshire."

They were approaching the red-roofed building, which was indeed a garage, and near to it was a cafeteria.

"I guess you could do with a cup of coffee and then some!"

It must be obvious that he had a hangover. The people passing in the cars had all slept in their beds, the men were newly shaven, wore clean linen.

He felt dirty, even inside. He had still not regained full control of his movements, and when he grasped the door to get down he was ashamed to see that his hands were shaking.

"Good luck!"

"Thanks."

He had not even offered him a cigarette. Perhaps he would have felt his position less acutely if it had still been raining, with the sky grey and windy. Even the garage was new, meticulously clean, with attendants in white duck overalls. He went up to one who was doing nothing.

"My car's stopped a little way back," he said in a voice so dismal that he must have sounded like a beggar.

"Better see the boss in the office."

He had to pass an open car in which three youths and three girls in shorts were already eating ice-cream cones. They stared at his dishevelled figure. His beard had grown. When he entered the office, in a corner of which new tyres were stacked, the proprietor, in shirt sleeves, smoking a cigar, waited for him to speak.

"My car's stopped half a mile back on the way to Boston. Flat tyre."

"You don't have a spare?"

168

He chose to say no rather than confess that he had left it by the roadside.

"I'll send someone. It'll take a good hour."

He saw a call-box, but decided to wait until he'd had some coffee.

He did not blame Sid Halligan for clearing out, realizing that the man had had no choice. What rankled was the disappointment he felt.

Looking at it more closely, he perceived that it was of himself he was really ashamed, above all of the fragments of recollection which were now returning to him, which he would have liked to blot out for ever.

"Have you the key?"

"It's on the dashboard."

As he said this he realized that he had no idea whether the key was there or not, since he had not been the last person to drive. What if Halligan had taken it with him or thrown it away in the bushes?

"I suppose you'll wait next door?"

"Yes. I've been driving all night."

"New York?"

"Yes."

Did the man's slight grimace mean that a whole night was a long time to come up from New York, and that Steve must have stopped a good many times on the way?

Steve was glad to get out of the office.

"You and me, Sid—we're brothers!"

It was these words, which he had repeated like a *leitmotiv*, that now shamed him. At that time he had been sprawled in his corner in the darkness, probably smiling beatifically and proclaiming to his companion that he was happier than he had ever been in his life. . . .

Perhaps he had talked less than he imagined? In any case he had thought he was talking, in a slow, sodden voice, his tongue stiff and too big for his mouth.

"Brothers. . . . You don't know what I mean, do you?"

Why, when he had been drinking, did he invariably suppose no one could understand him? Was it because things buried in the depths of his being, of which he knew nothing and in everyday life preferred to know nothing, then came to the surface to surprise and alarm him?

He preferred to think not. It was not possible. He had talked about Nancy. He had thought a great deal about her, not like a husband or a man in love, but like a superior being from whom no secret of human nature is concealed.

"She lives the kind of life she wanted, the kind she decided to live. Who cares if I. . . ."

He was reluctant to enter the cafeteria, to be examined again from head to foot. There was a big horseshoe counter with fixed stools and chrome-nickel appliances for cooking and making coffee. Two families were seated at tables in the bay window, both with children, one of them a little girl of Bonnie's age, and the smell of eggs-and-bacon filled the air.

"Do you want breakfast?"

He had seated himself at the counter. The waitresses wore uniforms and white caps. There were three of them, fresh, pretty girls.

"Give me some coffee first."

He had to telephone the camp, but he dared not do it right away. Glancing up, he was astonished to see by the electric clock that it was eight.

"Is it going?" he asked.

The girl answered gaily:

"What time did you think it was? Maybe you figure it's still last night?"

Everyone looked so clean! The mingled odour of coffee and eggs-and-bacon had a tang of their house in Scottville on a spring morning, with the sunshine streaming into the breakfast nook. They had no dining-room. A shoulder-high partition divided the kitchen in two. It was more cosy. The children came down to breakfast in pyjamas, eyes still gummy with sleep, and the little boy had a quaint look, as though his face had faded during the night. His sister would say:

"You look like a Chinaman!"

"And you? You look like—like. . . ." He always searched for a proper come-back and never found one.

It was clean and bright at home, too. It was gay. Where had he got all that stuff he had talked, or thought he had talked, to Halligan?

During that time he had seen nothing of him except a profile, a cigarette hanging from the lower lip, which he replaced as soon as it was finished, as though he were afraid of falling asleep.

"You're a man, Sid—a real man!"

That profile had seemed to him the most impressive in the world.

"You could have killed me just now."

The worst thing was that he seemed to remember that several times a disdainful voice had rasped:

"Shut up!"

So it was true he had talked, however laboriously, however indistinctly.

"You could have abandoned me at the side of the road. If you didn't do it because you were scared I'd give you away to the cops, you were wrong. You got me wrong. It hurts to think you got me wrong!"

He had to grit his teeth, in order not to cry out in anger, in fury. This, all this, was Steve Hogan! It had come from nowhere but himself!

"I know I don't look like it, but me, too, I'm a man. . . ."

A man! A man! A man! It had been an obsession. Was he so terrified of not being one? He had mixed everything up—the rails, the highway, his wife going off by coach.

"It was a good lesson I taught her!"

He was mechanically stirring his scalding coffee.

"When I came out of the bar and saw that note in the car. . . ."

Sid had looked at him, and Steve was almost sure he had seen him smile. If so, it was his only smile that night.

He must not think about it any more or he'd be unable to ring up Nancy. He had still not decided what he was going to say. Would she believe him if he told the truth, supposing he had the courage to do so? What she was sure to do, knowing her as he did, was to ring up the police, if only in the hope of getting back the things Halligan had taken. She had a horror of losing anything, of being cheated in any way, and once she had made him go three miles to collect twenty-five cents change that a shop had failed to give her.

Perhaps he had told Sid about those twenty-five cents. He didn't know and didn't want to know. He sipped his coffee, and the hot liquid had an atrocious taste as it went down and it brought the acidity welling up into his throat. He had to swallow some iced water for fear of vomiting, and he took the precaution of looking round to see where the toilet was, in case he had to make a dash for it.

He knew what he needed, but it was a remedy that frightened him. A peg of whisky would put him right in an instant. The trouble was, in an hour's time he would need another, and so it would go on.

"Have you found out if you're hungry or not?"

He tried to smile back.

"I guess I'm not."

She had understood. There was a knowing twinkle in the glance she gave him.

"The coffee won't stay down?"

"Hardly."

"If it's something else you want, there's a liquor-store a hundred yards from here, behind the garage. That's the fourth time I've told someone this morning, and I don't even get a percentage!"

He was not the only one in his condition all along the highways, of course. There must be thousands, tens of thousands, who that morning were feeling uncomfortable inside their skins.

He put a coin on the counter, went out, found the way which led between two rows of pine trees to a group of houses. He would sooner have had a drink in a bar, sure that he would have stopped at that; but there was none nearby, so he had to buy a bottle.

"A pint of whisky."

"Scotch?"

Rye had too evil a memory for him to touch it again to-day.

"A dollar seventy-five."

His hand went to his left-hand trouser-pocket and was suddenly motionless, like his gaze, because his wallet was no longer there. His face must have changed colour, if such a thing was still possible. The store-keeper asked:

"Anything wrong?"

"It's nothing. Something I left in the car."

"Your money?"

His other hand plunged into his right-hand pocket and he was somewhat reassured. He was in the habit of keeping one-dollar bills there, in a roll. Halligan had not searched that pocket, and Steve counted six dollars. He would need money for the garage. But perhaps they would accept a cheque?

He thought it necessary to take shelter in the woods before drinking, and he only had two sips, just enough to straighten him up. It did him good at once, and he slipped the bottle into his pocket and tried another cigarette which did not sicken him. As he turned he saw that he had not been mistaken earlier when he thought he could smell the sea: there it lay, calm and glittering between the dark green of the trees, with the red of a beach-umbrella making a splash of colour on a yellow strip of sand.

If he were questioned, what would he tell the police?

Gulls flew overhead, their white bellies gleaming in the blue of the sky, and he averted his gaze because they reminded him that Bonnie and Dan were waiting for him on another beach, less than seventy miles away. How had their mother explained his absence?

With his head bowed, he walked slowly towards the garage. There was no need now to worry about the police, because there was very little likelihood of their learning that he had driven Sid Halligan in his car.

The trouble with him was, he always created problems for himself. It was perfectly easy to explain the stolen suitcase and the other things. In any case he would be bound to admit that he had been drinking. Nancy already knew it. In two or three bars along the road—he wouldn't say exactly where—and when he had come out of one of them he had found the suitcase and the spare wheel gone.

And that was that! It wasn't exactly pretty, and he wasn't particularly proud of himself. But after all, he didn't get drunk every day like his friend, Dick, whom Nancy nevertheless considered an interesting and even a superior type of man.

As for his ringing up so late, he would say that at the place where he had been held up with tyre trouble the line had been damaged by the storm, and that it had only just been cleared. That's always happening.

He was nearly cheered up by his plan. One has to face facts. Everybody has to make small compromises with the truth, and pretty well every day of their lives. The sight of his car on the hydraulic lift in the garage was also reassuring. A mechanic was putting a new inner tube in the tyre.

"This yours?" he asked, seeing Steve watching him.

"Yes."

"You drove quite a way after the blow-out."

Steve chose to say nothing.

"The boss wants to see you."

He went into the office.

"We've patched up your tyre as well as we can. The car will be ready in a few minutes, if you want it. But if you're going any distance I advise you not to leave it like that. There's a six inch gash in the cover. We had to put in a new tube."

He was on the verge of ordering a new tyre, with the idea of paying for it by cheque, when another consequence of the loss of his wallet suddenly dawned on him. Nobody along the way would accept a cheque without seeing some evidence of his identity. But his driving-licence and all his other papers were in the wallet. Nor could he tell them to ring up his bank, because it was Saturday. Until then, perhaps owing to the weather, he had kept on thinking it was Sunday.

"I'm not going far," he murmured.

As he entered the garage he had decided, after having a look at the car, to go and get something to eat. Now that the whisky had settled his stomach he felt hungry. It would do him good to eat. He tried to reckon how much money he would have left, and how much the repair and the new tube would cost.

Supposing he hadn't enough? Suppose they wouldn't let him take the car away?

"I'll be back in a few minutes."

"Suit yourself."

He would sooner telephone from the cafeteria; the garage-proprietor made him feel uneasy, he didn't know why.

"Eggs-and-bacon this time?"

"Not yet. A cup of coffee."

He had some small change in his pocket. In the call-box he dialled the operator and asked for Popham Beach 7, the Keanes' number. It took some time. He could hear his call being relayed from station to station, and all the voices sounded cheerful, as though the people on duty also felt that this was a special day.

If his wife was worried about him she would very likely be keeping close to Gertrude Keane's office, and perhaps she would be the one to pick up the receiver. Turning to the wall he raised the bottle to his lips for a quick sip of whisky, just enough to clear his voice, which was more hoarse than usual.

"Walla-Walla Camp speaking."

It was Mrs. Keane, who so resembled her own voice that he seemed to be able to see her at the other end of the line.

"This is Steve Hogan, Mrs. Keane."

"Why, good morning, Mr. Steve! Where are you? We expected you last night, as you said, and I left the key in the door of the bungalow."

It took him a moment to grasp what her words implied, yet he made himself ask, checking a growing panic:

"Is my wife there?"

"She isn't with you? Why no, Mr. Steve, she hasn't arrived here. Three families got here this morning, all from Boston. Say, I can see your Bonnie at this moment, all sunburnt and with her hair more blonde than ever!"

"Tell me, Mrs. Keane, are you sure my wife isn't in the camp?

She wouldn't have stopped off at the boys' camp?"

"No, my husband was here a few minutes ago, and he'd have told me. Where are you?"

He did not dare tell her that he didn't know. It hadn't occurred to him to ask the name of the nearest village.

"I'm on the road about seventy miles away. Do you know what time the bus gets to Hampton?"

"The night Greyhound?"

"Yes."

"It gets in at four in the morning. But you don't mean to say your wife . . . ?"

"Just a minute. If she'd arrived at Hampton at four in the morning, would she have been able to find any way of getting to you?"

"Why, yes. There's a connexion on the local bus which gets here at half-past five."

He didn't realize that he had pulled a dirty handkerchief out of his pocket to wipe the sweat off his forehead.

"Do you know the hotels in Hampton?"

"There are only two, the Maine and the Ambassador. I hope nothing's happened to her! Would you like me to call Bonnie?"

"Not just now."

"What should I tell her? She's looking through the window. She must have guessed I'm talking to you."

"Tell her we had car trouble and we'll be late."

"And if your wife arrives?"

"Tell her I called up, that everything's all right and that I'll call again in a little while."

His hands were shaking; so were his knees. He dialled the operator again.

"Would you please get me the Maine Hotel in Hampton."

After a few moments a voice said:

"Deposit thirty cents, please."

He heard the coins drop.

"Maine Hotel."

"I want to know if a Mrs. Nancy Hogan checked in with you last night."

He had to repeat the name, spell it, and wait what seemed to him an interminable time.

"Would she have got here in the evening?"

"No—at four o'clock this morning on the Greyhound."

"Sorry. We didn't have anyone off the Greyhound."

Idiot! As though their hotel was so high-class that. . . .

He wasted another thirty cents on a call to the Ambassador, where no one was registered in the name of Hogan and where the last traveller had checked in at twelve thirty.

"You haven't heard anything about an accident to the Greyhound last night?"

"Nothing at all. We would have heard and it would have been in the papers. I've just read them. And anyway, the depot's right across the street, and. . . ."

He had to leave the call-box because he felt suffocated inside it. Even the waitress's smile hurt him. She couldn't know. She was gently teasing him.

"Made up your mind at last?"

How was he to find out what had happened to Nancy? He stared unseeing at his cup of coffee, and at that moment he loved his wife as he had never loved her; he would have given an arm, a leg, ten years of his life to have her there beside him, to beg her forgiveness, to beseech her to smile and be happy, to promise her that from now on she would always be happy.

She had gone off alone into the night, with nothing but her handbag, towards the lights at the cross-road, and he seemed to remember that it had been raining at the time, he imagined her tramping through the mud and being splashed by the cars streaming along the highway.

Had she been crying? Had the fact that he had felt the need to go and have a drink made her so unhappy? He had meant no harm when he took away the ignition-key. It had been just tit for tat, almost a joke, because she had threatened to take the car on alone.

Would she really have done so?

He knew she was sensitive, despite appearances, but he was not always ready to admit it, particularly when he had had a drink or two.

"At times like this you hate me, don't you?"

He had sworn it wasn't so, that it was just a sort of momentary, childish rebellion.

"No; I know it! I can see it in your eyes. You look at me as though you regretted having tied your life to mine."

It wasn't true! He must find her at all costs, he must know what had happened to her. He wondered frantically where to turn next, still with the idea in mind, for no precise reason, that she had reached Hampton. He paid no attention to the puzzled gaze of the waitress.

"Give me change for a dollar."

He added, however, by way of explanation:

"I've got to telephone. . . ."

As though she had read his thoughts she asked jokingly:

"Have you lost someone?"

The question nearly caused him to burst into tears in front of her. She must have realized, because she added quickly, in an altered tone:

"I'm sorry!"

The switchboard operator already recognized his voice.

"What number do you want this time?"

"Police headquarters, Hampton, Maine."

"Do you want the County Police or the City Police?"

"City Police."

"Thirty cents, please."

He would never forget the sound of the coins dropping one by one into the box.

"Hampton City Police."

"I want to know if anything has happened to my wife, who should have arrived in Hampton on the Greyhound at four o'clock this morning."

"What name?"

"Hogan. Nancy Hogan."

"Age?"

"Thirty-four."

It was always a slight shock to him to realize that she was two years older than he.

"Description?"

He had an awful premonition. If they asked for Nancy's age and description, it was because they had picked up a body and wanted to make sure it was her before telling him.

"Medium height, light-brown hair, wearing an almond-green suit and. . . ."

"Nothing like that on the file."

"You're sure?"

"Certain. All we have here is an old biddy too drunk to stay on her feet, who says she was beaten up by a stranger and. . . ."

"No one's been taken to the hospital?"

"One moment."

He checked the impulse to have another sip of whisky. Absurdly enough, what restrained him was having the police at the other end of the line.

"A road accident, husband and wife. The husband's dead. It's not the same name."

"Nothing else?"

"Only an emergency appendicectomy, a little girl. Local case. If it's anything that happened outside town you should call the Sheriff's office."

"Thanks."

"You're welcome."

The switchboard operator made no pretence of not having heard the conversation.

"Shall I get you the Sheriff's office?"

And as he grunted a vague affirmative——

"Thirty cents!"

The Sheriff knew nothing about Nancy either. The Greyhound had arrived without incident at its usual time, and had gone on ten minutes later.

He finally learned from the bus depot that no woman had got out at Hampton that night; and if he now took a gulp out of the bottle, turning towards the corner of the call-box after making sure that the waitress wasn't looking, it was genuinely in the hope of controlling the shaking of his hands and knees. Before leaving the box he even called in a low voice, because no one could hear: "Nancy!"

He did not know what to do next. If only he knew the name of the place where she had left him! He could remember the bar all right, and still more the fair-haired drunk who resembled him and whom he had thought of as a brother. Was there no way not to remember things like that just at this moment? He could also recall the stretch of road to the crossing, flanked by an open expanse on which he thought he had caught the outline of a factory, and more clearly, in a sort of village Main Street near the cafeteria, a bed draped with blue satin in the window of a furniture-store.

It was somewhere on the way to Providence, but because of the circuitous route he had taken afterwards he did not know whether it was twenty or fifty miles from there. He hadn't been worrying much about signposts just then! The world had been nothing but an endless highway with forty-five million motorists streaming at full speed past the red and blue lights of the bars. His night! he had bellowed with conviction.

"Bad news?"

He had returned to his seat, and he looked up at the waitress with the eyes of a lost child. She was no longer smiling. He could feel her sympathy. Slightly embarrassed at confiding in a young girl he did not know, he murmured:

178

"My wife."

"Accident?"

"I don't know. I'm trying to find out. Nobody can tell me."

"Where did it happen?"

"I don't know that either. I don't even know what has happened. We started out from New York yesterday evening, gaily, to get the children in Maine. Somewhere, for some reason or other, my wife decided to go on by bus."

His head lowered, he did not see that she was now gazing at him with more interest.

"Did you see her get on the bus?"

"No. I was in a bar about five hundred yards from the cross-road."

He had lost all sense of reticence. He had to talk to some-one.

"You don't remember the name of the place?"

"No."

She realized why, but he didn't care. He would have made a public confession in the middle of the highway if anyone had asked him to.

"It was in Connecticut?"

"Before Providence anyway. I think I'm going to hate that town all my life. I spent hours driving around it."

"What time of night?"

He made a helpless gesture.

"Does your wife have light brown hair, and was she wearing a green suit with matching suède shoes?"

He raised his head so sharply that he felt a stab of pain in the back of his neck.

"How do you know?"

From under the counter she had picked up a copy of the local paper, and as he reached for it he knocked over his coffee-cup, which crashed on the floor.

"It doesn't matter."

Then she said quickly, to reassure him:

"She isn't dead. If it's her, she's out of danger."

The astonishing thing was that outside the garage, fifteen minutes ago, he had seen the van bringing the Boston papers, had nearly bought one, then forgotten.

"On the back page," she said, leaning towards him. "That's where they put the latest news."

There were just a few lines under the heading:

"Unknown Woman Attacked on Highway."

179

CHAPTER FIVE

"A WOMAN of about thirty, whose identity has not yet been established, was found unconscious by the roadside on Highway Number Three, near Pennichuck Cross-road, at about one o'clock this morning.

"A head wound and the state of her clothes suggest that she was the victim of an assault. She was taken to Waterly Hospital, but it has not yet been possible to question her. Her condition is satisfactory.

"She answers the following description: height, five feet five inches; fair complexion, light-brown hair. Her pale-green suit and darker green suède shoes bear the label of a Fifth Avenue store, in New York. No handbag was found on the spot."

The waitress had had to leave the counter to serve an elderly couple who had just arrived in an open Cadillac. The man, who looked about seventy, stood tall and straight. His skin was tanned; he wore a white flannel suit and a pale blue tie, and his hair was the same silky white as that of his wife. Calm and smiling, they behaved as graciously in the cafeteria as they might have done in a drawing-room, showing an extreme courtesy towards the waitress and exchanging small attentions between themselves. One could imagine them in a white mansion surrounded by immaculate lawns, which they had just left to visit their grandchildren; and surely the parcels on the red leather seat of the car must contain toys. After thirty or thirty-five years of living together they still delighted in one another, still outdid each other in attentiveness.

Steve, with the newspaper on his knees, did not realize that he was taking in every detail as he waited for the waitress, who was taking down their order, to come back to him. He had nothing special to say to her. He had nothing to say to anyone except Nancy. All he needed was for someone to pay him a little attention, even if it was only a friendly glance; and his pretext for waiting for the girl to come back was that he needed more change for the telephone.

When she had put the bacon on the hot-plate he murmured: "It's my wife."

"I guessed it."

"Could you give me some more change?"

He handed her two dollars, and she picked out some ten-cent pieces.

"Drink your coffee first. Would you like a hot one?"

"Thanks."

He drank it to please her, almost out of gratitude, and went back to the call-box and shut himself in.

The switchboard operator did not know yet, and exclaimed as she recognized his voice: "You again? You'll go broke!"

"Get me the Waterly Hospital, in Rhode Island."

"Is someone sick?"

"My wife."

"I'm sorry."

"That's all right."

He heard her say:

"Providence? Give me the Waterly Hospital, and hurry up, honey. It's very urgent."

While she was waiting she spoke to him again.

"Did she have an accident? Was it she you were expecting to find in Maine?"

"Yes."

"Waterly Hospital? One moment please."

He had not prepared anything to say. It was all new to him and he was awkward.

"I'd like to speak to Mrs. Hogan, miss. Mrs. Nancy Hogan."

He spelt the name. She repeated it to someone else, adding:

"Do you know that name? I don't see it on the list."

"Try the Maternity Floor."

He cut in:

"No, miss. My wife was injured on the highway last night and taken to your hospital."

"One moment. There must be some mistake."

He could not understand why it should be so difficult to contact Nancy now that he had found her again.

"There's certainly a mistake," the voice confirmed after an interval. "The hospital has been full since eleven o'clock last night, and hasn't been able to accept any more patients. We even have beds in the corridors."

"The paper said. . . ."

"Wait a minute. She may have been given first aid in the emergency room and then transferred somewhere else. A weekend like this we do the best we can."

At the other end of the line, probably in the hospital yard, he heard an ambulance-siren.

"I'd advise you to try New London. That's where we generally send. . . ."

A man's voice called to the girl, who did not finish her sentence. Sure that the operator was listening, Steve said:

"Did you hear that?"

"Yes. They're rushed off their feet. Shall I get you New London?"

"Please. Will it take long?"

"I don't think so. Will you deposit forty cents please?"

He was suddenly so tired that if he had dared he would have asked the waitress to get the numbers for him. He had seen ambulances passing the night before, casualties waiting for first-aid at the side of the road, and he hadn't thought of the relatives who, like himself, had come up against silly difficulties in trying to find out what had happened.

"New London Hospital."

He repeated his little speech, spelt the name twice.

"You don't know if she's in Surgery?"

"I can't tell you. It's my wife. She was attacked on the high-way."

He suddenly realized his own stupidity. Nancy couldn't be registered under her name since, according to the paper, she had not yet been identified.

"Wait a minute! Her name isn't on your list."

"What name is she registered under?"

"None. I've only just found out from the paper what happened to her."

"How old is she?"

"Thirty-four, but she looks thirty. The paper said thirty."

He would have to call Waterly again. They had looked for her under Hogan. True enough, they had said they had taken in no patients since eleven o'clock last night, but the receptionist might be mistaken.

"I'm sorry. We have no one answering that description. Several ambulances had to be directed on to other hospitals last night."

He waited to get the operator again.

"I want Waterly again."

She seemed embarrassed at reminding him of the money that must be deposited. He took a sip out of his bottle. Neither for pleasure nor from vice. His head was beginning to spin in the airless booth, of which he kept the door shut, being loath to bother other people with his troubles.

The elderly couple were eating slowly, talking all the while, and he wondered what they found to say to one another after so long.

"I'm sorry to trouble you again, miss, but I've just realized my wife couldn't be registered under her name."

He explained the situation, laboriously making every detail clear. Beads stood out on his forehead. His shirt smelt of sweat. Was he going to Nancy in this condition, without even shaving?

"No, sir. I've checked thoroughly. Have you tried New London?"

He hung up in despair. It was the waitress who, after hearing the result, suggested:

"Why don't you try the police?"

He had two dollar-bills left. The garage would have to accept a cheque. In the circumstances they could scarcely refuse.

"I need some more change. Sorry to bother you."

He felt humbled, walked to the box with rounded shoulders, his head bowed.

"Pennichuck police?"

The resounding voice that answered seemed to fill the box. "What do you want?"

He explained again. How many times had he done so?

"Sorry. It isn't for us. There's no one here but me. I heard about something like that, but it happened outside our area. Try the Sheriff or the State Police. I guess the State Police would be better. They were patrolling all night. Better call Limestone 337."

Ever since he had contacted the police he had been haunted by the profile of Sid Halligan, a cigarette hanging from his lower lip.

"Yes. Yes. I heard something about it. The lieutenant who investigated isn't here. He'll be back in an hour. What? You're the husband? Well, give me your name, I'll make a note. H for Harry, O for Oscar . . . O.K. . . . Were you there? . . . No? You don't know anything? I suppose she was taken to Waterly Hospital. . . . She isn't there? You're sure? . . . Have you tried Lakefield? There was so much work last night that we put people wherever there was room. . . ."

After Lakefield, where they knew nothing, he very nearly gave up, then decided to make one last attempt. Another hospital had been suggested to him, at Hayward, almost in the same district.

He scarcely dared to say his piece again, which was beginning to sound meaningless to him.

183

"Was a young woman brought in to you last night after being attacked on the highway?"

"Who is speaking, please?"

"Her husband. I've just seen the morning paper, and I'm sure it's my wife."

"Where are you?"

"In New Hampshire. Is she there?"

"If it's the patient with a head injury, yes."

"May I speak to her?"

"I'm sorry, there are no telephones except in the private rooms."

"I suppose she isn't well enough to come to the phone?"

"One moment. I'll ask the floor nurse. I don't think so."

He had found her at last! There were about a hundred and twenty miles between them, but at least he knew where she was. If she was dead they would have told him already, at least the receptionist would have sounded embarrassed. What disappointed him was to learn that she was not in a private room. He pictured six or seven beds along a wall, the patients groaning with pain.

"Hello, are you still there?"

"Yes."

"Your wife can't come to the phone, and the doctor has left orders that she's not to be disturbed."

"How is she?"

"All right, I suppose."

"Has she recovered consciousness?"

"If you'll hold on a minute I'll put you through to the Head Nurse, who wants to speak to you."

The next voice, sharper than the receptionist's, was that of an older woman.

"I understand you're the husband of the injured woman?"

"Yes, Nurse. How is she?"

"As well as can be expected. The doctor examined her an hour ago and confirmed that the skull isn't fractured."

"Is she seriously hurt?"

"She's suffering mostly from shock."

"Has she recovered consciousness?"

There was a pause, a hesitation.

"The doctor wants her to rest, and he isn't allowing her to be questioned. Before leaving he gave her a sedative which should

184

keep her asleep for some hours. Will you please give me your name?"

Was this the last time he'd have to spell it that day?

"And what about your address and telephone number? The police were here first thing this morning, and they asked us to take down full particulars if anyone came to identify her. The lieutenant will come in again some time to-day."

"I'm leaving right away. If my wife should wake, would you tell her that. . . ."

Tell her what? That he was coming. There was nothing else to say.

"I expect to be there in three or four hours. I don't know exactly when. I haven't looked at the map."

He added in an almost supplicating voice:

"I suppose you couldn't put her in a private room? Naturally I'll pay whatever. . . ."

"My dear Mr. Hogan, you can think yourself lucky we've been able to find her a bed!"

Suddenly there were tears on his cheeks, for no reason, and he said with an uncalled-for fervour:

"Thank you very much indeed, Nurse. Take good care of her!"

When he got back to the counter the waitress, without a word, put a plate of eggs-and-bacon in front of him. He looked at her, surprised and uncertain.

"You must have something to eat."

"She's at Hayward."

"I know. I heard."

He had not realized he had been talking so loud. Other people had also heard and were gazing at him with a sympathetic interest.

"I'm wondering whether I should go and get the children first."

He started to eat, surprised at finding the fork in his hand.

"No. That would take at least three hours, and I don't want to take them to the hospital, I wouldn't know what to do with them."

He had to have some money; he hadn't enough left to pay for his breakfast, and there would be gasoline as well.

"Is it all right if I come back and pay you in a few minutes? I'll have to cash a cheque at the garage where I left my car."

He felt as though he were cheating. Everyone was nice to him because his wife had been attacked at the roadside and was

185

now in hospital; they spoke kindly to him, and thanks to Nancy's accident he no longer had any hesitation in offering a cheque. The garage-proprietor, in the office where the tyres were stacked, listened with increasing interest to his story.

"I must absolutely get to Hayward. I've lost my wallet and have no papers with me, but you'll find my name and address in the car."

"How much money do you need?"

"I don't know. Twenty dollars? Forty?"

"You'd better take a spare wheel and a new tyre."

"How long would that take?"

"Ten minutes. Where did you say your children were?"

"At Walla-Walla camp, in Maine, in charge of Mr. and Mrs. Keane."

"Why don't you call them up?"

He nearly said no, then realized that the garage-proprietor had found this way of checking his identity and went at once into the call-box, leaving the door open.

"Why, you've changed phone!" said the operator in surprise.

This time it was the husband who answered at the camp.

"Steve Hogan here."

He had to listen to all the old boy scout wanted to tell him, waiting for a chance to get a word in.

"Mr. Keane, I wanted to tell you. . . . My wife has had an accident on the highway. I've found out where she is, and I'm leaving right away for Hayward. . . . No! I don't want to talk to the children just now. Don't tell them anything. Only that we'll be coming for them in a day or two. It won't be too inconvenient for you? . . . What? I don't know. I don't know anything yet, Mr. Keane. . . . Just don't let them suspect their mother's been hurt. . . ."

As he finished talking the garage-proprietor had taken some notes from a drawer and had counted them out on to his desk.

"Make it out for forty dollars," he said.

He watched him closely as he signed the cheque and Steve wondered with discomfort whether he still had doubts as to his honesty. Only when he was at the door did the garage-man lay a hand on his shoulder.

"You can count on me. Your car will be ready in ten minutes."

His hand was still on Steve's shoulder, the fingers hard as tools.

"Weren't you travelling with your wife last night?"

To avoid a lengthy explanation Steve said no.

186

"My mechanic was puzzled when he found some women's clothes mixed up with the tools."

So ever since they had opened the baggage compartment they had been watching him suspiciously. What had they thought? What had they supposed he had done? If the police had happened to call in, would they have said something?

"They belong to my wife," he muttered, not knowing what else to say.

Cars were becoming increasingly numerous on the road, and some of them were from New York. It was the second wave. People who didn't like travelling at night and started first thing on Saturday morning. There was yet a third wave to follow, with all the shop-people, who had to work that morning and whose week-end did not begin until midday, Saturday. *Forty-five million motorists. . . .*

The waitress who had taken him under her wing said the wrong thing when he said good-bye.

"Don't drive too fast. Be careful," she admonished him. "And drop in with your wife to say hello when you come back this way with the children."

So that, because of her warning, of the state of exhaustion he was in, the highway with its throbbing sound of thousands of tyres speeding over the tarmac frightened him. He got in behind the wheel, and had to wait some time before a gap enabled him to turn into the stream of cars heading towards Boston.

The seat beside him was empty. Generally it was Nancy's place. He seldom drove without having her there. Unlike the elderly couple in the Cadillac they didn't talk much. He recalled the movement of his wife's arm as she reached out, switched on the radio after they had gone a few miles. On Sundays, in the spring and autumn, when they went out for a run the children would be in the back, not often sitting down but preferring to lean their elbows on the back of the front seat. His daughter would be just behind him, and he felt her breath on his neck; she talked incessantly about anything and everything, about the cars passing and about the countryside, assertive and self-assured, shrugging her shoulders condescendingly when her brother volunteered an opinion.

"Hurry on, camp-time!" Nancy and he were apt to sigh when they returned, worn out, from one of these expeditions.

And then when summer came they didn't take advantage of their freedom.

It seemed so strange to be alone that he had a feeling of shame.

187

Glancing at the empty seat he thought of Halligan, who had occupied it for part of the night, and once again his fingers began to twitch with impatience. He needed a mouthful of whisky if he was to drive even passably well. His very safety required it. He was so feverish that he was continually afraid of jerking the wheel and colliding with the cars in the next file.

He waited until no one could see and then put the bottle to his lips. Even Nancy would have understood and approved. The morning after the night when she had had to undress him and put him to bed, she had herself brought a glass of whisky into the bathroom, where he had stood looking more like a ghost than a man.

"You'll feel a bit more solid with this inside you."

He swore to himself that he wouldn't go into a bar whatever happened, or stop to buy another bottle.

Despite his impatience he did not let the speedometer exceed fifty, and he stopped as soon as the lights turned yellow. He had feared losing his way in Boston, where Nancy generally directed him, but he passed through the town as though by a miracle and found himself on the right road, over which he had travelled the night before without knowing it.

There was no way of avoiding Providence. He was surprised to find it a bright and pleasant town. Past it, he wouldn't have to follow last night's route, passing the bars where he had stopped, since he was to turn off at once towards the entrance to the bay.

Would this police-lieutenant of whom the nurse had spoken, want to question him? Would he be asked to account for his actions during the night? He would certainly have to explain why he had not been with his wife at the moment when she was attacked. The simplest thing would be to tell the truth, at least in part, and admit that they had quarrelled. Was there a married couple anywhere who did not have a quarrel of that kind? Were there many even who never drank a drop too much?

The most remarkable thing was that at the time when Nancy left the car he hadn't been drunk. He may have been "in the tunnel", to use his own expression, and he had had just enough to drink to make him short-tempered with Nancy, but if she hadn't gone off probably nothing would have happened. They would have bickered for the rest of the way. He would have complained that she did not treat him like a man, and perhaps, as usual on these occasions, he would have accused her of preferring the offices of Schwartz & Taylor to their own home.

It was unfair. If she had not gone back to work after the

children were born they would not have been able to buy that house, even on twelve-year terms. Neither would they have had a car. They would have been forced to live in the inner suburbs, because they could not have gone on indefinitely living in a three-room apartment as they had done at the beginning.

All this she pointed out to him in a calm voice, a little more flat than usual, her nostrils slightly pinched as happened only when she said something disagreeable.

But it was still true that she was happy in her office, where she was a person of consequence, treated with respect. For instance. when Steve telephoned her, the girl on the switchboard invariably answered:

"One moment, Mr. Hogan. I'll see if Mrs. Hogan's free."

And sometimes after handling the plugs:

"Could you call again a little later? Mrs. Hogan's in conference."

With Mr. Schwartz undoubtedly. Perhaps he never did make a pass at her. His wife was one of the prettiest women in New York, a former model whose name kept cropping up in the gossip-columns. Despite the exaggerated attention Schwartz paid to his appearance, Steve, who had met him a number of times, thought him repulsive.

He was quite certain there was nothing between them. Yet it still stung like a slap in the face whenever Nancy said:

"Max was talking to me to-day about. . . ."

Had she and Steve been discussing the theatre she would cut him short with:

"It isn't worth seeing. Max went last night."

Was he going to start on his grievances again? Had he forgotten already that Nancy was lying injured in a hospital bed? He had not dared ask the nurse on what part of the head she had been hit, or whether she was disfigured.

To try and stop himself thinking he switched on the radio, did not listen to it, and took some time to reflect that it was perhaps indecent to be listening to songs on his way to his wife's bedside. It hurt him to have left the children at the camp. He did not know when he would be able to fetch them. The Keanes closed the camp during the winter, which they spent in Florida. They were reputed to be very rich, and perhaps it was true.

The first signboard indicating Hayward made him feverish again. He had only another fifteen miles to go, on a road congested with cars making for the ferry to take them over to some islands. He took advantage of a pause in the traffic to bend low under cover of the dashboard and finish his bottle, which he threw in the ditch.

It would be time enough later on to think about shaving and buying clean clothes. A clock said twelve as he reached the town, and it took him a little while to get out of the procession of cars pushing him towards the ferry.

"How do I get to the hospital, please?"

Someone told him, but he had to ask again. It was a red-brick building with three storeys of windows behind which beds could be seen. Five cars parked in the front courtyard bore doctors' licence-plates and a stretcher was being carefully lowered from an ambulance. He found the patients' and visitors' entrance, and went to the reception-window.

"Steve Hogan," he said. "I'm the one who called a little while ago from New Hampshire about my wife."

There were two of them, dressed in white, and one glanced curiously at him as she telephoned. The other, plump and red-headed, murmured:

"I don't think you'll be able to go up. Visiting hours are two and seven."

"But. . . ."

Must they really stick to visiting hours in a case like his?

"The Head Nurse told me. . . ."

"Just a moment. Please have a seat."

There were six people seated in the entrance-hall, among them two little coloured boys who wore their best suits and never moved. No one paid any attention to him. He could hear the voices in the reception-office. They were ringing all the floors for a doctor whose name he could not catch, and when they got him they asked him to come to Emergency right away, no doubt for the patient who had just been brought in by ambulance.

Everything was as white and bright and clean as in the cafeteria, with sun streaming in through the bay-windows, and flowers in a corner, perhaps ten bunches and baskets, waiting to be taken up to the rooms.

The two little coloured boys, sitting with their caps on their knees, had the same expression they must wear in church. A middle-aged woman, near them, stared fixedly out of the window, a man was reading a magazine as absorbedly as though he had hours to wait, and another lit a cigarette, glanced at the watch on his wrist.

Steve was surprised to find himself more collected than he

had been a quarter of an hour earlier in the car. Everyone around him was calm. An old man in white hospital garb, his twisted body huddled in a rubber-tyred wheel-chair which he propelled with thin hands, travelled the entire length of the corridor to come and look at them. His lower lip hung and his expression was at once childish and cunning. After carefully examining each one, he turned the chair round and went back to his room.

Was it about Steve they were now talking over the phone? Steve did not dare ask, guessing that in this place nothing he said could serve any purpose.

"Will you come down? No? Shall I send him up?"

The one who was speaking gave him a quick glance through the window and said in reply to a question:

"It's hard to tell. . . . So-so. . . ."

In what way was he "so-so"? Did she mean that he did not seem to be too agitated and might be allowed to go up?

The girl put down the receiver and beckoned to him.

"If you will go up to the first floor, the Head Nurse will see you."

"Thank you."

"Turn to your right at the end of the corridor and wait for the elevator."

All the way along he saw open doorways, men and women lying or sitting up in bed, some sitting in armchairs, others with a leg in plaster that was held up by a pulley.

No one seemed to be in pain, or showed any annoyance or impatience. He nearly bumped into a young woman who wore nothing but a coarse cotton nightdress and was coming out of the toilet.

He spoke to a passing nurse:

"Excuse me, Miss . . . the elevator, please."

"The second door. It'll be down in a minute."

Indeed, a light on the wall, which he hadn't noticed, shone red. A doctor in a white smock, with a cap on his head and a white mask hanging down on his chest, also gave Steve a sharp look as he passed.

"First floor."

The old, white-headed lift-attendant seemed even more unconcerned than the rest of them, and the more deeply Steve penetrated into the hospital, the more he lost his personality, the ability to think and feel. He was very near Nancy, under the same roof. In a few moments, perhaps, he would see her, and yet he scarcely thought of her. Emptiness had insensibly taken hold of him, and he mechanically followed whatever instruction he might be given.

The corridors on the first floor formed a cross in the middle of which stood a long desk, a grey-haired sister in glasses was seated with a register in front of her. There was a notice-board on the wall opposite, and near the register a rack of phials plugged with cottonwool.

"Mr. Hogan?" she asked, having kept him standing there for at least a minute before she looked up from her papers.

"Yes, nurse. How is . . . ?"

"Please sit down."

She got up and went along one of the corridors, and for a moment he thought she was going to fetch Nancy. But she had gone to see another patient, and presently she came back with a phial bearing a label, which she put in the rack.

"Your wife hasn't wakened up yet. She'll probably go on sleeping for some time. . . ."

Why did he feel obliged to nod and smile with an appearance of gratitude?

"You can wait downstairs if you like, and I'll send for you when you can see her."

"Has she been in much pain?"

"I don't think so. She received treatment as soon as she was found. She seems to have a sound constitution."

"She's never been really ill."

"She has had children, hasn't she?"

The question surprised him, and the way she asked it; but he answered like a child in school:

"Two."

"Recently?"

"Our daughter is ten and the boy eight."

"No miscarriage?"

"No."

He dared not utter a word on his own account. In any case, what question would he have asked?

"You spent the day with her yesterday?"

"Not the day. We work in separate jobs in New York."

"But you saw her in the evening?"

"We travelled part of the way together."

"When you see her you mustn't forget that she has had a very severe shock. She will still be under the influence of sedatives. You mustn't get excited or say anything that might upset her."

"I promise. Has she . . . ?"

"Has she what?"

"I wanted to ask if she had recovered consciousness."

"Partly, on two occasions."

"Did she say anything?"

"Not yet. I thought I'd told you over the phone."

"I'm sorry."

"You must go down now. I've called up Lieutenant Murray to tell him you're here. He'll certainly want to see you."

She rose and he was obliged to do the same.

"You can go by the stairs. This way."

As on the ground floor, all the doors were open, including the one to the ward where Nancy was, no doubt. He would have liked to ask permission to see her for a second, even to look at her bed from the doorway.

He did not venture to. He pushed open the glass-paned door he had been shown and found himself on a stairway which a charwoman was busy cleaning. Down below he got lost again, but ended by finding his way back to the entrance-hall, from which the two little coloured boys had departed.

He went to the reception-window and said:

"I've been told to wait here."

"That's right. The lieutenant will be here in a few minutes."

He sat down. He was the only one in the place who wore a soiled and crumpled shirt, and was unshaven. He wished now that he had cleaned up before coming to the hospital, where he was no longer master of his own actions. He could have bought shaving things and a toothbrush and gone into one of the bus depots, for example, where there were washing facilities for travellers.

What was Lieutenant Murray going to think of him, seeing the state he was in?

However, he plucked up courage to light a cigarette, since someone else was smoking, and then went and had a drink at the water fountain. He was trying to foresee the questions that would be put to him and to think of suitable replies; but his mind was still cloudy, and like the woman near him he gazed fixedly through the open window at a tree outlined against the blue sky, its immobility, in the still, midday air, giving an impression of eternity.

It cost him an effort to remain fully aware of what he was doing here, of what had happened since last night, and even of his own identity. Was it really true that he possessed two children, one of them a fast-growing daughter, in a camp in Maine, and a fifteen-thousand-dollar house on Long Island; and that on Tuesday morning—in two days' time!—he would take his place behind the inquiry desk at World Travellers, to spend hours answering the customers' questions and operating two or three telephones?

From here, it all seemed improbable, ludicrous, and as though to enhance the feeling of unreality a steamship's siren rent the silence, close at hand, and looking through the other window he saw a black funnel ringed with red rising above the roofs, and he could clearly see the little white jet of steam.

A ship was setting off over the same sea that he had contemplated that morning through the New Hampshire pines, the sea at the edge of which Bonnie and Dan played at this very moment, wondering why their father and mother did not come for them.

The Head Nurse had not seemed worried about Nancy's condition. Would she have been worried even if Nancy had been at death's door? How many people died every week in that hospital? Did they talk about it? Did the word go round:

"The woman in No. 7 died last night"?

They must be taken out by some other door and the patients not know. The old man in the wheel-chair came round to see if there were any new faces, seemed disappointed at not finding any.

A car pulled up on the gravel drive. Steve did not rise to go and look. He did not have the strength. He was sleepy and his eyelids were pricking. He heard footsteps, felt sure they came for him, remained seated.

A lieutenant in the uniform of the State Police, his high boots shining, his cheeks as smoothly shaved and tanned as those of the old gentleman in the Cadillac, came in briskly and went to the reception-window, behind which the girl merely pointed to Steve.

CHAPTER SIX

HE HADN'T noticed when he'd gone up to see the sister that the first doorway on the left of the corridor was inscribed, "Director". The door was open like the others, and a bald-headed man in shirt-sleeves sat at a desk working. The lieutenant called to him familiarly:

"O.K. if I use the conference-room for a little while?"

The director recognized his voice and nodded without looking round. It was the room next door, bathed in golden half-light from the thin bars of sunshine filtered between the slats of the drawn venetian blinds. On the pastel walls hung photographs of venerable and solemn gentlemen, no doubt the founders of the hospital. A long table, so highly polished that it clearly reflected one's face, occupied the centre of the room, surrounded by ten chairs with seats of light-coloured leather.

The door of this room, too, was left open on to the corridor along which a nurse or a patient passed from time to time. The lieutenant sat down at the end of the table, his back to the window, got a notebook out of his pocket, opened it at a blank page and adjusted his propelling pencil.

"Sit down."

In the entrance-hall, he had scarcely looked at Steve, merely signing to him to follow; nor did he show any more interest in him now. He wrote a few words in a small hand at the head of the page, glanced at his wrist to see the time and wrote this down, too, as though it were a matter of importance.

He was a man of about forty, athletic in build, with a slight tendency to stoutness. When he pulled off his stiff-peaked cap and laid it on the table Steve thought he looked younger and less awe-inspiring, because of his short, reddish-blond hair, as curly as lamb's wool.

"Hogan, isn't it?"

"Yes. Stephen Walter Hogan. Everybody calls me Steve."

"Place of birth?"

"Groveton, Vermont. My father was an agent for chemical products."

It was silly to add this. It was because, whenever he said he came from Vermont, people always said:

"A farmer, eh?"

Actually, his father wasn't a farmer, nor his grandfather, who had been Lieutenant-Governor. It was Nancy's father who was a farmer in Kansas and was descended from Irish immigrants.

"Address?" asked the lieutenant in an impersonal voice, his head still bent over his notebook.

"Scottville, Long Island."

The window was open and a slight breeze stirred in the room where the two men occupied only a tiny part of the huge table around which eight chairs remained vacant. Despite the coolness of this draught Steve would have preferred to have the door shut, but it was not for him to suggest it. His attention was distracted by the coming and going of people along the corridor.

"Age?"

"Thirty-two. Thirty-three in December."

"Occupation?"

"I work for the World Travellers, on Madison Avenue."

"Since when?"

"Twelve years."

He could not see the sense of putting all this down in the notebook.

"You started there at nineteen?"

"Yes. Right after my second year in college."

"I suppose you're sure it's your wife who's been injured? Have you seen her?"

"They haven't let me see her yet. But I'm sure it's her."

"Because of the description of her and her clothes published in the papers?"

"And also the place where it happened."

"You were there?"

This time he looked up, but the glance he gave Steve, as though accidentally, remained indifferent. Steve blushed nonetheless, hesitated, gulped before saying:

"The fact is, I had left the car for a few minutes, outside a bar and. . . ."

The other cut him short.

"I think we'd better begin at the beginning. How long have you been married?"

"Eleven years."

"How old is your wife?"

"Thirty-four."

"Does she work, too?"

"She works for the firm of Schwartz & Taylor, 625 Fifth Avenue."

He took pains to answer precisely, gradually dismissing the idea that these questions were of no importance. The lieutenant was not much older than himself. He wore a wedding-ring, probably had children. For all Steve knew, they probably had about the same income, the same kind of house and family life. Why didn't he feel more at ease with him? For the past few minutes he had been afflicted with the shyness he had felt as a schoolboy in front of his teachers, the same as he'd felt for a long time with his boss and had never lost in the presence of Mr. Schwartz.

196

"Any children?"

"Two, a boy and a girl."

He did not wait for the next question.

"The girl is ten and the boy's eight. They both spent the summer at Walla-Walla camp, in Maine, with Mr. and Mrs. Keane, and we were driving up for them yesterday evening."

He would have appreciated a smile, a sign of encouragement. The lieutenant merely wrote away and Steve could not tell what was being written, had tried in vain to read it upside down. There was nothing surly in the officer's manner, nothing harsh or threatening. Very likely he, too, was tired after having spent the night on patrol and not having been to bed. At least he had been able to have a bath and a shave!

"What time did you leave New York?"

"A little after five—say twenty past, at the latest."

"Did you pick up your wife at her office?"

"We met as usual in a bar on Forty-Fifth Street."

"What did you drink?"

"A martini. Then we went home to get a bite to eat and collect our things."

"Did you have anything more to drink?"

"No."

He had hesitated to lie. He had to remind himself, to ease his conscience, that he was not testifying under oath. He did not understand why he was being questioned in so much detail when he was here simply to identify his wife who had been attacked on the road.

It increased his discomfort to see the old man in the wheel-chair loom in the doorway and stare at him, his hanging lip and his paralysed face making him seem to be sneering silently.

The lieutenant paid no attention.

"You probably took clothes to last you a couple of days. Is that what you call your things?"

"Yes."

Their interview scarcely begun, an apparently simple question already put him in an awkward position.

"What time did you leave Long Island?"

"Around seven or seven-thirty. We had to drive very slowly at first because of the heavy traffic."

"How do you get on with your wife?"

"We get on very well."

He had not dared answer, because of the notebook where he could see his replies being entered:

"We love each other."

Yet it was the truth.

"Where was your first stop?"

He did not even attempt to hedge.

"I don't know exactly. It was immediately after we left the Merrit Parkway. I don't remember the name of the place."

"Did your wife go with you?"

"She stayed in the car."

Apart from Sid Halligan he had nothing to hide, and what had happened with Sid had nothing to do with his wife, since he had met him long after the attack.

"What did you have to drink?"

"A rye."

"Is that all?"

"Yes."

"A double?"

"Yes."

"When did you start quarrelling?"

"We didn't exactly quarrel. I knew Nancy was annoyed that I'd stopped for a drink."

Everything around them was so calm and silent that they seemed to be living in an unreal world where nothing mattered any more except the doings of one Steve Hogan. The conference-room, with its long table, became a strange place of judgment where there was no judge, no prosecutor, only an official writing down his words and on the walls seven gentlemen, long dead, who represented eternity.

He felt no resentment. Not for an instant was he tempted to stand up and say that all this was nobody's business but his own, that he was in a free country and that it was for him to call the police to account for having allowed an unknown ruffian to attack his wife by the roadside.

On the contrary, he tried to explain.

"At those times I'm apt to get short-tempered, too, and I tend to be cross with her. I suppose it's the same in every family."

Murray did not smile, or agree, kept on writing indifferently, as though it were not for him to express an opinion.

A nurse whom Steve had not seen before stopped in the doorway and knocked on the woodwork to attract attention.

"Will you be coming soon to see the accident case, Lieutenant?"

"How is he?"

"They're giving him a transfusion. He has regained consciousness and says he can describe the car that knocked him down."

"Ask the sergeant, who's in my car, to take down his statement and do whatever's necessary. I'll see him later."

He continued his set of questions.

"In that bar where you stopped. . . ."

"Which one?"

He had spoken too quickly, but that shouldn't matter much, because they would have to come to it sooner or later.

"The first one. You didn't happen to strike up an acquaintance with anyone next to you at the bar?"

"Not in that one, no."

He was ashamed already of what was bound to follow. All his actions, which seemed so commonplace and innocent the night before, when there were one or two million Americans having drinks along the highways, now assumed a different aspect, even in his own eyes; and he rubbed his hand over his cheeks as though the beard which roughened them bore witness to his guilt.

"Your wife threatened to leave?"

He did not immediately grasp the implication of that question. Did the lieutenant realize that he hadn't been to bed, and that he was reaching a state of weariness that made it a great effort to understand the meaning of words?

"Only when I wanted to stop the second time," he said.

"She had already threatened to do so before?"

"I don't remember."

"Did she talk about a divorce?"

He looked at his questioner in sudden anger, frowned, and banged his fist on the table.

"But there was never any question of that! What are you driving at? I had a drink too many. I wanted another. We had a more or less bitter argument. My wife warned me that if I got out of the car again to go in a bar she'd drive on without me. . . ."

His anger was turning slowly into a painful stupefaction.

"You really thought she meant to leave me for good? But. . . ."

The thought opened up such horizons that there were no words to express what he felt. It was worse than anything he had imagined. If the lieutenant was so meticulously noting his replies, keeping an expressionless face, showing him none of the consideration one feels for any husband whose wife has been

199

seriously injured, it was because he thought he was the one who. . . .

He forgot all about the open door and raised his voice, though not in indignation, because he was too crushed with amazement to feel indignant any more:

"You really thought that! But Lieutenant, look at me, for God's sake, look me straight in the face, and tell me if I look like. . . ."

He did look, precisely, like a man who might have done anything, including what he had in mind, what with his watery eyes, his puffed lids, his two-day beard and his dirty shirt. His breath reeked of whisky and his hands, as soon as they no longer clung to the table, began to shake.

"Ask Nancy! She'll tell you that never. . . ."

He had to break off to repeat, because it choked him:

"You thought that!"

After which he slumped back on his chair, resigned, without the energy or the wish to defend himself. Let them do what they liked with him! In a little while, anyway, Nancy would tell them. . . .

And now another thought occurred to him, a hideous thought that kept growing, that engulfed all others. What if Nancy should not recover consciousness?

Almost haggardly, he stared at the lieutenant, who twisted the end of his propelling pencil and said evenly:

"For reasons which you'll learn later, we've known, since ten o'clock this morning, that you didn't assault your wife."

"And until ten?"

"It's our job to examine all the possibilities without rejecting any out of hand. Take it easy, Mr. Hogan. I never intended to frighten you with tricky questions. You're the one who's jumping to conclusions. But it could very well have happened, if quarrels like the one you had last night had been frequent enough, that your wife should think about a divorce. That's all I meant."

"It doesn't happen to us once a year. I'm not a drunkard, not even what you'd call a steady drinker. I. . . ."

This time, because a child had stopped in the doorway and was listening to them, the lieutenant went to shut the door. When he came back, Steve, who had been thinking about what could have taken place at ten o'clock that morning, asked:

"You've arrested the man who did it?"

"We'll come to that in a little while. Why, when you stopped in front of the second bar, didn't your wife drive on as she had threatened to?"

"Because I put the ignition-key in my pocket."

Would it become clear at last that it was all quite simple?

"I thought I'd teach her a lesson; I was sure she deserved one, because she's often too sure of herself. After two drinks, especially rye which doesn't suit me, things look different."

He argued the point without conviction, no longer believing in what he said. What else would they ask him about? He had supposed that the only embarrassing topic concerned Halligan, but so far he hadn't been mentioned.

"Do you know what time it was when you got out of the car?"

"No. The clock on the dashboard hasn't been going for a long time."

"Your wife didn't say that she'd go on just the same?"

He had to make an effort. He no longer knew where he was.

"No. I don't think so."

"You aren't sure?"

"No. Wait a minute. It seems to me that if she'd said anything about the bus I'd have reckoned she meant it and would have stopped her. I'm sure of that, now! I didn't think of the bus until afterwards, when I saw the lights at the cross-road. And another thing! I remember that when I didn't find her in the car I started calling her in the dark of the parking-lot."

He didn't remember about the message Nancy had left on the seat.

"Did you notice the other cars?"

"Just a minute."

He wanted to show good-will, to help the police as best he could.

"I thought they were mostly jalopies and trucks. Now maybe it wasn't at that same bar."

"Was it called Armando's?"

"It could be. The name seems to ring a bell."

"Would you recognize it again?"

"Probably. There was a television set to the right of the bar."

He preferred not to mention the little girl in the closet with the slab of chocolate.

"Go on."

"There were a lot of people, men and women. I remember a couple who never moved and didn't speak."

"You didn't notice anyone in particular?"

". . . No."

"Did you speak to anyone?"

"A man next to me offered me a drink. I was going to refuse when the bartender motioned me to take it, probably because the guy, who was a little high, would have insisted and perhaps started a row. You know how those things go."

"Did he have one on you, too?"

"I guess so. Yes. Probably."

"You talked to him about your wife?"

"Maybe so. More likely about women in general."

"You didn't tell him about the key?"

He was worn out. He didn't know any more. With the best will in the world he was beginning to mix everything up, confusing his conversation with the fair-haired man with blue eyes and the things he had said to Halligan. Even the two bars were running together in his memory. His head ached, the back of his eyes ached. His shirt was sticking to his body and he was aware that he smelt unpleasant.

"You didn't notice if this man went out before you?"

"I'm sure he didn't. I went out first."

"You're absolutely sure?"

He would reach the point where he was no longer certain of anything.

"I could swear I left first. I remember paying and walking towards the door. I turned around. Yes, he was still there."

"And your wife, she was no longer in the car?"

"That's right."

There was a knock at the door. It was a police-sergeant in uniform, who indicated to his chief that he had something to say to him. He only allowed one of his hands to appear, as though the other held something he did not want Steve to see.

The lieutenant rose to join him and they exchanged a few words in low voices outside the door. When Murray returned, alone, he threw a handful of clothes and under-garments on the table without saying anything—Nancy's things, which they had found in the baggage compartment of the car.

They must have suspected him of something, since they had searched the car, parked in the hospital courtyard.

The lieutenant sat down again at the end of the table, avoiding any reference to what had just happened. He went on in the same impersonal voice:

"We'd got to where you came out of Armando's and found that your wife had disappeared."

"I called her, thinking for sure she'd got out to stretch her legs."

"Was it raining?"

"No. . . . Yes. . . ."

"You didn't see anyone near the parking-lot?"

"Nobody."

"You left right away?"

"When I saw there was a cross-road not far off, and remembered Nancy's threat, I thought of the bus. We'd passed a Greyhound earlier in the evening. I guess that's what gave me the idea. I drove slowly, watching the right-hand side of the road, hoping I'd catch up with her."

"You didn't see her?"

"I didn't see anything."

"How long did you stay in Armando's?"

"I thought I stayed about ten minutes, a quarter of an hour at most."

"But it could have been longer?"

Steve smiled piteously at his inquisitor.

"The state I'm in . . ." he murmured bitterly.

He scarcely knew any longer that he had found Nancy, that she was a few steps away from him, that before long he would see her, speak to her, perhaps take her in his arms. Was he sure that they would allow him to?

The strange thing was that he bore them no grudge, that he had no resentment, that he felt genuinely guilty.

By a cruel irony, there came back to him now things he had said to Sid Halligan in a sodden voice. It had started with the railroad tracks, of course, the tracks and the highways, and he had gone on to talk about people who are afraid of life because they aren't true men.

"So, you see, they make rules that they call laws, and they call sin anything that scares them in other people. That's the truth, brother! If they didn't shake in their boots, if they were real men, they'd have no need for police-forces and law-courts, for preachers and churches, no need for banks, for life-insurance, for Sunday Schools and red and green lights at the street corners. Does a guy like you give a damn for all that? But here you are, thumbing your nose at them! There're hundreds looking for you along the roads and bawling your name in every news bulletin, and so what do you do? You quietly drive my car, smoking a cigarette, and you say 'nuts' to them!"

It had been longer, involved, and he remembered that he kept seeking his companion's approval, just a word, a sign, and that Halligan had seemed not to be listening. Perhaps he had snapped, once again, with the cigarette glued to his lower lip:

"Shut up!"

That morning it was Nancy's forgiveness he had resolved to ask. But it was not only to her that he owed atonement; it was to a whole world, embodied in this police-lieutenant with curly, ginger hair, which had rights over him.

"When I got to the cross-road I inquired at the cafeteria on the corner. The waitress at the counter can confirm it. First, I asked her if she'd seen my wife."

"I know."

"She told you?"

"Yes."

He had never imagined that his words and actions would one day assume so much importance.

"Did she also tell you that it was from her I found out that the bus had gone?"

"That's right. You got back in your car and, to use her own words, drove off like crazy."

This was the only time the lieutenant allowed a faint smile to break through.

"I planned to overtake the bus and persuade her to come with me."

"Did you overtake it?"

"No."

"What speed were you driving at?"

"Sometimes over seventy. It's surprising I didn't get a speeding ticket."

"It's even more surprising you didn't have an accident."

"Yes," he admitted, hanging his head.

"How do you explain that, going at that speed, you weren't able to overtake a bus that wasn't going over fifty?"

"I got on the wrong road."

"Do you know where you went?"

"No. Once before, earlier in the evening when my wife was still with me, I'd taken the wrong road but we had ended back on the highway. By myself, I just went round in circles."

"Without stopping anywhere?"

What was he going to do? The moment he had been fearing since he first opened his eyes, alone in the car at the edge of the pine-wood, had come. That morning, he had decided to say nothing, without knowing exactly why. Of course, it was humiliating to have to tell Nancy about his encounter with Halligan. But his decision had also been prompted by the wish to avoid a lengthy interrogation by the police.

And now, like it or not, he had been subjected to the interrogation for nearly an hour; he wondered how he had been caught in the web; he saw himself following the lieutenant into the room with the long table, sufficiently easy in his mind to study the photographs of the old gentlemen.

He had expected some formality. Right at the start he had said more than he had been asked. Now he was beginning to think of himself as a cornered animal. It was no longer a question of Nancy or of Halligan but of himself, and he would have been scarcely surprised to be told that his life was at stake.

For thirty-two years, nearly thirty-three, he had been an honest man; he had followed the tracks, as he had proclaimed last night with so much vehemence, being a good son, good student, employee, husband, father, and the owner of a house on Long Island; he had never broken any law, never been summoned before any Court and every Sunday morning he had gone to church with his family. He was a happy man. He lacked nothing.

Then where did they come from, all those things he said when he'd had a drink too many and started by attacking Nancy before assailing society as a whole? They had to spring from somewhere. The same phenomenon occurred each time, and each time his rebellion followed exactly the same course.

If he believed the things he said at those times, if they were a part of his personality, of his character, would he not continue to believe them next morning?

But the next day, his feeling was invariably one of shame, accompanied by a vague apprehension, as though he realized he had been unfaithful to someone or something, to Nancy first of all, whose forgiveness he always asked, but also to the community, to a more indefinable power which had a claim upon him.

This payment of accounts was now being demanded of him. He had not yet been accused. The lieutenant had not reproached him in any way, merely asking questions and noting down the replies, which seemed even more ominous, and he had tossed

205

Nancy's belongings on to the table without once referring to them.

What deterred Steve from confessing everything without waiting to be compelled to do so?

This question he did not dare answer. Besides, it was complicated. After what had happened between them, wouldn't it be a dirty trick, and cowardly, to give Halligan away?

More and more he was convinced that he had made himself his accomplice, and in law this was true. Not only had he not attempted to hinder his escape, but he had helped it, and not because of the revolver levelled at him.

It had to be remembered that at the time he was living his night!

In the morning he had telephoned hotels, hospitals, the police. Had he said a word about the fugitive from Sing Sing?

He had a few seconds left in which to choose. The lieutenant did not press him, waiting with remarkable patience.

What had the last question been?

"Without stopping anywhere?"

"I stopped once more," he said.

"Do you know where?"

He stayed silent, staring at the golden reflections on the table, certain that the policeman was weighing his silence.

"At a log cabin."

The lieutenant repeated:

"Whereabouts?"

"Just outside Providence. There was a road-house next door."

Why did he feel a sudden break in the tension? How could the reply relieve the lieutenant who now looked at him not merely with the eyes of an official carrying out a routine assignment, but, it seemed to him, with the eyes of a man.

Steve was touched by it. This morning, too, people had looked at him that way; but then, to the waitress in the cafeteria and the telephone operator he had been simply a man who has just received bad news. They knew nothing of the night he had spent. The garage-proprietor was the only one who suspected anything.

Had the man with the cigar in fact passed his suspicions on to the police? It could be. Steve had offered no reasonable explanation about the baggage compartment which was an unlikely place in which to find women's underwear mixed up with the tools. Nor had he explained how or where he had lost his wallet and papers.

Anything was possible, and he was now convinced that long before they both sat down at the end of the long table where eight chairs remained empty, Lieutenant Murray already knew.

The lieutenant also seemed sensitive to the slightest change and it took him only one look at Steve to know that he was ready to make a clean breast of everything.

"Did he tell you his name?" he asked as though he were sure of being understood.

"I don't remember if he was the one. Wait a minute. . . ."

He was smiling now, almost amused by his own perturbation.

"I've got everything so mixed up. . . . I was the one. . . . Yes, I'm almost certain I was the one who guessed when I found him in the car. . . . They had just been talking about him on the radio. . . ."

He was coming to the surface, taking a deep breath, and looked round in annoyance as someone knocked at the door.

"Come in!"

The sister from the first floor spoke, not to Steve, but to the policeman whom she seemed to know well.

"The doctor says he can come up."

She went up to the lieutenant, leaned forward and whispered something in his ear. The lieutenant shook his head and she said something else.

"Listen, Hogan," Lieutenant Murray said at last. "There are certain facts I still haven't had a chance to tell you. It's partly your own fault. First, I had to find out. . . ."

Steve nodded to show that he understood. If he had talked at once it would have been over long ago and now he found his own obstinacy absurd.

"Your wife is out of danger. The doctor's definite about that. But she's still in a state of shock. Whatever her attitude may be, whatever she may say, it's important that you should keep calm."

He did not quite understand what this meant, and, with a lump in his throat, he said obediently:

"I promise."

All he knew was that he was going to see her, and at the thought a shiver ran down his back. He followed the sister out into the corridor, while the lieutenant came behind, moving noiselessly in his boots.

They didn't take the elevator, but went up the stairway and came to the crossing formed by the corridors. He would have been incapable of saying, later, whether they turned to the right or to the left. They passed three open doorways, and he avoided looking in; a doctor came out of the fourth room, nodded to the sister that all was well, looked hard at Steve and shook hands with the lieutenant.

"How are you, Bill?"

Those words became etched on his memory as though they had possessed the utmost importance. His legs felt weak. On his left, he saw three beds against the wall—not six as he had pictured them that morning—an old woman sitting up in her bed near the window, reading; another, with her hair hanging down in plaits, seated in a chair, and a third who seemed to be asleep and was breathing with difficulty. None of them was Nancy. She was on the other side, where there were three more beds, in the one that had been hidden from him by the door.

When he saw her he spoke her name, at first in a whisper; then he repeated it more loudly, trying to make his voice sound cheerful for her sake, so that she shouldn't be frightened. He did not understand why she was looking at him with a sort of terror, so that the sister thought it necessary to go over and pat her shoulder, murmuring:

"He's here, you see? He's happy to have found you. Everything's going to be all right."

"Nancy!" he called, no longer able to hide his anguish.

He did not recognize the look in her eyes. The bandages that encircled her head down to the eyebrows and hid her ears perhaps changed the appearance of her face. It was so white that it seemed to be without life, and her lips, so pale, seemed different. He had never seen them so thin, so pinched, like the lips of an old woman. He had expected all this; he could, he should have been expecting it all, but he did not expect those eyes which were afraid of him and abruptly turned away.

He came closer and held one of her hands lying on the sheet.

"Nancy, honey, forgive me. . . ."

He had to bend down to catch her reply.

"Don't talk . . ." she said.

"Nancy, I'm here. You'll get well quickly, the doctor's sure of it. Everything's fine. We. . . ."

Why would she still not look at him? Why did she turn her face to the wall?

"To-morrow I'm driving up to camp for the children. They're fine, too. You'll see them. . . ."

"Steve!"

He thought she wanted him to bend still lower.

"Yes, I'm listening. I'm so glad I've found you! How I hated myself, for being such a fool!"

"Ssh!"

She wanted to speak, but first she had to get her breath.

"They told you?" she asked them, as he saw tears rolling down her cheeks and he clenched his teeth so that he could hear them grating.

The sister touched his arm as though to convey a message, and he murmured:

"Why, sure. They told me."

"Can you ever forgive me?"

"But Nancy, I'm the one that needs to be forgiven, I'm the one . . ."

"Ssh . . . !" she said again.

Slowly, she turned her face to look at him, but as he bent down to touch it with his lips she pressed her arms against him weakly, crying:

"No! No! No! I can't!"

He straightened up in astonishment, and the doctor came into the ward and went to the head of the bed while the sister whispered:

"You must come now. It's better to leave her alone."

CHAPTER SEVEN

IT MIGHT have been happening on another planet. The idea of asking any question did not occur to him, or of making any decision, of taking the slightest initiative; he would scarcely have been surprised if someone had walked through him like a ghost.

With a hand on his shoulder the lieutenant guided him towards a window at the end of the corridor and they had to thrust their way through a torrent of people who, as though at a signal, had invaded the first floor, men, women and children in their Sunday clothes, many carrying flowers and fruit or a box of candies, and a man his own age with a little brown moustache and a straw hat, who was struggling to reach Heaven knew what destination with an ice-cream cone in either hand.

Steve did not even wonder what was happening, or how two little coloured boys whom he had seen somewhere before, he did not remember where, should again have entered his world, holding hands in order not to get lost.

"It's no use my trying to question her just now, with all these visitors," said Lieutenant Murray, addressing him suddenly as though he felt he had to account for his actions, or as though he needed his approval. "Anyway it's better to give her a little time to recover. I've asked the doctor to ask her the only question that matters at the moment."

The sister, to whom everyone was struggling to speak, no longer concerned herself with them or with Nancy. The lieutenant offered Steve a pack of cigarettes, then a lighted match.

"If you don't mind waiting for me here I'll drop in on my accident case. It'll save us time."

Three minutes or one hour made no difference to Steve now. Leaning against the window he gazed in front of him with no more interest than if he had been watching fishes swim in clear water, and he did not realize that the smiles of encouragement which the sister darted from time to time in his direction were intended for him

The doctor came out of the ward, glanced up and down the corridor, looked surprised, and then went over to the sister who spoke a few words and pointed towards the stairway down which he vanished in his turn.

A young woman in hospital dress walked slowly along the corridor between the two same doorways, supported on one side by her husband, her other hand holding a little girl's hand, and she smiled with ecstasy, as though she were hearing celestial music. There were people everywhere, talking, going in and out, gesticulating for no apparent reason; and when at length the lieutenant appeared at the glass-paned doors at the head of the stairway, and signalled to Steve to join him, he too became a part of the general movement, relieved of having to think for himself.

"The doctor thinks, just as I do, that you'd better not see her again until this evening, maybe not till to-morrow morning. He'll let you know after his seven o'clock visit. If you want to come with me, I have to go to my office; but I have to make a phone call first."

He went to the sister's telephone, stood by the desk, asked for his number, and Steve waited without attempting to listen to what the policeman said. He heard only words which he made no sense of:

". . . just as we thought, yes. . . . Simply for the record. . . . I'm leaving right now. . . ."

Steve followed him downstairs, along the ground floor

corridor, through the entrance-hall again and out into the hospital garden where the drives were now crowded with cars.

The sunshine, the noise and the movement of so many people dazed him. The whole world was astir. He got mechanically into the back of the police-car, while the lieutenant got in beside him and slamming the door said to the sergeant at the wheel:

"Headquarters."

As they drove past Steve caught a glimpse of his own car, which no longer looked the same and seemed not to belong to him any more.

Crowds swarmed in all the streets through which they passed, mostly people in shorts, men bare to the waist, children in brightly-coloured swimsuits; everywhere there were people eating or licking ice-cream cones, and cars sounded their horns, girls laughed throwing back their heads or hanging on the arms of their escorts, and over it all loudspeakers spread as it were a coverlet of music.

"Maybe you'd like to buy one or two shirts?"

The car pulled up outside a shop with beach gear hung up in the doorway.

He was clear-headed enough to ask for two short-sleeved white shirts, tell them his size, pocket the change and get back into the car, where the two men awaited him.

"I have a razor and everything in the office. You can clean up a little. If I don't come back with you I'll have one of the cars take you over. The only thing is, you may have trouble finding a room."

They emerged from the town, and along the road were still other shanties selling refreshments and ice-cream.

The lieutenant waited until it had become a real road, with trees on either side.

"Did you understand?" he asked when he thought the moment had come.

Steve heard the words, but it took some time before they acquired a meaning.

"Understand what?" he asked then.

"What happened to your wife."

He considered with difficulty, shook his head and said:

"No."

He added in a lower voice:

"It's as if I scared her."

"I was the one who picked her up by the roadside last night," his companion went on, his voice more subdued. "She was lucky that some people from White Plain got car trouble not far from where she was lying. They heard her groaning. I was only a few miles away when the office notified me by radio and I got there before the ambulance."

Why did he not talk naturally? It was as though he were saying all this simply to gain time. An artificial note had crept into the conversation. Steve was not thinking of what he was saying either when he asked:

"Was she in much pain?"

"She wasn't conscious. She lost a lot of blood, which is why you found her looking so pale. She was given first aid on the spot."

"Did they give her an injection?"

"The ambulance attendant gave her one, yes. I think so. Then we had to find a hospital with a bed available, and we tried four before . . ."

"I know."

"I'd have liked her to be in a private room. But it was impossible. You saw for yourself. It's distressing to have to interrogate her in front of the other patients."

"Yes."

Nancy's terror-stricken eyes continued to haunt him, and still he did not ask the question. They were travelling fast; the other cars, seeing the police shield, slowed abruptly and it was like a procession. As they passed a restaurant the lieutenant suggested:

"Would you like a cup of coffee?"

He said no. He did not have the courage to get out of the car.

"There's some in the office anyway. You see, Hogan, the reason why your wife was so frightened when she saw you is that she thinks she was responsible for what happened."

"I'm the one who took the key. She knows that."

"Just the same she went off by herself, in the dark, along the road."

Steve did not know why his companion had brought him along. He hadn't wondered about it. He was only surprised that a man like Murray should lay a hand on his knee and, without looking at him, should say in an even more expressionless voice:

"It wasn't just to steal her handbag that the man attacked her."

Steve turned towards him, his forehead wrinkled, his gaze intense, and the words seemed to come from a long way off.

"You mean that . . . ?"

212

"That she was raped. That's what the doctor confirmed to us this morning at ten."

He did not move, did not say anything more, rigid, not a muscle stirring, with the pathetic picture of Nancy before his eyes. Who cared what words the lieutenant was now saying? He was right to talk. Silence must not engulf them.

"She defended herself with a lot of courage, the state of her clothing and the bruises on her body prove it. So the man hit her on the head with a heavy object, a length of lead piping, a wrench or the butt of a revolver, and she lost consciousness. . . ."

They came on to a highway which Steve had already seen in a near or remote past, they travelled a few more miles, and then the car pulled up in front of a red-brick building of the State Police.

"I thought it would be easier to talk about it on the way here. Now, let's go into my office."

Steve could not have spoken, he walked like a man in his sleep, he crossed a room where there were several men in uniform, and went through a doorway which was shown him.

"Excuse me a minute, will you?"

He was left alone, perhaps because the lieutenant had instructions to give or perhaps from tactfulness, but he did not weep, if that was what they had thought he would do; he did not sit down, did not walk another step; he simply opened his mouth to say:

"Nancy!"

No sound came. Nancy had been afraid of him when he had walked over to her. It was she who was ashamed and wanted to ask forgiveness!

The door opened and the lieutenant came in with two cartons of coffee in his hands.

"It's sweet. I hope you take sugar?"

They drank together.

"With any luck, in an hour or two we'll get him."

He went out again, this time leaving the door open, and came back almost immediately with a map of a kind Steve had never seen before, which he spread out over the table. Certain crossroads, certain strategic points in Maine and New Hampshire, not far from the Canadian border, were marked with red pencil.

"About a mile from the spot where he had to abandon your car and leave you by the side of the road, a truck-driver picked him up and gave him a lift as far as Exeter. After that. . . ."

Steve suddenly found his voice and asked harshly:

"What are you saying?"

He was almost shouting, menacingly, as though challenging the lieutenant to repeat what he had just said.

"I said that at Exeter he found. . . ."

"Who?"

"Halligan. Right now he's somewhere in this area. . . ."

The lieutenant stretched out his arm to point to a section of the map, and Steve pulled it roughly down.

"I'm not asking where he is. I want to know if he's the one who . . ."

"I thought you'd understood that a long while ago."

"You're sure?"

"Yes. Since this morning, when I showed his photograph to the bartender at Armando's. He has identified him positively. Halligan left the bar around the time you were there."

His fists clenched, his jaw set, Steve continued to gaze steadily at the policeman, as though awaiting proof.

"We picked up his trail again at the log cabin where he had a drink on you and where they gave us a description of you and your car."

"Halligan!" he repeated.

"Just now at the hospital, while you were waiting in the corridor and I was down with my accident case, the doctor, at my request, showed your wife a photograph which she recognized also."

The lieutenant added after a pause:

"You understand now?"

Understand what? There were too many things to understand for one man.

"At nine o'clock this morning a garage-owner called up the police from a small place in New Hampshire and gave them the number of your car's licence-plates, which we'd already had from the owner of the log cabin."

Had they followed his trail, too, with red pencil-marks on the map, as they were busy doing for Sid Halligan?

"Would you like to shave?" asked the lieutenant, opening the door of a lavatory. "There's one thing certain. Up till now all he risked for jailbreaking was an extra five or ten years. Now, it's the chair!"

Steve slammed the door and, bent double, was violently sick. An acrid smell of alcohol rose up from the bowl, his throat burned, he held his stomach with both hands, eyes streaming, his whole body shaken with the spasms.

He could hear the lieutenant talking on the telephone next

door, then the footsteps of two or three men, and the murmur of a sort of conference taking place in the office.

It took a long time before he was able to douse his face with cold water, to smear cream over it and shave, looking as harshly at his own image as he had glared at the policeman. A terrible anger seethed in him like a tempest rumbling simultaneously at the four corners of the sky, a painful hatred only to be expressed by the word "kill", not kill with a weapon, but kill with his hands, slowly, fiercely, in full knowledge of the act, without losing a single look of terror, a twitch of agony.

The lieutenant had said:

"Now, it's the chair!"

And this recalled another voice which, the night before, had also referred to that same chair, Halligan's voice, saying:

"I don't want to go to the chair."

No. That wasn't quite right. The scene came back to him. Steve had asked if he had used his gun. He had asked the question in a calm voice, without indignation, with only a quiver of curiosity. And Sid had answered casually:

"If I'd fired they'd have sent me to the chair."

Wasn't it about then that Steve had thought of the two youngsters who had committed a hold-up on Madison Avenue, thinking how, for ten years, they wouldn't see a single woman?

Halligan had just served four years in Sing Sing. He had not wanted to hurt the little girl he had locked in the closet with a slab of chocolate to prevent her from yelling. He had bound and gagged the mother so as to be able to search undisturbed for the household savings in the drawers. He didn't have a gun then. He also needed the husband's clothes, because he was still wearing the prison uniform. Later, he had stolen a weapon from a shop-window. And, finally. . . .

Stripped to the waist, his hair damp, he opened the door.

"I left the shirts in the car."

"Here they are," said the lieutenant, pointing to the parcel on his desk.

He was glancing quickly at Steve to judge his state of mind.

"You can put your shirt on in here. We aren't talking about anything confidential."

A sergeant was reporting on a telephone call he had just received.

"The car stolen in Exeter has been found between Woodville and Littleton, on Highway 302. The tank was empty. Either he thought he had more gas and hoped to get to the Canadian

215

border, or else he was afraid to show himself in a garage."

The two men bent over the map.

"The New Hampshire police are keeping us informed. They've already notified the F.B.I. Road-blocks have been set up all through the area. Because of the woods, which make it harder to track him down, they sent for bloodhounds, which they're expecting any time now."

"You hear that, Hogan?"

"Yes."

"I hope they get him before dark and that he won't have a chance to hold up some isolated farm. After what's happened he won't hesitate to kill. He knows he's playing for keeps. O.K., that'll be all!"

The sergeant went out.

The lieutenant remained seated in front of the map. He had taken off the jacket of his uniform, and with his shirt-sleeves rolled up above his elbows, he was smoking a pipe which he probably never used except in the office or at home.

"Sit down. It's a bit quieter to-day. Most of the people have arrived wherever they were going. To-morrow, there'll be hardly anything but local traffic, a few drownings, some dance-hall fights. It'll pick up again on Monday, when everybody starts rushing back to New York and the big towns."

Forty-five million. . . .

He was repelled by the words which reminded him of the motion of the car, the suction of all the wheels on the tarmac, the headlights, the miles covered in the darkness of a kind of no-man's-land and the neon signs looming suddenly into sight.

"He threatened you with his gun?"

Steve looked straight in the man's eyes, as he leaned back in his chair, pulled at his pipe in short little puffs.

"When I got into the car, he was sitting there and pointing his gun at me," he said, choosing his words.

Then clipping each syllable he added, as though in defiance: "It was not necessary."

The lieutenant didn't stir, gave no sign of surprise; he asked another question:

"At the log cabin place. . . . By the way, it's called the 'Blue Moon'. . . . At the 'Blue Moon', as I say, did you already know who he was?"

Steve shook his head.

"I knew he was a prowler, and I guessed he was hiding. It excited me."

"Did you do all the driving?"

"We stopped somewhere at a garage to get some gas and I bought a pint of whisky from the attendant. I guess I drank it down in a few minutes."

He added a detail nobody was asking him for:

"Halligan had fallen asleep."

"Ah!"

"Then, we had a blow-out, and he had to change the wheel because I was no good for anything, and I just stayed slumped on the roadbank. After that I don't know any more. He could have left me there or put a bullet through my head to stop me giving him away."

"Had you told him you knew who he was?"

"As we were leaving the 'Blue Moon'."

"How do you feel now?"

"I threw up everything in my stomach. What will be done with me?"

"I'm going to have you driven back to Hayward. It's five o'clock. At seven, the doctor will examine your wife again and tell you if you can see her to-night. I suppose you plan to sleep there?"

He had not thought about it. He had not considered the question. It was the first time he had ever found himself without a bed to sleep in, with his house empty in Long Island, the children waiting for him at camp, and his wife, surrounded by five other patients, lying on a hospital bed.

"You'd be wasting your time to try the hotels and the inns. Everything is jam-packed. But there are people who, in the summer, rent out rooms by the night. You might have some luck there."

The lieutenant did not pursue the question of his relations with Halligan; he said nothing more about the matter, and that annoyed Steve. He wanted to talk about it, to confess to all the thoughts that had passed through his head during the night, sure that it would do him good, that afterwards he would feel relieved.

Did his companion guess what was in his mind? Did he want to avoid this confession for his own reasons? In any case he rose there and then to end the interview.

"You'd better get started right away if you don't want to sleep on the beach. Call me up when you've got an address. I'll let you know how things are going."

He called him back just as he reached the door.

"Here's your other shirt!"

Steve, who had forgotten buying two, took the package.

"I threw the dirty one in the basket," he said.

In the outer office, the same sergeant, who was listening through ear-phones, reported to his chief:

"The dogs have arrived and, after sniffing the seat of the abandoned car, they picked up a scent."

Steve did not want to wait, did not venture to hold out his hand.

"Thank you, lieutenant, for the way you treated me. And for everything."

He was shown to a car with a uniformed policeman at the wheel. He got in beside him.

"Hayward. Drop him in the hospital yard, where he left his car."

The motion of the car caused him little by little to close his eyes. He fought against it for a time, then his head fell forward on his chest and he dozed off, without entirely losing the sense of where he was. Only the notion of time was obscured; events came back in a jumble to his memory, isolated images intermingled, forming and reforming new patterns.

For example, he would see Halligan not as the nervous, thin-faced figure, but as the fair-haired man in the first bar, and he imagined Nancy with him, drinking at the counter, that wasn't the one at the roadside bar but the counter at Louis' on Forty-Fifth Street.

Then, he protested excitedly:

"No, that's not him! That's the wrong one!"

The real Halligan was dark-haired, sickly-looking, and his pallor was not surprising since he had spent four years in prison. He was driving the car with a mysterious smile on his lips when Steve suddenly cried:

"But it was my wife! You didn't tell me it was my wife!"

Crying the words "my wife" more and more loudly, he grasped the man's neck in both his hands as one of the tyres burst and the car came to a stop under the pine trees.

"Hey, Mister. . . ."

The policeman, smiling, was tapping him on the shoulder.

"We're here."

"I'm sorry. I guess I fell asleep. Thanks."

Most of the cars had disappeared from the hospital court-yard, and his stood alone in the middle of a great emptiness. He did not need it. Where would he go in a car? He looked up at the windows, unable to tell which was Nancy's. There was no sense in standing there staring up in the air. He must do what he had been told.

The lieutenant had advised him to look for a room first of all. There were houses quite near, most of them made of wood, painted white, with a veranda all round, and on the verandas were people, mostly old people, taking the air in their rocking-chairs.

"I'm sorry to bother you, Mam. You don't know where I might find a room?"

"You're the third person who's asked me that in the last half-hour. Try the house at the corner. They haven't anything left, but they might know of something."

He saw the sea, quite close, at the end of a street. The sun had not yet disappeared in the opposite direction, behind the houses and trees, but the surface of the water was already a chilly green.

"Excuse me, Mam, do you. . . ."

"You're looking for a room?"

"My wife's in the hospital, and. . . ."

He was sent elsewhere, and again elsewhere, into streets further and further away from the centre of the town, where the people sat on their doorsteps.

"Just for yourself?"

"Yes. My wife's in the hospital. . . ."

"You had an accident?"

They found it strange that he hadn't a car.

"I left my car over there. I'll go and get it as soon as I find a place to stay."

"All we can offer you is a camp-bed on the back porch. It's a screened porch, but I warn you it won't be warm. I'll give you two blankets."

"That'll do fine."

"I have to charge you four dollars."

He paid in advance. Almost directly after letting him have that money the garage-proprietor had thought it his duty to notify the police. Steve had not suspected, as he drove towards Hayward, that they knew exactly where he was.

Instead of disturbing him, the thought rather reassured him. It was comforting to find that the world was well-organized, society well-knit.

The police couldn't prevent everything. Nancy hadn't been

able either to stop him drinking last night. She had tried all she could, and it was she in the end who had paid.

"What time do you expect to be back?"

"I don't know. I must go to the hospital and see my wife. I won't be late."

"At ten, I go to bed and lock the door. I'm warning you. Fill in your form."

Writing his name made him think of the news item in the paper. There would be more about the attack in the evening papers, inevitably. The radio must have already announced that the victim had been identified. He had often read news of that sort without attaching any importance to the words, *"the victim had been raped."*

Everyone would know. He thought of Mr. Schwartz, of the switchboard girl who took a secret pleasure in telling him that his wife was in conference, of Louis and his five o'clock customers. And then to his distress, so apparent that his landlady eyed him with some misgiving, was added pity of an especial kind. It was not only as her husband that he pictured Nancy. He thought of her as a woman seen in the street, in daily life, a woman after whom people gazed, murmuring sadly:

"Is she the one who was raped?"

This gave rise to new problems. Perhaps Nancy, lying alone in her bed, had already faced them? Knowing her as he did, it seemed to him that she would never agree to meet the people they knew or return to her former life.

"If you're going to the hospital and want a short cut, take your first right and keep walking till you come to a restaurant with its front painted blue. You can see the hospital from there."

What would be wonderful would be for them to live quite alone, just the two of them and the children, without seeing a soul, not even Dick and his wife, who always wore a jaundiced smile and was jealous of Nancy anyway. Nancy would stay at home. He would go to work as usual, because he had to earn his living, but he'd come straight back without dropping in at Louis' and without ever wanting a martini. No one would ask them any questions, or pass any remarks.

The noise and the blare of music from the centre of the town came to him, muffled by distance; radios were going in a good many of the houses, and in others one could make out motionless figures in a half-light, in front of the lunar-pallor of the television screen.

He reached the restaurant with a blue-painted front and went in, not for a drink, but to get something to eat, because he had cramp in his stomach. In any case, there was no bar. They did not serve alcoholic drinks. He would not have been tempted anyway. If they let him talk to Nancy that evening, and if she were not too exhausted, he intended to swear to her there and then that he would never again touch a drop of alcohol; and he was firmly resolved to keep the promise, not only for her sake but for his own.

A girl smelling of perspiration wiped the table in front of him with a dirty cloth, and thrusting a menu into his hand stood awaiting his order with her pencil poised.

"Just bring me anything—a sandwich."

"Why not a lobster salad? That's to-day's special."

"Will it be quicker?"

"It's all ready. Coffee?"

"Please."

An afternoon paper was lying on a nearby table, but he preferred not to look at it. The clock on the wall pointed to ten past six. At that hour yesterday his wife and he had still been in their home. So as not to waste time they had not sat down to eat their sandwiches, and he could hear again the hum of the frigidaire as his wife had opened it to take out a coca-cola.

"Do you want one?"

He could not tell her that he had just had a rye. That was where it had all started. She was wearing the green summer suit she had bought on Fifth Avenue, never dreaming that the Boston papers would be talking about it next morning.

"Ketchup?"

He was impatient to get back to the hospital. Even if they didn't let him go up right away, he would feel nearer to her. Besides, at the hospital he was not tempted to think. He did not want to think any more to-day. His weariness had reached the point where it set up an ache throughout his body, as though inside the bones. It had happened to him often enough to be up all night, even to be up drinking all night, and to feel sick in the morning; but he had nearly always pulled himself together with the help of alcohol. It would probably have worked this evening, too. That morning, the Scotch had enabled him to bear up and drive here, and had even steadied his nerves enough to enable him to telephone all over and find Nancy.

He was sorry the waitress in the cafeteria was not here to give him support. Everyone in this place was in a hurry, there was a constant clatter of dishes, the girls bustled about without being able to satisfy the customers, and there was always some noise-lover to put five cents in the juke-box.

"Dessert? There's apple pie and lemon-meringue pie."

He preferred to pay and go. All the windows in the hospital were lighted up, and if Nancy had not been on the side of the door he might have been able to see her bed. Not all the curtains were drawn. One caught a glimpse here and there of a nurse's white cap, or the outline of a patient bent over a magazine.

As he passed his car he looked away uneasily, because of all it brought to mind, and he resolved to trade it for another, even an older one, if he got the chance.

He had forgotten to call the lieutenant, who had asked him to do so. He remembered seeing a call-box in the hospital entrance-hall. As soon as he had any news, he would have to telephone the Keanes as well. He must not forget the children. But first he needed to have a clearer idea of what they were going to do.

"You don't know if I may see my wife?"

The girl recognized him and put a plug in the switchboard.

"It's the husband of the patient in 22. You know who I mean? Yes. What? The doctor's not due before seven? I'll tell him."

She repeated:

"Not before seven."

"May I use the phone?"

"The one in the booth is public."

He rang police headquarters.

"Steve Hogan here. I'd like to speak to Lieutenant Murray."

"This is the trooper who was with him at the hospital, Mr. Hogan. I know all about it. The lieutenant's out to dinner."

"He asked me to call up and give him my address here."

"You found a room?"

He read out the address his landlady had written on a scrap of paper.

"Is there any news?"

"We've had some in the past half-hour."

The voice was happy.

"It's all over. At first, the dogs went off on a wrong scent, and that wasted a good hour. So they were brought back to the car, and that time they got it right."

"Did he put up a fight?"

"When he saw he was cornered he threw his gun away and put his hands up. He was scared green and kept on begging

222

them not to hurt him. The F.B.I. took charge of him. They'll come here to-morrow when they bring him back to Sing Sing."

"Thank you."

"Good-night. You can tell your wife the news. She'll be pleased, too."

He left the call-box and went and sat down in a chair in the hall, where he was alone. Through the glass pane he could see the upper half of the receptionist's face as she sat typing and occasionally glancing curiously in his direction.

He did not at first recognize the doctor, who came from outside and whom he had not yet seen in ordinary clothes, but the doctor knew him, nearly passed him by, then turned back to him, worried. Steve rose.

"Don't get up."

The doctor sat down beside him, resting his elbows on his knees as though for a quiet man-to-man talk.

"The lieutenant told you?"

Steve nodded.

"I suppose you realize that she's the one for whom it's most tragic. I haven't seen her this evening. The head wound isn't nice, but that heals rapidly. By the way, you'd better know, so that you don't hurt her by looking shocked, that we had to cut off her hair and shave her head."

"I understand, doctor."

"We can't keep her here long, turning away urgent cases as we've done all day. Do you have a good doctor? Where do you live?"

"On Long Island."

"Is there a hospital nearby?"

"About three miles away."

"I'll see just how she is and if she'll soon be able to make the trip without risk. The most important thing, in her case, is her state of mind, and that's up to you. Wait a minute! I'm sure you're ready to give her all the care in the world. Unfortunately this isn't the first such case that I've had to attend. The reaction is always violent. It will be a long time before your wife considers herself a normal person again, or reacts like a normal person, particularly after all the publicity that there'll be about her, which no one can prevent. If they catch her attacker there'll be a trial."

"He's been arrested."

"You'll have to be patient, resourceful, and if her progress is slow you may have to call in a specialist."

223

He got to his feet.

"You may come up with me and wait in the corridor. Provided there's nothing new, I'll only be a minute or two. I think she told me you have children?"

"Two. We were on our way to Maine, where they're waiting for us to take them home from camp."

"I'll talk to you about them later."

They went up. The sister at the desk wasn't the one Steve knew, and the doctor exchanged a few words with her.

"Just take a seat. . . ."

"Thanks."

He preferred to remain standing. The corridors were empty, bathed in a soft yellow light. The doctor had gone into Nancy's ward.

"Did she sleep?"

"I don't know. I came on duty at six."

She glanced at a record-sheet. "I can tell you that she took some bouillon, some meat and vegetables."

The words had a reassuring sound.

"Have you seen her?"

"Last night, when they brought her in."

He didn't press the matter, preferring not to know the details. From the nearest doorway came the monotonous murmur of a conversation between two women.

The doctor appeared and called:

"Nurse, will you come here a minute?"

He said a few words and she went into the ward as the doctor came towards Steve.

"You'll see her. The nurse will let you know when she's ready. Unless there are complications which I don't expect, there's no reason why she shouldn't leave on Tuesday. The week-end will be over and the roads won't be so congested."

"Will she need an ambulance?"

"If you have a good car and drive without shaking her too much it won't be necessary. I'll see her before she goes. I'm telling you now so that you an make arrangements. As for the children, if you have someone to look after them at home. . . ."

"We have a part-time baby-sitter and I can ask her to stay longer."

"It will help your wife's recovery if life around her can be as normal as possible right from the start. Don't stay with her now more than twenty or thirty minutes, and don't let her tire herself talking."

"I promise, doctor."

The sister reappeared, but still not for him. She had come to get something he couldn't quite see out of her handbag, which was in a cupboard, and then she went back into the ward.

A good ten minutes dragged by and at last she beckoned to him from the doorway.

"She's waiting for you," she said, standing aside for him to pass.

A screen had been put round the bed to separate it from the rest of the room, and there was a chair beside it. Nancy kept her eyes closed, but she was not asleep, and he could see tremors passing over her face. He noticed that her lips were redder, saw traces of powder near the bandage which encircled her head, about level with her ears.

Without a word he sat down, and his hand reached for the hand lying on the sheet.

CHAPTER EIGHT

WITHOUT opening her eyes, she whispered:

"Don't say anything. . . ."

Then she herself was silent, motionless, except for her hand which moved in Steve's hand the better to nestle in it. They were both in an oasis of peace and silence where no sound reached them save the hissing breath of the woman with fever.

Steve avoided even the least movement, and it was Nancy who presently said in a voice that was still very low:

"First, I want you to know that I didn't ask for the powder and lipstick. The nurse did it. She insisted for fear I'd scare you."

He opened his mouth but did not speak, and finally closed his eyes, too, because they were even closer together that way, not seeing one another, with only the touch of their intertwined fingers.

"You aren't too tired?"

"No. . . . You see, Nancy. . . ."

"Ssh! Don't move. I can feel your pulse beating."

This time she remained silent so long that he thought she had fallen asleep. But at last she said:

"I'm very old now. I was already two years older than you. Since last night, I've become an old woman. Don't say anything. Let me speak. I've done a lot of thinking this afternoon. They gave me another injection but I managed to stay awake and I was able to think."

He had never felt so close to her. It was as though a circle of light and warmth surrounded them, giving them shelter from the rest of the world, and in their joined hands their pulses were beating with the same rhythm.

"In a few hours I've aged at least ten years. Don't be impatient. You must let me finish."

It was at once good and heart-rending to hear her, talking always in a whisper, so that it might be more secret, more intimately theirs; her voice had no expression, and she made long pauses between the sentences.

"You've got to understand, Steve, if you haven't thought it out for yourself yet, that our whole life will be changed, that from now on nothing will ever be the same again. I shall never be a woman like other women, I shall never be your wife again."

And as she sensed he was going to protest, she hurried on to stop him.

"Ssh! I want you to listen and to understand. There are things that can't exist any more, because, each time, the thought of what happened. . . ."

"Don't . . . !"

He had opened his eyes, and he saw her with her eyelids still closed, with her lower lip trembling in a slight pout as it did when she was going to cry.

"No, Steve! You couldn't, either. I know what I'm saying. You know it, too, but you're trying to deceive yourself. For me, it's finished. There's a kind of life I shall never know again."

Her throat tight, she swallowed, and he thought he caught, for an instant, the gleam of her eyes beneath the fluttering lids.

"I won't ask you to stay with me. You'll go on living a normal life. We'll do the best we can to make it easy."

"Nancy!"

"Ssh . . . ! Let me finish, Steve. Sooner or later, you'd find out for yourself the things I'm saying this evening, and then it would be much harder for both of us. That's why I wanted you to know right away. I was waiting for you."

He didn't know he was crushing her hand, and she moaned:

"You're hurting me."

"I'm sorry."

226

"It's silly, isn't it? A person doesn't realize until it's too late. When people are happy, they think nothing of it, do foolish things, even rebel at times. We've been happy, the four of us."

And then, suddenly, he forgot the doctor's warning, forgot to think, forgot the wound on Nancy's head, the hospital ward where they were. A tide of warmth had welled up in his breast and words came crowding into his mind which he had to speak to her, words he had never spoken to her and perhaps never even thought.

"It's not true!" he protested at once, as she had just spoken of their past happiness.

"Steve!"

"I believe I've done some thinking, too, without knowing it. And what you just said is a lie. It's not as though we were happy yesterday."

"Don't . . . !"

His voice was as thick as his wife's and yet he managed to give it a restrained vehemence that was the more eloquent.

This was not how he had imagined their talk together and he had never thought that he would one day tell her the things he was about to say. He felt himself to be in a state of utter sincerity and it was as though he were naked, as sensitive as if the skin had been stripped off him.

"Don't look at me! Keep your eyes shut. Just listen to me. The proof that we weren't happy is that the minute we strayed from our everyday routine, from our ordinary habits, I felt so lost that I had a violent need to drink. And you, you needed, every day, to go to an office on Madison Avenue to convince yourself that you had an interesting life. How many times have we stayed alone together, at home, without feeling the need, after a few minutes, to pick up a magazine or listen to the radio?"

Nancy's eyelids were damp at the lashes, her lips pouted more and more; he had nearly let go her hand, and she clung to his nervously.

"Do you know just when it was, yesterday, that I started to betray you? You were still in the house. We hadn't yet started. I told you I was going to fill up the gas tank."

She murmured:

"You had first talked about getting cigarettes."

Her face had already lightened.

"It was to have a rye. I stayed on rye all night. I wanted to feel strong and uninhibited."

227

"You hated me."

"You, too!"

Didn't the trace of a smile appear on her lips as she whispered: "Yes."

"So I continued to rebel all by myself until I woke up this morning at the edge of a road where I didn't remember stopping."

"You had an accident?"

He had the feeling that, for the first time since they had known one another there was no deception between them any longer, nothing more, nothing as thick even as a veil, to prevent their meeting face to face.

"Not an accident. It's my turn to say that you've got to know, and right now. I met a man in whom, for hours, I tried to see another me, another me that wasn't a coward, a man I wished I could be like; and I spilled out everything that was on my mind, all the rottenness fermenting inside me. I told him about you, perhaps about the children as well, and I may even have said I didn't love them. Yet I knew who that man was and where he came from!"

He had shut his eyes again.

"I had a drunkard's determination to soil everything, and the man I confided in like that was. . . ."

He scarcely heard her repeat:

"Don't. . . ."

He had finished. He wept in silence, and the tears running down from beneath his closed lids were not bitter. Nancy's hand lay inert in his.

"Do you understand, now. . . ."

He had to wait for the tightness in his throat to pass.

"Do you understand that it's only to-day we shall begin to live?"

Opening his eyes, he was surprised to find that she was looking at him.

Had she been watching him all the time he was talking?

"That's all. You see, you were right to say that, since yesterday, we've come a long way."

He thought he caught a last hint of incredulity in her eyes.

"It'll be a different life. I don't know what it will be like, but I'm sure we'll be living it together."

She still tried not to give in.

"Is it true?" she asked with a candour that he did not recognize in her.

The sister passed behind him to attend to the fever patient who must have rung for her. All the time she stayed in the room, they avoided talking.

It did not matter now. Perhaps when he got back into everyday life Steve would feel slightly embarrassed at the recollection of his outburst. But wasn't he still more ashamed when he woke up the morning after holding forth as a drunkard?

They gazed at one another unselfconsciously, each feeling that this moment would probably never come again. Each was straining towards the other, but this was apparent only in their eyes, locked in a gaze in which grew a look of grave enchantment.

"O.K., folks?" called the sister, as she was leaving.

The commonplace words did not disturb them.

"Five minutes more and that's all!" she announced, going out of the door with a bedpan covered with a cloth in her hand.

Three of the five minutes had elapsed when Nancy spoke, her voice firmer than before:

"You're sure, Steve?"

"And you?" he answered with a smile.

"Maybe we can try."

What was important was not what was going to happen, but that this moment should have existed, and already he was trying not to lose its warmth, was in a hurry to leave, because anything they might say could only weaken their emotion.

"May I kiss you?"

She nodded and he stood up, bent over her, put his lips cautiously to hers and pressed them gently. The two remained thus for several seconds, and when he stood upright Nancy's hand still clung to his own; he had to loosen her fingers one by one before hurrying to the door without looking back.

He almost failed to hear when the sister called to him. He had not seen her as he passed close by.

"Mr. Hogan!"

He stopped, saw her smiling at him.

"I'm sorry to break in on you like that. I just wanted to tell you that from now on you must only come during visiting hours, which are posted downstairs. We made an exception this time because it was the first day."

Seeing him glance towards Nancy's ward she added:

"Don't worry. I'll see that she sleeps all right. By the way, the doctor gave me these for you. Take both of them when you go to bed and you'll have a good night."

There were two tablets in a small white envelope which he slipped into his pocket.

"Thanks."

The night was clear and the stones of the courtyard shone beneath the moon. He got mechanically into his car and drove, not towards his lodgings but towards the sea. He still needed to live a little while with the things he felt inside him, upon which the lights of the town, the music, the shooting-galleries, the swings had no hold. The things surrounding him had no substance, no reality. He drove along a street which grew darker as he went and at the end of it he found a rock with the sea lapping almost soundlessly against it.

A cooler air came from the open sea, a rich scent with which he filled his lungs. Without shutting the door of the car behind him he walked to the extreme edge of the rock, stopping only when the water touched the tips of his shoes, and furtively, as though he were ashamed, he repeated the gesture he had made as a child when for the first time he had been taken to see the sea, bending down and dabbling his hand in the water, keeping it there for a long time to enjoy its living freshness.

Then he waited no longer, looked for the blue-fronted restaurant which served him as a landmark, and found the road along which he had walked, and the house where he was to sleep.

The landlady and her husband were sitting together in the darkness of the veranda, and he did not see them until he had started up the steps.

"You're early, Mr. Hogan. To be sure, you wouldn't have the heart to be enjoying yourself. You have no suitcase? Wait, I'll switch on a light in the house."

A very white bulb suddenly lit up the flowered wallpaper in the hall.

"I won't let you sleep in your clothes after what you've been through."

She knew now, and she spoke to him as one does to someone bereft.

"How's your poor wife?"

"Better."

"What a shock it must have been for her! Men like that ought to be shot down without taking the trouble to try them. If anything like that happened to my daughter I think I'd be capable. . . ."

He would have to get used to it. Nancy too. It would be a part of their new life, at least for a time. He waited patiently for the woman to finish and then she went into her bedroom for a pair of her husband's pyjamas.

"They may be a bit short, but it's better than nothing. If you'll come with me I'll show you the bathroom."

She was switching on lights, fetching one room after another out of darkness.

"I found you a third blanket. It's a cotton one, but it'll be some help. You'll appreciate it towards morning, when the dampness comes in with the mist from the sea."

He was in a hurry to get to bed, to withdraw into himself. But he got out again when he remembered the doctor's tablets, and went to get a glass of water to take them with. The low muffled voices of the couple came to him from the front of the house, but he paid no attention.

"Good-night, Nancy," he said in a whisper recalling the hospital ward.

There were crickets in the garden. Later, there was an opening and shutting of doors, heavy footsteps went up the stairs to the first floor, someone struggled violently to open or close a window that seemed to be jammed, and all he remembered of the night was a sensation of cold creeping into him, against which the blankets were useless.

He had no dreams, nor did he awake until the sun was shining directly on him and he felt his face almost scorched. The town was already full of movement and voices, cars were passing along the street, cocks were crowing somewhere and a clatter of crockery came from within the house.

He had left his clothes hanging on the bathroom door, with his watch in them. When he went into the hall, his landlady called from the kitchen:

"Well, you certainly slept good! You can't say fresh air doesn't agree with you!"

"What time is it?"

"Half-past nine. I expect you'd like some coffee? I've just made some. By the way, the police-lieutenant called in to see you."

"What time was it?"

"About eight. He was in a hurry because he was going to the hospital with someone. I told him you were asleep, and he wouldn't let me wake you. He said he'll be in his office all morning and you can go there any time you like."

"Did you see who was with him?"

"I didn't dare have a look. There were three men in the back of the car, all in plain clothes, and I could swear the one in the middle was handcuffed. I shouldn't be surprised if it was the man they caught in New Hampshire who's in the paper this morning, the one that escaped from prison two days ago and managed to do so much harm in such a short time. You know about it. Do you want the paper?"

It must have surprised her that he should say no. She must have thought him cold, but his calm was not coldness. He went into the kitchen to drink the cup of coffee she poured for him, then had a shower and shaved; and when he came out on to the veranda some women neighbours were at their windows or on their doorsteps to look at him.

"May I sleep here again to-night?"

"As many nights as you like. I'm only sorry it's not more comfortable."

He drove into the town and stopped to have breakfast at the restaurant where he had dined the night before. When he had finished eating and had drunk two more cups of coffee he went into the call-box, asked for the number of Walla-Walla camp and waited nearly five minutes, staring through the glass pane at the counter behind which eggs were being fried by the dozen.

"Mrs. Keane? This is Steve Hogan."

"It's you, poor Mr. Hogan? We worried a lot all day yesterday in spite of your phone call. We were wondering what had happened to you. It was only in the evening that we learned about your wife's misfortune. How is she, poor dear? Are you near her? Have you seen her?"

"She's getting on all right, thank you, Mrs. Keane. I'm in Hayward. I'm planning to come up and get the children to-morrow. You haven't told them anything?"

"Only that their Mummy and Daddy were held up. Imagine, Bonnie said you must be having a very good time on the trip! Do you want to speak to them?"

"No. I'd rather not say anything over the phone. Just tell them I'll be there to-morrow."

"What are you going to do?"

And still he did not grow impatient.

"We'll go back home Tuesday, when the roads are clearer."

"Will your wife be fit to stand the trip?"

"The doctor's sure of it."

"To think that a thing like that should have happened to her! All the parents who come tell us about it, and if you only knew

232

how sorry they are for you both, Well, it could have been even worse. . . ."

He surprised himself by replying indifferently:
"Yes."

He could not go to Maine, come back, pick up Nancy and return to Long Island in a single day, except by driving like mad. The children would have to spend a night in Hayward. Luckily on Monday night everyone would be gone, and he would easily find hotel accommodation.

He thought of everything, for example that he would not need to tell Mr. Schwartz that Nancy would not be at the office on Tuesday morning, because by now he would know the news from the papers. The same applied to his own boss. He would simply send a wire the next day, which would reach Madison Avenue first thing on Tuesday, saying, "Returning office Thursday."

He was allowing himself Wednesday in which to organize the household. He could not make arrangements any earlier with Ida, their coloured girl, because she had told them that she was going to spend the week-end with relations in Baltimore.

He was clearing things up, little by little, trying to think of everything, including the story he would tell the two children, which must not depart from the truth more than was absolutely necessary because they would hear their schoolfriends talk.

He looked forward to seeing them again. But not in the same way as he had at other times. There was a new sort of closeness between them and him now; Bonnie and Dan, too, would be part of their new life.

After his two o'clock visit to the hospital he would see about trading the car. There was certainly a used-car dealer's somewhere, and those places do more trade over the week-ends than on any other days. And he must not forget to ask the lieutenant to draw up a temporary paper, some kind of certificate to replace his driving-licence, unless, perhaps, his wallet had been recovered.

There was yet another thing to do, much more important, which he could not postpone. He was calm. It was essential that he should retain all his self-control. He drove right on to the highway without having the curiosity to switch on the radio, and it was half-past ten when he pulled up outside the police building. One of the cars by the entrance, which bore New Hampshire number-plates but no other distinctive sign, must be the one in which the F.B.I. detectives had brought Sid Halligan.

It was also necessary that he should grow accustomed to hearing this name, to speaking it in his own mind. The weather was as fine as the previous day, but a little more oppressive, with a slight haze in the air which could lead to a thunderstorm towards the end of the day.

He crushed his cigarette under the sole of his shoe before going up the flight of stone steps and into the outer office, where one of the policemen was busy questioning a couple. The woman, her make-up smudged, had the voice and manner of a cabaret-singer.

"Is the lieutenant in his office?"

"Step right in, Mr. Hogan. I'll tell him you're here."

In the time it took him to reach the door which he knew from before, he had been announced over the inter-com. system, so a hand pulled the door open just as he was pushing it. Lieutenant Murray greeted him, seemed a little surprised by his attitude.

"Come in, Hogan. I thought you'd come. I needn't ask if you slept well. Take a seat."

Steve shook his head as he looked about him. He said in a quieter voice than usual:

"He's here?"

The policeman nodded, still surprised, perhaps at finding him so composed.

"Can I see him?"

The lieutenant in his turn became more grave.

"You'll see him in a moment, Hogan. But first I insist that you sit down for a few minutes."

He did so, obediently, and listened in the same way as he had listened to the landlady and to the condolences of Mrs. Keane. The other man felt it so keenly that he spoke without conviction, filling his pipe with short thrusts of his index finger.

"He was brought here last night, and first thing this morning we took him to Hayward. I didn't want to speak to you about it yesterday, and I hope you aren't angry at me. It was better to get a formal identification right now. In an hour, the F.B.I. men will start off with him for Sing Sing. If it hadn't taken place this morning, your wife would have had to see him later on, and. . . ."

"How was my wife?"

"We found her remarkably self-possessed."

Steve could not quite repress the smile which rose to his lips unbidden, and seemed to take the lieutenant aback.

"At six o'clock this morning, a private room in the hospital became free, and I arranged for her to be transferred."

"Did someone die during the night?"

The change in him must indeed be considerable, because he had hardly to open his mouth, and the lieutenant would practically lose his poise.

Without answering the question, he asked in his turn:

"You had a talk with your wife yesterday evening?"

"We straightened things out," Steve said simply.

"I guessed as much this morning. She seemed at peace. First, I went alone into the room to ask her if she felt strong enough to stand the identification. As a precaution, the doctor waited all the while in the corridor, just in case. Contrary to what I'd expected, she was neither nervous nor afraid. She said as naturally as you're talking to me this morning:

" 'I suppose it's got to be done, Lieutenant?'

"I said yes. Then she asked where you were, and I said you were still asleep, and she seemed pleased. She said:

" 'Do be quick.'

"I motioned to the detectives to bring in the prisoner. Ever since his arrest he's denied the assault and claimed mistaken identity. He admits everything else, which is less serious. I expected that.

"When he came into the room, he held his head high and he started to grin insolently. Standing in the middle of the room, he stared at your wife, challenging her.

"She didn't move. Her expression didn't change. After a moment she wrinkled her forehead, as though to see him better.

" 'Do you recognize him?' one of the detectives asked, while the other took down shorthand notes.

"She merely said:

" 'It's him.'

"He still stared at her with the same look of defiance while the F.B.I. man went down the list of questions which each time your wife answered with a distinct:

" 'Yes.'

"That's all, Hogan. All told, it took less than ten minutes. Reporters and photographers were waiting in the corridor. When Halligan had left the room and only then, I asked your wife if I could let them in, warned her that it's never a good idea to get on the wrong side of the Press. She answered:

" 'If the doctor doesn't mind, let them in!'

"The doctor allowed only the photographers in, just for a few minutes, forbidding the reporters to go and question her.

"She was plucky, I can tell you. I don't mind admitting that before I left I couldn't help shaking her hand."

Steve looked straight in front of him, saying nothing.

"I don't know whether she'll have to appear in person when the case goes before the jury. Anyway, there are so many charges, and they're so complicated, that it'll take some weeks; and by then your wife will have recovered. Maybe the Court will even be satisfied with an affidavit."

The lieutenant looked more and more embarrassed. Watch Steve as he might, he didn't understand. It seemed to be beyond him.

"Do you still want to see him?"

"Yes."

"Now?"

"As soon as possible."

Murray left him alone. Steve got to his feet and stood facing the window, as though collecting himself.

He heard the sound of coming and going in the corridors, the opening of doors, the footsteps of several people. After a rather long time the lieutenant came in first, leaving the door open, and went over to sit at his desk.

The first to enter the room then was Sid Halligan, his wrists linked by the handcuffs, and behind him came the two F.B.I. men.

Everyone except the lieutenant remained standing. Someone had shut the door.

Steve still faced the window, his head low, his fists clenched at the end of his hanging arms. The blood had left his face. There were beads of sweat on his forehead and his upper lip.

They saw him close his eyes, steel himself as though he needed all his strength and then, slowly, he turned partly around and faced Halligan.

The lieutenant, who was watching them both, saw the gradual disintegration of the smile on the prisoner's face.

For a moment he feared he would have to intervene; he even moved ever so slightly in his chair, because Steve, whose eyes seemed unable to detach themselves from those of his wife's aggressor, had begun to stiffen, his body had grown hard, his jaw out-thrust.

His right fist moved an inch or two and Halligan, who was

236

aware of it, quickly raised his arms fettered in the handcuffs, and threw a frightened look at his guards as though calling them to his rescue.

They had not spoken a word. Not a sound had been heard. Once again, Steve relaxed, the lines of his body became rounder, his shoulders sagged slowly, his face crumpled.

"I'm sorry . . ." he stammered.

And the others did not know whether it was for the blow he had so nearly struck.

He could look Halligan in the face now, with the expression he had a moment before when the lieutenant was talking to him, the expression that had been his since the previous evening.

He gazed at him for a long time, as he had set himself to do, because it had seemed to him necessary before starting on their new life.

No one suspected that it was some part of himself that he had nearly struck when he had raised his fist, or that it was something of his own past which he outfaced in the prisoner's eyes.

Now, he had seen the end of the road. He could look elsewhere, return to everyday life; he gazed about him, surprised to find them all so tense, and said in his normal voice:

"That's all."

He added:

"Thank you, Lieutenant."

If they had questions to ask him, he was ready. It did not matter now.

Nancy, too, had been brave.

THE WATCHMAKER OF
EVERTON

CHAPTER ONE

UNTIL midnight, indeed until one o'clock in the morning, he followed the routine of every evening, or more exactly of Saturdays, which were a little different from other days.

Would he have spent that evening differently, or would he have tried to enjoy it more, if he had foreseen that it was his last evening as a happy man? To this question and many others, including that of whether he had ever been really happy, he would later have to try to find an answer.

As yet he knew nothing of it, and contented himself with living, without haste, without problems, without even being fully conscious of living them, hours so similar to others that he might have thought he had already lived them.

It rarely happened that he shut the shop at six o'clock precisely. Nearly always, he let a few more minutes pass before getting up from his work-bench, in front of which the watches under repair hung from little hooks, and removing from his right eye the magnifying-glass framed in black ebonite which he wore nearly all day like a monocle. Perhaps, even after years, he still had a sense of working for an employer and was afraid of seeming to grudge his time.

Mrs. Pinch next door, who kept the estate-agency, closed at five o'clock sharp. The hairdresser on the other side, for fear of being late, began to refuse customers at half-past five and Galloway, at the moment of opening his display-window, nearly always saw him getting into his car to drive home. The hairdresser had a nice house in the residential quarter, on the hill, and three children at school.

In a few minutes, moving with the precise, rather slow gestures of a man accustomed to handling delicate and valuable objects, Dave Galloway cleared the display-shelves of their watches and jewels, which he stored away in the safe at the back of the shop.

The most expensive of the watches was worth not quite a hundred dollars and there was only one at that price. The others were very much cheaper. All the jewels were in plated settings, with imitation stones. He had tried at first to sell engagement-rings adorned with a real diamond, a diamond of about a half-carat, but for purchases of this sort the Everton people preferred to go to Poughkeepsie or even to New York, perhaps because it would have embarrassed them to buy their engagement-rings by monthly instalments from someone they knew.

He put the contents of the till in a drawer in the safe, took off his unbleached working-smock which he hung on a hook on the inside of the door of the cupboard, put on his jacket and glanced round to see that everything was in order.

It was May; the sun was still quite high in a sky of very soft blue and, all day long, the air had been motionless.

When he had slipped the spring-lock of the door and gone out, he glanced automatically towards the cinema, the "Colonial Theatre," whose neon sign had just lighted up, although it was still broad daylight. The same thing happened every Saturday, because of the seven o'clock performance. There was a lawn in front of the theatre, a few lime-trees on which the leaves scarcely stirred.

Standing on his doorstep, Galloway lit a cigarette, one of the five or six he smoked in a day, then walked slowly round the long building of which the ground floor was occupied by shops. He lived on the first floor, exactly over his own shop, but since there was no communication between the latter and his apartment, he had to turn to the left past the hairdresser's establishment, go round to the back, where the entrance to the dwellings was situated.

As happened nearly every Saturday, his son had come in during the afternoon to say that he would not be home for supper. No doubt he would get a hot-dog or a sandwich somewhere, most probably at Mack's Lunch.

Galloway went upstairs, turned the key in the lock and went at once to open the window, from which he had almost exactly the same view as from his work-bench, with the same trees, the cinema display, whose lights, in the full sunshine, were out of place, almost disturbing.

He no longer noticed that every day he went through the same motions, in the same order, and that it was this, perhaps, which gave him so peaceful and reassuring an aspect. Nothing was left lying about in the kitchen, where he always washed up after the midday meal before going downstairs again. He knew what cold meat he would find in the frigidaire and precisely whereabouts, and he handled the objects as though by magic; his place was very quickly laid, with the glass of water, the bread, the butter, the coffee beginning to bubble in the percolator.

When he was alone, he read while he ate, but this did not prevent him hearing the birds in the trees, or the noise of a car

241

someone was starting, which he recognized. From his seat he could even see the youngsters beginning to move towards the cinema, which they would not enter until the last minute.

He drank his coffee in little sips, washed up, cleared away the breadcrumbs. So far as his activities and movements were concerned, nothing unusual took place and, shortly before seven, he was out in the street again, greeting the garage-keeper, who with his wife was on the way to the cinema.

He saw some young lads and some girls in the distance, did not spot Ben, did not try to meet him, knowing that the boy did not like him to seem to be keeping an eye on him.

It was not really a matter of keeping an eye on him, as Ben knew. If sometimes his father went out of his way to catch a glimpse of him, it was not in order to supervise his actions and behaviour, but simply for the pleasure of making contact with him, even at a distance. A boy of sixteen can't understand this. It was natural that, when he was with boys and girls of his own age, Ben should prefer his father not to be watching. The matter had never been referred to between them. Galloway felt it simply, did not insist.

The building in which he had his shop and apartment was nearly on the corner of Main Street; along it he now went, passed the drugstore which stayed open till nine, then the Post Office with its white columns, then the newsagent's shop. Cars went by, scarcely slowing, some not slowing at all, as though they did not notice they were passing through a village.

Beyond the gasoline-pump, scarcely a quarter of a mile from his own house, he turned to the right into a street bordered with trees, where the white houses were surrounded by lawns. This street did not lead anywhere, and the only cars to be seen were those belonging to its inhabitants. All the windows were open, children were still playing out of doors, men without jackets, their shirtsleeves rolled up, were driving motor-mowers over the grass.

Every year brought similar evenings of this almost oppressive mildness and the hum of mowers, just as every autumn brought the sound of rakes on the dead leaves and the smell of these leaves being burnt, in the evening, in front of the houses, and later still there was inevitably the scraping of shovels on the hardened snow.

From time to time, with a gesture or a word, he returned a "good evening."

On Tuesdays, he also went out, to go to the village hall for the meeting of the School Committee, of which he was secretary.

On other evenings, except Saturday, he most often stayed at home, reading or watching television.

Saturday was the evening for Musak, who must at that moment be awaiting him in one of the rocking-chairs on his porch.

His house, built of wood, like the other houses in the neighbourhood, was the last of the row, backing on to a steep slope, so that what was the first floor on one side became the ground floor on the other. It was painted pale yellow instead of white and, less than fifty yards away, was a stretch of waste land where people were in the habit of dumping anything they wanted to get rid of, iron bedsteads, broken-down perambulators, split metal drums.

From the terrace one looked over the sports-ground, where, every evening in summer, the baseball team practised.

The two men treated each other without ceremony. Galloway could not remember ever having shaken hands with Musak, who, when he arrived, contented himself with uttering a grunt and pointing towards the second rocking-chair.

It was the same that evening as on other Saturdays. They followed at a distance the white costumes of the players against the steadily darkening green of the field, and they heard their cries, the whistle of the trainer, who was very fat and worked during the day behind one of the counters of the hardware store.

"Nice evening," was all Galloway had said, after sitting down.

A little later, Musak had grumbled:

"If they don't make up their minds to change their damned pitcher we shall be bottom of the list again at the end of the season."

Musak talked in a surly voice no matter what he said, and it was rare for him to smile. In fact, Dave Galloway could not remember ever having seen him smile. What he sometimes did was to burst into a loud laugh which must have alarmed those who did not know him.

In the village, people were no longer alarmed by Musak, because they had grown used to him. Elsewhere, he ran the risk of being taken for one of those elderly convicts broken out of jail whose photographs, full-face and in profile, are to be seen in post-offices above the notice, "Wanted by the F.B.I."

Galloway, who did not know his age, would never have thought of asking him what it was, any more than he had asked him what European country he had come from when he was

243

still just a child. He knew only that he had made the crossing in an immigrant ship with his father, his mother and five or six brothers and sisters, and that they had first lived in the outskirts of Philadelphia. What had become of the brothers and sisters? The subject had never been mentioned between them, any more than what Musak had done before settling all alone in Everton, twenty years ago.

He must have been married, because he had a daughter somewhere in southern California, who wrote to him from time to time and sent him photographs of her children. She had never been to see him. He had never gone out there, either.

Was Musak divorced? or a widower?

At some period in his life, he had worked in a piano-factory, this was all Galloway knew, and he had had enough money, when he came to Everton, to be able to buy a house.

He was probably sixty or even older. Some people claimed that he was in his seventies, which wasn't impossible, either.

He still worked from morning till night in the workshop situated behind the house, on the side where the first floor became the ground floor, so that the workshop communicated directly with his bedroom. This was where they often sat in the winter, when they could not sit on the porch. Musak would finish off some job or other, always a delicate one, with hands so large that one might have thought them clumsy. There was an iron stove in the middle of the room which was cluttered up with work-benches, glue heating in the water-bath, wood-shavings on the floor.

His speciality was doing work that called for extreme patience, repairing old furniture or old clock-cases, or making small, elaborate articles, boxes inlaid with mahogany or woods from the West Indies.

They could remain for a long time without talking, the two of them, satisfied to be there watching at a distance the players running to and fro while the sun sank slowly behind the trees and the air little by little became the same blue as the sky.

For Dave Galloway what characterized the winter evenings in the workshop was the smell of wood-shavings mingled with that of strong glue.

In the summer evenings, on the porch, there was another smell, equally recognizable, that of the pipe which Musak smoked in small puffs. He must have adopted some special tobacco, which had an acrid and yet not unpleasant smell. It came to Galloway in waves at the same time as that of the grass cut in the neighbouring gardens. Musak's garments were impregnated with it, his very body, one could have sworn, smelt of the pipe, and also the living-room of his house.

Why had he, so adroit with his hands, so meticulous in everything he undertook, been content to mend his favourite pipe with a piece of wire? A little air passed through the crack each time he sucked and it made a queer sound, like the breathing of certain sick people.

"Who are they playing against to-morrow?"

"Radley."

"They'll be beaten hollow."

There was a baseball game every Sunday and Galloway took his seat on the benches while old Musak contented himself with watching from his porch. He had astonishingly good eyesight. From that distance, he could recognize every player and, on the Sunday evening, could have given a list of all the local people who had watched the game.

The movements on the field grew slower, the voices less piercing, the referee's blasts of the whistle more infrequent. They could scarcely see the ball any longer in the half-light and a certain freshness began to prevail; one would have said that the air, hitherto motionless, was awakening at the approach of night.

Perhaps both men were equally impatient to go indoors and begin their Saturday night pastime, but, as though of one accord, they awaited the signal; neither of them moved before all the figures in baseball clothes had gathered together in a corner of the field to hear the comments of the trainer.

By that time the darkness was almost complete The radios were growing more strident in the neighbouring houses, some windows were lighting up, others, because of television, remained in obscurity.

Only then did they look at one another and one seemed to say:

"Shall we go?"

Theirs was a strange friendship. Galloway could not have said, any more than Musak, how it had begun and they seemed to take no account of the twenty years which separated them.

"If I remember rightly, I have to get my revenge."

It was the cabinet-maker's only fault, he did not like losing. He did not get angry, never thumped the table with his fists. As a rule he said nothing, but his face became sulky like that of a child and sometimes, after an evening when he had been badly beaten, he would go two or three days without seeming to see Galloway when he passed him in the street.

He switched on the light and they entered another atmosphere even quieter, more enveloping than that which they had left. The living-room was comfortable, as well cared for as by any woman, with handsome furniture carefully polished, and Galloway had never detected in it the slightest disorder.

The backgammon board was ready on a low table, always in the same place, between the same armchairs, with a standard lamp which shone on it, and they liked to leave the rest of the room in the shadow where only reflections existed.

The bottle of rye was also in readiness, and the glasses, and there was nothing more to be done, before beginning the game, except to go and fetch ice from the kitchen.

"Your health."

"And yours."

Galloway drank little, two glasses at the most during the evening, whereas Musak took five or six without their seeming to have the least effect on him.

Each threw a dice.

"Six! I begin."

For nearly two hours their life was attuned to the rhythm of the falling dice and the sound of the yellow and black counters. The pipe made its whistling noise. Its acrid scent gradually enveloped Galloway. At long intervals one of the two uttered a remark such as:

"John Duncan has bought a new car."

Or:

"They say Mrs. Pinch has sold Meadow Farm for fifty thousand dollars."

These called for no reply. These prompted neither question nor comment.

They played until half-past eleven, which was about their limit. Musak lost the first game, won three others, which averaged out with the previous time.

"I said I'd beat you! I only lose when I can't bring myself to concentrate. A last drink?"

"No thanks."

The cabinet-maker poured himself one, and this drink he always took neat. Also, towards the end of the contest, his breathing always became noisy, his nose made almost the same sound as his pipe. He must snore at nights, which would not disturb anyone, since he lived alone in the house.

Did he wash the glasses before going to bed?

"Good-night."

"Good-night."

"Still pleased with your son?"

"Very pleased."

Galloway felt uncomfortable whenever Musak asked in this fashion after Ben. He was convinced that his friend was not malicious, still less cruel, and had no reason to be jealous of him. Perhaps, in any case, he was imagining things? One would have said that it ruffled Musak that Ben should be a well-behaved boy of whom his father had never had reason to complain.

Had he once had difficulties with his daughter? Or was he sorry that he had not a son as well?

There was something different in his voice, in his look, when he touched upon that subject. He seemed to be saying:

"All right! All right! We shall see how long it lasts!"

Or again did he suspect Galloway of deceiving himself about his son?

"He's not playing baseball any more?"

"Not this year."

Last year, Ben had been one of the best players in the High School team. This year, suddenly he had decided not to play. He had not given any reason. His father had not asked. Wasn't it the same with all youngsters? One year, they are crazy about a game or a sport, and the next year they don't talk about it any more. For months, they meet the same group of friends every day, and then one day they break away from them for no apparent reason to join another group.

Galloway, needless to say, would have preferred it to be otherwise. He had been greatly distressed when Ben had given up baseball, because his greatest pleasure had been to watch the school games, even when the team travelled thirty or forty miles to play on some other ground.

"No doubt he's a good boy," said Musak.

Why did he say it with an air of concluding an argument, of putting a full-stop to the conversation? What exactly did the words signify?

Perhaps Dave Galloway was too touchy where Ben was concerned? It was natural for people to ask:

"How's your son getting on?"

Or again: "It's a long time since I saw Ben."

He had a tendency to look for some special significance in these passing remarks.

247

"I've no reason to complain of him," he most commonly replied.

And it was true. He could formulate no complaint. Ben had never caused him any trouble. They never quarrelled. It was rare for Galloway to have to reprimand his son and, when it happened, he did so quietly, as man to man.

"Good-night."

"Good-night."

"Till Saturday."

"Yes."

They saw each other a dozen times during the week, notably at the Post Office, where they both went almost every day at the same time to collect their mail. Galloway had a card which he hung on his door whenever he had to be away, or to go up to his apartment—"Back shortly."

They also met at the garage and at the newsagent's. Nevertheless, when they separated on Saturday nights they invariably said: "Till Saturday."

The tobacco's bitter smell followed Galloway for a dozen yards and, as he went along the lane towards Main Street, where nearly all the lights were out, he heard, in two of the houses only, the echoes of the same boxing-match.

Did it take him six minutes to return home? Scarcely. Nothing remained open, at the end of the village, except the Old Barn tavern, with its red and green lights which, even at a distance, made one think of brands of beer and whisky.

He walked round his building, and only as he was entering the alleyway, past the hairdresser's shop, did it occur to him that he had not seen any light in his window.

He did not remember raising his head either, but he was sure he had done so because he always did so, with a mechanical movement, when he returned home in the evening. He was so accustomed to seeing the lighted window that he no longer thought about it.

But now, as he went towards the staircase, he could have sworn that the window was in darkness. There was no dance that night, no party, nothing special to keep Ben out late.

He started up the stairs and after going a few steps he knew, without the possibility of error, that there had been no light in the apartment, because he would have seen a streak under the door.

Had Ben come in early and gone to bed? Who knows. Perhaps he hadn't been feeling well?

He turned the key in the lock, called as he pushed open the door:

"Ben!"

The echo of his own voice in the room told him that there was no one there but he would not admit it, switched on the light in the living-room, went towards his son's room repeating in a voice as normal as possible:

"Ben!"

He must show no anxiety because, if Ben were there, if he were really in bed, would he not look at him in annoyed surprise as he asked:

"What's the matter?"

There was nothing the matter, of course. Nothing could be the matter. One must never let one's fears be seen, especially by a boy in the process of becoming a man.

"Are you there?"

He tried to smile in advance, as though his son were watching him.

But Ben was not there. The room was empty. The bed was untouched.

Perhaps he had left a note on the table, as he sometimes did?

There was nothing. The cinema-sign, opposite, was switched off. The second performance had finished more than half an hour ago and the last cars had gone. On his way back from Musak's house, Dave Galloway had not met a soul.

Only twice before had Ben returned home after midnight without having warned his father. On both occasions, the latter had waited up for him, seated in his armchair, incapable of reading or listening to the radio. Only when he heard the boy's footsteps on the stairs had he hastily picked up a magazine.

"I'm late. I'm sorry."

He spoke lightly, to make the thing seem unimportant. Had he expected a scolding, a scene?

Dave had simply said:

"I was worried."

"What could have happened to me? I was in Chris Gillespie's car and we had a breakdown."

"Why didn't you telephone?"

"There were no houses near and we had to put it right ourselves."

That time, it was at the beginning of the winter. The second time, between Christmas and the New Year, Ben had come upstairs more loudly than usual and, once in the room, had deliberately turned away his head, avoided coming near his father.

"... So sorry.... Was held up by a friend.... Why didn't you go to bed?... What are you scared of?"

It was not his voice. For the first time, there was something changed in him, almost aggressive. His attitude, his gestures were those of a stranger. Galloway, however, had pretended to notice nothing. On the Sunday morning, Ben had slept late, a restless slumber, and when he had appeared in the kitchen his face had been ashen.

His father had allowed him time to have his breakfast, trying to appear as casual as possible, and only at the end had murmured:

"You were drinking, weren't you?"

It had never happened before. Dave lived in sufficiently close intimacy with his son to be sure that, until then, he had never touched a glass of liquor.

"Don't be cross with me, dad."

And, after a silence, in a low voice:

"Don't be afraid. I'm not keen to do it again. I wanted to do the same as the others. I loathe it."

"Sure?"

Ben had smiled as he repeated, meeting his eyes.

"Sure."

Since then, that's to say since December, he had not once come home after eleven. Generally, when he returned from his visit to Musak, Galloway found him seated in front of the television receiver, watching the boxing programme, the one whose echoes had just now reached him as he walked along the lane. They sometimes watched the finish of it side by side.

"Aren't you hungry?"

Galloway would go into the kitchen, make sandwiches, return with two glasses of iced milk.

With the window open, so as to hear Ben's footsteps at a greater distance, he sat down in the same place as on the two previous occasions when he had awaited him. The air from outside was cold, but he didn't bring himself to shut the window. He thought for a moment of putting on his overcoat, told himself that if he found him seated like that in his armchair Ben would have a shock.

The first time, he had come home at midnight, the second time at about one in the morning.

He lit a cigarette, then another and yet another, smoking them nervously without being conscious of doing so. At one moment, he went and switched on the television, but no picture appeared on the luminous screen. All the programmes one could get in Everton were ended.

He did not walk up and down, despite his interior tension, stayed motionless, his eyes fixed on the door until they became cold with the strain, without any precise idea in his head. More than three-quarters of an hour had passed when he got up, calm in appearance, and again went towards his son's room.

He did not switch on the light, did not think of it, so that the room, lighted only by the reflection from the room next door, was a little ghostly, the bed in particular, of a dull white which evoked tragic images.

One would have said that Galloway knew what he had come in search of, what he was going to find. A pair of dirty shoes lay crosswise on the rug, and a shirt had been thrown over the back of a chair.

At some time during the evening, Ben had come in to change his clothes. His everyday suit lay on the floor in a corner of the room, his socks a little farther off.

Slowly, Dave opened the wardrobe and what struck him instantly was the absence of the suitcase. Its place was on the floor, below the clothes hung on hangers. It was two years since Galloway had bought it for his son, on the occasion of a trip they had taken together to Cape Cod, and since then it had not been used.

It had still been there that morning, he was sure of it, because it was he who tidied up the apartment every day. The charwoman only came twice a week, for a few hours, on Tuesday and Friday, to do the heavy cleaning.

Ben had come back to put on his best suit and had gone off taking his suitcase with him. He had not left any message.

Curiously, there was no surprise in Galloway's eyes, as though for a long time, always, he had lived in the expectation of a catastrophe.

Perhaps, however, he had never envisaged this particular catastrophe. With slow movements, even more slow than usual, like a man struggling to postpone disaster, he thrust open the door of the bathroom which served them both and switched on the light.

On the glass shelf, there was now only one razor. The electric razor he had bought Ben for his last Christmas had disappeared.

251

His comb was not there either, nor the toothbrush in its holder. He had even taken the tube of toothpaste.

Because of the bathroom ventilator, still open, a draught blew through the apartment, stirred the curtains, caused the pages of a newspaper lying on the television to flutter.

He returned to the living-room to shut the window, stood for a moment staring out, his forehead pressed to the cold glass pane.

He felt as exhausted as after a walk of several hours and there was no more strength in his limbs. He was tempted to go and lie flat on his stomach on his bed and talk by himself, talk to Ben, with his head in the pillow. But what good would that do?

There remained one thing for him to know and he was going to find it out immediately. He did not hurry. He had no reason to hurry. He even took the time to put on his light overcoat and a cap, because he felt frozen.

The moon had risen, almost full, brilliant, and the sky resembled a bottomless sea. On that side of the building, garages occupied all the ground floor and he went towards his own, pulled a bunch of keys out of his pocket, thrust one into the lock.

He had no need to turn the key. The door moved at once and a split in the wood showed that it had been forced with a screwdriver and another tool.

What need was there to make sure that the garage was empty? It was, the van was no longer there. He knew it already. He had realized it instantly, upstairs. He did not switch on the light. It was not worth the trouble.

He closed the door, nevertheless, with as much care as usual. What was he doing, standing, alone, in the sort of courtyard which lay behind the house where only one window, his own, was lighted?

He had no reason to remain out of doors. He had nothing to do there.

But henceforth what had he to do at home?

He went upstairs again, however, treading slowly, as though at every stair he paused to reflect, locked the door once more, took off his coat, his cap, which he put back in their place, and went towards his armchair.

Then, his body limp, he stared at the blankness around him.

CHAPTER TWO

It happens that in dreams we find ourselves suddenly trans-
ported to the border of a countryside at once strange and
familiar, agonizing as a precipice. Nothing in it resembles what
we have known in real life and yet we feel something stir in our
memory, we have the near-certainty of having been that way
before, perhaps of having lived there in a previous dream or in
a former life.

Dave Galloway, too, had already lived once before the hour he
was now in the act of living, with the same sense of total collapse
in his body and in his spirit and the same emptiness around him;
on that previous occasion too he had lain limply in the green
armchair, opposite the matching sofa which they had originally
bought on credit, his wife and he, in a furniture-store in
Hartford, together with the two low tables, the two chairs and
the radio-console, because television did not yet exist.

The room, there, was smaller, the house, like all the others on
the lot, was new; they had been the first to live in it and the
trees were only just beginning to come to life on the two sides
of the newly made road.

It was at Waterbury, in Connecticut. At that time he was
working in a factory making watches and precision-instruments.
He recalled details of that evening as minutely as, no doubt, he
would later recall the evening he had just spent with Musak. He
had gone to the house of a friend, who worked in another department, to repair a pendulum-clock dating from the time of his
great-grandfather.

The clock, of German origin, had a finely engraved pewter
face and the movement had been made by hand. Dave had stood
on a chair in his shirtsleeves, his head almost touching the ceiling,
and he remembered moving the hands to regulate the striking of
the hours, the half-hours and the quarters. The windows were
open. Then too it had been the spring, a little earlier in the
season, and a big bowl of strawberries had stood on the table
beside the rye and the glasses. His friend's wife was named
Patricia. She was dark-haired, of Italian origin, with a skin of
very fine texture. In order to be with them, she had brought her
ironing-board into the living-room and, all the time he had been
there, she had ironed diapers, except when one of the children
had awakened and she had gone to soothe it back to sleep. She
had three, aged four years, two and a half and one year, and she
was pregnant again, calm and glowing as a ripe fruit.

"Your health!"

"And yours!"

On that occasion also he had had two ryes. His friend had wanted to pour himself a third, but Patricia had gently called him to order.

"Aren't you afraid of having a headache in the morning?"

They were delighted at hearing the striking of the clock, which had not gone since they had inherited it. Galloway had been happy too, at having passed the evening with them and handled beautiful pieces of mechanism. He remembered that they had tried to calculate what a clock like that would cost if it were made in these days.

"A last drink?"

Like Musak!

"No, thanks."

He had gone on foot. He lived only two streets away. The moon was bright. From the corner, Galloway had noticed that there was no light in his house. Ruth must have gone to bed without waiting for him. This was curious because, at night, she never wanted to go to bed and found all sorts of pretexts for delay. He had perhaps been wrong to stay so long?

He quickened his pace, accompanied by the sound of his soles on the cement of the alley. Twenty yards from his house, he was already searching in his pocket for the key. And, with the door open, he had instantly had the same impression of emptiness that he had had that evening on entering his apartment. He had not even pressed the switch. The moon shed enough light in the rooms through the uncurtained windows. He went towards the bedroom, a name on his lips: "Ruth!"

The bed was undisturbed. There was no one there. An old pair of shoes lay on the rug. Then he had opened the other door and stood motionless, trembling with the fear he had suddenly felt. Ruth had not taken the baby! Ben was there, in his cradle, quite warm, peaceful, spreading a good odour of fresh bread.

"Don't you think he smells of warm bread?" he had once said to his wife.

She had answered, without unkindness, he was sure, simply because it was her way of thinking:

"He smells of wet, like all babies."

He had not picked him out of his cradle to clasp him in his arms as he wanted to do. He had only bent down to listen to his breathing for a long time, then, on tip-toe, had returned to their bedroom where he had switched on the light.

She had not shut the wardrobe and a drawer of the dressing-table was pulled out wide, with two black hairpins in it. The room was still impregnated with the strong, vulgar scent she affected, which she must have used at the moment of leaving.

She had taken all her things with her, except a flowered cotton house-coat and two torn pairs of pants.

He had not wept or clenched his fists. He had gone and sat down in the armchair in the living-room, near the radio. Long afterwards, he had gone into the kitchen to make sure she had not left a note for him on the table. There was none. Nevertheless, he had not been entirely mistaken. In the garbage-pail, by the sink, he found a number of scraps of paper which he had sufficient patience to fit together like the pieces of a puzzle.

She had meant to leave him a message, but had not managed to write one. She had started several, in her scrawling hand, with spelling mistakes.

"My dear Dave. . . ."

She had crossed out "dear" and substituted "poor" and, on that sheet, there was nothing more except the beginning of a sentence:

"When you read this. . . ."

She had torn it up. She had written on the scribbling-pad hanging in the kitchen, which was used for noting orders to be given to the grocer who called every morning. She must have been seated at the same table where, every day, she sat down to peel vegetables.

> *"My dear Dave,*
>
> *I know I'm going to hurt you, but I can't stand it any longer and it's better for it to happen now than later. I've often wanted to talk to you about it, but. . . ."*

Incapable, no doubt, of expressing exactly what she had in mind, she had torn this one up as well. The third had no form of address.

> *"We aren't right for one another, I knew it from the start. It has all been a mistake. I'm leaving you the baby. Good luck."*

"Good luck" had been crossed out, replaced by:

> *"Be happy both of you."*

At the last minute she had changed her mind again, because this note had been torn up like the others, thrown in the pail.

She had preferred to leave without saying anything. What was the use? What could words have added? Wasn't it better for him to think what he chose?

He had gone back again to his armchair, convinced that he would not sleep that night, and Ben's crying had awakened him at six in the morning when the house was already bathed in sunshine. It was always he, morning and evening, who gave him his bottle. After a few weeks cereals were added, and vegetable-purée during the last days. He knew how to put on diapers as well. It was the first thing he had wanted to learn when Ruth and the baby had come out of hospital.

That was fifteen and a half years ago and he had never seen Ruth again; the only time he had had indirect news of her had been when, three years later, he had received a visit from a lawyer who had got him to sign papers in order that his wife might obtain a divorce.

He was not asleep. His eyes remained wide open, staring at the sofa which had followed him with the rest of his household when he had left Waterbury.

It was he who had brought up Ben, by himself, because he only entrusted him to a woman neighbour, who had four children, during his working hours. All his free time, all his nights, he had passed with his son and he had not once gone out in the evening, had not put his foot inside a cinema.

The war had prevented him from leaving the house in Waterbury when he had intended, because he was mobilized in the factory, which turned over to national defence work. Only later had he looked round for a place where he could set up on his own so as not to be obliged to leave the house. It was on purpose, for Ben's sake, that he had chosen a village where existence was peaceful.

Suddenly, he had a wild hope. Footsteps had sounded behind the building where no one had any reason to be at that time, and for an instant the thought had crossed his mind that it was his son returning. He forgot that Ben had gone off with the van, and that he would first have heard the engine, the brakes, the slam of the door.

The footsteps drew nearer, not those of one person, but of two, and their rhythm was strange, one felt in it a sort of stumbling. Someone down below put a foot on the first step of the stairway at the same time as the murmur of a woman's voice was audible. Heavy soles that seemed to hesitate came down on the second step, on the third. He went and opened the door, switched on the light and asked:

"What is it?"

He did not understand, stood there, astounded, above the well of the staircase, watching Bill Hawkins who, completely drunk, his moustache damp, his hat filthy, looked him up and down besottedly.

Isabel Hawkins, in indoor clothes, in her apron, without hat or coat as though she had had to leave her house in a great hurry, was trying to squeeze in front of her husband.

"Don't take any notice of him, Mr. Galloway. He's in his usual state again."

He knew them just as he knew all the people in Everton. Hawkins worked as a cowhand on a neighbouring farm and about three nights a week got so drunk that he sometimes had to be brought in from the road where he might have been run over by a car. One saw him pass, with a lurching gait, muttering indistinctly into his reddish moustache which was beginning to turn a dirty white.

They lived near the railway track, a little outside the village; they must have had eight or nine children; the two oldest, married, lived at Poughkeepsie, one daughter at least went to High School and the ones best known were two twin boys about twelve years old, red-haired and shaggy, wild in appearance, who were the terror of the village.

Hawkins, incapable of coming any higher, his body swaying, his two hands clinging to the stair-rail, attempted to speak and could not find words. All the way there, his wife must have been trying to persuade him to return home. She must have said to him:

"Stay here if you want to. I'll go on there. . . ."

Despite the size of her family, she found time to go out as a domestic help and, for some months, had been working at the Old Barn.

"I'm sorry to disturb you at this hour, Mr. Galloway. Bill, let me pass. Just lean against the wall."

The man fell down and she struggled to get him on his feet again while Galloway, at the top of the stairs, did not move. There was in this scene, lighted by a single yellowish electric bulb, something grotesque and a little unreal.

"I suppose your son hasn't come home?"

He did not understand. Incapable of grasping any connexion between these people and Ben's departure.

"Wait while I get by so I don't have to shout. There are probably people asleep in the house."

There were a few. Most of the tradespeople occupying the shops on the ground floor lived in the residential quarter. It was an old woman, a Pole, who lived next door to Galloway; she had witnessed the massacre within a few minutes of her husband, her three children, her son-in-law and her granddaughter, a few months old. She still did not understand why she had been spared, scarcely spoke any English, lived by doing small dressmaking jobs, mending, because she would not have been able to cut out a dress. Her hair entirely white, her face almost without wrinkles, she looked attentively at the people who spoke to her and, understanding only an occasional word, she smiled at them gently as though to apologize. A married couple lived at the end of the corridor, people whose children were married and in New York; the husband worked as a mechanic in the garage across the way. Had the Hawkinses awakened them?

Bill Hawkins was still trying to manifest his indignation, and not succeeding except with grunts. His wife had reached the top of the stairs.

"I had to come out just as I was, to run after him, because I didn't want him to come alone to see you. Do you know anything?"

He could not invite her in, because of the drunken man still on the stairs, and they remained standing on the landing, in front of the half-open door.

Isabel Hawkins saw that he did not understand her. She was not angry.

"Know anything about what?" he asked.

"About Ben and my daughter. They've gone off together."

She had tears in her eyes, but one felt that they were mechanical, conventional tears, that in reality she was not affected by any violent grief.

"I knew he'd taken a fancy to her. He used to hang around the house every evening and more than once I've caught them clinging to one another in the dark. I didn't pay much attention. I didn't think it was serious. But you, you didn't know?"

"No."

She exclaimed, gazing at him:

"Ah!"

Then she was silent for a moment, as though this had quite upset her ideas.

258

"He didn't tell you he was going away?"

"He didn't tell me anything."

"When did you find out?"

"Just now, when I came home."

It was painful to him to have to account for Ben to this woman whom he scarcely knew.

"He took the van," she said, as though she knew it already.

"Yes."

"I heard the engine somewhere near the house."

"At what time?"

"Perhaps ten. I didn't look at the clock."

"Did you think it was him?"

"No. I just heard a car starting up. I was busy in the front room, mending the children's shirts. The car was on the road at the back."

"Your daughter was out of doors?"

"I suppose so. At home, you never know, because everyone comes and goes in the house, goes in and out without anyone bothering."

Her husband, down below, made a wide gesture with his arm, as though telling her to be quiet, shouted a word which must have been:

"Bastard!"

"Be quiet, Bill. It isn't Mr. Galloway's fault, and I'm sure he's just as worried as we are. Aren't you, Mr. Galloway?"

He said yes, reluctantly, asked in his turn:

"You're certain your daughter's with him?"

"Who else would she have gone with? It's more than two months now that they've been going together and she hasn't seen any other boys, she hasn't even been seeing her girl friends. She never had a sweetheart before him, and I was almost worried about it, because she wasn't like other girls her age."

"What made you certain she'd gone?"

"It was after half-past eleven when Steve, who's seventeen, who's at High School too, came home from the cinema, and I asked him if his sister was with him. He said he hadn't seen her. At first I thought your son must have brought her back and that they were still hidden somewhere in the dark. I opened the door. I called:

" 'Lillian! Lillian!'

"Then I stopped calling, for fear of waking the children. When I came in again Steve said:

" 'She isn't in her room.'

259

"He had been to look.

" 'You're sure she wasn't at the cinema?'

" 'I'm sure.'

" 'You didn't see Ben either?'

"They are friends, Ben and he. In fact that's how things started with Lillian. The boys were always going out together and your son often came and had a sandwich with us.

"I could see Steve was starting to think. He's the most serious of them all and he gets the best marks at school.

" 'Did Ben come this evening?' he asked me.

" 'I didn't see him.'

"And then he rushed up to his sister's room for the second time. I heard him pulling out the drawers. He came back and said :

" 'She's gone.' "

The voice was not dramatic. The tone was as monotonous as a lament. Now and then, she wrinkled her forehead, in her desire to say everything, to forget nothing, and she continued to keep an eye on her husband who had ended by sitting on one of the stairs with his back towards her, pursuing his interior monologue and wagging his head.

"I went up in my turn to have a look and I found that Lillian had taken her best things with her. When I got back to the kitchen, where father seemed to be asleep in his armchair, I told Steve about the car I'd heard and Steve said :

" 'I don't understand.'

"I asked him what he didn't understand, seeing Ben had been running after his sister for months.

" 'Because he hasn't any money,' he said.

" 'How do you know?'

" 'Only yesterday, some of the boys went to have ices at Mack's, and Ben wouldn't go with them because he said he hadn't any money.'

" 'Perhaps it wasn't true.'

" 'I'm sure it was true.'

"They know each other among themselves better than we know them, isn't that so?"

Galloway said :

"Won't you come in?"

"I'd rather not leave him all alone. Mark you, he wouldn't do anyone any harm. I don't know exactly at what moment he woke up, or what he heard. Every Saturday he's like this. An idea suddenly occurred to me and I went and looked in the box where we keep the week's money. At half-past six, I'd put in the thirty-eight dollars my husband had brought me."

In a non-committal voice, without inflection, Galloway questioned:

"The money wasn't there any more?"

"No. She must have taken advantage of a moment when I'd left the kitchen or else when I had my back turned. Don't think I'm blaming anyone. It's not your son I'm accusing. Most likely they don't either of them realize what they're doing."

"What did your son say?"

"Nothing. He had something to eat and went to bed."

"He doesn't like his sister?"

"I don't know. They've never got on very well. It was my husband who suddenly went out, without a word, before I had a chance to stop him, and I came running after him along the road. What are you going to do?"

What could he do?

"Do you think they're going to get married?" she asked him. "Lillian's only fifteen and a half. It's not that she's big, but she looks so serious that people think she's older than she is."

She had come to his shop a few times, like all the girls in the district, to buy knick-knacks, a bracelet, a tinsel necklace, a ring, a pin. He did not recall her as red-headed, like all the other Hawkinses, but rather as a brunette. He tried to understand, to see her through Ben's eyes. She was thin, slightly round-shouldered, less developed than the other girls of her age. But perhaps this picture of her dated from some months back and she had changed since? He had thought she had a sulky manner, almost sly.

"I read somewhere," Isabel Hawkins went on, "that there are States in the south where they marry them from the age of twelve. Do you think that's where they've gone and they'll write to us afterwards?"

He did not know. He did not know anything. On that other night, fifteen and a half years ago, he had not lost everything, something had remained for him to cling to, a baby in its cradle which, at six in the morning, cried for its bottle.

This time his distress was so great that he was almost tempted to cling to this woman with her shapeless body, whom he scarcely knew.

"Your daughter never talked to you about her plans?"

"Never. I've an idea that in her heart she was a bit ashamed of her family. We're poor people. Her father isn't always

261

presentable and I can understand that it isn't nice, for a young girl. . . ."

"How did my son behave when he was with you?"

"He was always very nice, very polite. Once when I was trying to repair a shutter which the wind had dismantled, he took the hammer out of my hand and did it very well. Whenever he had a glass of milk, he always washed the glass and put it back in its place. But there's no use our talking about all that to-night. It's time I put Bill to bed and you went to bed, too. I was only wondering if we should tell the police."

"You have the right to do so if you think you should."

"That isn't what I mean. What I was wondering was whether we were obliged to tell them. The way things are, the police couldn't do anything about it anyway, could they?"

He did not reply. He was thinking of the thirty-eight dollars, of Ben who, indeed, did not ordinarily have more than three or four dollars in his pocket and never asked for money. Every week, his father gave him five dollars and Ben slipped them into his pocket with an embarrassed air, saying thank-you.

Dave thought also of the van, which was not in a condition to make a long journey. He had had it over six years and had bought it secondhand. He scarcely used it except when he went to work on other premises. Like his friend at Waterbury, people often asked him to put an antique clock in order. It was he, too, who looked after the Council Office clock, those of the school, the Episcopalian and Methodist churches. The back of the van was arranged as a sort of workshop, equipped with tools like an electric-cable repair truck.

Months ago, he should have changed the tyres. Moreover, after a few miles, the engine began to heat up and, if Ben did not remember to refill the radiator frequently, it would not do a hundred miles without a serious breakdown.

He was suddenly annoyed with himself for not having bought a new van, for having always postponed that expense.

"I hope they won't get themselves arrested on the road," went on Isabel Hawkins, sighing.

She added as she turned towards the stairs:

"Well! Let's hope everything will turn out all right. One can't do just what one would like with children and it isn't for our own sakes that we have them. Get up, Hawkins!"

She was strong enough to be able to lift him by one arm and push him in front of her, gently, without his now bothering to make any resistance. Raising her head, she concluded:

"If I hear any news, I'll let you know. But I'd be surprised if my daughter's the first to write!"

He still heard her, outside, murmuring:

"Look where you're going. Hold on to me. Don't drag your feet like that."

The moon had vanished and it would take them half an hour, perhaps an hour, to get home, stopping every ten yards in the darkness of the road.

Ben was on the road, too, no doubt with Lillian pressed against him, and he would have his eyes fixed on the luminous track of the headlights. These gave a bad light, the left-hand one especially, which sometimes went out for no reason and then started working again, like some radio receivers, after one gave it a few jolts. Would Ben remember this? If the police stopped him to examine his papers, as happens at night, would they consider his driving-licence valid?

It was perhaps deliberately, in order not to think of other things, that he occupied his mind with these minor problems. He was once more alone, in the apartment where only the living-room was lighted, and, like fifteen and a half years previously, it did not occur to him to go to bed, or to light a cigarette; he remained seated in his armchair staring straight in front of him.

Legally, the driving-licence was not valid, at least not in New York State, where the age limit is eighteen years. It was curious that two months ago, in March, Ben should have gone to a little town in Connecticut, thirty miles from Everton, to pass his driving-test. He had not told his father, had simply said that he was going out with a friend who had a car. It was not until a week later, one evening when they were alone in the apartment, that he had pulled his wallet out of his pocket, extracted from it a slip of paper.

"What is it?" Dave had asked.

"Look."

"A driving-licence? You know that just the same you aren't allowed to use the car in New York State?"

"I know."

"Well?"

"Well, nothing. I passed the test for fun."

He was proud of the scrap of printed paper which bore his name and, in his eyes, made a man of him.

"You could answer all the questions?"

"Easily. I'd studied the instruction-book."

"Where did you say you lived?"

"In Waterbury. They don't ask for proof. I'd borrowed a car with Connecticut plates from my friend's uncle."

Ben had known how to drive for at least two years, had been familiar with the car for much longer. At the age of ten, he was capable of putting it into the garage and taking it out and, later, he often practised behind the building.

Dave had returned the licence to him with a smile.

"Mind you don't use it!"

According to Isabel Hawkins, at that time he was already meeting Lillian in the evenings. He went to call on her parents, as a friend of Steve, ate a sandwich with the others, helped himself to milk and washed his glass as though he were one of the household.

The most difficult thing to picture was Ben, who in his own home never did anything with his hands, who had never even learnt to make a bed properly or to clean his shoes, taking the tools and offering to repair Mrs. Hawkins' shutter.

Dave suddenly realized that he was jealous and that, just now, when the woman had told him her story, it was jealousy that had pumped the blood into his face.

He had never entered the Hawkins' home. He had seen the house in passing, a big, ramshackle, wooden shanty which had not been repainted for years, with garbage scattered over a patch of waste land and always, round the porch, children and puppies squealing. For fear of running over one or the other, since they rushed out on to the road when one least expected it, he was always careful to sound his horn.

The twins, with coppery red hair, were the boys who were always riding bicycles along the village sidewalks without holding the handle-bars, uttering Red Indian cries.

For at least two months, perhaps for three, Ben had seen these people every day and no doubt he had ended by considering himself to some extent one of the family.

In his talks with his father, he had divulged none of this. At no moment had he felt any need to confide in him. Young as he was, he already took care not to reveal himself. Dave recalled the first time he had taken him to nursery-school, when he was only four years old. He had not cried, had simply given his father a long, reproachful look as the latter went away. When he came to fetch him home, Dave had asked anxiously:

"How did you like it?"

Imperturbably, without smiling, the child had answered:

"All right."

"Is the teacher nice?"

"I think so."

"And the other children?"

"Yes."

"What did you do?"

"Play."

"Nothing else?"

"No."

Day after day, during the following months, Dave had asked similar questions and the answers had always been the same.

"You like it at school?"

"Yes."

"Do you have more fun than at home?"

"I don't know."

Long afterwards, by means of questions and deduction, Dave had discovered that there was a bigger and stronger boy in the class who had made Ben his especial victim.

"Does he hit you?"

"Sometimes."

"What with?"

"With his fists, with anything, or he pushes me to make me fall in the mud."

"You don't defend yourself?"

"I'll beat him when I'm as big as he is."

"The teacher lets him do it?"

"She doesn't see."

His legs were short, in those days, and his head seemed too big for his body. His father often caught him, when he thought he wasn't being watched, gravely murmuring sentences under his breath.

"What are you saying, Ben?"

"Nothing."

"Who are you talking to?"

"To me."

"And what are you telling yourself?"

"Stories."

He did not say what stories. It was his secret domain. For a long time, Dave had wondered what answers he would give the child when he asked him questions about his mother. It was repugnant to him, from a feeling akin to superstition, to pretend that she was dead. How explain to him that she had gone away and that he would probably never see her?

But at no age had Ben put the question. He was nearly seven

when they had been able to leave Waterbury. Had his little schoolfellows, having heard their parents talk about it, told him the truth?

If so, he had betrayed no sign of the fact. He was not a morose boy. He was not repressed either. Like all children, he had explosions of noisy gaiety.

"You're happy, Ben?" his father often asked him, trying to speak lightly.

"Yes."

"You're sure you're happy?"

"Sure."

"You wouldn't want to change places with any other boy?"

"No."

It was an indirect way of knowing. Once, when Ben was thirteen and they were walking together in the country, Dave had murmured:

"You know I'm your friend, Ben?"

"I know."

"I'd like you always to think of me as your friend, never to be afraid to tell me everything."

Galloway had not dared to say more, because he had a feeling that the boy was embarrassed. Ben had always been very shy of his feelings.

"If, someday, you want to ask me questions, ask them and I promise to answer absolutely frankly."

"What questions?"

"I don't know. Sometimes one wonders why people do this or that, why they live in one way or another."

"I haven't any questions."

And he started to throw stones into a pond.

It was seven in the morning when the telephone rang in the shop, setting up a vibration which could be felt through the floor. Dave instantly recollected himself, wondered if he would have time to go downstairs, walk round the building and enter the shop before the switchboard-operator gave up.

This had sometimes happened. If it was Ben, he knew and would call again in a few minutes.

At the corner of the alleyway Dave could still hear it ringing, but by the time he had opened the door it had stopped.

The sun had the same kind of brilliance as the moon during the night. The streets were empty. Birds were hopping on the lawn in front of the cinema.

His limbs stiff, he stayed there waiting, his eyes fixed on the

266

telephone, while the open door let in the fresh morning air.

One or two cars passed, people from New York or its suburbs on their way into the country. He felt mechanically in his pockets for cigarettes. He must have left them upstairs.

They didn't ring back. He had not really believed that it was Ben who had called, he could not have explained why.

A half-hour went by. Then another quarter of an hour. He wanted a cigarette, a cup of coffee, but he dared not go upstairs in case he should miss another call.

Ben, who often wanted to ring up his friends in the evening, had asked him to have a telephone installed in the apartment. Why had he always put off this expense?

It must have been very late when he had fallen asleep. His slumber had been both heavy and disturbed, so that now he felt more tired than he had done the previous evening.

He nearly rang up Musak. To say what to him? To tell him what had happened? They had never talked together about their personal affairs. Dave had never talked about them to anyone.

He stood with his elbows on the counter, his eyelids smarting, and he was still in that posture when a car drove along Main Street at high speed, turned the corner and pulled up right in front of the shop.

Two men in the uniform of the State Police got out, both of whom had faces that were fresh and rested, close-shaven. They raised their heads to look at the name over the window and one of them consulted a notebook he had pulled out of his pocket.

Without waiting, Galloway went to meet them, well knowing that it was himself they sought.

CHAPTER THREE

STANDING in the doorway, blinking because of the morning sunlight which hit him full in the face, he half-parted his lips to ask:

"Has my son had an accident?"

He could not have said what stopped him, whether it was his intuition or something in the attitude of the two men. They seemed surprised to find him there, exchanged glances as though questioning one another. Were they astonished at his unshaven face and his clothes creased by the hours he had spent in his armchair?

There was a State Police station at Radley, almost opposite the High School, and Galloway knew, at least by sight, the six men attached to it, two of whom were in the habit of stopping their car outside his shop when the clock wanted repairing.

These two were not from Radley. They must have come from Poughkeepsie or further off.

He would probably have ended by asking his question none-theless, if only for the sake of form, if the shorter of the two had not said:

"Your name is Dave Clifford Galloway?"

"It is."

After consulting his notebook, the police officer went on:

"You are the owner of a Ford van, number 3M-2437?"

He nodded. Now, he was on the defensive. His instinct warned him that he must protect Ben. He said in a casual voice, as though he did not think it important:

"Has there been a smash?"

They looked queerly at one another before one of them answered:

"No. No smash."

He must not talk any more. From now on he would simply answer questions. When they tried to see into the shop over his shoulder, he stepped back to let them enter.

"Were you at work, at eight o'clock on a Sunday morning?"

It was no doubt intended to be ironical, since the display-window was empty and the watches under repair were not hanging on their hooks about the bench.

"I wasn't working. I live on the floor above. About half an hour ago, I heard the telephone ringing through the floor. I came down. I had to walk round the building and, when I got here, the caller had hung up. I stayed, thinking they might call again."

"It was we who called up."

From their disconcerted aspect, Dave could have sworn they had expected something else. They were not threatening. Embarrassed, rather.

"Did you drive your van last night?"

"No."

"It's in your garage?"

"It isn't there any more. It disappeared last night."

"When did you find out?"

"Between half-past eleven and midnight, when I came back from the house of a friend where I'd spent the evening."

"Can you give me his name?"

"Frank Musak. He lives in the first street on the right after the Post Office."

The one with the notebook wrote down the name and address.

Galloway did not lose his calm. He was not afraid. The fact of being questioned in this fashion by police officers in uniform nevertheless gave him the feeling of being no longer a citizen quite like others. People occasionally went by outside, in particular young girls, children in Sunday clothes, who were on their way to the Catholic church and cast a curious glance at the open shop and the two policemen.

"You found that your van was no longer in the garage when you got home?"

"That's right."

"You didn't go out again during the night?"

"No."

He was not lying, but he was deceiving them nonetheless and he was afraid he would start blushing. Once again, they exchanged glances, withdrew to a corner of the shop where they talked in undertones; Galloway, mechanically, had gone behind his counter, as when he was receiving a customer, and he did not try to hear what they were saying.

"Will you allow me to use your telephone? Don't worry: we'll have the call charged to us."

The man called the operator.

"Hullo? State Police. Will you give me the Hortonville station? . . . yes . . . thank you."

The weather was brilliant. The bells began to ring in full strength and the lawn opposite, over which the trees cast long blue shadows, was dotted with yellow flowers.

"That you, Fred? Dan here. Put me through to the lieutenant, will you?"

He had only an instant to wait. He talked in an undertone, almost a whisper, his hand to his mouth.

"We've arrived, lieutenant. He's here. . . . Hullo! . . . Yes. . . . We found him in his shop. . . . No. . . . Apparently he wasn't doing anything. . . . He lives on the first floor and heard the phone ring. . . . It's a little hard to explain. . . . The way the place is arranged, he has to leave his apartment and walk round the building, which is fairly long . . . yes. . . . Yes. . . . It seems the van disappeared from the garage last night before half-past eleven. . . ."

The voice of the lieutenant sounded, causing the diaphragm to vibrate, but one could not hear what he was saying. The policeman, with the receiver in his hand, still seemed rather perplexed.

"Yes. . . . Yes. . . . Obviously. . . . There's something strange. . . ."

During this time he continued to scrutinize Galloway with a curiosity free from hostility.

"Maybe that would be better, yes. . . . In about an hour. . . . A bit more. . . ."

He hung up, lit a cigarette.

"The lieutenant would like you to come with me to formally identify your van."

"Can I go upstairs and shut the doors?"

"If you want to."

Dave slipped the spring-lock and they both followed him to the other side of the building. One of the officers at once noticed the fresh scratch on the garage door.

"Is this yours?"

"Yes."

He pulled open a wing of the door to look inside, where there was nothing but a black oil-stain on the concrete floor where the van should have been.

Dave started up the stairs and the shorter of the two policemen followed him, as though, again with a sign, they had concerted their actions.

"I suppose I haven't time to make myself a cup of coffee?"

"It'll be quicker for us to stop at a restaurant on the way."

The man was gazing about him, still surprised, rather like someone who fears he has come to the wrong door. While Dave was combing his hair and splashing cold water on his face, he looked inside the two bedrooms.

"You don't seem to have been to bed!" he remarked.

Then, as Galloway sought for a reply, he hurried to add:

"It's not my business. You've no need to tell me anything."

A little later, in the same detached voice, he questioned again —and it was more a remark than a question:

"You aren't married?"

Dave wondered what there was about the apartment which caused him to think this. He had always tried, for Ben's sake, to prevent their home seeming like the habitation of men alone. At Musak's place, for example, this had always struck him. No one could mistake it. The very odour revealed that there was no woman in the house.

"I used to be married," he contented himself with replying.

He was behaving like certain sick people who are so afraid of unleashing a crisis that they live in slow-motion, with careful movements, only speaking in a lifeless voice.

In his heart, he had not been surprised at seeing the police officers. Neither had he seriously believed that Ben had had an accident. Besides, if it had been an accident, they would have told him at once. Since he had returned last night to the empty apartment, he had known that it was more serious and he was hunching his shoulders to make himself less vulnerable to fate.

No matter what had happened, he had to protect his son. Never had he felt so sharply, so carnally, the bond that existed between them. It was not a separate person who was in trouble somewhere, God knew where—it was a part of himself.

He was bearing himself like an honest man, respectful of the laws, a little apprehensive, but having nothing with which to reproach himself.

"I suppose it doesn't matter that I haven't shaved?"

He was red-headed, not the red of the Hawkins family, a vivid red. His very fine hair was beginning to grow thin and the sun drew glints of gold from his cheeks. Why did he go into the kitchen to make sure that the electric cooker was not switched on? From force of habit! He locked his door, downstairs rejoined the second police officer to whom his colleague went and spoke a few words.

"Are you coming?"

He had been going to get into the back of the car, but they signed to him to sit in front and, to his astonishment, only the shorter of the two men got in and took his place at the wheel, while the other remained standing on the sidewalk and watched them go.

"It's always on a Sunday morning that we run into cases of this sort," said his companion in the tone in which he might have chatted to someone in a bar. "On Saturday night, people can't stay quiet!"

It was truly Sunday all along the road. In every village, one saw white churches with open doorways, women wearing white gloves and, in one place, little girls walking in line, each with a bouquet in her hand.

"Don't forget my cup of coffee," Dave permitted himself to say with a forced smile.

"We'll come to a good place just past Poughkeepsie."

They went through the town without stopping, crossed the bridge over the Hudson which sparkled in the sunlight and where at that moment an excursion steamer was passing. . . .

The car entered the first ramparts of the Catskills and the road, twisting, rose and fell, plunged into dark, cool forest, ran alongside a lake, sometimes passed farms and meadows on a plain. In front of a drive-in standing at the edge of the highway, festooned with posters advertising brands of soft drinks, the police officer pulled up, called to a girl in slacks who came towards them:

"Two coffees."

"Black?"

"Black for me," said Dave. "With two lumps of sugar."

"Same for me."

For most people it was a wonderful Sunday. Further on, they crossed a golf-course over which little groups were scattered, their golf-bags slung over their shoulders. Nearly all the men were wearing white caps, and a good many of the women were already in shorts, with sun-glasses.

Judging by the phone-call and the phrases Dave had overheard, it was to Hortonville that he was being taken. He had been there before. It was a village situated on the border between New York State and Pennsylvania. He seemed to remember a police-station built of brick, with no upper storey, at the edge of the highway. From Everton to Hortonville it was sixty miles, and they took only a little more than an hour and a quarter to cover it.

He was compelling himself to keep silent, to ask no questions, and his hands were damp with the effort, there was sweat on his upper lip.

"You don't smoke?"

"I left my cigarettes behind."

The policeman offered him his pack, pointed to the electric lighter. They had just passed through a little town still asleep, Liberty probably, then they had seen a lake of considerable size on which numerous vessels appeared motionless. They again entered a forest and Dave suddenly almost stopped his companion, started to lay a hand on his arm.

He had thought he recognized his chestnut-coloured van at the side of the road, its right-hand wheels in the grass, and he had had time to make out in the shadow the figure of a policeman.

The movement had not escaped his companion.

272

"That's yours . . . ?" he asked as though it were of no importance.

"I think. . . . Yes. . . ."

"We have to see the lieutenant first, about two miles from here, and we'll probably come back afterwards."

The bricks of the police station were of tender pink and there was a flower-bed on either side of the door. In contrast with the light outside, the interior seemed dark and Galloway felt almost cold, perhaps partly owing to his nervous tension. He even felt, when they left him alone in the passage, a genuine shudder.

"Will you come this way?"

The lieutenant was young, athletic. Dave was surprised when he held out a vigorous hand to him.

"I'm sorry to have caused you this inconvenience, Mr. Galloway, but it was difficult for me to do otherwise."

What had the lieutenant told the police officer who had brought him, with whom he had had a fairly long talk? The latter was not looking at him now in quite the same way. Dave had the impression that there was a great deal more sympathy in his gaze, indeed a sort of respect.

"You noticed your van on the way here?"

"I thought I recognized it."

"We'd better start with that. It'll only take us a few minutes."

He got down his cap with its badge of rank, put it on, and went out to the car, signing to the other man to come with them.

"It seems you didn't have much luck at backgammon last night?"

They had questioned Musak. They were not attempting to hide the fact. It was as though this were a means of proving that they were dealing with him openly.

"You mustn't be angry with us, Mr. Galloway. You should know that it's our job to check up on everything."

They were already coming within sight of the van and Dave's first glance was at the tyres, of which not one was flat; the palms of his hands now were really wet and, as he got out of the car, he wondered for an instant if he was going to be capable of walking.

"You recognize the bus?"

"Certainly."

"Those are watchmaker's tools you have in the back?"

"Yes."

"For a moment I was puzzled, because I couldn't figure out what trade they belonged to. Do you want to have a look inside?"

273

They opened the door for him and what he instinctively looked at first was the place where Ben had sat. He passed his hand over it furtively, as though the leather had been able to retain a little of his son's warmth. The white, crumpled object, near the clutch-pedal, was a woman's handkerchief smelling of *eau de Cologne*.

"One of our patrols found the van around two in the morning, but it must have been here some time, because the engine was cold. The headlights had been switched off."

Galloway could not prevent himself from asking:

"Does it go?"

"That's just what intrigued my men. The engine works. So it wasn't a question of a breakdown."

He called to the man in charge.

"You can drive it to Poughkeepsie," he said.

Dave was on the verge of protesting, of asking why his van wasn't given back to him.

"You coming, Mr. Galloway?"

He was silent while he drove and did not speak a word until they were in his office where the officer who had come to Everton followed them.

"Shut the door, Dan."

The lieutenant's manner was grave, embarrassed.

"Cigarette?"

"No, thanks. I didn't have time for any breakfast and. . . ."

"I know. You didn't sleep much last night. You didn't even go to bed."

Was Galloway really doing his utmost? Was he doing everything in his power to protect Ben? His fear was that he might not be equal to the occasion. He was not used to trickery.

It seemed to him that the lieutenant read his thoughts on his face. Why did he show him so much consideration when he was only a small village watchmaker of no importance?

The other man suddenly decided to sit down and ran his hand through his hair, which was stiff, cut short.

"Since you left Everton, Mr. Galloway, we've had news from various sources and it's my duty to tell you about it. We've heard, for instance, that the Hawkinses paid you a visit during the night."

He did not start, did not blink, but it was as though his heart had ceased to beat because, now, they must inevitably come to the subject of Ben.

"One of the Hawkins boys, passing on his bicycle this morning,

274

saw men in uniform in your shop and rushed home to tell his mother. She hurried there at once, hoping they'd be able to give her news of her daughter."

The lieutenant's hands must have been damp as well, because he got his handkerchief out of his pocket and fiddled with it.

"Do you know your son well, Mr. Galloway?"

They had reached it. Dave had hoped that this moment would never come, had tried to hope against all possibility, against all reason. His eyes began to burn, his adam's-apple rose and fell and the lieutenant turned away his head, out of delicacy, as though to allow him to express his feelings freely.

Was it Dave's voice that answered:

"I think I know him, yes."

"Your son didn't come home last night. The Hawkins girl. . . ."

He glanced at his notes, corrected:

". . . Lillian Hawkins left her parents' house during the evening taking her belongings with her."

He allowed nearly half a minute to pass.

"You knew they had gone off together in your van?"

Why deny it? It was he, and not Ben, who was being accused.

"It's what I supposed after the Hawkinses had been."

"It didn't occur to you to notify the police?"

He said frankly:

"No."

"You've never felt any anxiety regarding your son?"

Meeting the lieutenant's eyes, he answered firmly:

"No."

It was not altogether true, but his anxieties had never been of the kind to which the lieutenant was referring. Even an ordinary father could not understand.

"He has never given you any trouble?"

"No. He's a quiet boy, rather studious."

"I've already been told that, last year, he was one of the three best pupils in his class."

"That's true."

"This year, his markings have changed. . . ."

He was about to explain that children are not the same every year, that they grow interested first in one thing, then in another, that in a few years they have to complete a whole cycle. It was the compassion he read in the lieutenant's eyes which prevented him from speaking, and then, very low, his chin on his chest, as though he had given up the contest, he stammered:

"What has he done?"

275

"Would you like to read the report for yourself?"

He pushed several large-sized sheets of paper across the desk. Dave shook his head. He would have been incapable of reading.

"One mile from here, in the direction of Pennsylvania, but still in New York State, a motorist this morning saw a human form lying at the side of the road. It was half-past five and only just beginning to get light. At first the man drove on, then, conscience-stricken, thinking it might be someone who was injured, he turned back."

The lieutenant was speaking slowly, in a monotonous voice, as one does when reading a report, but he only gave an occasional glance at the papers which he had again pulled towards him.

"A few minutes later, this man came in here to report that he had found a dead body. I'd just gone on duty at Poughkeepsie when I was notified and I arrived on the spot only a short time after the police officers from the station."

Was Dave listening? He could have sworn that the words were no longer words, but pictures passing in front of his eyes like a coloured film. He could not have repeated a single one of the phrases uttered and yet he had the impression of having followed in their comings and goings each one of the persons evoked.

While all this was going on, he had been asleep himself, in his green armchair, facing the window beyond which the sun was rising and the birds were beginning to hop about the lawn.

"From the papers we found in the dead man's pockets, we have established that he was a certain Charles Ralston, of Long Eddy, about twelve miles from here. I called up his home, where his wife told me that yesterday evening her husband went to dine with their daughter, who's married and lives in the suburbs of Poughkeepsie. His wife has not been well for some weeks, so she couldn't go with him and went to bed early. When she woke up in the middle of the night and found her husband wasn't beside her, she didn't worry, thinking he had decided to stop the night at their daughter's house, which was a thing he sometimes did, particularly when he had had a drop too much. Charles Ralston was the regional representative of a well-known brand of refrigerator and was aged fifty-four."

He made a pause, let fall:

"He had been killed by a bullet in the nape of the neck, fired at point-blank range, probably when he was seated at the wheel of his car. Then he was dragged to the side of the road, as the surface indications show, and his wallet was searched, the money it contained was taken. According to his

276

wife, he probably had twelve or fourteen dollars on him."

There was a heavy silence, such as prevails sometimes in a court of law when the judgment is read. The first to make any movement was Galloway, and it was to uncross his legs which were hurting him.

"I can go on?" asked the lieutenant.

He nodded. It was better to get it over.

"The bullet, a 38-calibre, was fired from an automatic. When he left his daughter and son-in-law, Ralston was driving an Oldsmobile sedan, painted blue, with New York State number-plates."

He glanced at his wrist watch.

"It is three hours, now, since the description of this car was sent out by radio in all directions, especially to Pennsylvania, where the car seemed to be heading. A short time before your arrival, the police at Gagleton called up to tell me that, last night, about two o'clock, the occupants of a car answering to that description had stopped at a filling-station, right out in the country, and had got the owner out of bed to fill their tank."

Dave's mouth was dry, burning, and he was unable to swallow; his adam's-apple, stuck, gave him a sense of strangulation.

"The blue Oldsmobile was driven by a young man of medium height, light-complexioned, wearing a fawn-coloured raincoat. A very young girl, who was inside the car, pulled down the window to ask for cigarettes. So as not to have to open up the office where there was an automatic machine, the garage-proprietor gave her his own partly used pack. The young man paid with a ten-dollar bill of which we shall soon have the number."

That was all. What more could one say? The lieutenant waited, without looking at Galloway, finally got up and signed to the policeman to follow him outside. Dave did not move, took no account of the time that passed and, twice, caught himself dreaming that he was taking a little boy to school. They were merely pictures that passed very quickly over his mind's eye. He was not thinking. The telephone rang and he paid no attention. He could, if he had listened, have heard what was being said over the instrument installed in the other office.

He had not wept. It was certain, now, that he would not weep, that he had passed the point of tears.

When, much later, he raised his eyes, he was surprised to find himself alone; it troubled him and he nearly called out, not daring, of his own accord, to leave the room.

Perhaps they were keeping an eye on him, had heard him move? The lieutenant, in any event, appeared in the doorway.

"I guess you'd like to go home?"

He nodded, astonished that they did not keep him prisoner. He would not have protested. It would have seemed to him natural.

"I have to ask you to sign this statement. You can read it. It's simply a declaration by which you formally identify your van."

Didn't this constitute a betrayal of Ben?

"Do I really have to sign?"

The other lowered his eyelids and he signed submissively.

"I may tell you, between ourselves, that they've gone a long distance since last night and that they're already out of Pennsylvania. The last place where they were reported is in Jefferson County, Virginia."

Wouldn't Ben, who'd been driving like this since last night, have to stop and get some sleep?

"They aren't travelling on the highways, they're turning off along lanes and secondary roads, which makes it more difficult to catch up with them."

Galloway was standing and the lieutenant laid a hand on his shoulder.

"If I were in your place—and I'm speaking as a man, not as a police officer—I'd make sure, right away, of getting a good lawyer for your son. He has the right, as you know, not to say anything except in his presence, and that sometimes makes all the difference."

"*He*" meant Ben, incredible though it seemed, Ben of whom they were suddenly talking as though of a grown man responsible for his actions. He nearly protested, so monstrous did this seem to him. He was tempted to cry:

"But he's only a child!"

He had given him his bottle. At four years old, Ben had still wetted his bed and, in the morning, was all upset about it. It had mortified him for more than a year.

How many weeks had passed since the last time his father had asked him:

"Happy, Ben?"

He had answered without hesitating, in his voice which, during the past two years only, had grown curiously grave:

"Yes, Dad."

He did not use high-flown phrases. He did not easily unbosom

278

himself. But surely Dave, who had spent sixteen years of his life watching him, must know him better than anyone?

"You'll drive Mr. Galloway home?"

"Shall I bring Dan back?"

"No. He's had instructions by telephone."

A broad, muscular hand was again held out, used a little more pressure than the first time.

"Good-bye, Mr. Galloway. If this case doesn't pass out of my responsibility, as it may do, I'll keep you informed."

He added after glancing at his desk:

"I have your phone number . . . ? Yes. . . ."

Dave had to close his eyes entirely, so dazzling did he find the sunshine, and the air trembled about him, flies buzzed among the flowers in the beds. He found himself seated again in the car where a voice was saying:

"Perhaps I'd better open all the windows."

An arm stretched in front of him to turn the handle and he started.

"Sorry! Come to think of it, you'd have been glad of another cup of coffee, wouldn't you? There was some at the station and I didn't think of offering you any."

He answered mechanically:

"It doesn't matter."

"The lieutenant's a nice man. He has three children. The youngest was born exactly a week ago, when he was on duty like to-day."

The policeman reached out, turned a knob, and, after a sound of crackling, they began to hear a nasal voice repeating a figure, the registration number of a car. It was only when his companion hastily switched off, as though without thinking he had been guilty of tactlessness, that Galloway realized that it was the blue Oldsmobile.

The man in uniform made two or three further attempts at conversation, observing the watchmaker from the corner of his eye, and finally resigned himself to silence. The same woods, the same golf-course, the same villages swept past, with more cars on the road and parked outside the roadhouses. Ben had passed that way a few hours earlier, with Lillian clinging to him. Would it serve any purpose, at this moment, if Dave cried with all his strength, as though a human voice could be heard across all the States of America, as though distance did not exist:

"Ben!"

He so longed to do so that he clenched his teeth and drove his finger-nails into the flesh of his hands. He did not even recognize Poughkeepsie, did not notice when they passed through a town and its suburbs.

And when the car passed the signboard announcing the approach to his own village, he had no sense of returning home, looked at the Old Barn, the First National Store, finally the lawn, the shops, his own shop, that of Mrs. Pinch, that of the hairdresser, as though it were all no more than the empty shell of what had once been his village.

He did not know what time it was. He had lost all sense of time. Time had ceased to exist, like space. How could he believe, for instance, that Ben was now driving over the roads of Virginia, perhaps even over those of Ohio or Kentucky?

Dave had never been as far as Kentucky and Ben was only a child. Dozens, hundreds of men in the prime of life, trained for that kind of hunt, with perfected appliances, were nevertheless in pursuit of him or trying to track him down.

It was not possible. Nor that in the evening and to-morrow all the newspapers in America would publish his photograph on the front page as that of a dangerous criminal.

"Shall I drop you behind the building?"

There was never anyone on the sidewalks, on Sundays, during the middle of the day. Directly after church service, the streets emptied, became more echoing, and life did not return to them until later for the baseball game.

The policeman went round to the other side of the car to open the door for him and it was Galloway who held out his hand and said politely:

"Thank you very much."

A strip of adhesive tape, with a wax seal at either end, barred the door of the garage, and sticky paper had been put over the split to protect it. He went upstairs without meeting anyone and he seemed still to see old Hawkins huddled on the third step, talking to himself and wagging his head.

Perhaps at that moment everything had been done. It was almost certain. He did not want to think about it too precisely. And, on the landing, Isabel Hawkins had been talking to him about her daughter and the thirty-eight dollars that had disappeared from the box in the kitchen.

He heard footsteps behind the door of the old Polish lady who went about all day in slippers because of her swollen legs. They always made a furtive sound, a curious slithering, like that of an invisible animal in the forest.

He opened his door and it was the time when the sun lighted a third of the living-room, including a corner of the green sofa. Ben had a habit of stretching out on it, in the evenings, and holding a book above his face.

"You find that position comfortable?"

He'd answer:

"I'm all right."

Galloway did not know what to do with himself. He had not taken off his hat. He no longer thought of making himself coffee, or of eating. He was waiting, at any moment, for the burst of shouting which would indicate the beginning of the baseball game. Through the bathroom ventilator, if you stood on a stool, you could see part of the ground.

What had he come to do in the kitchen? Nothing. He had nothing to do there. He went back into the living-room, saw his cigarettes on the radio, didn't touch them. He had no desire to smoke. His knees were trembling agonizingly, but he did not sit down.

The window was closed. It was hot. When he started to sponge his face he found that he still had his hat on and he took it off.

Then, suddenly, as though this were what he had come to the apartment to do, he went into Ben's room and stretched himself out at full length, face down, on his son's bed, his two hands gripping the pillow, and moved no more.

CHAPTER FOUR

At the beginning, he did not do it deliberately, was aware of nothing. If he stayed motionless, it was from lassitude, because he hadn't the strength to move, nor any reason for doing so. Little by little, a heaviness somewhat resembling that of fever took possession of his limbs, of his whole body, and it seemed to him that his mind, in yielding to it, acquired a more intense life, but on a different plane. It was rather as though—he would not have said it to anyone, for fear of being laughed at—he gained access to a higher reality, where all things took on a sharper significance.

This had often happened to him when he was a child. He remembered one time in particular, when he was five years old, in Virginia. It had perhaps lasted an hour, perhaps only a few minutes, because it was a state like that of dreams, which give the impression of lasting a long time, precisely because time is abolished. It was in any case his most vivid memory, sufficing in itself to sum up all his childhood.

He had been lying down then too, not on his stomach, that time, as he was at present on Ben's bed, but in the open air, on his back, his hands clasped behind his head, and, with his face turned to the sun, he had kept his eyes closed while red and golden gleams pierced his eyelids.

At that period, he was losing his first teeth and, in a half-wakeful state, he worried with the tip of his tongue a tooth that was loose. It didn't hurt. On the contrary he derived from it a sensation so exquisite, spreading in waves, like a fluid, through his being, that he couldn't believe it was not a sin and afterwards was always ashamed of it.

Never, since then, had he so acutely felt the mingling of his own life and that of the universe, his heart beating with the same rhythm as the earth, as the grass which surrounded him, as the leaves of the trees which rustled above his head. His pulse became the pulse of the world and he was conscious of every-thing, of the movements of the grasshoppers, of the coolness of the earth which he felt against his back and of the rays of the sun which were scorching his skin; sounds as well, ordinarily confused, detached themselves from one another with a mar-vellous clarity, the clucking of the hens in the yard, the drone of the tractor on the hillside, the voices on the porch, that of his father above all, who, while he drank his glass of bourbon in little sips, was giving instructions to the coloured overseer.

He couldn't see him then, and yet he was sure that the picture he retained of him was as he was on that day, in the violet shadow, with his russet moustache which he wiped with his forefinger after each sip.

The syllables came to him very distinctly and he had not tried to grasp their sense, because what the words meant was of no importance, what mattered was that his father's voice rose, calm and reassuring, with the other sounds of the earth to lend it a sort of accompaniment.

Sometimes, the coloured man punctuated a sentence with a—

"Yes, sir."

And his voice too was different from those he had heard since, coming from the depths of his chest, heavy and pulpy as the flesh of a ripe fruit.

"Yes, sir."

The southern accent greatly prolonged the "sir," from which

the final "r" disappeared, and it became an incantation.

It was in the house where his father had been born. The earth was dark red, the trees of a greener green than anywhere else, and the summer sun had the colour and consistency of honey.

Was it not on that occasion that he had vowed to himself to be like his father? When his mother, with the van, drove him to school in the neighbouring small town and someone exclaimed that he took after her, he spent the next few days looking in the glass and feeling unhappy.

In the town too, the dust was red, the wooden houses painted the same syrupy yellow as Musak's house. Perhaps Musak had lived in Virginia?

Everton was arousing itself from its midday torpor, he knew it. He knew where he was, forgot nothing. But he was capable, without becoming confused, of mingling past and present, of making them one whole, because, finally, they were probably nothing but one whole.

Someone spoke down below, a woman's voice:

"Do you think he's at home?"

When the husband replied, he recognized his voice. It was the Post Office clerk, the man who headed the Fourth of July procession carrying the flag. He murmured, no doubt tugging his wife's arm:

"It seems they brought him back a little while ago. Come on."

Although they spoke in an undertone, he heard everything.

"Poor man!"

They were on their way to the baseball field. Other people passed by. Footsteps scuffled over the dusty stones of the sidewalks, growing more and more numerous. Not everyone stopped, but each one probably raised his head to glance at his windows.

They knew. Through the radio, of course. Early that morning, the call had been sent out on the ultra-short police wave-length, then they had decided to make the news known to the public in the ordinary midday news-bulletin.

He had a small radio near him, on the night-table, he had no need to look to know that it was there. It was Ben's radio, which he had given him for his twelfth birthday, during the period when he listened every evening, his gaze intent, to the cowboy programme.

Was it not strange that Ben, at this moment, might be in that same Virginia, of which Dave had so often talked to him but where he had never before set foot?

283

"Is the soil really red?" he had still been asking only a few years ago, incredulously.

"Not red like blood. But it's red. I don't know any other word."

Had they been able to stop for a bite to eat at a "drive-in" or to buy sandwiches at some place along the road?

Someone passing, an urchin probably, gave two or three little knocks on his shop-window. Then, like a theatre orchestra, cries burst out on the sports-ground, there were blasts of the whistle, the usual Sunday tumult, with the spectators getting up on the benches and waving their arms.

One day, not very long after that midday in the grass and the sunshine, it wasn't his mother who came to fetch him from school, but one of the coloured men on the farm and, when he got home, Dave hadn't seen his parents, but had found the maidservants in tears gazing compassionately at him.

He had never seen his father again. He had died, about one o'clock, alone in the waiting-room of a bank in Culpeper where he had gone to try to obtain a new loan. His mother had been told by telephone and the body had been taken straight to the undertaker's.

His father had been forty. It was then that the conviction had been implanted in him that, since he resembled him, he too would die at forty. The idea had gained so strong a hold that even now, at the age of forty-three, he was sometimes astonished to find himself alive.

Had Ben, too, ever imagined that he resembled him? that their lives would follow a similar pattern? He had never dared to ask him. He hesitated to put direct questions to him, observed him covertly, tried to guess.

Had his own father had these curiosities, these fears where he was concerned? Was it the same with all fathers and all sons? Very often, he had behaved in a particular way only because of the memory of his father and, when he was seventeen, he had let his moustache grow for several months in order to be more like him.

Perhaps, if he had retained so heightened a memory of him, this was connected with the fact that his mother had remarried two years later? He was not sure. The thought often occurred to him, precisely because of Ben, when he had feelings of uneasiness on his account.

Scarcely two weeks after the funeral, they had sold the farm in Virginia and had gone to live in a town of which the memory was hateful to him, Newark, in New Jersey. He had never known why his mother had chosen that particular town.

"We were ruined," she had told him, later, without convincing him. "I had to earn my living and I couldn't go out to work in a place where everyone knows my family."

She was a Truesdell and one of her ancestors had played a part in the Confederation. But the family of Galloway, which had included a governor and an historian, was no less well-known.

At Newark, they had no servants, lived on the third floor of a house of dark brick, with an iron outside-staircase, in case of fire, which passed in front of their window and stopped on the level of the first floor.

His mother worked in an office. Often she went out in the evenings and a young girl whom she paid for the service came to look after Dave.

"If you're good, we'll soon go and live in the country again, in a big house."

"In Virginia?"

"No. Not far from New York."

She meant White Plains where, sure enough, they went to live when she married Musselman.

If he switched on the radio, would he hear something about Ben? Two or three times he had been tempted to do so, but had not had the courage to wrench himself out of his stupor, to return suddenly to naked reality. And, if he made the slightest movement, he knew that this would happen, that he would get up, begin to walk about, go and open the window, because it was beginning to grow warm in the apartment. No doubt he would even eat something. He felt gnawing pains in his breast.

Later, there would be time. So long as he was in his present state, like the little boy in Virginia, it seemed to him that he was closer to Ben.

Perhaps his son had no desire to be like him? Once when he had been playing with other children on the sidewalk, outside the shop, he had heard one of them, the garage-keeper's son, proclaim:

"My father's stronger than yours. He could knock him down with one punch."

It was true. The garage-keeper was a colossus and Dave had never gone in for sport. He had remained in suspense, waiting for Ben's reaction, and Ben had said nothing.

285

This had hurt him. It was ridiculous. It hadn't meant a thing. Nevertheless he had felt a twinge at his heart and, after seven years, still remembered it.

What troubled him most of all was when his son, thinking himself unobserved, silently regarded him. At those moments, his face was grave, thoughtful. He seemed very far away. Was he making a picture of him such as Dave had made of his own father?

He would have liked to know that picture, to ask: "You aren't too ashamed of me?"

Those words had often trembled on his lips and it was then that he would say, approaching the matter indirectly:

"Are you happy?"

His mother had never put that question to him. Would he have had the courage, if she had done so, to answer: "No!"?

Because he had not been. The mere sight of Musselman, who was a quite important man in the insurance business and felt the need to prove it to himself all day long, was enough to make the house at White Plain intolerable to him. It was because of Musselman, because of his mother, that when he left High School he had gone to a school of watchmaking, in order to be able to earn his living straightaway and not live with them any more. . . .

Last night, Ben had gone away, he too. In the room, a cupboard, big as a closet, was still packed with his toys: clockwork cars, tractors, a farm and its animals, cowboy belts and hats, spurs and pistols. There were at least twenty pistols of all kinds, all broken.

Ben never threw anything away. It was he who hoarded his old toys in the cupboard and, one day, not long ago, his father had caught him solemnly trying to play a tune on a ten-cent whistle which dated from his ninth or tenth year.

A loud-speaker, out there, on the sports-ground, was giving a running commentary on the game, and the people on the benches must be talking about him. Had Musak listened to the radio? Or perhaps someone had come and told him the news? Just the same, he would be sitting on his porch, smoking his patched-up pipe which whistled when he sucked.

A car pulled up in front of the shop, two people got out, two men, to judge by their footsteps, who went to the window and looked inside.

"Isn't there a bell?" one of them asked.

286

"I don't see one."

There was a knock on the glass pane of the door. Dave did not move. Then one of the men stepped back into the middle of the street to look at the first-floor windows.

The old Polish woman must have been leaning out of her own, because they shouted to her from below:

"Mr. Galloway, if you please?"

"The next window."

"Is he home?"

Half in English, half in her own language, she tried to explain to them that you had to go round the building, enter by the small door between the garages and go upstairs. They apparently understood, because finally they went off.

Dave knew that at any moment they would be knocking at his door and did not even ask himself who they were.

It was time, in any case, for him to emerge from his torpor. It had worn off by degrees and, in the end, he had been obliged to maintain it artificially. The thing was a trick, a certain way of tensing his muscles as he bore down on the mattress. He did not wait to hear footsteps on the stairs before raising his head and opening his eyes and it was strange to rediscover his every-day background, the objects with their exact shape, the bright square of the window, a corner of the living-room which he could see through the half-open doorway.

There was a knock and, without answering, he sat on the edge of the bed, his mind still vacant, without having fully regained awareness of the drama which was unfolding.

"Mr. Galloway!"

The knocking grew louder. The woman above, having emerged from her apartment, was talking volubly.

"I heard him come in about one o'clock and I'm sure he hasn't gone out again. What is so strange is that, since then, I haven't heard any sound in his apartment."

"Do you think he's the sort of man who would commit suicide?" asked another voice.

He knitted his eyebrows, astounded, because this idea had never for a moment occurred to him.

"Mr. Galloway! Do you hear?"

Resignedly he got up, went to the door and unlocked it.

"Yes?" he said.

They were not police. One of them had a leather case slung from his shoulder and a big camera in his hand.

The stouter of the two gave the name of a New York newspaper, as though there were no need of any further explanation.

"Get your picture, Johnny."

He explained by way of apology:

"That way, it'll arrive in time for the evening edition."

They didn't wait for his permission. There was a white flash, a click.

"One minute! Where were you when we arrived?"

He answered without thinking, because he was not in the habit of lying:

"In my son's room."

He regretted it instantly, too late.

"That room there? Would you mind going back in for a moment? Like that, yes. Stand in front of the bed. Look down at it."

Another car pulled up in front of the house, a door slammed, there were hurried footsteps on the sidewalk.

"Hurry up! Got it? Rush it to the office. Don't worry about me. I'll fix some way of getting back. Excuse me, Mr. Galloway, but we were here first and there's no reason why we shouldn't have the benefit."

Two more men thrust their way into the apartment, of which the door was no longer locked. All four knew one another, chatted among themselves while they looked about them.

"From what we've been told, the police-car brought you back here about one o'clock and you hadn't eaten. Haven't you had anything to eat since?"

He said no. He felt powerless before their energy. They seemed so much stronger than he, so sure of themselves!

"Aren't you hungry?"

He no longer knew. This noise, these comings and goings, these lights that flashed every minute were making him dizzy.

"Was it you who cooked the meals for your son and yourself?"

It was now that he wanted to weep, not from grief, but from weariness.

"I don't know," he answered. "I don't even know what you want of me."

"Have you a photograph of him?"

He nearly gave himself away, said no, fiercely, resolved, this time, to defend himself. It was a lie. There was an album filled with photos of Ben in a drawer in his bedroom. At all costs they must not be allowed to know.

288

"You should eat something."

"Perhaps."

"Would you like one of us to make you a sandwich?"

He preferred to do it himself and was photographed again in front of the open frigidaire.

"Do they still not know where he is?" he asked in his turn, timidly, ready to draw back.

"You haven't been listening to the radio?"

He was ashamed of having to admit it, as though he had failed in his duty as a father.

"From now on, the police aren't relying on the information that's coming in because the blue Oldsmobile has been reported from five or six different places at the same time. Some people claim to have seen it an hour ago near Larrisberg, in Pennsylvania, which would mean that they've turned in their tracks. On the other hand, a restaurant-keeper in Union Bridge, Virginia, says he served them with breakfast before hearing their description over the radio. He has even given details of the meal they ordered: shrimps and fried chicken."

He tried to keep his face expressionless. It was Ben's favourite meal whenever they ate in a restaurant.

"I suppose it was your automatic they took with them?"

He protested, relieved by the diversion:

"I've never owned any kind of weapon."

"Did you know he had one?"

They were taking notes. Galloway, still standing, tried to eat his sandwich while he drank a glass of milk.

"I never knew him to have anything but toy pistols. He was a quiet boy."

It was for Ben's sake that he was enduring this. He wanted to avoid setting the newspapers against him and so he was patient with the reporters, doing his best to please them.

"Did he play a lot with pistols?"

"No more than other boys."

"Up till what age?"

"I don't know. Twelve, maybe."

"And after that, what games did he play?"

He was incapable of remembering, like that, at point-blank range, and this embarrassed him. It seemed to him that he should have been able to remember everything that concerned his son. Wasn't that the time when he went crazy about football? No. The football phase, that had come at least a year later. There had been an interim period.

"Animals!" he exclaimed.

"What animals?"

"All kinds. Anything he could get hold of. He kept white mice, young rabbits which he caught in the fields and which died after a few days. . . ."

This did not seem to interest them.

"His mother died when he was very young?"

"I'd rather not talk about that."

"Look, Mr. Galloway, if we don't talk about it, other people will. Within the next hour, other reporters will probably have got here. And what you don't tell them, they'll find out elsewhere."

It was true. It was better to help them.

"She isn't dead."

"Divorced?"

He murmured reluctantly, as though he were surrendering a part of his secret life:

"She left me."

"How old was the kid?"

"Six months. But I'd so much rather. . . ."

"Don't be afraid we won't be tactful."

They were doing their job, Dave realized and bore them no grudge. Like everyone else, he had read stories of this sort in the papers, but it had never occurred to him to put himself in the place of the people they were about. Those things had seemed to happen in a separate world.

"You knew about his affair with Lillian Hawkins?"

He said no, because it was the truth.

"Did you know her?"

"By sight. She came to my shop two or three times."

"I take it you and your son were great friends?"

How could he answer them? He said yes. That was his conviction. At the very least it had been his conviction until the previous night and he could not yet bring himself to abandon it. One of his interviewers, tall and thin, looked more like a young Harvard professor than a reporter and it worried Dave to feel his eyes upon him. This one had not yet asked him anything and, when at length he spoke, it was to say:

"In fact, you've been both a father and a mother to your son."

"I've done my best."

"It didn't ever occur to you that by marrying again you might have procured him a more normal life?"

He blushed, felt himself blushing and was all the more unhappy. Without thinking he stammered:

"No."

As though he were pursuing a definite line of thought, the reporter continued, implacably:

"Were you jealous of him?"

"Jealous?" he repeated.

"If he'd asked you for permission to marry Lillian Hawkins, how would you have reacted?"

"I don't know."

"Would you have given it?"

"I suppose so."

"Willingly?"

One of the others, the stout one who had been the first to arrive, gave his colleague a slight nudge with his elbow and he beat a retreat.

"I'm sorry if I've pressed you too far, but you see, it's the human angle that interests me."

The Everton team must have scored a home run, because there was a burst of cheering that lasted several minutes.

"How did you hear the news?"

"From the police. First they tried to call me up. The telephone's down below, in the shop."

On this subject, he was quite ready to give them all the details. It was a relief to him. He explained in far too many words how he had to walk round the building to get to his shop and how two uniformed police officers had appeared from their car and read his name over the window, then had consulted their notebook.

"You'd no idea what was coming?"

They talked together in low voices. After which, the photographer asked:

"Would it bother you to come and pose for a moment in your shop?"

He agreed, still for Ben's sake. He was a little ashamed of the part they were making him play but he would have done anything to gain their favour.

They went down in single file and Dave, who had forgotten the key of the shop, had to go back to fetch it. The apartment, where all the men had been smoking, no longer had the same odour and had lost its intimacy.

It was only at that moment, while he was gazing round the room looking for the key, that he realized that a certain life

291

was finally ended and that, whatever happened, the existence he had shared with Ben between those walls would never be resumed.

This was no longer his home, their home. The objects it contained had no identity and Ben's bed, on which he, Dave, had been stretched a little while ago, was no longer anything but an ordinary bed bearing the impress of a body.

In the yard, they were talking about him in undertones. They must be feeling sorry for him. The one like a professor had hurt him unintentionally with his questions, because he had spoken words which, henceforth, would torment him. No doubt he would have thought of it for himself. He had already thought of it, before what had happened, but not in the same way. Expressed in a certain way, the truth became disturbing, sordid, like the photographs of women in certain poses which young men surreptitiously pass round.

Someone asked him from below:

"You've found it?"

He picked up the key and went down, then they all walked together.

"Is that your garage?"

"Yes."

"Get a picture of it later on, Dick. We shall probably have the whole centre spread to fill."

Two women, seated on the grass, were keeping an eye, while they gossiped, on the children playing around them and they watched, from a distance, as the party went into the shop. One of them, the younger, was pregnant.

"What are the hooks for?"

"That's where I hang the watches under repair, during the day. It takes several days to regulate a watch."

"You work at this bench, do you? Where are the watches?"

"In the safe."

They asked him to hang them on the hooks, to put on his white smock and to fix the black-ringed magnifying-glass in his right eye.

"You couldn't hold a tool in your hand? . . . . Yes . . . like that. . . . Don't move."

He pretended to be working.

"Hold it one second more. I'll take another."

He should have had someone to protect him and the thought of his father passed through his mind. He hadn't the courage to resist them, submissively did everything they told him, so much so that his readiness to co-operate surprised them.

Was he entitled to lock himself in and see no one? Just now, if he had not opened to them, they would no doubt have gone for a locksmith or else broken the door down for fear lest he had hanged himself!

"You haven't found any photos of the girl among your son's belongings?"

"I haven't searched his belongings."

"Aren't you going to?"

"Certainly not."

He had never opened Ben's wallet, not even the time, when he was eleven, when a dollar had vanished from the cash-drawer. It was in any case, so far as he knew, the only time this had happened. He had spoken of it to his son without pursuing the matter. Just two sentences, in a sorrowful voice.

His own mother, when he was young, had been in the habit of going through his drawers and his pockets and he had never forgiven her for it.

"The police haven't searched the place?"

He stared at them, horrified.

"Do you think they will?"

"It's more than likely. I'm very surprised they haven't done so already."

When all was said, what did it matter? After his father's death, they had stacked part of the furniture on the porch encircling the house, and the rest on the lawn, and people had come long distances to examine it, to sniff at every nook and cranny. The auction had taken place on a Saturday and had been interrupted while lemonade and hot-dogs were served to everyone there. They had sold everything, including frames which still contained photographs.

He had not been allowed to see his father in his coffin, lest it should frighten him, but no one had thought of preventing him from being present at that carnage.

It was something rather similar that was now happening, after all. All their private life would be brought out into the open, their intimacy exposed, their past, their habits, their smallest doings and gestures discussed by the public.

What they did not know was that, while they were questioning him in this fashion and making him pose for photographs, he was more with Ben than with them. Throughout that afternoon, he had had in his mind's eye, like an overprint, a picture of the red soil of Virginia, the trees taller, more stately, with darker foliage than the ones here, and he had thought of the blue car speeding along the side-roads.

They would have to stop somewhere. Would they run the risk of spending the night at a "motel", or would they drive the car into some wood to sleep there?

They hadn't much money. Dave had mechanically calculated the amount, that morning, when the lieutenant had told him of the twelve or fourteen dollars in Charles Ralston's wallet. With the thirty-eight dollars Lillian had taken from her parents' kitchen, this made roughly fifty dollars. If Ben, in addition, had saved as many as ten. . . .

They had to eat, to buy gasoline several times a day.

It was at this moment that the reporter whose questions had disturbed him said:

"Tell me, Mr. Galloway, has it occurred to you that you might be able to send him a message?"

He gazed at him in astonishment, not understanding.

"I represent the Associated Press. Your message would be sent out by teletype to every newspaper in the States and I'm certain they would all print it. It's likely, again, that your son will have the curiosity to buy papers as he goes, if only to get some idea of which way the search is heading."

He had seen that Dave was hesitating and perhaps had anticipated his thoughts. Otherwise, why should he have added:

"It would be better for him, don't you think?"

Galloway recalled the words one nearly always reads on criminal notices displayed in the post-offices.

"Warning! This man is armed."

Ben also was armed. Which meant that the police, rather than run risks, would be tempted to shoot first.

Was that what the reporter was suggesting? That he should advise Ben to give himself up?

"Let's go back to your apartment, shall we?"

It was better to do so, because the baseball game had just finished and the first cars were passing. The crowd would follow in a stream, as when they came out of mass or the cinema. Dave, preoccupied with this new idea that had just been implanted in his mind, nearly forgot to slip the spring-lock on the door.

The plump reporter, the first to arrive, stood hesitating at the corner of the alleyway.

"How does one get to the Hawkins' place?"

"You turn left at the garage, then you take the first on the right."

Evidently considering that he had got as much out of Galloway as there was to get, he went off to question them in their turn. The other, however, seemed to take no interest in Lillian, but only in Ben and his father. He was cold and understanding at the same time. The photographer also left them, stood waiting for the crowd to come in order to photograph them outside the shop.

Back in the apartment, the representative of the Associated Press said in a detached voice:

"The police know as well as you do how much money your son has in his pocket. It's easy to figure out what it's costing them to travel by road. They reckon that, by to-morrow evening, they'll have come to the end of their bank-roll."

"Did the lieutenant tell you that?"

"Not him. The F.B.I., who are taking part in the search, know that the fugitives have crossed one or more State frontiers in the stolen car. I must apologize for. . . ."

"It's all right."

"Perhaps if your son read in the newspaper that you begged him to give himself up. . . ."

"I understand."

"Take your time before you decide. I don't want you to reproach yourself afterwards. It's not as though he could hope to reach a foreign country. And, even if he did, he would come under the extradition laws, whether it was Canada or Mexico."

The reporter had stationed himself in front of the window and was staring at the trees across the way, the children who had left the baseball-field and were running across the grass.

The police would shoot first, Dave was convinced of it. The reporter wasn't trying to trick him. No doubt he knew more about the F.B.I.'s plans than he was allowed to say.

He was tempted, to the point of being overtaken by a sort of giddiness. And it was not only with the idea of preventing his son's being killed. For no precise reason, simply by intuition, he didn't believe in that possibility. It existed in theory. It seemed logical, almost inevitable. Nevertheless, he could have sworn that things would not happen that way.

It was not possible that he would not again see Ben alive.

His companion still stood with his back to him as though to avoid influencing him. Dave got out his handkerchief, mopped his forehead, the palms of his hands. Twice, before speaking, he opened his mouth.

"I'll do it," he said finally.

And his hands trembled at the thought that in a sense he was going to make contact with Ben.

CHAPTER FIVE

OTHERS had come: five, it seemed to him, each accompanied by a photographer, and one had brought his wife who waited down below in an open car. For one reason or another, there were more than five cars, some with the name of the paper painted on the coachwork, parked anyhow in front of the house, and people went incessantly up and down the stairs; the door remained open almost all the time. One of the photographers, who found that the smoke interfered with his work, went and opened the window and the draught made the curtains tremble, and the leaves of the scribbling-pads. People talked, moved, smoked in every corner.

Each asked more or less the same questions and Dave was answering mechanically, without trying to think, with the feeling that all this was no longer of any importance. His knees were shaking with fatigue, but he could not bring himself to sit down, remained standing in the midst of them, facing now this way and now that.

In the street, groups passed slowly along the opposite side-walk, bordering the lawn, couples walking arm-in-arm, families with children going in front or being led by the hand, and everyone looked up to try and see in through the window; some stopped altogether. As for the boys and girls who, ordinarily, hung about outside Mack's, they had set up their headquarters round the press-cars.

Twice, Dave had seen in the distance the policeman of that morning, one of the two in uniform, the one who hadn't left the village and seemed busy.

Without noticing it, he smoked cigarette after cigarette, because those who questioned him offered him their pack, and they didn't look round for the ash-tray any more, they just threw the stubs on the floor and crushed them with their heels.

The sky, by six o'clock, was overcast, the weather had become oppressive, as though a storm were approaching, and occasionally a sharp gust of wind shook the leaves of the trees opposite.

They had ended by going away one after the other. All went sooner or later to the Hawkinses' house which must be in the same state of disorder. Some went to the Old Barn, to telephone their stories.

At the moment when Galloway fancied himself at last alone and was about to sink into his armchair, there was yet another knock on the door and he went to open, found a man carrying a suitcase that seemed very heavy.

"Have they all gone?" he asked in astonishment.

He put down the case, mopped his forehead.

"I represent the biggest radio network. A short time ago, the appeal you've made to your son was sent in to us, for our newsbulletin. My chiefs and I thought it would be more likely to make an impression on him if he heard your own voice."

What Dave had mistaken for a suitcase was a tape-recorder which the radio-man was setting up on one of the tables. He looked round for a power-point.

"Do you mind if I close the window a minute?"

Dave's message had been difficult to word and, like Ruth fifteen and a half years before, he had torn up several drafts. At the time he had been alone in the apartment with the journalist who was like a professor and the latter had kept discreetly in the background all the time he was writing, without offering a single suggestion.

None of the phrases he had tried had given him the feeling of making contact with his son.

"Your father urges you. . . ."

That would not do. He knew what he wanted to say, but the words were lacking. Since they had never been separated, Ben and he, they had never had occasion to write to one another, except notes which one of them might leave on the kitchen table. *"Back in an hour. Have your meal, there's some cold meat in the frigidaire."*

He had wished this were as simple.

"Ben, I implore you," he wrote. . . .

It did not matter if other people laughed, or failed to understand. He was talking to no one but his son.

"Ben, I implore you, give yourself up."

He had nearly handed over the sheet of paper without adding any more, then he had taken it back and scribbled:

"I'm not angry with you."

He had signed it, *"Dad."*

The representative of the Associated Press had read it, had raised his eyes towards Galloway who was watching him and expecting some criticism.

"I can say that?"

He thought he was going to be asked to delete the last words. Instead, almost solemnly, the man folded the sheet of paper and put it in his wallet.

"You certainly can!"

He had said it in a queer voice and he shook him by the hand before leaving.

Now, Dave asked the radio-man:

"Do you want me to use the same words?"

"The same ones or fresh ones if you like."

He set the apparatus going, tested it, began his introduction in the manner of a professional broadcaster.

"Now, ladies and gentlemen, we are interrupting our programme for a moment to relay a message which Mr. Galloway, from his apartment in Everton, is going to send out over the air to his son. We can only hope, like all of you, that the latter is listening."

He held out the microphone, signed to Dave to speak.

"This is Dad, Ben. . . ."

At that moment, his eyes filled with tears and the outline of the microphone grew blurred; he vaguely perceived the gesture of the other man urging him to continue.

"It's better for you to give yourself up. . . . Yes. . . . I honestly think it's better. . . . I shall always be on your side, no matter what happens. . . ."

His voice became stifled and he was only just able to finish:

"I'm not angry with you. . . ."

The radio-man switched off.

"Very good. Fine. Do you want to hear yourself?"

He shook his head. The blue Oldsmobile had a radio. It was probable that Ben and Lillian were on the alert for every news-bulletin.

"What time will it go out?" he managed to ask as his visitor moved towards the door.

"Probably in the nine o'clock bulletin."

It wasn't in order to hear his own voice but so that, when the time came, he might be near Ben in thought.

Before sitting down, he went and opened the window again, indifferent to the procession in the street, to the curiosity he aroused in the village and everywhere else.

By half-past seven, the clouds were so dark and low that he had to switch on the light and it was then that he received another visit, that of an F.B.I. man, in plain clothes, who was not more than thirty years old and whom he seemed to have seen before.

"I must apologize for bothering you after the day you've had, but believe me, Mr. Galloway, I wouldn't trouble you, if it weren't absolutely necessary."

He held out an official document at which Dave merely glanced. It was a search-warrant.

"I should like to examine your son's possessions. Is that his room on the left?"

Dave did not ask what he was looking for, noted that it was Ben's papers, letters, exercise-books, that principally interested his visitor.

"Some time, I shall have to ask you for as complete a list as possible of your son's friends, including those who may have left the district. Have you relatives in the South or West, Mr. Galloway?"

"Some aunts, in Virginia . . . if they're still alive. I haven't seen them since I was six and I've never heard from them."

"You've never been to the Middle West with your son?"

"The only places we've been to together are Cape Cod and New York."

"You know, it's unusual for anyone to start out by road the way he has done without having a definite objective. If we knew what that objective was, it would obviously narrow the field of search."

He spoke as though he took it for granted that Dave was on their side.

"The idea of making for one place rather than another could be derived from various sources, from something he'd read or from a film, or again from a conversation with a friend."

Ben possessed few books other than his school-books. There were only two shelves of them in a quite small bookcase and for the most part they were the animal books that had interested him four years ago.

Why did Dave feel the need to say, as though he were being accused, or as though he wanted to make a good impression:

"You know, it isn't here that he got the weapon. I've never owned one."

He had said it already that morning. He repeated it.

"We've found out where the automatic came from."

While he went on leafing through the books, the F.B.I. man explained: "I suppose you know Dr. Van Horn?"

"Very well. He's our doctor. His son Jimmy has been to play in this room for years."

It had happened more especially just before Ben went to High School. Jimmy Van Horn, at that time, had been small and thin, of an astonishing vivacity. Then suddenly, two years ago, he had started to grow in height and now he was a half-head taller than any of his schoolfellows, seemed embarrassed by his size, by his voice, which had been very late in starting to break.

"Have you seen him lately?"

"He hasn't been here, if that's what you mean, but I've every reason to believe that Ben often sees him."

"Dr. Van Horn bought an automatic twelve years ago, when he was still living in Albany and was often called out at night to visit places in the outer districts. It was his weapon, almost forgotten in a drawer, that Jimmy sold to your son for five dollars. He admitted it this afternoon to one of the State Police. The deal took place a fortnight ago."

Dave had no comment to make. The Van Horns passed for wealthy people, possessed the most handsome house in Everton, surrounded by a real park. Each of the girls had her own horse, Mrs. Van Horn was the heiress of a manufacturer of chemical products whose trademark was known from coast to coast.

"Was it you who bought this booklet?"

He was shown an almanac that he didn't remember having seen before in the apartment. The General Information section contained a list of former Presidents of the United States, population figures for the big towns, statistics, the speed-limits imposed in the different States.

It was on another page that the detective found, almost instantly, as though he had been looking for them, two pencilled crosses.

The first column on this page bore a list of the States in alphabetical order, parallel columns gave the minimum ages at which marriage-licences were granted, first for men, then for women, and finally the number of days' notice required.

"I'm afraid I shall have to take this booklet with me."

"May I see it?"

The two States marked with a cross were Illinois and Mississippi. In Illinois, the minimum age for boys was eighteen, for girls sixteen, while in Mississippi the figures were fourteen and twelve respectively. Neither State required notice, so that it was possible to go to the house of any Justice of the Peace and be married in a few minutes. Ben looked eighteen.

"I don't think I shall need the list of names I asked you for just now. This seems to me to answer the question."

"You think they're making for one of those States? It would have been so simple to——"

He broke off. It was not for him to pretend not to understand.

"I'm sure," he went on, "that when he explains to us. . . ."

The other looked at him curiously, as though he had said something enormous.

"You should try to get some rest, Mr. Galloway. To-morrow will probably be a hard day."

He, too, shook him by the hand. Dave was almost tempted to try and keep him back, terrified, suddenly, at the thought of being left alone. He no longer knew where to put himself in the apartment which so many people had invaded and now had no more intimacy than a station waiting-room. The very lamps seemed to give less light than usual.

Should he have made sure, before the police searched it, that there was nothing in Ben's room that could put them on the track? It seemed to him that he had failed his son, for lack of sufficient astuteness, and he wanted to ask his forgiveness. Who knows? Perhaps he had also been wrong to write his message, to send out his appeal over the radio. People were certain to think that he had done so in order to put himself on the side of the law.

But please, God, don't let Ben think that! Dave had not thought of it until then. The idea suddenly occurred to him and he was filled with remorse, he would have liked to take back the message he had written and later naïvely repeated into the tape-recorder.

It wasn't true! He was not trying to show himself in a favourable light, or to evade his responsibilities. Ben was himself, he was ready to stand judgment in his stead and to accept the punishment.

Would Ben understand this when he heard:

"I'm not angry with you."

On the spur of the moment, he had been able to find no other words. These were the only ones that had come to his lips. Only now did he begin to realize that they implied a degree of accusation.

He was not accusing, not explaining either. Later on would be the time to try to explain.

Ben was his son and Ben couldn't have changed from one day to the next. Even when he thought of Charles Ralston lying at the side of the road and of the scene which must have taken place in the car, he could not bring himself to reproach him. He was simply horrified, as one is by a cataclysm.

It exhausted him to think. He would have liked to be able to stop the little wheels of his mind as one stops the mechanism of a clock. Outside large drops of rain were falling more and more rapidly but it was not thundering; there was no lightning to be seen. Dave was at a loose end. His thoughts were at a loose end, too. It was only a quarter past eight and his radio message would not be broadcast until nine.

He was on the point of going out of doors, bareheaded, so that the cold rain might refresh him, and it was a relief, this time, to hear footsteps on the stairs.

Someone came up making as little noise as possible, then whoever it was stood outside the door, without knocking, without saying anything, while, inside, he waited in suspense.

A good minute passed before he heard a soft rustling on the floor. Someone was slipping a sheet of paper under the door and it was so mysterious that he hesitated for a time before picking it up.

The message had been written with a thick pencil such as carpenters use:

"If you don't want to see me, don't open. I'll leave a little package on the landing."

It was signed *"Frank"*, Musak's Christian name, which no one ever used. He was waiting and when Dave opened the door he found him standing in the half-darkness, with a parcel in his hand.

"I thought maybe you wouldn't want to see anyone, or that you were asleep."

"Come in, Musak."

He was the first person, that day, to wipe his feet on the mat, and, for the first time that he could remember, Galloway saw him take his cap off.

During all the years they had known one another, and had played backgammon every Saturday, Musak had never come up to the apartment because, when he had anything to say to his friend, it was in the shop that he always stopped.

"I brought this," he said, pulling the paper wrapping off a bottle of rye.

He had remembered something Dave had once said to him:

302

that, because of Ben, he never kept liquor in the house, both for the example and so as not to put temptation in his way.

"When you want me to go, you only have to say so."

He seemed even bigger and rougher here than in his own home and yet he moved without a sound, almost without causing a stir in the air, as he might have done in a sick-room. He found glasses in the kitchen cupboard, got cubes of ice from the frigidaire.

"Have you had anything to eat?"

Dave nodded.

"What?"

"A sandwich."

"When?"

"I don't know. The baseball game hadn't finished."

He recalled the shouting on the ground while he had the sandwich in his hand.

Musak held out one of the two glasses and he could not refuse.

"It's time you had something more solid. Sit down. Leave it to me."

He talked in his grumbling voice, less loud than usual, went back into the kitchen, again opened the frigidaire where he found two large steaks.

Every Saturday, Dave bought two thick steaks for Sunday dinner, for Ben and himself. And this tradition was more than ten years old. Only when he saw the meat on a plate did he reflect that yesterday had been Saturday, and that, at about ten in the morning, as he had done so many times before, he had shut his shop to go and do his marketing at the First National Store.

The notice he left on the door read:

"Back in a quarter of an hour."

That afternoon, at about five, he had been working on a woman's watch when Ben had come into the shop. Although Dave had had his back turned, he had known it was his son, from the way he opened the door.

"You won't mind if I don't come in for supper, Dad?"

Dave had not turned, had remained, with the glass in his right eye, bent over the movement of the watch. No doubt he had said:

"Don't be too late."

It was his usual phrase.

"You going to Musak's?" Ben had asked.

303

This had not seemed to him out-of-the-way. Ben had probably asked the same question on other Saturdays.

"Yes. I shall be back around half-past eleven."

" 'Night, Dad."

Galloway suddenly called:

"Musak!"

"What?"

"I can't eat anything."

The steak continued nevertheless to splutter on the cooker.

"They asked me to send out an appeal over the radio for him to give himself up."

The cabinet-maker gave him a curious glance from the kitchen, contented himself with saying:

"Yes."

"I agreed. They recorded it."

Musak made no comment.

"I'm wondering now if I was right."

It was raining hard. The raindrops rattled on the roof. He went to shut the window, because a puddle was beginning to form on the floor.

"I was afraid they'd kill him."

"Come and sit here."

Musak had laid a place for him on a napkin, not knowing where the tablecoths were kept, and, seated opposite Galloway, with his elbows on the table, he waited as one does when one is persuading a child to eat.

"I listened to the radio all afternoon," he muttered.

"What are they saying?"

"They're repeating almost the same words every hour. Their idea now is that the car's heading for Chicago. However, there are people who claim to have seen it on the roads in South Carolina."

Almost without realizing it, Dave had begun to eat and Musak, for his part, had poured himself a second glass of whisky.

"A State Police officer spent the day questioning people in the village. He came to see me."

"To confirm that we were together yesterday evening?"

"Yes. And there are two reporters still here, who've taken rooms at the Old Barn."

It was the first time since that morning that Galloway had relaxed, without knowing it. Musak's presence was comforting. It did him good to hear his voice, to see his gross, familiar face.

"Would you like some apple-pie? I saw some in the frigidaire."

The apple-pie was also part of the Sunday menu.

"Won't you have some?"

"I had supper."

He lit his pipe instead, the one he had mended with wire, and for an instant, because of the acrid smell of the tobacco, Dave thought himself in the yellow house at the end of the lane.

"Do you mean to listen at nine o'clock?"

Galloway nodded and Musak looked at his old silver watch which had never needed mending.

"We've plenty of time. There's still twelve minutes to go."

When Galloway rose to take his plate into the kitchen, he stopped him:

"We'll do that later."

He pointed to his armchair, as though he knew his habits.

"Coffee?"

Without awaiting a reply, he went to make some, huge and silent, and not even the rattle of a cup was to be heard.

Dave glanced at his own watch and grew more nervous as the time approached. At five minutes to nine, he went to get the radio from Ben's room, plugged it into one of the points in the living-room and turned the knob to give it time to warm up.

Musak had poured out coffee for himself as well. They heard the end of a symphony. Then, after a commercial, the latest news of the day was announced.

It did not start with Ben, but with a declaration by the President on the subject of customs tariffs, then went on to a frontier incident between the Lebanon and Palestine.

The announcer was speaking rapidly, with a staccato delivery, not making a pause as he passed from one topic to the next.

"Home news: the police of six States, joined by the F.B.I., are still searching for the sixteen-year-old killer, Ben Galloway. With his girl-friend, Lillian Hawkins, aged only fifteen and a half, Galloway left Everton, in New York State, on Saturday evening, driving his father's van. After killing a man named Charles Ralston, aged fifty-four, domiciled in Long Island, with a bullet from an automatic, on the border of Pennsylvania, the couple took possession of the victim's blue Oldsmobile and continued to drive in a south-westerly direction."

The two men, motionless, avoided each other's eyes. Contrary to his expectation, Dave was more impatient than moved, as though the event, recounted in this fashion, no longer concerned either him or his son.

"The car, registration-number 7G-1624, has been reported successively in Pennsylvania, Virginia and, according to the latest news, Ohio. It is, however, difficult to determine the exact route taken by the fugitives owing to the large number of contradictory reports which are reaching the police."

Another voice took possession of the microphone.

"And now, ladies and gentlemen, we are interrupting our news bulletin for a moment to broadcast an appeal which Mr. Dave Galloway is making to his son."

It was the voice of the radio-man who had come earlier on, but it seemed to Galloway that the words were not quite the same.

There was a pause, then a scratching sound, and then with a strange resonance, as though they were spoken in the resounding emptiness of a cathedral, came the words which were familiar to him but which, all of a sudden, made him feel ashamed.

"This is Dad, Ben. . . . It's better for you to give yourself up. . . ."

The pauses between the sentences seemed interminable.

"Yes, I honestly think it's better. . . . I shall always be on your side, no matter what happens. . . ."

He heard himself breathe very hard, and pause as though he were asking someone's permission to continue, before ending:

"I'm not angry with you."

"And now, ladies and gentlemen, here is the latest weather forecast. . . ."

He reached out his hand to switch off. Musak said nothing. Galloway had no wish to speak either and now hoped that Ben was not listening.

If he were listening, somewhere on the road, his eyes intent on the track of the headlights, wouldn't he, too, have already switched off?

"I thought . . ." began Dave.

He had thought he was acting for the best. He had imagined he would be making contact with Ben. He had received them all politely. He had answered their questions, accepted their cigarettes.

He had betrayed his son, it was only now that he realized it. He had seemed to be excusing himself, coming to their help.

Did Musak understand what he felt? In silence, he drank a mouthful of rye and wiped his lips. A crash of thunder sounded, so loud that the lightning might have struck one of the trees opposite or the belfry of the Catholic church. It was not followed by any other. For several minutes, the rain doubled in intensity, set up a real pandemonium on the roof, after which, suddenly, it ceased as though by magic and there was silence.

Dave had let his head sink a little on his chest but, tired though he was, he did not sleep, did not doze, continued to reproach himself. When he saw Musak get up, he took no notice, nor of the sound of the tap in the kitchen.

The police of six States. . . .

And they were two children in the car, glancing in terror at the cars that overtook or passed them, gazing into the darkness of the night in constant apprehension of seeing a police-barrier rise up ahead of them.

The F.B.I. man had taken away the almanac in which two crosses designated Illinois and Mississippi.

Were they still intent upon the same objective as they wound blindly between the traps? Were they continuing this mad flight simply in order that, having crossed a given frontier, they might rush to a Justice of the Peace and cry to him, panting: "Marry us!"

They might, if they had not made too many detours, reach Illinois that same night, perhaps were there already. It was not improbable that, in some remote village, they would arouse some elderly judge who had not listened to the radio all day.

Were they, too, having to pass through storms, down there on the plains of the Middle West? He regretted not having listened to the weather forecast, began to grow restless, wished Musak would come back and sit opposite him to prevent him thinking. He, too, was on the highway, with the monotonous sound of the windscreen-wipers seeming to tick off the seconds.

The police of six States. . . . Plus the F.B.I.

He got up suddenly to pour himself a mouthful of whisky, gazed at the radio calculating that there were still thirty-five minutes to go before the ten o'clock bulletin. He had a feeling that, this time, there would be news.

"You shouldn't have washed up, Musak."

The other shrugged his shoulders, poured himself a drink and sat down in an armchair.

"Don't forget I'll go directly you want me to."

Dave shook his head. He didn't want him to go. He dared not imagine what that evening would have been like if Musak hadn't come and humbly slipped a sheet of paper under the door.

307

"People don't know, they can't know," Galloway said as though to himself.

And Musak murmured, as though he, too, were talking to himself:

"When my daughter went off, it was a year and a half before I had any news of her."

It was the first time he had ever made any allusion to his private life and no doubt it was to come to the aid of his friend.

"In the end I had a letter from a hospital in Baltimore where she'd landed up, without any money, and was expecting a baby."

"What did you do?"

"I went there. She refused to see me. I left some money with the office and came away."

He said no more and Dave didn't venture to ask whether he had seen her again later, nor if this was the daughter who wrote to him now and then from California and sent him snapshots of her children.

"I wonder what they're thinking. . . ."

His thoughts were still with the couple in the car.

"Everyone thinks differently," sighed Musak.

He added after a moment, during which the whistle of his pipe could be heard:

"Everyone figures he's right."

Galloway looked at his watch, impatient to hear the radio.

"You should sit down."

"I know. I've been on my feet nearly all day. I can't help it."

Every time he sat down, a fit of trembling overcame his legs, a nervous twinge spread through his body. He said suddenly:

"Dr. Van Horn must be terribly upset."

He did not explain why; although he realized from Musak's expression that he had not heard the story of the automatic.

"In one minute, you will hear our latest news bulletin."

The commercial was given first.

"During the last few minutes we have learned that Ben Galloway, the sixteen-year-old killer, whose father broadcast an appeal to him in our last bulletin. . . ."

They held their breath.

". . . arrived with his companion, at about the time of that appeal, at the home of a Justice of the Peace in Brownstown, on the frontier of Indiana and Illinois, and asked him to marry them immediately. The judge, who had chanced to hear a description of the couple over the radio a short time previously,

308

*left the room on the pretext of fetching the necessary papers
and rushed to the telephone.*

*"Before he could get through to the Sheriff, the sound of the
car's engine told him that the two young people, no doubt
guessing what he intended to do, had made a dash for it.*

*"In any event, this narrows the area of search. It also indicates
that the blue Oldsmobile had covered a lot more ground, in the
past twenty-four hours, than had hitherto been supposed and
that Ben Galloway can scarcely have left the wheel.*

*"The Illinois police are watching all cross-roads and it seems
that an early arrest may be expected."*

Had Musak noticed? At a certain moment, during the broadcast, Galloway had not been able to prevent a slight, scarcely
perceptible smile from rising to his lips. It was not a smile of
satisfaction, or of irony. It signified nothing precise. Only a sort
of contact with Ben, down there. He shut his eyes to recapture
the feeling but, like a breath of air, it had already passed, subtle,
impalpable.

There remained only two men in their armchairs.

CHAPTER SIX

THAT night was a little like the night one spends on a train, at
times dozing, at times plunged in exhausted slumber through
which one is nevertheless conscious of the rhythm of the wheels,
of the stations where one pulls up with a hiss of steam, of the
man with a lantern who hits the axles with a hammer while
unknown voices call from one platform to another.

When, for example, Musak touched him on the shoulder, he
knew that he was in his armchair and not in bed, and that he
was being awakened for the midnight news. He wondered
whether Musak had fallen asleep, too, did not venture to ask,
rubbed his eyes, saw that the whisky had sunk to a lower level
in the bottle. The tubes in the radio were already warming up,
voices came out of the silence, growing so loud that the volume
had to be reduced.

It was the end of a play. A man and a woman were resolving
to patch up their life together as best they could. He did not
notice the commercial.

*"Ladies and gentlemen, as we announced a quarter of an hour
ago in a special bulletin. . . ."*

Neither Musak nor he had thought that there might be a special announcement and they had simply turned on the radio at the usual times.

"... the hunt for the sixteen-year-old murderer, Ben Galloway, which had gone on for nearly twenty-four hours, came to an end this evening, a little before eleven o'clock, at a farm in Indiana, where the couple sought to take refuge using the threat of an automatic. Shots were exchanged with the police and a sergeant was wounded by a bullet in the hip. Ben Galloway and his fifteen-and-a-half-year-old companion, Lillian Hawkins, both uninjured, have been taken to Indianapolis.

"For fuller information, see your usual daily paper to-morrow morning."

Perhaps Musak was a little surprised by his friend's reaction? Galloway uttered a sigh which resembled a sigh of relief, his nerves instantly relaxed and he stood up, rubbed his eyes as he looked about him with an air of disgust, as though sickened by the atmosphere in which he had been immersed since the morning.

It was over. He had no more need to wait, to stay there as though in suspense. His first thought was that before leaving he must have a bath and shave, because he had a feeling that he smelt unpleasantly of sweat.

"I'm going down to the shop to call up the airport," he said.

It seemed to him natural. He was going to see Ben, he would talk to him. Ben would explain everything, would tell him the whole truth because, to his knowledge, his son had never lied to him.

He was a little irritated that Musak came down with him. He no longer needed anyone. Everything was quite simple, now; he would take the first plane to Indianapolis and he would see Ben.

Down in the shop, Musak, going ahead of him, took up the receiver saying:

"It's better for me to telephone."

He didn't understand why. Then as he looked at the empty hooks, he reflected that, if he were away several days, customers would doubtless come to collect their watchs. There was nothing he could do about that. They would just have to understand.

"What time did you say, Miss? . . . Six seventeen? . . . Will you please book a place in the name of Musak? . . . Frank Musak."

Now Dave knew why his friend had insisted upon telephoning: it was to spare him another assault by reporters and photographers at the airport.

"Thank you. . . . No. . . . Not a return. . . ."

Musak did not consult him. A little later, he found himself outside with him. The moon had risen. Low clouds, dark at the centre and brilliant at the edges, were gliding as though on calm water. For two or three minutes, they remained there without speaking, standing on the sidewalk where the rain was drying in patches, listening to the silence.

"We might as well go and fetch my car now."

He understood that, too. Dave hadn't got his van, which the police had kept. Musak intended to drive him to La Guardia. He did not protest and the two started to walk along Main Street where there wasn't a soul. There were no lights to be seen except in the Old Barn tavern, where two of the journalists were spending the night.

When they turned into the lane, the grass, after the rain, smelt good.

"I'll get the car out," said Musak going towards his garage.

Ben, too, must have relaxed, down there. If only they would let him sleep! He had always needed a lot of sleep and, in the morning, when his father woke him, it took him a long time to shake off his drowsiness, it even happened sometimes that, as he went, barefooted, in his pyjamas to the bathroom, he bumped against the doorpost because he had not yet got his eyes properly open.

That was the time when he was grumpy. Only after his bath, and even more after he had begun his breakfast, did he regain his normal spirits.

For the first time, Galloway entered Musak's car and he found in it the same odour as in the carpenter's house.

"It's less than two hours from here to La Guardia. Allowing half an hour for you to get ready and have something to eat, that gives you nearly three hours' sleep."

He nearly protested; but his lids were drooping and it cost him an effort to hold his head upright. He could, easily, have fallen asleep in the car.

He wondered whether Musak intended, for his part, to sleep in Ben's bed. This would have shocked him. But Musak, back in the apartment, gave no sign of undressing, but settled down on the sofa as though for the rest of the night.

Dave went and undressed, was a little embarrassed at showing himself in pyjamas.

"You'll wake me at not later than a quarter past three?"

"Make it half-past," said Musak, setting the alarm, as a precaution. "Go to sleep."

Two minutes later, Dave had sunk deeply into slumber, but he could have sworn that he was conscious all the time of the presence of his friend who had picked up a book and was smoking his pipe while he drank rye. Nor did he lose sight of the fact that he had to catch the plane at La Guardia at six seventeen, or that the ticket was in Musak's name. Two or three times, he turned over in a lump, as though to bury himself more deeply in the mattress, and when he again felt a touch on his shoulder, he sat up instantly. He had not heard the alarm sound. The apartment smelt of fresh coffee.

"Go and have your bath."

He had never got up at this hour, except when Ben was ill, one time, in particular, when he had a bad cold and had to be given medicine every two hours. On one occasion, during the latter half of the night, he had looked at his father with a frightened air and cried:

"What do you want?"

"It's time for your pill, Ben."

Did he hear? Did he understand? Frowning, his face screwed up, he continued to stare at his father as though he were seeing him for the first time and his eyes were hard.

"Can't you let me alone?" he said in a voice made husky by fever.

Dave had thought he sensed a resentment. Ben had taken his pill, drunk a mouthful of water, fallen asleep again and, in the morning, when his father referred to the episode, seemed not to remember it. But Galloway had never been quite sure that his son had not been in possession of his faculties at that moment. He avoided thinking about it. There had been three or four incidents like that in their life, which he preferred to forget.

He was too susceptible, paid too much attention to Ben's least reactions. All children, like grown-ups, have moments of bad humour, even of instinctive rancour.

The smell of bacon reached him in the bathroom and it was that of the apartment on other mornings. He shaved carefully, chose his best clothes, as though this were of importance. Ben liked him to be well-dressed. When they had first come to live in Everton and Dave had worn iron-grey smocks to work in, instead of the unbleached smocks he later adopted, his son had once said to him:

"You look like an old sick man."

It was perhaps on this subject that he was most sensitive. He could not resign himself to appearing old in his son's eyes. In his presence, he was less cordial with the customers, for fear of seeming obsequious.

"Feeling rested?"

"You've given yourself a lot of trouble," he said looking at the laid table, the eggs and bacon on a big dish, the toast in the electric toaster.

He knew it had been a pleasure to Musak, just as it was for him to do all the things he used to do for his son.

Around them, an absolute calm prevailed in the village and, when they started the car, they were almost ashamed of the noise they set up.

"Have you been to Indianapolis before?" asked Musak, as they reached the highway.

"Never."

"I have."

He said nothing more, allowed his companion to sleep, keeping in his mouth his unlit pipe on which he drew mechanically and it made its familiar sound. At the airport, they had nearly half-an-hour to wait. On the newspaper-stalls, headlines announced:

"Sixteen-year-old Killer."

For, because of Sunday, the papers had not yet been able to report the events of the previous night. Galloway frowned as he caught sight of his son's photograph which he scarcely recognized. He didn't remember that photograph. Ben seemed younger, with a curious, vague stare and a sort of smirk at the corners of his mouth. He had to look at it more closely to see that the head had been cut out of a group taken at High School. One of Ben's friends, no doubt, had given the newspapermen a copy.

The was also a photograph of Lillian, in which she did not look more than twelve years old.

A sub-heading said:

"Twenty-four hour manhunt ends in shooting on Indiana farm."

He bought three different papers while Musak watched him without saying a word, looking displeased. On the centre page his own photograph was displayed, standing in front of Ben's bed, of which one only saw a part, and another in which he was pretending to work on a watch in his shop.

Everything here was grey and gloomy. People were sleeping on the settees. Those who had their eyes open stared in front of them with a depressed air. A couple were embraced, the woman was crying, clinging to her companion as though they were separating for life.

His plane was announced. He went towards the doorway indicated by the loudspeaker and no one seemed to take any notice of him. An official called out the names of the passengers. "Musak," he murmured as he passed.

He had shaken the cabinet-maker's hand saying simply:

"Thanks. Now, everything will be all right."

He was convinced of it. He did not look at the papers until after they had loosened their safety-belts and he turned at once to the last paragraphs, those dealing with events on the farm:

"While the Illinois police were keeping watch for the fugitives at all the cross-roads, the latter turned back and again drove into Indiana. Was Ben Galloway at the end of his strength, after spending twenty-three hours at the wheel, or was he afraid to run the risk of filling his tank? In any case a little later the car stopped at an isolated farm, twenty miles from the border.

"It was about ten in the evening. The farmer, Hans Putman, aged fifty, was still up, as was his wife, and both were in a room on the ground floor.

"When Putman answered the knocks at the door, he found himself facing Galloway who levelled his automatic at him and told the girl:

" 'Cut the telephone-line.'

"He seemed exhausted. His hands were trembling with fatigue.

" 'Get us something to eat and don't anyone try to leave the house.'

"By that time, the Putman son, who had been upstairs when the car arrived, had slipped out by a back way and was bicycling to the nearest house, so that ten minutes later the Sheriff was notified and in a little while three police-cars were converging on the farm."

Other passengers were reading the same story as himself and had seen his photograph, but no one seemed to recognize him.

"With the house surrounded, the Sheriff and one of his men went towards the door and what happened then is still not very clear. Galloway and his companion certainly tried to escape by way of the farmyard. The inquiry will establish who was the

*first to shoot. A burst of shots was fired and one of the policemen
was hit by a bullet on the hip.*

*"In the end, the young man shouted, using his hands as a
megaphone:*

" 'Don't shoot any more, I surrender.'

"His automatic was empty.

*"While he was being taken to Jasonville, where he was to be
handed over to F.B.I. agents who were to take him to
Indianapolis, he expressed no regret for his actions.*

*" 'If it hadn't been for a boy of my age, you wouldn't have
caught me,' he said, referring to the Putman boy, who is also
apparently sixteen years old.*

*"He ended by falling asleep in the car while his companion
kept her eyes wide open as though to watch over him."*

It was probably not wholly true, because it is impossible to
report the words and deeds of anyone with entire accuracy.
Ben's words, however, must surely be authentic:

"If it hadn't been for a boy my age. . . ."

And also, perhaps, the fact that Lillian Hawkins had kept
awake during the journey to watch over him. This detail disturbed Galloway, made him sullen. It seemed to him, without
his being able to explain why, that because of her, things were
going to be less simple than he had thought.

He dozed, a lighter sleep than in the apartment, broken into
by three or four awakenings. Once, he saw a woman with a baby
in her arms gazing intently at him. A newspaper lay open on the
seat beside her. She must have recognized him. When he met
her gaze and glanced mechanically at the child, she shuddered,
as though she were mentally making Heaven knew what comparison, and clasped the baby more tightly to her.

When he had been left alone with him, Ben had been scarcely
older than that baby. Galloway had not suffered, in reality,
from his wife's departure. One would have said that he had
always expected it. Who knows? After the first shock, it was
perhaps a relief to him that she should have vanished from their
life.

He did not like remembering Ruth, or that time. Until he was
twenty-five, the idea of marriage had never occurred to him and
he associated with women only to the extent that was necessary:
he was over twenty before he first had sexual relations with a
woman.

At Waterbury, Ruth worked in the same shop as he. He knew
she went out every evening with one man or another and

haunted the taverns where, after a couple of drinks, she became vulgar and noisy.

She was not yet twenty, but she had left her parents' farm, in Ohio, when she was scarcely sixteen and had lived in New York, in Albany, perhaps in still other places before landing, God knows how, in Waterbury.

She worried neither about to-morrow, nor about what people thought of her. For months he had watched her, convinced that she had for him a sort of contempt, because he did not amuse himself like the others. She attracted and frightened him both at once. She was a female rather than a woman and the very movement of her hips sufficed to disturb him.

One evening as he came out of the workshop and was about to go towards the streetcar, he found her standing motionless beside him on the sidewalk.

He never knew if she had been waiting for him.

"Do I scare you?" she asked him as he looked at her with embarrassment.

He said no. She had a hoarse voice, stood very close to men whom she talked to.

"Are you waiting for someone?"

She laughed, as though he had said something comic, and, blushing, he had been on the point of going away. Even now, he did not know what had held him back.

"What's so funny about me?"

"The way you look at me."

"Shall we have dinner together?"

He had been wanting to, in reality, for a long time, but until then had never thought it possible. Throughout the evening he was embarrassed by the way she behaved, first in the restaurant, then in the two or three bars where she led him and where, at the end, she had drunk neat whisky.

He could have spent the night with her. She had been surprised when he had left her at her door. All next day, in the workshop, she had watched him as though she were trying to understand and his manner had been cold towards her.

For a week, he had practically not said a word to her, but one night after he had seen her getting into a friend's car it had taken him at least two hours to get to sleep. The next day, he had asked her:

"Are you free this evening?"

"My! Has it come over you again?"

He had looked at her in such a way that she had been sobered.

"If you really want to, wait for me outside."

They had followed the same programme as the first time. His manner had been sombre and he had deliberately drunk more than usual. At the moment of taking leave of her, on her doorstep, he had said as he looked at her in the same hard, hostile fashion as that morning:

"Will you marry me?"

"Me?"

She laughed, then laughed no more, studied him more attentively and her face betrayed both astonishment and a certain unease.

"What's got into you? Is it the whisky?"

"You know very well it isn't."

And it was true that she knew it.

"We'll talk about it some other time," she murmured, turning towards the door.

He had grasped her wrist.

"No. To-night."

She had not asked him in. She was genuinely frightened of him.

"Let's walk!"

For nearly two hours, they had walked up and down the pavement, between the same two lamp-posts, and they had held each other by the arm, not stopped to embrace.

"Why do you want to marry me?"

His forehead stubborn, he replied:

"Because!"

"And if you could have what you want in any case?"

"I'd still marry you."

"You aren't the sort of man to live with a woman like me."

Why was she the one he suddenly thought of, in his half-sleep, after just seeing a child in its mother's arms? For years, he had repulsed that memory.

"Do you reckon you'll be happy with me?"

He hadn't answered. It wasn't a question of happiness. He could not have explained himself, and in any case it was too turbulent to be expressed. What mattered was that he had made his decision and was sticking to it.

"Is it yes?"

"I'll give you my answer to-morrow."

"No. Right now."

He had married her two weeks later, without having previously

317

had relations with her, and, the next day, had forbidden her to go to work.

She was Ben's mother. She had left him one night, twenty months later, without being tempted to take the child with her. He had not been angered by her going. What he had felt that first night in the empty house was chagrin, as though he had suffered a set-back. He knew what he meant by this. This set-back was one he was bound to encounter sooner or later, because it went back a very long way, to things that had existed in him when he was still a child.

It was nobody's business. He had to forget it. Ben remained with him and that alone mattered.

Someday, much later on, when Ben would be quite a man, they might perhaps talk it over together and Dave would tell him the truth.

The notion that perhaps there would never be a "later on", that his son would not be given time to become a man, had never entered his head and, at Indianapolis, he nearly rushed straight to the Police Court without stopping to leave his suitcase at the hotel. He changed his mind on the way, in the taxi.

"Drop me first at a hotel," he said.

"In the centre of the town?"

"As near the Police Court as possible."

Now that he was so near his son, he was overtaken by feverishness. He saw a huge square surrounded by stone buildings, recognized what must be the Capitol, then, further off, the Post Office with capitals supported by white columns.

The driver thrust down his flag outside a hotel which looked luxurious.

"I'd like you to wait for me."

"The Police Court's right there," the man replied, pointing to a building.

He passed through a revolving door behind a porter who carried his case and led him to the reception-desk.

"Did you make a telephone reservation?"

"No. I'd like a room."

A pad of forms was handed to him and he wrote his real name, which the clerk read upside down. Perhaps because he knew at once why he had come, he did not ask how many days he expected to be staying.

"Show Mr. Galloway up to 662."

He had not wanted to go up to his room, but did not venture

to protest. Being there, he took advantage of the fact to wash his hands, bathe his face and comb his hair.

He hoped they had not started interrogating Ben immediately and had let him sleep. Had they allowed him to wash and change his clothes?

When he crossed the hall, several people followed him with their eyes.

This no longer had any effect on him; he felt no self-consciousness.

It was ten in the morning. At the Police Court, lawyers, judges, messengers were going from one door to another, pre-occupied, with dossiers in their hands, and, feeling suddenly lost, he turned for help to the uniformed attendant standing by the door.

"Do you know if Ben Galloway is in the building?" he asked.

"Who?"

"Ben Galloway. The one who. . . ."

"Oh! Sure."

The man looked at him more closely. He must have seen his picture in the paper.

"He isn't here," he went on in an altered voice. "I know there was a conference, this morning, in the District Attorney's office. The newspapermen have been here three or four times already. If you want my opinion, you're most likely to find him at the F.B.I."

"Where are the F.B.I. offices?"

"In the Federal Building, over the Post Office. You know where the Post Office is?"

"I saw it as I came along."

People stopped to look at him. One man, he thought, was about to come up and speak to him, changed his mind at the last moment. It was probably an official, perhaps one of the District Attorney's assistants, or perhaps a lawyer wanting to offer his services.

The sun was brilliant, the day already hot, women were wearing light-coloured dresses and many of the men already had on their panama hats. He was walking quickly. In a few minutes, he would know, perhaps would be face to face with Ben.

The Federal Building was bright, with wide marble-paved corridors, mahogany doors each bearing a brass number. He knocked on the one which had been pointed out to him. A voice called to him to come in and a middle-aged woman, with grey hair, for a moment stopped typing.

"What can I do for you?"

"I want to see my son. I'm Dave Galloway, Ben's father."

It was not the sentence he had prepared. He was wasting no words, looking at a half-open door on his left, at another, on his right, which was shut.

"Please sit down."

"Can you tell me if my son's here?"

Without answering, she picked up the telephone-receiver and said into the mouthpiece:

"Mr. Dave Galloway's in the ante-room."

She sat listening, punctuating the utterances of the person at the other end with:

"Yes. . . . Yes. . . . Very well. . . . I understand. . . ."

He had obeyed mechanically when she asked him to be seated but he was already on his feet again.

"I'm going to see him?" he asked.

"The inspector's busy right now. He'll see you in a little while."

"You aren't allowed to tell me if my son's here, straight out?"

Embarrassed, she murmured as she started typing again:

"I've had no instructions."

The venetian blinds, lowered, let through even spaced bars of light which were reflected on the walls and the ceiling. A fan was turning almost soundlessly.

Resigned to remaining seated, his hat on his knees, he followed with his eyes the carriage of the typewriter, then the movement of the second hand on the electric clock built into one of the partitions.

A youngish man came out of the office on the left, papers in hand, glanced at him, frowned, examined him again more closely while he was pulling open the metal drawers of a filing-cabinet. When he had found what he wanted and made some notes on a document, he leaned over the secretary and spoke to her in a low voice.

It was something to do with Galloway. But neither of them addressed him and the man disappeared through the door by which he had come.

Dave was attentive to every sound. Apart from the tapping of the machine, he could hear nothing but footsteps in the big corridor, now and then knocks on a door. The telephone rang, the woman answered:

"One minute, please. Hold on."

She pushed buttons.

320

"Albany's on the line."

He nearly rose to his feet again. Albany, that must certainly be something to do with Ben. While he was waiting, powerless, in an ante-room, it was his son's fate that they were discussing!

This was something he had not foreseen, this impossibility, not merely of seeing Ben immediately upon his arrival, but of talking to someone, no matter whom, someone who could tell him what was happening.

A half-hour went by, the longest, most painful of his life. Twice more the telephone rang, messages were passed to the mysterious inspector who lurked in one of the offices, hidden from sight. Once, the woman simply announced:

"The Governor."

He could understand at a pinch that they would not be able to receive him immediately. At least they could have told him whether Ben were here or not. He was his father. He had a right to see him, to speak to him.

"Listen, Miss . . ."

"Be patient, Mr. Galloway. It won't be much longer."

She knew what was happening herself! He tried to glean something from her expression, but she paid no attention to him, continued to type with a dizzy rapidity.

At one moment, a door opened in the corridor nearby, perhaps the one next to them, and, if he had obeyed his instinct, he would have darted out to look. He dared not, too subdued, fearing a rebuke from the grey-haired lady. Almost immediately afterwards, the right-hand door, the one which had hitherto remained closed, opened in its turn, a man about his own age stood in the doorway, looked towards him.

"Will you come in, Mr. Galloway?"

There were the same venetian blinds over the windows, the same reflections quivering on the light-coloured walls. The man pointed to a chair, sat down himself behind a huge metal desk on which, in a frame, Dave noticed the photograph of a woman and two children.

He opened his mouth to ask the question to which he was at length to receive a reply, when the other spoke first, in a quiet voice, a little cold, in which however he thought he could discern some sympathy or pity.

"I suppose you got here on the first plane?"

"Yes. I . . ."

"You know, you shouldn't have left before hearing from us. Unfortunately you've made the trip for nothing."

He felt his limbs grow cold. "My son isn't here?"

"He's to be taken to New York, and from there to Liberty all in the course of to-day."

Dave didn't understand, stared at the other man as he tried to do so.

"The murder at the start, which was committed in New York State, is more important than the assaults which took place here. The question was whether your son was first to be tried in Indiana for having fired at the police and wounded an officer, or whether he should go for trial right away in New York State. The Governors of the two States got in touch by phone this morning and came to an agreement."

"He hasn't already gone?" he protested.

The man glanced at a clock exactly like the one there was in the ante-room.

"No. Right now, they're probably having a meal."

"Where?"

"I'm sorry I can't tell you, Mr. Galloway. In order to avoid all unnecessary publicity and possible incidents, we have arranged matters so that even the newspapermen don't know they spent the night here and they're waiting for them at the door of the prison."

"Ben was *here*?"

With his finger, he indicated the room in which they were seated and the other nodded.

"He was in here when I arrived, wasn't he?"

The inspector nodded again.

"And I was made to wait, deliberately, in the ante-room, so that I shouldn't see him?" he cried finally, unable to control himself any longer.

"Take it easy, Mr. Galloway. It wasn't I who prevented you from meeting your son."

"Who was it?"

"It was he who refused to see you."

CHAPTER SEVEN

"I'M AFRAID, Mr. Galloway, that all of us, without exception, are the last people to know our own children."

The inspector, at that moment, was filling his pipe with slow, careful movements and, as though to emphasize the fact that he

322

did not except himself, he allowed his gaze to rest for a moment on the photograph on his desk.

Dave uttered no protest, because all his life he had had an instinctive respect for everything that represented authority. What the inspector had just said, in any case, was probably true for certain fathers, for ordinary fathers, but it was not for him.

What good would it do to try and explain their life, Ben's life and his, the nature of their relationship, which was not merely the relationship of father and son?

"I don't know," the inspector went on, leaning back in his chair, "what they will decide about him. Our part, here, is over. I imagine his lawyer, if not the District Attorney himself, will insist on his being examined by one or more psychiatrists."

Galloway almost smiled, so absurd did it seem to him to suppose that Ben was not in full possession of his reason. If he was not normal, then his father was not normal either. But Dave could not have reached the age of forty-three without the fact being apparent.

"I had him here from midnight until a few minutes ago and I must confess I haven't been able to make up my mind about him."

"Ben's not easy to get to know," his father hastened to say. The inspector seemed surprised.

"Well, at least," he retorted, "he showed no signs of shyness, if that's what you mean. I've seldom seen anyone at any age so much at ease in similar circumstances. They were brought into my office together, he and his girl-friend, and you'd have thought they were delighted to be here, as though in spite of everything they'd done what they set out to do. When the handcuffs were taken off them, they drew close to one another and held hands.

"It didn't matter that they were dirty and tired, their eyes were clear. They took pleasure in looking at one another with a sort of jubilation, as though they shared a marvellous secret.

"I said to them:

" 'You can sit down.'

"And your son said coolly:

" 'We've had enough sitting down on the trip.'

"He was watching me, ironically I could swear.

" 'Is this where you give us the Third Degree?' he shot at me with a smile that was just a bit nervous all the same. 'If you're wanting confessions, I confess everything, the murder of the old boy on the highway, the theft of the car, the threats to the farmer and his wife and the shots fired at the police. I'm not accused of anything else, am I?'

" 'There's no question of interrogating you at present,' I said. 'You're almost asleep on your feet.'

"That seemed to upset him, as though I weren't playing the game according to the rules.

" 'I'm still capable of lasting out the night if necessary. As far as Lillian's concerned, you can let her go. She hasn't done anything. She didn't know my plans. I just told her we were going to Illinois or Mississippi to get married and she didn't know I was armed.'

"The girl interrupted him.

" 'That's not true!'

" 'You've got to believe me, Inspector. When we left the farm, she begged me to give myself up without shooting.'

" 'He's lying. What we did, we did together. The Justice of the Peace in Illinois didn't marry us, but since last night I've been his wife just the same.' "

Galloway had withdrawn into himself and now nothing of his feelings showed.

"I thought they were going to start an argument between themselves and I sent them to bed. Your son slept on a camp bed in the next room and Lillian Hawkins spent the night in another office in charge of a wardress.

"The girl slept restlessly. As for the boy, he slept as though he were in his own bed and they had some trouble waking him."

"He has always been a heavy sleeper."

"It's true that I had no intention of putting him through a proper interrogation, because that's the business of the District Attorney, in Liberty, the capital of the county where the crime was committed. It's only about fifty miles from your home, if I'm not mistaken. Do you know anyone in Liberty, Mr. Galloway?"

"No one."

"That's where your son and his girl will be tried if the psychiatrists decide that they should go for trial. This morning, I had coffee and rolls sent up to them and they both had good appetites. While I was putting through some phone-calls, I watched them. They were sitting just there . . ."

He pointed to a dark leather settee, against the wall.

". . . they were holding hands, like last night, whispering, gazing ecstatically into each other's eyes. Anyone not knowing the facts who had come in at that moment would have taken them for the happiest pair on earth. When I was notified of your arrival, I said to your son:

324

" 'Your father's here.'

"I don't want to cause you pain, Mr. Galloway, but I think it's important you should know the truth. He turned towards his girl, scowling, and he muttered between his teeth:

" 'Hell!'

"I went on:

" 'I can allow you to see him for a few minutes, alone if you like.'

" 'But I don't want to see him at all!' he cried. 'I've nothing to say to him. Is it absolutely necessary that you let him come in?'

" 'I can't compel you to see him.'

" 'Well then, it's no!'

"Other people will be handling the rest of the business and I confess to you that, personally, I'd rather not have to come to a decision where he's concerned."

"He's not mad," Dave repeated with conviction.

"Just the same that's his only chance, I wonder if you realize it? Now if you'll promise me to do nothing that might cause an incident, if you think you're capable of seeing your son pass close by you without rushing towards him . . ."

"I promise."

"I'll give you a piece of information which is still confidential. At twelve forty-five, your son and Lillian Hawkins will arrive at the airport, with a police officer and a wardress, to catch the New York plane. They'll just go through the hall where there will certainly be a few reporters and one or two photographers. If you happen to be there . . ."

"They're travelling in an ordinary plane?"

The inspector nodded.

"I'm entitled to catch the same one?"

"If there's room."

He had an hour and a half to spare, but he was so afraid of being late that he hurriedly left the Federal Building and ran to his hotel.

"I have to leave by the twelve forty-five plane," he said. "I've come to fetch my suitcase. How much do I owe you?"

"Nothing, Mr. Galloway, since you haven't used the room."

He returned in a taxi along that morning's route, ran instantly to the booking-office.

"Is there any room left in the twelve forty-five plane for New York?"

"How many seats?"

"Only one."

325

"One minute."

It was very hot. The girl had beads of sweat on her upper lip, damp circles under her arms, and her odour recalled that of Ruth. She telephoned another office.

"What name?" she then asked, preparing to fill in a ticket.

"Galloway."

She looked at him, astonished, hesitated.

"Do you know that in the same plane . . ."

"My son will be there, yes."

He had lunch at the airport restaurant. What the F.B.I. inspector had told him did not yet trouble him, perhaps because he was still living on his built-up momentum. Only when he had been told about Lillian, and what she had proudly proclaimed on the subject of their relationship, had he felt a tightening at his heart.

If Ben had refused to see him, it was obviously because he was embarrassed at the thought of being confronted by him. He, too, was in a nervous state. He must be allowed time to recover.

At a quarter past twelve, already, Galloway was at the entrance to the airport, watching the cars arrive, and he had asked two different attendants if they were sure there was no other way in. He saw some photographers arrive with their cameras and the three men who joined them were no doubt reporters. They formed a group in the middle of the hall and one of them caught sight of him, wrinkled his forehead, spoke to the others, went and questioned the girl in the ticket-office who nodded.

He had been recognized. He didn't care. They all came up to him together.

"Mr. Galloway?"

He said yes.

"Did you see your son this morning?"

He was on the verge of lying, so much did it cost him to have to admit that he had made the journey for nothing.

"I wasn't able to see him."

"Were you refused permission?"

He was tempted to say yes, but his reply would appear in the papers and the F.B.I. inspector would probably contradict it.

"It was my son who didn't want to see me," he confessed, forcing a smile as though he were talking of a piece of boyish naughtiness. "You should be able to understand his reaction. . . ."

"You're going to make the trip with him?"

"In the same plane, yes."

"The trial will be held in Liberty?"

"That's what I was told an hour ago."

"Have you chosen a lawyer?"

"No. I'll get the best, I can afford it."

He was ashamed of himself, suddenly, realizing that he was behaving ridiculously.

"Do you mind?" he was asked. "Take a step forward. Thanks."

He was photographed. And it was at this moment that he saw his son getting out of a car, his wrist linked by a handcuff to the wrist of a police officer in plain clothes who was young and looked like his elder brother. Ben was wearing his fawn-coloured raincoat. He was bare-headed. Lillian Hawkins was following him accompanied by a plump woman, tightly enclosed in a dark suit which made one think of a uniform.

Two big bay-windows were open. Had Ben recognized his father, at a distance, under the photographers' flashes? These latter made a rush for the doorway, the reporters as well, and the crowd, which quickly grasped what was happening, was already beginning to form itself into a hedge, as though for the passing of an official personage.

Dave was using his elbows, working his way into the front row and, when his son was only a few yards from the inner door, their eyes met, Ben frowned and went straight on, turned a little later, not to look at him again, but to say something to Lillian.

She was a little more pale than he, no doubt from fatigue, and, in her cheap coat covering a flowered cotton frock she looked, beside the wardress, like a little ailing child.

Ben had made no movement towards his father and Dave began to understand, now, what the inspector had tried to tell him. It was as though sixteen years of shared life and daily intimacy had suddenly ceased to exist. There had been no glint in his son's eyes, no emotion on his face. Nothing but a knitting of his brows, as when one sees something unpleasing in one's way.

"My father!" he must have said to the girl as he turned to her.

They had already vanished on to the airfield where they were to board the plane before the barrier was opened for the other passengers.

"Did he see you?" one of the reporters asked him.

"I think so."

He added:

"I'm not sure."

He followed the queue, was one of the last to enter the plane where the stewardess showed him to one of the back seats. Ben and Lillian, on the other hand, were right in front, he on the left with the policeman, she on the right with the woman escorting her, and there was only the gangway between them.

By rising in his seat, Dave could catch sight of them. He could see nothing but their heads and the backs of their necks, and this only when they were not leaning back, but it was enough for him to realize that they were turned towards one another the whole time. They sometimes leaned sideways and exchanged remarks and their escorts did not interfere. A little later, the stewardess went and offered them tea and sandwiches, as she did the other passengers, and they refused.

Was it possible that neither of them realized their position? One might have thought they were on holiday, happy to be making a trip by plane, and Dave saw that the other passengers were as astonished at their behaviour as himself.

After about half an hour in the air Lillian's head slipped gradually sideways and she must have slept nearly all the rest of the journey. As for Ben, after chatting for a time in a low voice with the policeman, he read the paper the man offered him.

All this was nothing but a misunderstanding, Galloway was sure of it. The actions of others always appear strange to us because we do not know their true motives. When he had married Ruth, way back, everyone, in the workshop, had regarded him with a mingled astonishment and commiseration and he had turned to them very much the same face that Ben turned to the crowd.

He knew what he was doing when he married Ruth. He had been the only one to know.

People were sorry for him. They imagined he had let himself be bewitched, that he had yielded to a passing infatuation, not realizing that she was the only kind of woman he could have any desire to marry. Who knows? Perhaps some of them had thought that he had temporarily gone out of his mind?

He too had held his wife's hand in public, gazing defiantly at the world. And, when she was pregnant, he had walked proudly beside her through the centre of the town.

Most of his friends had had her. In spite of this, he hadn't permitted himself to touch her before their marriage, and this, strangely, had so moved her that she had wept as she thanked him. It was true that they had been drinking that night. They drank every night.

Everyone would have predicted that he would be unhappy with her and it had not been the case at all. He had insisted upon living in one of the new houses on the building lot, like most young couples, on buying the same furniture, the same knick-knacks. His mother had not been present at the wedding because he had only told her about it a month later, casually, at the end of a letter, as though it were news of no importance. The following spring, she had paid them an unexpected visit with Musselman and he was sure she had never been so surprised in her life. He didn't know what she had expected; it certainly wasn't Ruth, or the little household which her eyes beheld.

"Are you happy?" she had asked him when for a moment they were alone together.

He was content to smile and she didn't believe his smile. She'd never believed him. She'd never believed his father either. Did she believe Musselman?

"Well! children, it's time for us to be going!"

She had not accepted their invitation to a meal.

"Good luck!" she had called, once on the sidewalk.

She wished the pair of them every conceivable disaster. So he had not written when Ruth left him. He had gone nearly two years without answering her letters, which were in any case not frequent.

Was this what the inspector had tried to make him understand that morning? The difference lay, precisely, in the fact that he trusted Ben. They were of the same breed. He was truly his son. To-night, to-morrow, they would have a talk and everything would be explained. What Ben had to know was that his father already understood. It was implied in his message:

"I shall be on your side no matter what happens."

He had added, to emphasize it still more:

"I'm not angry with you, Ben!"

It was not a matter of being angry in the strict sense of the word. It was bigger than that. Ben had probably not heard his radio message since, at about the time when it was broadcast, he had been calling on the Justice of the Peace in a village in Illinois.

Was he the one who, later that evening, had stopped the car in the darkness, regardless of the police on their trail, and proposed to Lillian that they should belong to one another? Had it been her idea? He preferred not to think about that, nor to try to guess what they were saying now that the girl had just woken up.

They were flying over New York, whose skyscrapers could be seen almost golden in the sunshine, and the plane was steadily losing height. They had put out cigarettes, buckled their safety-belts. Dave had intended to stay in his seat until his son went out so that he would be obliged to pass very close to him and even brush against him, but the stewardess made all the passengers go first, himself included.

He was obliged to follow the others through the barriers and, when he reached the waiting-room and looked round, he saw that Ben and Lillian were being taken to another part of the airfield.

"Where are they going?" he asked an attendant.

The man looked in the direction to which he was pointing.

"Most likely to catch another plane," he said indifferently.

"What line is that, down there?"

"Syracuse."

"Does the plane call at Liberty?"

"Probably."

He tried in vain to catch it. By the time he had found the right ticket-office the plane had already taken off.

"There's another airplane in an hour's time which stops at Liberty. You'll still get there faster than by train."

He no longer let himself grow impatient, was beginning to get used to the fact that everything turned out differently from what he hoped, and did not lose courage, being convinced that it was he who would have the last word.

It was five o'clock when he reached the county capital which he had only driven through by car before. The last time was the previous day, in a police-car, and everything was shut because it was Sunday. He took just time to leave his suitcase at the hotel, without going up to his room, this time, and hurried to the Police Court, which was not far off.

He arrived there a few minutes too late. A group of sightseers, a photographer were still standing on the stone steps.

"Is Ben Galloway in the building?" he asked.

"He's just been taken away."

"Where?"

"To the County Jail."

"Has he seen the District Attorney?"

"They were both taken to his office, but they only stayed a few minutes."

He had not been recognized. He tried to push through the glass-paned door and it wouldn't open. From inside, a doorkeeper with a chevroned cap, who had lost an arm, signed to him to stop.

"He won't open," said an old gentleman. "At five sharp they shut the doors and then no one's allowed in."

"Is the District Attorney still in his office?"

330

"Probably. I haven't seen him come out. But he won't see you after hours either."

The old man, whose denture did not fit very well, regarded him with a sly smile.

"You're the father, aren't you?"

And, as Galloway nodded, he added in a shrill voice:

"A fine son you've got there! Something to be proud of!"

It was the first gratuitous insult he had suffered because of Ben and, taken aback, not understanding, he stared after the little old man as he went off chuckling.

He had gone about it the wrong way, from the start. He should have listened to the lieutenant, who had advised him to engage a good lawyer immediately. What did he know about the formalities with which one had to comply in order to visit a prisoner? He undoubtedly had rights, but he did not know what they were. Ben had to be protected. He must not be allowed to go on talking and acting like a child.

He went back to the hotel, not knowing where else to turn.

"Could I see the manager?"

Without being kept waiting, he was shown into a small office near the reception desk. The manager was jacketless, his shirt-sleeves rolled up.

"Sid Nicholson," he introduced himself.

"Dave Galloway. I suppose you know why I'm here?"

"Yes, I know, Mr. Galloway."

"I want to ask you if you can tell me the best lawyer in the county."

He added with unnecessary bravado:

"Never mind if he's expensive. I can pay."

"You should try to get Wilbur Lane."

"Is he the best?"

"He's not only the best in Liberty, but he has cases pretty well every week in New York and Albany and he's a personal friend of the Governor. You'd like to see him this evening?"

"If possible."

"In that case, I'd better call him up right away because, when he leaves his office, it'll be to go to the golf course and you won't have another chance."

"I'd be glad if you would."

"Get me Wilbur Lane, Jane."

There was a secretary at the other end of the line whom he also called by her Christian name.

"Is the boss still there? Sid Nicholson here. I'd like to have a word with him. It's urgent. . . . Hullo, Wilbur? Sorry to disturb you. You were just getting ready to leave? . . . I have someone here who wants your help. . . . Can't you guess? . . . That's who it is. . . . He's in my office. . . . You can see him? . . . I'll send him right over. . . . So long. . . ."

"Where is it?" asked Galloway who had heard.

"You go down the street till you see a little Methodist chapel, on your right. Exactly opposite, there's a big, white, colonial-style house with the names 'Lane, Pepper and Durkin' on the nameplate. Jed Pepper only handles taxation and wills. As for Durkin, he died six months ago."

The offices had been shut since five o'clock, but the secretary must have been keeping watch for him at one of the windows because she opened the door the moment he set foot on the flight of steps.

"Mr. Lane's waiting for you. This way, please."

A white-haired man, his face still youthful, who stood a head taller than Galloway and had the build of a rugby footballer, stood up to shake hands with him.

"I won't go so far as to say I was expecting you, which would be fatuous on my part, but I wasn't surprised when my friend Sid called me up. Sit down, Mr. Galloway. I've been reading in the afternoon paper that you made a fruitless trip to Indianapolis."

"My son's here."

"I know. I've just this minute contacted George Temple, the District Attorney, who's an old friend. He, too, understood at once what it was about."

"I want you to undertake my son's defence. I'm not rich, but I have about seven thousand dollars saved and . . ."

"We'll talk about that later. Whom did you see, in Indianapolis?"

"A man who seemed to be chief of the F.B.I. there. They didn't tell me his name."

"What did you say to him?"

"That I was convinced everything would be explained when I'd had a talk with Ben."

"And your son refused to see you."

Noting Galloway's surprise, he explained:

"It's in the papers already. You must understand, it's important, from now on, that you avoid talking about this business to anyone at all and especially to newspapermen. Even if they ask you questions about your son which seem quite harmless, don't answer. Temple didn't want to take advantage of the situation and interrogate the pair directly they left the plane. So they only spent a few minutes at his office for the usual formalities and he sent them straight to the jail. To-morrow, since you want me to undertake your son's defence, I will be present when he undergoes his first interrogation. Probably I shall have a chance to talk to him even before then."

He asked bluntly, while thrusting a cigar into a cigar-holder with a gold band:

"What's he like?"

Dave flushed, because he did not understand the exact sense of the question, and was afraid of going wrong again.

"He's always been a quiet, thoughtful boy," he said. "In sixteen years, he has never once given me any trouble."

"What was he like when you saw him in Indianapolis? According to the papers you came face to face in the hall at the airport."

"Not quite face to face. I was in the crowd."

"He saw you?"

"Yes."

"He seemed embarrassed?"

"No. It's hard to explain. I suppose he was annoyed at finding me there."

"Is his mother still alive?"

"I imagine so."

"You don't know where she is?"

"She left me fifteen and a half years ago, leaving me the child, who was then six months old. Three years later, someone brought me some papers to sign so she could get a divorce."

"Any weaknesses on that side?"

"What do you mean?"

"I'm asking you whether his antecedents, on his mother's side, might explain what has happened."

"To my knowledge, she has never been ill."

"And you?"

He had not expected questions of this sort and was non-plussed by them, the more so since the lawyer was writing down his replies. His hands were carefully tended, his nails manicured. He was dressed in a double-breasted blue suit, admirably cut. For some moments, Dave had been wondering whom he reminded him of.

"I've never had any serious illness either."

"Your father?"

"He died of a heart attack at the age of forty."

333

"Your mother?"

"She married again and is in good health."

"No aunts, uncles, cousins male or female, who, at any time, had to be put in a mental home?"

He realized where these questions were heading, protested: "Ben isn't mad!"

"Don't shout it so loud, because it may very well be our only chance of saving his skin. You know, when I read what the papers said about his attitude, I thought at first he was doing everything he could to get himself sent to the electric chair. I'm sorry to put it crudely. We have to look the facts in the face. Afterwards, thinking it over, I wondered, and I'm still wondering, whether he isn't more crafty than we think and if he hasn't adopted the best tactics."

"I don't understand."

"He doesn't cry, doesn't say he's sorry, doesn't collapse, doesn't shut himself up in a mistrustful silence either. On the contrary he talks and behaves as though he were delighted at having killed a man, in cold blood; at having stolen his car and having, later on, opened fire and gone on shooting until his automatic was empty.

"It is difficult, my dear sir, to conceive of an intelligent youth, who has attained his sixteenth year and has been normally raised in the middle section of society, it is difficult, I say, to imagine him behaving in this way unless his mind is deranged.

"The word 'madness' frightens you, as it does everyone, and in any case it's not precise enough. The psychiatrists will use more exact terms in establishing first your son's degree of understanding, secondly his capacity for reacting to a good or evil impulse.

"This expert examination is the first thing I shall demand to-morrow of the District Attorney and it's more than probable that I shall call in a New York specialist."

Had Dave been going to persist in repeating that his son was not mad? He was not listened to. He was given to understand that this was no longer his business, that Ben's defence was no longer in his hands.

"I take it you intend to stay in Liberty until the case goes before the jury? Unless the expert examination I have just mentioned takes longer than I expect, the jury will be summoned in two or three days.

"I don't want to prevent you staying, but it's preferable that you should show yourself as little as possible and above all that

334

you should avoid saying anything. There's a telephone in every room in the hotel. I promise to keep you informed. If I think it desirable that you should have an interview with your son, I'll make arrangements with the District Attorney.

"While waiting you can help me and occupy your mind by trying to remember every more or less unusual incident in the course of your son's life. Don't tell me there haven't been any. You'll be surprised how much you'll discover."

He glanced at his watch and stood up. Was he perhaps telling himself that there was still time for his game of golf? It was as they shook hands that Dave suddenly realized of whom he reminded him.

It was of Musselman, his mother's second husband.

It was too late to change his mind. Besides, Musselman was efficient at his job. This one, too, no doubt.

He was thrust into the background, he was told to keep quiet, almost to hide himself, and it was the lawyer who would decide whether or not an interview between father and son was desirable!

He walked along the street and people turned to look at him. When he pushed through the revolving door of the hotel, he saw, in a corner of the entrance-hall, Isabel Hawkins, wearing her best dress and hat. She was talking to someone whom he did not immediately recognize because his back was turned.

It was Evan Cavanaugh, the Everton lawyer. They must have arrived together a short time previously. Dave had not once thought of the Hawkinses, still less that Lillian Hawkins would need a lawyer, also. It gave him a queer feeling.

Isabel Hawkins had seen him. They both looked at each other. Instead of greeting him, of giving a sign of recognition, she pressed her lips together and her little eyes became hard.

He was almost gratified to learn that they were enemies.

CHAPTER EIGHT

TOWARDS eleven, through his window, he saw Isabel Hawkins leave the hotel with Cavanaugh and go in the direction of the Police Court, and he could not help envying her. His own lawyer had not yet telephoned and, in the expectation of a call, Dave had not left his room for an instant.

He was still at the window, still without news, when Isabel

came back, alone this time, after having spent three-quarters of an hour at the Court. Had she been with her daughter all this time? She only entered the hotel and came out again and, carrying her small suitcase, walked towards the bus depot.

She was going back to Everton. Perhaps he should telephone Musak, who had helped him as best he could to get through Sunday night and had driven him to La Guardia in his car?

What could he say to him? It seemed to him that an eternity had passed since then and he wondered if he would ever see Everton again.

Wilbur Lane rang him up a few minutes later. Did he really speak more coldly than the previous evening, or was that merely the impression his voice gave over the telephone? In any event, he wasted no time with unnecessary words, didn't ask Galloway how he was.

"I've fixed an interview with your son for three o'clock this afternoon at the District Attorney's office. Be in the entrance-hall a few minutes earlier, and I'll pick you up there."

Lane hung up without giving him time to ask any questions. Musselman was like that, even when he had nothing to do, just to make himself look busy. Galloway went down to the restaurant for lunch, reached the Police Court long before the time, walked up and down, then began to read all the administrative announcements on the notice-boards.

The lawyer arrived at two minutes to three and, without stopping, signed to him to follow him down a long corridor.

"The interview will take place in the presence of the District Attorney," he said as they went.

"Did he insist on that?"

"No. Your son did."

"You've spoken to him?"

"For half an hour, early this morning, and I came round later to be present at his interrogation."

What had been said, the way Ben had reacted, was apparently not his business, since he was told nothing about it.

Lane knocked at the door, opened it without awaiting a reply and touched his pearl-grey hat as he passed through a room where two secretaries were working.

"They're there?" he asked in the manner of a regular visitor.

He pushed open the second door and Ben was there, in the middle of the room, seated in a chair with his legs crossed, smoking a cigarette. The District Attorney sat facing him, on

336

the other side of his desk. He was a man of about forty who did not look in the best of health and was worried—over-conscientious probably.

"Come in, Mr. Galloway," he said, standing up.

Ben did the same, turning towards him:

"Hullo, Dad."

He said it nicely, but without feeling, as he did, for example, when he came home from High School. They did not approach one another. Embarrassed by the presence of the two men who pretended to be talking in low voices in a corner, Dave could find nothing to say. Perhaps he would have been equally at a loss if he had been alone with his son?

He finally murmured:

"Did you hear my message?"

He had seldom seen in Ben an attitude so casual. He seemed, in two days, to have rid himself of all the shyness and uncouthness of the awkward age, bore himself naturally, without constraint.

"To tell you the truth it never occurred to us to switch on the radio, but I read it yesterday on the plane."

He made no comment on what his father had said. Everyone had pictured the fugitives hanging on the radio in the hope of guessing the police plans. As Ben said with simplicity, the thought had not occurred to them. And he added with an amused smile:

"It was the same with the route we followed. They were looking for us on the side roads when, except the two times we went astray, we were driving quietly along the highway."

He was silent, Dave for his part remained speechless, gazing with avid eyes at his son who had slightly turned his head away and he saw him now in profile. He noted that Ben had shaved and wore a clean shirt.

"You know, Dad, you'd do better to go back to Everton. They don't know yet when we'll go before the jury. That depends on the alienists, who are due from New York to-morrow."

He was referring to the jury and the psychiatrists without a trace of embarrassment.

"If you see Jimmy Van Horn, tell him I'm terribly sorry for his sake. It wasn't I who gave the show away."

"You haven't anything to say to me, myself, Ben?"

He was almost begging. His son replied:

"What do you want me to say? Anything I might say would only hurt you. Go back to Everton. Don't worry about me. I

337

don't regret anything and, if I had it over again, I'd do exactly the same."

He turned towards the District Attorney.

"Will that do?" he asked, as though he had only consented to see his father at the magistrate's persuasion.

The District Attorney was not at his ease and would undoubtedly have preferred not to be landed with an affair that was being discussed in every newspaper in the United States.

"It seems he has nothing more to say to you, Mr. Galloway." He added after a pause, as though to avoid the appearance of turning him out too brutally:

"It's quite true we can't fix a date for the Grand Jury until after the psychiatrists have reached their conclusions.

Ben leaned forward to stub out his cigarette in the ash-tray.

"So long, Dad," he murmured to induce his father to go.

"So long, son."

Lane followed him out. Dave did not remember having taken leave of the District Attorney and nearly went back to apologize.

"The way you've just seen him, that's the way he was with me this morning and, afterwards, at his interrogation."

The lawyer spoke angrily, as though he were accusing Galloway of being responsible.

"There was a chance, at a pinch, we could deny premeditation and claim that the idea of attacking a motorist only occurred to him after he was on the road."

Dave had no sense of listening; he was surrounded as it were by a zone of emptiness that protected him.

"He insisted, on the contrary, on telling the District Attorney that he had made his plans in detail three weeks earlier. He chose a Saturday, it seems, because that's the day you go and spend the evening with a neighbour. Actually, the start, fixed for the previous Saturday, had to be postponed because you had a cold and didn't leave the apartment. Is that correct?"

"That's correct."

"Lillian Hawkins' lawyer is doing no better with her. Your son tried again to take everything on himself. According to her, she not only worked out the whole plan with him, but it was she who took the initiative. It was also she, in the Oldsmobile, who signed to Ben when it was time to fire."

He was in a bad temper.

"The thing I don't understand is that you've lived sixteen years with a boy like him without noticing anything."

Dave almost wanted to ask his forgiveness. What could he

338

do? So much the better if they blamed him, if the whole world blamed him. It was no more than justice that he should be held responsible.

"Do you intend to take his advice?"

"What advice?"

"To go back to Everton."

He shook his head. He would stay near Ben to the end, even if he could only see him at a distance and from time to time.

"As you please. The psychiatrist I have selected is Dr. Hassberger, who will be here to-morrow morning at the same time as the expert called in by the District Attorney. As things are now, I must warn you not to expect miracles."

Galloway saw him again, standing there in the half-light of the corridor, in his blue suit, with his silky white hair. Finally, Lane touched him on the shoulder with a protective gesture.

"Go and get some rest. Stay in your room in case I need you."

It was a room with twin beds. The tinted wallpaper had wide vertical stripes, dark green on light green, and one of the springs in the armchair protruded slightly. Dave spent the best part of his time at the window, watching the comings and goings round the Police Court, but either Ben was not taken there, or he was taken in and out by a back door. On the other hand, he saw Wilbur Lane come out, at about five, in company with one of the secretaries he had seen in the District Attorney's office.

After dinner, he again nearly telephoned Musak, but lacked the courage. Lane was angry with him, he wondered why. As for the District Attorney, he was uncomfortable in his presence.

He fell asleep finally, was surprised, when he awoke, to find that it was eight in the morning. Until ten, he waited for some word from the lawyer and, unable to bear it any longer, rang him up at his office. Lane was a long time coming to the phone and, while he talked, he seemed to be listening to what some visitor was saying.

"I promised to call you if I had any news. I've nothing to tell you at present. . . . No. . . . Dr. Hassberger arrived at eight, and, since then, he has been examining your son at the jail. . . . That's right. . . . I'll call you. . . ."

At midday, he had still not been rung up. Not until one o'clock did the telephone ring.

"The case will go before the Grand Jury at ten o'clock Thursday morning," Lane snapped almost brutally.

"That means?"

"That means that Hassberger has found him sound in body

and mind and a hundred per cent responsible for his actions. If that's our expert's opinion, we can't hope for anything better from the prosecution's expert. I shall probably call you as a witness and, in that case, I'll have to talk to you, probably, some time this afternoon."

He gave no further sign of life. Dave remained without news all the next day and, at about half-past four, ended by going to the lawyer's office. It served no purpose. The secretary told him that Lane was in conference and could not see him.

Galloway was surprised, not merely at not suffering any more, but that he should have become insensible to petty vexations of this kind. Since he had had nothing to do, time had ceased to count; he passed hours in the armchair in his room, or at the window, and the chambermaid had to take advantage of meal-times to come in and clean.

At a certain moment, there was a knock on the door and a stranger, who looked like a policeman in plain clothes, handed him a summons to appear as a witness before the Grand Jury on the following day.

He arrived at the Police Court half an hour early and it appeared to him that Wilbur Lane, who was talking in a group of people, pretended not to see him.

About thirty people only, mostly women, were seated on the light-coloured benches in the courtroom, and the rest strolled up and down the corridor or chatted in corners smoking cigarettes.

He saw Dr. Van Horn with Jimmy, but Van Horn turned his back on him and went towards the lawyer with whom he talked familiarly as though they had known one another a long time. Isabel Hawkins was there, too, accompanied, this time, by her son Steve, and neither of them greeted him.

A young reporter asked him, almost gaily:

"Excited?"

He could only give him a forced smile. He was hoping to see his son's arrival, not knowing that for the past half-hour he had been in the District Attorney's office.

A few moments before the usher came along the corridor ringing his bell, Lane seemed to become aware of his presence.

"I had you subpœna'd just in case. I shall ask you two or three unimportant questions. It's even possible I shan't call you at all. In any case, don't get impatient."

"I shan't be in the courtroom?"

"Not until you've testified."

340

Hadn't Lane caused him to be subpœna'd deliberately, in order to be relieved of him during the proceedings? They called the witnesses and showed them into a room flanked by backed benches where there were copper spittoons and a drinking-tap with carton cups. The lieutenant who had questioned him on Sunday morning was there, freshly shaven, and gave him a warm handshake. Isabel Hawkins was seated on one of the benches accompanied by her son Steve who was talking in an undertone to Jimmy Van Horn.

There were other people whom he did not know, in particular a woman of about forty, dressed in black, whose eyes he often felt fixed upon him.

It was not the lieutenant, but another policeman in uniform, who was first sent for, no doubt the one who had found the van at the side of the road. They could not hear what was being said in the next room, because there was a padded inner door, but they sometimes caught a murmur of voices and, more clearly, the tap of the presiding judge's gavel on the rostrum.

A second policeman passed through the door to the court-room, then at length the lieutenant, who stayed longer than the two others. After they had testified, one didn't see them return. Perhaps they remained in Court. Perhaps they went away? Dave didn't know what happened because he had never in his life been at a trial before a Grand Jury. A little earlier, in the corridor, he had heard someone who looked important say that it would be very quickly over, that it was really no more than a formality, since the youngsters did not deny anything.

The fourth witness looked like a doctor, probably the one who had examined the body of Charles Ralston.

If Galloway understood rightly, they were engaged in establishing the facts from successive testimonies. It was the woman in mourning who was next called, after which the hearing was adjourned and one heard footsteps in the corridor where everyone hurried in order to smoke. The witnesses themselves were not allowed to leave the room and there was a constable, seated by the door, to prevent them doing to.

When the usher reappeared, Isabel Hawkins half-rose, thinking it was her turn, but it was to Galloway that he beckoned.

The courtroom was very much brighter than the little room he had left and, because of the heat, they had opened the two big windows giving on to the park, so that one heard the noises from outside. Between a hundred and a hundred and fifty people were seated on the benches and he recognized the Everton garage-keeper, the hairdresser, and even old Mrs. Pinch. The garage-keeper alone raised his hand in greeting.

Not until he turned round did he discover the judge, alone at his rostrum, on a sort of dais at the foot of which the District Attorney and his assistants were seated at the same table as the press reporters.

Ben was seated on a bench, to the left, facing the jury, with Lillian beside him, and the two of them, attentively following what went on in the Court, occasionally leaned towards one another to exchange a remark when they recognized a new face.

Galloway raised his hand, repeated:

"I swear."

After which he was made to sit down facing the jury and the public and Lane advanced towards him.

"First of all I should like the witness to tell us his son's age when Mrs. Galloway left their home. Answer, please."

"Six months."

"Since then, your son has never left you?"

"Never."

"There has never been any question of your re-marrying?"

"No, sir."

"You have no sister, no woman relative of any degree living with you in your home or visiting it regularly?"

He thought he saw an amused smile on Ben's lips, as though he could see what the lawyer was driving at.

"You had no maidservant either?"

He shook his head.

"Did friends visit your home with their wives?"

He could still only answer in the negative, and Ben was not the only one to smile; others, in the courtroom, were amused at his embarrassment.

"If I understand you rightly, your son passed his childhood, then part of his adolescence, without ever seeing a woman in his home?"

It was the first time this had ever struck him.

"It's quite true. Except the help, two days a week."

He corrected himself.

"But there again! Now I come to think of it Ben was at school at the times she came to work."

There was a burst of laughter and the judge used his gavel. He was a middle-aged man of insignificant appearance.

"Thank you, Mr. Galloway," said Lane.

He turned to the District Attorney.

"If you wish to cross-examine my witness. . . ."

Temple hesitated, consulted a young man on his left.

"Just one question. On Saturday, May 7th, that is to say, a week ago last Saturday, was the witness prevented by a cold from visiting a friend as he is in the habit of doing every Saturday?"

"Quite correct."

"That's all," murmured the District Attorney, writing a few words on a sheet of paper.

Dave did not know what to do, wondered whether he should leave and, seeing an empty place on the front bench, went and sat there.

He was just opposite his son, within five yards of him. Without Ben's appearing to act deliberately, he never turned his head his way and not once did their eyes meet.

It was not he who counted in Ben's eyes, but Lillian, at whom he smiled from time to time, perhaps also the crowd who were watching them.

All the time the session lasted, Dave sought in vain to attract his attention, going as far as to cough so loudly that the judge gave him a look of reproof.

It was important that Ben should look at him, because then he would realize the transformation that had taken place in him. He was not tense, his face was serene. He wore on his lips a faint smile resembling his son's smile. It was like a message which Ben continued not to see.

Isabel Hawkins had taken her place on the chair Galloway had just left, her handbag on her knees, and Cavanaugh moved forward to question her, very much more simply than Lane had done.

"How long have your daughter and Ben Galloway been seeing each other regularly?"

She answered in a low voice:

"So far as I know, it would be about three months."

"Speak up!" said someone on the public benches.

She repeated loudly:

"So far as I know, it would be about three months."

"He came regularly to your house?"

"He used to come long before that, because of my son, Steve, but he didn't take any notice of my daughter."

"What happened last Saturday?"

"You know quite well. She went off with him."

"Did you see her go?"

"If I'd seen her I wouldn't have let her go."

"Did you not then pay a certain visit?"

"I went to the Galloways' house, because I was afraid my husband would do something silly if I let him go alone."

"Did Mr. Galloway know that his son had gone off with Lillian?"

"He knew his son had gone, but he didn't know who with."

"Did he seem surprised?"

"I can't say he did."

There must have been other questions, but Dave did not listen to them, he still wore on his face the sort of message he was trying vainly to communicate to his son.

It was the District Attorney who asked, in the course of cross-examination:

"After finding that your daughter had gone, did you not make a second discovery?"

"My husband's pay was no longer in the box."

Then came the turn of Jimmy Van Horn, who looked round the room for his father and invariably replied:

"Yes, your Honour. . . . No, your Honour. . . . Yes, your Honour. . . ."

One day when Ben had been at their house, he had shown him the doctor's automatic and Ben had asked him to sell it to him.

"He paid you five dollars for it?"

"Yes, your Honour."

"Did he give you them?"

"No, your Honour, only three. He was to give me the other two next week."

Again there was laughter. The members of the jury, for the most part, held themselves as rigid and immobile as in a family photograph and there were two women among them.

Galloway did not at once understand why the judge rose and put on his cap, muttering unintelligible words as he did so. It seemed that the hearing was again adjourned, this time for an hour to enable everyone to have lunch. Only the members of the jury and the witnesses who had not yet been called were not allowed to leave.

"I suppose," his lawyer came and said to him, "it would be no use asking you not to come to the afternoon session?"

He merely shook his head. Why shouldn't he be present, when there was still a chance of seeing Ben and being near him?

"The two psychiatrists are going to testify. If they don't take

344

too long, there's a chance that the District Attorney will make his speech for the prosecution to-day and even that I may make my speech for the defence, in which case everything may be over by this evening."

Dave did not react. He had come to view what was happening around him as though it did not concern him personally. Since his son had been taken out of the courtroom, he didn't stay there either, but went and had a sandwich in a restaurant resembling Mack's Lunch. Nearly everyone was there, but no one took any notice of him, only the Everton garage-keeper came and shook him by the hand saying:

"My, but it's hot in there!"

One of the psychiatrists was old, with a foreign accent, the other middle-aged, and Wilbur Lane made a great display, questioning them, using their own jargon, with which he seemed to be familiar.

Several times, Dave felt the judge's eyes rest upon him; perhaps it was accidental: having to sit facing the crowd for hours on end, he was bound to look somewhere.

There was another adjournment, of only a few minutes, during which Ben and Lillian remained in the Courtroom. Isabel Hawkins took advantage of it to go and talk to her daughter and the constable allowed her to do so. Dave, himself, did not venture to approach his son, for fear of displeasing him. He longed with all his heart for Ben to look at him and see the distance he had travelled.

The District Attorney spoke for twenty minutes, in a monotonous voice, after which it was the turn of Cavanaugh, who was even more brief, and finally of Wilbur Lane.

The jury were absent not more than half an hour and, shortly before their return, Ben and Lillian were brought back seeming still quite at their ease; the girl even waved to someone she recognized among the public.

Less than five minutes later, it was over. The jury had unanimously decided to convict Ben Galloway of murder in the first degree, Lillian Hawkins of complicity, and to send them both before the County High Court.

Dave watched his son's face so intensely during the reading of the verdict that it made his eyes ache. He was almost sure he saw a slight quivering of the lips and nostrils, then, instantly, Ben recovered his smile and turned to Lillian, who smiled back at him.

He did not look at his father. In the confusion which followed, the latter tried in vain to thrust himself into his field of vision, lost sight of him, heard a voice, that of Lane, saying to him resentfully:

"I did everything that was humanly possible. It was he who wanted it that way."

Galloway bore him no grudge. He didn't like him, any more than he'd liked Musselman, but he had nothing special against him.

"Thank you for everything," he said to the lawyer politely.

The latter, surprised at finding him so submissive, went on:

"The High Court won't be sitting for a month and, maybe, between now and then I'll find new weapons."

Dave did not know that as he shook the lawyer's hand he was smiling at him with almost the same smile that his son had had on his lips all day.

The sun was shining outside and the garage-keeper was driving the hairdresser and old Mrs. Pinch away in his car.

CHAPTER NINE

HE REOPENED his shop two days later at the usual time and, on the Saturday, went to Musak's house, spoke of nothing, watched at a distance the baseball players in the setting sun, then played his game of backgammon with the cabinet-maker who smoked his mended pipe.

Widowers, in the beginning, must have the same sensation that he had during the first days, when he sometimes turned round to speak to Ben, or when, at certain times of day, he glanced impatiently at the clock, thinking his son was late; once at least, in the morning, he found himself breaking eggs for two over the cooker.

This soon passed, however. Ben was always there, not only in their apartment, but in the shop, in the streets, everywhere he went, and Galloway no longer so greatly needed his physical presence.

Perhaps the travail which had taken place in him had begun before the session of the Grand Jury, or on the Saturday night, for example, when, seated in his green armchair, he had still awaited Ben's return without much believing in it, or perhaps even before that?

He had spent his life watching his son, and, until the moment when he saw him before the tribunal, carefree, a smile on his lips, he had not understood.

One week-day morning, he hung the sign on his glass-panelled door and went to call on Musak who was in his workshop. Almost blushing, as though he feared to betray his deepest secret, he took three photographs out of an envelope.

"I'd like you to make me a single frame for the three of them," he said, arranging them in a certain order on the bench. "A very simple frame, just a rim of unstained wood."

The first was a picture of his father, at about the age of thirty-eight, exactly as Dave remembered him, with his moustache emphasizing his slightly mocking expression. The second was a photograph of himself, when he was twenty-two and had just entered the works at Waterbury. His neck looked longer and thinner than now. He had his head in half-profile and the corner of his lip was slightly drawn in.

The last photograph was the one of Ben which a schoolfellow had taken a month ago. He, too, had a long neck and it was the first time he had been photographed smoking a cigarette.

Musak brought him the frame the same day towards the end of the afternoon and Dave at once hung it on the wall. It seemed to him that those three photographs contained the explanation of everything that had happened, but he realized that he alone could understand and that, if he tried to communicate his feeling to any other person, to Wilbur Lane for example, he would be stared at in consternation.

Didn't the gaze of the three men reveal a shared secret life, a life, rather, that had been made to recoil upon itself? A look of timidity, almost a look of resignation, while the identical drawing-in of the lips hinted at a suppressed revolt.

They were of the same breed all three of them, the breed opposed to that of a Lane, or of a Musselman, or of his mother. It seemed to him that, in the whole world, there were only two sorts of men, those who bow their heads and the others. As a child, he had already thought it in more literal terms: the whipped and those who whip.

His father had bowed his head, spent his life soliciting loans from the banks, and it was while he was once again waiting in a banker's ante-room that he had died. Had not that irony of fate caused him to smile at the last moment?

Once only in his life had he accomplished an act that might pass for a revolt and, subsequently, he had been made every day

347

to pay for it; years later, Dave's mother was still using the incident to besmirch his memory, saying to her son:

"You'll never be anything but a Galloway!"

It had happened before Dave was born. No one, except his father, knew exactly what had taken place. One Fourth of July night, he had simply not come home. His mother had telephoned his club, and various friends, without obtaining news of him, and he had not returned until the following day at eight in the morning. He had tried in vain to get to his room without being seen, just as he had tried to remove the traces of lipstick from his shirt-collar.

He had listened all his life to reproaches for this escapade, and, each time, he bowed his head. Dave was none the less convinced that he was glad he had done it. Sometimes, when his wife spoke harshly to him, the father winked at his son, as though the child were already able to understand.

Wasn't it for the same reason that every day he drank a certain quantity of bourbon, never enough to make him drunk, but sufficient to dull the edge of reality?

Dave had never drunk. He had fitted his life to his own measure, which he knew well, but he, too, had made his revolt, going a stage further in violence than his father. When he had married Ruth, he had performed an act of defiance, he didn't know precisely of what or of whom, defiance of the world, of all the Musselmans, all the Lanes on earth.

He had deliberately chosen her for what she was and, if he had found a girl on the streets, he would doubtless have preferred her.

He might one day tell Ben of his father's revolt in Virginia, but he could not, alas, tell him of his own. Who knows? Perhaps his son would come to understand of his own accord?

What Dave looked for in Ben's eyes, even when he was still a child, was perhaps a hint, a sign of that revolt. In those days, he was afraid of it. He could almost have wished that his son were of the other breed.

But Ben had the same look, that of his father and himself, of all the others who resembled them. Some were able all their lives to prevent their revolt from coming to the surface. With others, it breaks out.

The two psychiatrists had discussed Ben without knowing that once in his life his grandfather had spent the night out, and that his father had married a slut who had been had by all his friends. Ben, at sixteen, had felt the need to make an end.

348

It was not without reason that Dave had put the three photographs in the same frame. The three men stood together. Each was in some sort no more than a stage in one single process of evolution.

Even before, it was rare for Dave to pass a whole day without thinking of his father. Now, he was nearly as much present in the house as Ben.

His mother had not written, had not come to see him. She must certainly have read the story in the papers. She must have said to Musselman:

"I always prophesied that would end badly!"

It was true. Wilbur Lane, too, had at once predicted that Ben would be found guilty and sent before the High Court. Those people are invariably right.

From then on, it was a little as though the cycle were complete. Dave worked as usual, opened and closed the shop with the same meticulous movements, moved the watches and jewels from the display-window into the safe for the night, did his shopping at the First National Store and went upstairs to prepare his meals.

The people in the village had already ceased to look curiously at him. It was he who sometimes surprised them, who shocked them perhaps, by talking to them of Ben as though nothing had happened. Ben was with him, within him, all day long, no matter where he went.

The month passed without a drop of rain and the men went about without jackets. The police had brought back his van which he used when necessary.

Wilbur Lane spent a day in Everton, questioning school-teachers, Ben's friends, shop-people, but he saw Dave only briefly.

"The trial's fixed for next Tuesday."

"How's Ben?"

The lawyer's face darkened.

"The same as ever, unfortunately!"

This occasion was much more important than the first, and the hearing lasted three days, during which Dave occupied the same room at the hotel, with light and dark green stripes. The hotel was full. Reporters had come in great numbers from New York and elsewhere, not only with press photographers, but with cinema and television cameramen. The judge, at the first session, ordered that no camera was to be allowed in the court-room and one saw them everywhere in the hall, in the corridors, even in the reception-hall of the hotel, where most of the witnesses were stopping.

Ben had not grown thinner, if anything was a little less angular. All the first day, his father remained shut in the witness-room as the first time. He had resolved, if he had the chance, to try to explain, if only for Ben's benefit, what he had discovered. Not necessarily everything, but the essentials, and he was careful to say nothing of this to Lane.

The lawyer evidently mistrusted him, because he asked him only a few unimportant questions, cutting him short when he threatened to say more.

All he managed to say, thrown in hastily when he was about to leave the witness-box, was: "My son and I stand together."

There was no one to understand. He even had the impression that his words had caused embarrassment, as though he had been guilty of a solecism.

When he looked at Ben a little later, he had the conviction that he had not understood either. Several times, during the trial, his son glanced curiously at him. He was no longer seated beside Lillian, as on the first occasion, because a warder and a wardress separated them. The proceedings took place in a large room, with greater solemnity, but, during the adjournments, the people were in no less of a hurry to go out and smoke or drink a coca-cola.

On the last day, he recognized more than thirty Everton people who had come by bus and the door was left open to allow the spectators crowding the corridors to hear.

A place was kept for him, always the same place, in the second row, between a young lawyer from Poughkeepsie and the wife of one of the judges. Wilbur Lane spoke for two and a half hours and the jury withdrew to deliberate shortly before five in the afternoon.

Everyone, or nearly everyone, left the courtroom. At six o'clock, at seven, the stone steps, at the foot of the white columns of the Court, were still crowded with people and the men returning from a nearby bar smelt of liquor.

Some made little signs of recognition to Dave as they passed near him. Others must have been astonished to find him so calm. He knew they would not dare to kill his son. Later, as he had the right to do, he would visit him in prison, and little by little, without trying to go too fast, he would manage to make Ben understand that they were one. Hadn't he himself taken years to make the discovery?

The street-lamps sprang to light all together in the dusk, the neon signs shone on either side of Main Street, midges began to buzz round heads. People who were in the know, and went from time to time to get the latest news, came back and said to the others:

"They still can't manage to agree, particularly about the girl. They've sent for the President of the Tribunal."

At half-past ten, at last, there was a movement in the crowd and everyone converged on the courtroom. In the artificial light, it made one think more than ever of a Methodist temple or a lecture-hall.

Ben and Lillian's places remained empty for nearly a quarter of an hour and, when they were brought in, Dave thought both their faces seemed drawn, perhaps, in part, because of the lighting.

The Court entered, then the jury. The foreman of the jury rose in an absolute silence, a sheet of paper in his hand, to read the verdict.

The hereinafter-named, Ben Galloway, sixteen years, and Lillian Hawkins, fifteen years and a half, both of Everton, in the State of New York, were convicted of murder in the first degree and sentenced to death. In view of their age, however, the jury recommended that the sentence be commuted to imprisonment for life.

From someone, on the benches, came a sob which resembled a cry. It was Isabel Hawkins, whose husband, now sober, dressed as though for a wedding, accompanied her.

Was it his father whom Ben sought with his gaze at the moment when they were preparing to take him away? In any event, their eyes met and Ben's lip quivered, was drawn in on one side only, as in the three photographs.

Dave strove to put into his eyes all that was in him, to pour his spirit into his son, who finally disappeared through a small varnished door.

He had had no time to observe Lillian.

The papers and the radio announced a few days later that Ben Galloway had been taken to Sing Sing while the girl had been sent to a women's penitentiary.

Then he received a letter from Wilbur Lane notifying him of the total amount of his fees and expenses and informing him that he was entitled to write his son a letter every fortnight and, if the latter's conduct was good, to visit him once a month.

It was quite near, scarcely twenty-three miles, on the bank

351

of the Hudson. He paid Lane and there remained to him almost none of his savings. This no longer mattered. Indeed it was better so. What could he have done with the money?

The first visit was the most sterile, because Ben had grown no tamer, continued to regard his father as though they were not both of the same kind.

Dave would take as much time as was needed to make him understand that each of the three had had his revolt, that each of the three was responsible and that, outside prison, he was paying the same price as his son.

Hadn't all three imagined that they were going to set themselves free?

"You're eating well?" he asked.

"Not badly."

"The food isn't too bad?"

It wasn't the words that mattered. These, like the "Yes, sir" of the coloured man in the Virginia sunshine, were in some sort no more than incantations.

"Is the work hard?"

They had put Ben in a book-binding shop and his fingers were covered with pricks, some of which seemed to be inflamed.

At the end of the second month, the papers suddenly revived the affair to announce that Lillian Hawkins was pregnant and would be transferred at the appropriate time to another penitentiary where she could keep the baby.

When Dave next saw his son, the boy did not speak to him of this, but more than ever he had the resigned and melancholy look of the Galloways, with, somewhere, for those who could see, a little secret flame.

Who knows? Now that Fate had been conjured, perhaps it was a different cycle that was about to begin?

Often, in his apartment, in his shop, and even in the street, Dave talked in a low voice to his father and to his son who went with him everywhere. Soon, he would talk to his grandson as well to reveal to him the secret in men.